What the critics are saying about
Empire State

"A solid, gritty suspense novel."
—*The Kirkus Reviews*

"A fast-moving suspense novel with plenty of murder and sex and a close look at the newspaper world of the big city."
—*Library Journal*

"Provocative, flawless, and possessed of a message well worth reading."
—*Desert Sentinel*

"*Empire State* is . . . a big, entertaining pot-boiler that delivers."
—*The Plain Dealer*

"Despite the feeling that we've met this governor, mayor and publisher before, *Empire State* transcends such tricks to present believable characters and a plot that thrills to the very end."
—*Book World*

EMPIRE STATE

EDWARD A. POLLITZ, JR.

PINNACLE BOOKS **NEW YORK**

For Knox and Kitty

Empire State is a work of fiction. Any resemblance to actual
events or persons, living or dead, is entirely coincidental.

EMPIRE STATE

A Pinnacle Books edition, published by special arrangement with
Macmillan Publishing Company.

Macmillan Publishing edition published 1983
Pinnacle edition/July 1984

ISBN: 0-523-42257-1

Can. ISBN: 0-523-43249-6

Cover art by Tom Galasinski

Printed in the United States of America

PINNACLE BOOKS, INC.
1430 Broadway
New York, New York 10018

9   8   7   6   5   4   3   2   1

ACKNOWLEDGMENTS

During the several years that *Empire State* was written, I had cause to thank many people. Among them, Joe Nicholson, who brought me up to date on the newspaper business; Tom Gervasi, who helped me to organize my ideas; and, most of all, Knox Burger, whose editorial skills and patience seem to be equally without limit.

PART ONE

1

Cloaked in a gray mist that was both shroud and caul, Uhuru Towers hung in the air of gathering night, massive but sterile, separated by the morbid gulf of Harlem from its counterparts in midtown Manhattan, which were already alive with sparkling lights. Its fifty-story skeleton, only partly fleshed in concrete and brickwork, dwindled in the distance, and when viewed from downtown, seemed insubstantial. But from 125th Street and Seventh Avenue, where it stood, it dominated.

February is a somber month in New York, colder than any other, short of daylight and given to chilling damps and cruel winds. Lloyd Gibbons stood on the eighth floor of the uncompleted tower with his clipboard under his arm, trying to tighten the drawstrings of his hood, to fit it more snugly under his construction helmet. The wind moaned eerily through the exposed wire of incomplete electrical installations that hung loosely from gray structural steel girders, creating atonal chords that set his nerves on edge.

Gibbons pulled on his gloves and stepped around one of the pyramidal stacks of pipe awaiting installation by the plumbing crew. He was an experienced construction supervisor and felt pride in his work. As a black, he felt a special pride in Uhuru Towers. While it did not guarantee the promise of its name—which meant "freedom" in Swahili—he saw it as a step in that direction for the residents of Harlem's core.

The high rise was to be an apartment house for upper-,

middle-, and lower-class tenants and was to provide high-quality office space and facilities for retail stores on the street level and in the subterranean mall. While the practical impact of one such building might be debated, the psychological and moral effect of the commitment that the investment implied to the alienated community could not.

On the eighth floor, the work of enclosure to the elements was about to begin. In short order, it would be closed to the elements by brickwork and masonry, which were Gibbons's specialty. Already, pallets of glazed brick stacked higher than a man's head stood at random, interrupting the view across the open floor.

Gibbons turned toward the center of the building, where regularly spaced columns of reinforced concrete marched across the floor to a dimly lit shaft which contained the main construction elevator. The area was a jumble of compressors, small cement mixers and troughs, distorted in the shadows by the last vestiges of daylight.

He walked in among the skids of bricks, taking a flashlight from his coat pocket to check his path. He stopped before a stack of bricks and played the light over it, then looked down at the clipboard. He squinted at the paper, shook his head, and wiped at the masonry dust that had blown onto his dark brown cheek.

He walked closer to the elevator shaft, checking the red stacks at random, occasionally referring to his papers. Among the skids on the floor stood a small cable-lift crane. Suspended from its arm, several feet from the floor, a skid of bricks, neatly squared and tethered in black steel strapping, swung slightly in response to the intermittent wind.

So engrossed was Gibbons in his papers, totally puzzled by the numbers before him, that he failed to hear the click of the pivot pin that locked the crane arm in place. He didn't have time to register a look of horror as gravity and centrifugal force launched the skid and its four-ton cargo against his body, flinging him backward onto a concrete column, leaving him impaled like a badly mounted specimen on the rusty steel reinforcing bars that projected from it.

In a moment, the clatter of cascading bricks subsided and the dust settled. A tall man in a suede coat and a snap brim hat walked briskly across the floor from behind the crane. He took the papers from Gibbons's clipboard, extinguished the flashlight that still flickered where it had been dropped, and then hid in a stairwell.

He heard the elevator start up with the watchman, coming to check on the noise. The man waited calmly as the watchman, guessing at the location, stopped on the sixth and then the seventh floors. When the elevator reached the eighth floor, the man in the hat walked quickly but quietly down the stairs. Once on the ground, he strode unconcernedly across the building, out of the gate and into the night. As he turned the corner of 125th Street onto Seventh Avenue, he checked his watch. It was 5:00 P.M. At the same time, the watchman emerged from the elevator and ran to the hut at the entrance of the construction site to phone the police.

Phil Seelig, one of a half dozen police reporters for the *New York Advocate*, was sitting in the *Advocate*'s office in the Press Room on the second floor at Police Plaza, headquarters of NYPD. He sat with his feet propped on the desk, reading a western, to kill time until six, when his shift would be over.

The room was ten by fifteen, just large enough for one desk, a couple of chairs, and a row of filing cabinets. Stacked on the cabinets were a shortwave radio and four speakers which gave him immediate access to the broadcasts of the police and fire departments and a dozen other civil services as they tracked the parade of crime and accident that marches across the city of New York every day of the year. There were three phones on his desk; one was linked to the Operations Room of the Police Department, six stories above, and the others to the *Advocate* for instant relay of urgent leads. Down the hall, similar offices covered the police beat for the *Times, El Diario, News World.* At the end of the complex, a bull pen housed the three reporters that the *Daily News* keeps on the job nineteen hours a day.

Understanding the short static-marred transmissions on the emergency frequencies was like becoming fluent in a foreign language. Trained by twenty years of experience to the nuances of the broadcasts, he had hardly stirred all day. After he had balled up the brown bag in which he had brought his lunch, there had been a promising possible child molestation. He sighed and turned the page. But it had turned out that the lady in Queens overstated the case. There is no law against her eighteen-year-old daughter screwing her boyfriend on the living room couch—even if she's supposed to be in school and mistakenly thinks her mother's at the supermarket.

Patrol car calls and minor fires blared out across the room, along with petty stickups and muggings. Seelig kept reading, subliminally screening and rejecting the broadcast information. When the call went out for a police car and ambulance at Uhuru Towers, he lifted his head, then turned back to his book. Probably, he thought, just a routine accident which could be collected from the communal telex out in the hall at a later hour and submitted for possible inclusion in the morning editions.

Seelig put down the book and made a short note to himself on the pad. The door opened to admit Bert Harvey, who was coming in to relieve him, and Frank Ruggieri, the *Advocate* police photographer.

Harvey, tall and thin with a graying pompadour, shuddered in his coat. "Oy, is it cold."

"Find anything interesting out there?"

"I found out that I'd rather be in here. That's what I get for standing near an editor when a call comes in. Got any coffee?"

Seelig pointed at the urn on the windowsill. "Just made."

Ruggieri, a plump man of medium height with rosy cheeks, took a proffered cup and sat on the edge of the desk. "We found that you can spread two Puerto Ricans of average size over a twenty-five square foot area if you push hard enough on them with two cars."

"Did you drop off the film?" Seelig asked.

Harvey said, "Yes. And stopped off long enough to turn in the story. A hundred words. It'll get chewed up in the overnight. They'll use the pictures, though. What a mess."

Seelig checked his watch. "I know it's a little early, but why don't you take over, Bert? There was an accident up at Uhuru Towers. I'd like to drop by for a quick look."

"Ah, yes," Harvey replied, in his best W. C. Fields voice. "The governor's project to renovate the inner city."

"Tut-tut, my dear. Respectable housing for black Americans of all colors." Seelig got up, dog-eared his place in the book, and stuffed it into his jacket pocket. "It also happens that I'm off at six and that Uhuru Towers is closer to Riverdale than Police Plaza. So, I'll kill two birds with one stone." He put on his coat, called in to the metropolitan desk about his plans, and left.

By the time that he had gotten his car out of the municipal garage it was close to 5:30, and the traffic going uptown from Wall Street, ten blocks south of police headquarters at the end of Manhattan Island, had begun to thin out. As it was, it took nearly a half hour to get to the off ramp at 125th Street and to fight his way west.

He double-parked the car near the entrance of the construction site, walked up and showed his identification to a red-faced policeman with earmuffs, who waved him by. Because of the cold and the darkness, the crowd had been kept to a minimum, called in only by the sound of sirens. Seelig joined several officers, including a uniformed lieutenant, and watched as two hospital attendants, their whites protruding from their overcoats, wheeled the blanket-covered remains of Lloyd Gibbons to the waiting ambulance.

Seelig recognized the lieutenant and moved to intercept him as he headed toward the construction hut. "Hey, Joe," he cried. "Lieutenant Healy, can I talk to you?"

Healy stopped and motioned to him. "Hi, Phil. Come inside. I'm freezing my ass off."

They walked together up the few crude wooden steps. There were two desks pushed together in the middle of a twenty-foot space, a couple of trestle tables at the walls covered with rolled blueprints, and some filing cabinets. On a couch in a corner a skinny middle-aged black man in a watchman's uniform sat, disconsolate, hugging his knees.

Lieutenant Healy told Seelig, "Lovinski has all the details, names and such."

"What happened, Joe?"

"From what we can tell, he was up on the eighth floor." He shrugged. "Maybe a cable broke. Anyway, he got slammed by a skid full of bricks. It knocked him into a concrete column. Got a couple of those wire things right through the back. He was just hanging there when we found him."

"Anything in it?"

Healy shook his head. "Forensics is looking into it. Seems like just another industrial accident."

"You know what he was doing up there?" Seelig asked.

"Not really," Healy replied. He pointed toward the guard on the couch. "He says he was a supervisor. One of the people in charge of masonry. Not unusual for a guy like that to stay a little late. It was about a quarter to five when he got killed. The crew goes home at 4:15."

There was a knock at the door. Healy opened it to find the red-faced cop shivering on the steps. "There's a man out here named Hawkes, Lieutenant. Says he's the head of the company that's building this place."

Healy walked outside and down the steps. Seelig followed him unobtrusively to a deep-brown Lincoln sedan parked at the entrance.

As Healy strode forward, he was met by a light-skinned black of medium height, but great bulk, enveloped in a dark woolen coat. He extended a gloved hand and said, "I'm Marcus Hawkes, Lieutenant. My company is the general contractor here. I'm told there's been an accident."

Healy took his hand. "I'm afraid so. Gibbons is dead."

"I know. The security agency called me at home." Healy was surprised to hear a high tenor voice coming from the rotund body, only accentuated by a Jamaican twang. "He was one of our best people, was Lloyd. Conscientious. One of few blacks ever admitted to the Masonry and Bricklayers Union. A sad thing. How did it happen?"

"It appears that he was struck by a load of bricks." Hawkes made Healy uncomfortable and he shifted from one foot to another. "Well, we're going to take the guard to the hospital, too. He's pretty badly shaken. He found the body. Anyway, the company said they'd send another man right out."

"I'm sure that they will," Hawkes said. "I'd like to talk to the guard. There's a lot to consider. This isn't just another building, you know. This is the key to the renewal of the urban core." He stopped short, realizing that his voice had risen half an octave, and that Healy was staring at him oddly. He lowered his voice decorously, and said, "And, of course, he was a family man—tragic."

There was an awkward silence, during which Phil Seelig slipped around Healy and into Hawkes's view. "Oh, yeah," the Lieutenant said, "Mr. Hawkes, Phil Seelig. He's with the *Advocate*."

Hawkes turned a smile upon him, all white capped teeth behind thin lips, his eyes large and round. "A pleasure. What brings you this way?"

Seelig shuffled uncomfortably. "I'm a police reporter, Mr. Hawkes. I cover violent death a lot. Nice to meet you, too."

Hawkes tipped his hat. "I must speak to the guard, now." He continued past them toward the shack. When the guard emerged, shakily, his elbow held by a policeman, Hawkes strode forward and put his arm around the man's shoulders. "Are you all right, brother? This must be a terrible thing for you. Can you talk?"

"Yes, sir. I'm okay, Mr. Hawkes."

"You made a statement to the police, I guess."

"Yes, sir. I told them how I found him. I heard this big noise. I went up there and there he was, hung up there, all smashed up. Blood everywhere." He began to shake.

Hawkes patted his arm. "You go with the policeman. That's all right. Thanks for your help." As the cop led him away Hawkes turned and said, "You will let me look at that report, won't you, Lieutenant? There may be some information that will keep this kind of thing from happening again."

"Yeah. You told me that, Mr. Hawkes. If you come over to the station house tomorrow, you can look at it."

Hawkes smiled in acknowledgment and thanked him, then turned to Seelig. "I hope that we'll get a fair shake out of the press on this matter. This project is important to the whole community. I'm sure that Lloyd would have wanted it that way."

"Lloyd?" Seelig asked puzzled.

"Lloyd Gibbons," Hawkes said. "The deceased."

Seelig nodded in agreement. Hawkes stripped his glove from his short fat fingers and extended it to the reporter, a diamond in a Florentine setting gleamed from his pinky. Seelig shook his hand and said, "It's just another accident."

"It'll be reported and forgotten before tomorrow's statistics start to come in. But, Gibbons, he'll still be dead."

Seelig drove up the Henry Hudson Parkway to his Riverdale apartment, gabbed alternately during dinner with his wife about her bridge game and with his son about the Knicks, then settled into his living room chair to read the Sixth Race Final edition of the *New York Advocate*.

He'd gotten a little space on page nine, a couple of hundred words. Some guy named Halloran in Queens had come home drunk and shot his wife. Nothing fatal—just in the arm. His son had broken a candlestick over his head. Nothing serious—just a concussion. Both the old lady and the old man had battled the cops for trying to take him and the kid away on various assault charges.

Seelig leafed through the paper starting with its tabloid front page, featuring a large photograph and a banner headline. The rest of the space was taken up by the masthead bearing the paper's name, and a few words of follow-up on the headline. The lead story always continued on page three. When he finished it, he looked across to page two. Half of its six-column width and its full length was occupied by a feature story by Paul Curtin. Seelig scanned it quickly, then went back again.

The subject was three sick people, dead or maimed by substandard drugs in a public hospital. Seelig, who knew Curtin well, could sense his frustration through the crisp prose. Since Paul had come up from the *Washington Post* four years ago, he'd been the paper's watchdog in the affairs of the state of New York. He'd been hired to sell papers, half-columnist and half-reporter in the way of the new journalism, newsman and entertainer. It was election year, and the publisher of the *Advocate* was determined to unseat Francis Xavier McCarthy O'Neil, the governor of New York.

Seelig put the paper on the table and looked through his pocket note pad. He had scribbled "check possible Curtin interest Uhuru." Glancing at a mimeographed list of *Advocate* personnel, he dialed Curtin's home number, and waited.

He was about to hang up when Curtin answered the phone, breathless. "Hello, Paul Curtin."

"Hi, Paul. This is Phil Seelig. Did I pull you out of the john?"

"Close, the shower. What's up?"

"Maybe nothing. I covered an industrial accident today. Around five o'clock a construction superintendent named Gibbons got killed up at Uhuru Towers. That's a pet project of your buddy Frank O'Neil's."

"And you smell a rat?"

"A black-run construction company building a fifty-million-dollar building with public money and no rats? You jest, of course."

"Cynical, Phil. Nasty, even. Accidents happen. You know this is Big Frank's Harlem trump card. I'm sure it's being looked over through a magnifying glass."

"You never know, Paulie."

Curtin paused for a minute. Phil Seelig was no fool. "You got a hunch?"

Curtin could imagine his indifferent shrug as he replied. "It looked like an ordinary accident to me. Some poor spook got smacked by a ton of bricks. Then this guy Hawkes who runs the construction company—you know him?"

"I've seen him a couple of times. A little fat guy."

"That's the one. He shows up full of crocodile tears and platitudes to make sure that he didn't get a bad press."

Paul laughed. "And that was enough to turn you off. Never trust a man who proclaims his own honesty."

"Not to the working press, anyway. Go dry off." Seelig hung up the phone and dumped his copy of the *Advocate* into the wastebasket on his way to his bedroom to watch TV.

2

Paul Curtin jotted a few words about his phone conversation on the yellow pad that he kept by his bedside. He glanced at the clock in annoyance and trotted back to the bathroom, his feet squishing on the carpet, and stepped back into the running shower.

He rinsed the shampoo from his hair and stood for a moment, turning his stiff left shoulder into the stream. The scar, a Vietnam War souvenir that ran from the top of his arm to his elbow, had whitened in ten years, but damp weather still caused it to ache. He watched the droplets trace a random path to the floor of the tub, then remembering the clock, turned off the shower, grabbed a towel, and began to dry himself vigorously.

He tugged in disgust at a modest roll of excess flesh that had begun to take shape at the waist of his otherwise trim thirty-six-year-old body. "Oh, Paul," he said aloud, "you ain't so lovely as once you was." He finished with the towel, threw it on the floor, and then as an afterthought, retrieved it and hung it folded on the bar. It took a few minutes for the blower to dry his blond hair. He shifted from foot to foot impatiently, running a brush over his head to speed the process.

Although he had laid out his formal attire that morning, down to putting the links and studs through the impossibly small holes in the pleated front of the shirt, he was going to be late.

As he pulled on his pants, stumbling in his haste, he cursed aloud at the reason for his delay. Humberto Valenzuela, M.D., assistant director of Medicaid for the state of New York, had resigned under fire—much of it provided by Paul himself.

He looked up into the mirror to snap his bow tie into place, then reached for his jacket. When he had called the doctor's office, Valenzuela had flown the coop.

Dr. Valenzuela was either incompetent, on the take, or both. He had approved the appointment of a small wholesaler of drugs as a supplier to Stuyvesant Hospital in the poorest section of Brooklyn. There had been some substandard insulin. A couple of deaths. One patient blinded. A kid.

He'd got it down on paper. It was a tight, angry story. He'd tried to keep it low key. Bare facts. He kicked a wastebasket out of his way. He knew it would slip from the public imagination in twenty-four hours. Therefore, no support from the editorial board of the paper, and no follow-up. There had been a brief mention in the *Times*. TV had passed it over.

The company's appointment would be cancelled. There would be no indictment. Too tough to prove criminal intent. Courts that release knife-wielding rapists on their own recognizance don't have time to fool with the fine points. Perhaps they would be sued by the Health and Hospitals Corporation, which ran New York's public medical facilities. So what? It was a storefront with no assets. They'd open up across the street with a new name in a week.

"File it and forget it, Paul," he said, looking at himself in the full-length mirror on the bathroom door. The jacket still closed. He smiled, showing his teeth. Almost perfect. There was one that was crooked on the bottom.

As he reached for the light switch on the wall, his eyes flickered over the picture in the five-by-seven frame. The face was like his, oval with a straight nose and blue eyes. But where Paul's were acute with intelligence, the child's were vacant. The mouth hung slack in the six-year-old face, the features oddly flattened. As he walked to the door, Paul recalled with mixed emotions that since it was Tuesday, in two days it would be Thursday—That Thursday—the day every other month when he went to Stamford to visit his son, Jerry.

As he waited for the elevator, he mused that things holding promise seemed fewer to him as time went on. He had been looking forward to this evening for a month. The annual charity function for the Sloan-Kettering Cancer Institute was to be a cocktail party and buffet dinner, its high estate in the social firmament underscored by its prestigious setting—the Great Hall and Egyptian Wing of the Metropolitan Museum of Art.

The women would be bejeweled and beautifully dressed, the conversation witty and enlightened. In all, a lot of New York's movers and shakers would be in attendance.

Paul liked the cosmopolitan crowd and the visual impact of the rich at their charities. And it was to be a professional feast. The governor would be there, and his rivals, Mayor Christopher Greene, the Democratic candidate, and George Allen Mason, the Conservative. One could hope for a few sparks to be struck, Paul thought, or at least, more cynically, a few sacred promises to be made.

He turned and looked back at his building, and thought fondly of Maryanne. During the first two years that Paul had lived in New York, he'd rented a space in an uninspiring dormitory of studios and one-bedroom flats on Second Avenue in the seventies. Then he had met her, and with her inside position at a major real estate broker, she had found him his lovely rent-stablized apartment in a converted six-story limestone mansion on Eighty-third Street between Madison and Fifth avenues. He walked down the block toward the museum, which was just across the avenue. If he hung out of his window far enough, he thought, he could see the fountains from his bedroom.

As Paul waited for the light to change, a converted De Ville limousine thirty feet long, sprouting TV and telephone antennas like a ship of war, pulled up to the broad steps that front the museum. There was a buzz from the little crowd of onlookers that hovered on the sidewalk as the door opened. Autograph books and pens were brought to the ready. A few strobes from free-lance paparazzi threw splashes of light on an impeccably dressed couple as they emerged and climbed toward the bronze doors. There was a sigh of disappointment, and the books and pens were lowered.

Amused, Paul crossed the street and trotted up the stairs behind them. It was probably just one of the ten richest men in the world instead of a rock star. He caught a glimpse of the couple as he showed a guard his engraved invitation. They looked Latin, he thought, as he watched them swirl through the throng in the Great Hall.

After getting rid of his coat he stood for a moment orienting himself. Jonas Salk was in from the coast and stood in the middle of the hall holding court.

Paul stepped up to the bar, and asked a waiter for a scotch and soda, sidled over to a marble column, and looked across the Great Hall of the Metropolitan Museum of Art.

A voice behind him whispered, "I left an animated conversation with Harry Lesser to find you. You are an hour late."

Without turning, Paul said, "Who is Harry Lesser?"

"One of the biggest co-op converters in the real estate business in New York. He says he is interested in the Walsh house on Sixty-second Street."

"And that's important?"

"To me it is, my love. I've been trying to sell it for six months. It would pay a lot of tuition." She slid around the beige and rose pillar and touched her glass to his own. "Wish me luck?"

He looked down at Maryanne, a head shorter than his six foot two. She was dressed in a shimmering gown of royal blue silk, draped across her left shoulder toga-style, leaving her back bare. His eyes followed the soft fabric from where it clung to her bosom to the skirt, slit to mid-thigh revealing a long and shapely leg.

He smiled tenderly at her and replied, "I hope you sell him the Empire State Building."

She touched his cheek lightly with her palm. Her blue eyes flashed under blond curls that tumbled over a high forehead. "To my dismay, it isn't mine to sell. But I appreciate the thought."

He bent forward and brushed his lips lightly against hers. "Well, my heart was in the right place anyway. How are you?"

She put her arm through his and leaned against him. He could see that her makeup disguised little lines of fatigue at the corners of her too-wide mouth, beneath an upturned nose. "I'm pooped. I had to take Petey for a shot, and then back to school. I never got any lunch." Her eight-year-old son by her ex-husband, Forrest Middleton, had recurring asthma attacks that were more frightening than dangerous. "Between tuition for two kids at private school and doctor bills, it's a miracle I can afford lunch. Jesus, would I love to sell the Walsh house to Harry Lesser."

"You must be starved. What did you do besides tend to Petey?"

"I showed nine apartments to a couple from Switzerland. Très riche. Très Teutonic. Très demanding."

He led her toward a waiter bearing a rapidly emptying tray of hors d'oeuvres.

She grasped the waiter's elbow firmly, extracted a paper napkin, balanced it on top of her glass and took three canapes from the tray. Paul followed suit. "Technique is everything," she said.

"Mmmmm."

"Is that all you can say, Paul? I have it on the best authority that this caviar is from Oregon."

"Down with the Ayatollah," Paul said, washing it down with a swallow of scotch. "Damn good, too."

"A trifle bland, and a bit too salty."

"Now you're the purist. The caviar is delicious. Ah, look what I see. Follow me." Setting his glass in a convenient niche, Paul took Maryanne's arm and swept her across the marble floor through the swirling mass. A tall man, so painfully thin as to raise questions about his health, stood talking to the couple that Paul had seen emerge from the limousine.

"Good evening, Pierre," Paul said.

Pierre Du Fresne, the society columnist for the *New York Advocate*, turned his narrow patrician face in the direction of his companions. His voice was nasal and Oxford-cultured with only the trace of a rolling French R. "Guido and Rafaela Bronzini, may I present Maryanne Middleton, one of New York's most charming ladies. She has been a member of the Sloan-Kettering benefit committee for years—she was merely a child when she began, you understand. And this is Paul Curtin." He smiled dryly. "Dare I call you a star reporter?"

Paul extended his hand with a grin. "In front of anyone but our publisher. Good evening, Mr. Bronzini. I'm glad to meet you." Bronzini took his hand and shook it firmly. Paul took his wife's proffered elbow-length white glove and brushed it lightly with a kiss. "Signora."

"Signor Bronzini is in chemicals," Du Fresne said airily. "Just in the process of moving to our fair city."

"Yes, we will be spending much more of our time here now. Our children are enrolled in school here for the fall."

"How many have you?" Maryanne asked.

"Three girls and a boy."

"Let me guess," Maryanne said. "Three to the convent and one to St. Ignatius."

"Almost perfect," Bronzini said in a cultured and slightly accented voice. "Three to the Convent of the Sacred Heart and one to St. David's. Tell me, has it to do with Italians? Is that all we shall find there? A kind of ghetto for the Catholic rich?"

Maryanne burst into laughter. "They're fine schools. You'll find Catholics of every national and ethnic flavor, and a number of non-Catholics, as well."

Bronzini smiled a knowing smile. "But still a ghetto."

She acknowledged him with an amused nod. "Of the best sort, of course. A pleasure to meet you, signora. I wish you luck in your new home."

As she drifted away with Paul, she said, "Did you see the rock?"

"I would like to lie, but a blind man couldn't have missed it. Tell me where it falls on the Middleton Index."

"Oh, maybe ten carats. First class, too. Shall we say two-fifty?"

She looked around at the uniformed security men who stood at regular intervals against the walls. "There are probably more guards here than in the Bank of England."

"And you can't even see the plainclothesmen," Paul added.

"Sure I can. They're the ones whose tuxes don't fit."

"Let's eat."

Paul steered Maryanne across the floor. A class act, he thought, in the year-old dress that her father had bought her. He gave her a squeeze. It wasn't easy for Maryanne to raise

two kids in Manhattan on her grand a month in alimony and the
two or three more that hard work pulled out of the real estate
game.

"Would that I could smoke my salmon over hundred-dollar
bills like the Bronzinis," she said. "Where's the food?"

"Don't you know?"

"I told you. I had Harry Lasser cornered right over there by
the gift shop entrance. I didn't move till you finally showed
up."

"The food must be in the Egyptian Wing. Shall we, then?"
He walked her past the ancient stones that herald the beginning
of the finest collection of Egyptology in the Western World.
"It's crazy, but I think Bronzini views us in the same light that
Peter Stuyvesant saw the Indians. Twenty-four dollars worth of
beads. . . ."

"Hey, to him it's a bargain. Twenty-four dollars worth of
beads, plus two million dollars for the house. It's cheaper than
he could buy the same property in Milan, or in Paris or
London, for that matter. He thinks he's taking us for a ride."

"And none of the other worries about raising kids in New
York. He's not going to have to worry about whether his kids
will be able to evade their classmates and make it home alive
every night. Or whether or not they're going to blow their
allowance on drugs in the school yard. And all of that for a
lousy twenty-five thousand a year."

"Whoosh. A little down on the Big City. You sound like
you're ready to leave town."

He cocked his head and looked down at her, saying with
some annoyance, "Well, maybe I am."

She fixed her gaze at the end of the hall and walked on. She
was not amused.

Paul and Maryanne strolled down a long corridor covered
with facsimiles of Egyptian tomb paintings until they came to a
pair of enormous stone sarcophagi standing like guardians
before bronze-framed glass doors, where another guard asked
to see their invitations.

They stepped through into a glass-walled gallery three
hundred feet long and a hundred feet wide, which gave onto
Central Park to the north and to Fifth Avenue's opulent
apartment buildings to the east.

In its center, a raised platform extended two thirds of the

room's width and length, surrounded by water-bearing channels, with a pool twenty feet wide at its foot. At the far end of the platform stood the Temple of Dendur, a classic form, whole and serene, its walls incised with hieroglyphics, telling the story, two millennia old, of the two drowned brothers in whose memory it had been erected.

Maryanne tugged at his arm. "If the nice people on the benefit committee have been thoughtful enough to provide this lovely diversion for you and to put together all of this lovely nourishment, and the Doctors Sackler have been kind enough to build this lovely room for your pleasure, I think that the least you can do is stop gnawing at your intestines about the bastard Valenzuela for the moment and enjoy my company."

"I guess I'm just a little out of sorts with the system."

A long table was set against the far wall of the building, to the rear of the temple. Despite her hunger Maryanne took sparingly of a rich chicken curry with rice. Paul filled his plate twice. He left Maryanne for a moment to go to the bar. When he returned, she had disposed of both plates. He smiled. He had opened his jacket.

"I almost lost the damn button."

"I noticed."

He glanced at his watch. "I'd better dip my pen in poison. I think that my quarry is approaching. How shall I malign thee? Let me count the ways."

"Do you think he will bring his girl friend?"

"Do you think she would miss a shindig like this? This is her element. And besides," he said with sarcasm, "do you think she'd want to miss a chance to see the governor's favorite critic—me?"

They stood together and looked across the gallery, now seemingly crowded despite its vast open space, as two thousand people drifted in to partake of the buffet and to look at each other.

Maryanne shook her head in admiration. "It's better than a fashion show. Galanos and Halston, Versace and Armani, Dior and Givenchy, Kenzo and Hanae Mori."

"And only two grand and up. I don't like the last two, though. I can't tell Oriental designers apart."

"Oh, God."

Paul perked up and pulled her along. "Here comes the Boss."

The doors to the Sackler Wing opened to admit Francis Xavier McCarthy O'Neil, governor of the Empire State. He stood in the midst of an admiring throng, and portable TV lights competed with flashes from still cameras for the opportunity to illuminate the familiar face, tan from a brief vacation in Puerto Rico the previous week. Graying sideburns framed a strong jaw, balanced by a substantial nose above a sensuous mouth, and the piercing dark eyes of the Black Irish. His six-foot-three-inch frame was flattered by a well-cut tuxedo, his arm graced by Allison Vance Forrestiere.

Paul waited for a few minutes for the initial rush to die down. His focus shifted from the governor as he parried questions with his customary ease to his companion who was always referred to by both her maiden and married names, a convention meant to both recall and reinforce the fortuitous accident of her birth into an American industrial dynasty whose wealth was built on soap flakes. Paul's role as the governor's critic had earned him Allison's angry dislike.

She was tall and languid, shoulders sloping from a swan's neck, with a small-featured face framed by soft reddish-blond hair. From time to time, when she frowned, Paul thought that he could see a trace of the iron will that passed from her father, Wallace Harley Vance III, chairman of Vance Products, and the fourth in the founder's line.

The governor, a widower for a dozen years, had been her regular companion since soon after her divorce from a dashing but eminently unsuitable Italian count.

She pivoted slightly from side to side before the audience of anxious reporters and photographers to give each a view of her impressive décolletage, set off by a brilliant cascade of diamonds and amethysts. She made eye contact with Paul, and by the merest gesture of lowered lids, chilled him to the bone.

The governor spotted Paul as the crowd around him thinned out. "Ah, look who's here," he said in his lilting tenor. "It's my man Paul. How are you doing this evening?"

"Struggling along, thank you, Governor. A little weary from the chase, but otherwise all right. How has your day been?"

"Outside of a minor misunderstanding with some of the press about problems in health care in the city," he pushed back a bit, "I've had a rousing day, I signed the Law Enforcement Aid Bill and kissed a dozen babies. I'm on the road to reelection, in case you hadn't heard."

Paul smiled at the combination of his geniality and his gall. This was the Frank O'Neil who handled Big Labor with the back of his hand and gave them boondoggles with the palm, who taxed businessmen to their knees, and then drew their contributions as he compared himself to the alternatives. "I don't suppose all of the other guests here will share that sentiment," Paul parried.

"Is Chris Greene going to be here?" the governor asked in mock surprise. "I didn't think that His Honor was going to grace us with his presence. Is he going to read us an old Teddy Kennedy speech? Or is tonight the night for William Jennings Bryan?"

"I heard from his campaign headquarters," Paul said off-handedly, "that he was going to say that when he was governor, the redistribution of wealth would be from the rich to the poor instead of the other way around."

The governor flashed a broad smile. "That sounds like him. If he's governor, with his platform, Robin Hood will starve to death, because we'll all be poor."

Paul nodded politely to the governor, acknowledging the barb. "Anything to say about Dr. Valenzuela's sudden departure?"

Some of the humor went out of the voice, but the smile remained. "I believe that was pretty well hashed over in the papers. The man was tired. He withdrew from his post because he didn't feel up to its continuing pressures. It was a matter of health."

Paul stifled the temptation to ask whether it was public or private health. "Do you think that the departure will promote an improvement in the department?"

O'Neil raised an eyebrow. "He was a dedicated public servant. But he was very tired. Let's just say his replacement will have . . . a fresher outlook toward the job." The smile faded. "I'm afraid we'll have to continue this in another forum, Paul. I came here to extoll Sloan-Kettering's virtues, and to pay my respects. I'm being called."

Paul turned to see that the chairman of the charity dinner, and parenthetically of the city's largest store, was waving to the governor across the multitude. Paul stepped aside graciously, and watched Frank O'Neil, confident and unruffled, work his way through the rich crowd, shaking hands here and there. Paul stared after him. Had he acknowledged Valenzuela's culpability? Not certainly enough to print. But Paul felt some satisfaction all the same. The crowd melted away with the governor, and in a moment, Paul stood alone.

"A penny and a half for your thoughts."

Paul started, then his eyes focused on Maryanne, who had come to stand with him. "Has the value of my thoughts gone up?"

"Just compensating for inflation. What were you thinking?"

"Shit. I don't know. Let's go get another drink. I wonder when the mayor will show up. This is supposed to be a theatrical presentation staged for my benefit. Instead of my chasing the candidates, they're all supposed to present themselves to me."

Ten minutes later, having fought and won the battle of the bar, they drifted back to the center of the room. Maryanne touched Paul's arm and said, "Look, here comes the prodigal son, now."

There was a repetition of the governor's entrance scene at the bronze doors, flashguns popping and people crowding forward. Paul raised his glass irreverently to the life-sized bas-relief of hawk-headed Horus on the temple wall before him, and sallied forth.

As Paul watched the mayor take on his questioners, he saw him give a characteristic hitch of his thin shoulders that always gave the impression that he was stepping up onto a soapbox. Not, Paul thought to himself, that he ever got off for very long. Even flat on his feet, he had an advantage. Chris Greene was six foot two and thin. He costumed himself in Brooks Brothers pinstripes and button-down shirts, and favored regimental ties. Paul stared at him critically. Maryanne said she couldn't go to bed with a man who wore a toupee. Chris Greene's was carefully combed to form a casual wave above the high forehead and the aquiline nose. Maryanne said she wondered if he could change his political opinions with the same ease as he could his hairstyle.

As was his habit, Mayor Greene pointed a bony finger at the reporter whose question he was answering. His voice was sharp and slightly nasal. His lips were thin, and high cheekbones gave him a saturnine air. He looked younger than his forty-one years, and his expression was meant to convey an air of seriousness to his words.

"We shouldn't wait around forever while the clubhouse hacks and the banks decide what's going to happen to the greatest city in the greatest state in the country. You have to instill a sense of confidence in the people. Give them a sense of participation and dignity, then we'll realize our richest asset, a productive and willing work force. Good workers mean fat profits, and profits are what attract industry and jobs. If we make the people able, then industry will come to seek their services." As he finished the sentence, his dark eyes cast about the audience like a bird of prey, then flashed and fixed on Paul, whose hands were in his pockets.

"Hey, Paul, very provocative article today on Valenzuela. Reporting at its best. Guess we won't be seeing much of him anymore. But it'll take more than that to clean up the Health and Hospitals Corporation in this state. Keep digging."

Paul felt queasy. He was as fond of public praise as the next man, but Greene's pat on the head had been nothing but a cheap shot at the governor.

Paul listened to another question, letting his eyes wander around the fringe of the crowd. They fell upon a pretty, thin-faced blonde. Jennifer Ashton was in the background, as usual, rooting her candidate on. Unlike Maryanne, she didn't mind sleeping with men who wore toupees.

Stanley Greenberg's son had done well for himself, Paul thought. He was a New Yorker born and bred. He had gone to Horace Mann, then on to Columbia and Columbia Law School. When he had graduated, he had cast about for a career and decided on politics. He claimed that he changed his name to avoid profiting unfairly from his father's position as a nationwide publisher of taxi guides and street maps, and from association with his substantial wealth. With the collapse of the city under Beame, he had staked out a sparsely populated corner of the Democratic Party and had quickly risen from assemblyman to councilman and then to mayor. And now, Paul thought, he has a *shiksa* girl friend. What constituency could ask for more?

A reporter from the *Times* raised his hand and asked, "Do

you think there ought to be a broader program in job development, Mr. Mayor?"

How much did he pay him to ask? Paul thought cynically.

"How else can we provide the work force I was talking about? Unemployment is just the dark side of skills development and training programs. If you don't have one, then you have the other. Establish projects to fill the needs in the capital spending program, then join the state and industry together in providing jobs and training for the urban poor. You have your cake and eat it. The development of needed public works and the elimination of the unskilled and poverty ridden."

Paul stopped chewing at a hangnail and raised a hand. Greene recognized him immediately. "Would you put Uhuru Towers in that category, Mr. Mayor?"

There was a brief hesitation, then Greene said, "I would consider Uhuru Towers a triumph." He grinned showing even, capped teeth. "Do you know how much pushing and shoving it took to get our Republican governor to do something for the people? It's his project, but it's the city's victory." He turned to the sea of upraised hands. "Next."

Paul stood politely for the ten minutes that the question and answer period occupied, and when it ended, drifted away to the corner of the temple where he had left Maryanne.

She was engaged in conversation with a petite fortyish woman in blue tulle with a cymbidium orchid pinned to one shoulder.

As Paul approached, the woman said, "No need to charm me, Mr. Curtin. Your job is already being done for you."

"Thank you, Dr. Mason. It's always nice to know that one can be easily replaced."

"Oh, dear. Don't tell me that I've brought on a crisis in confidence."

"Where is the congressman?" Paul asked. "I've been out talking to the opposition and haven't had a chance to have his views this evening."

"As a matter of fact, he's standing right up there by the temple door talking to one of your cohorts." Eleanor Mason pointed over his head where her husband was deeply involved with Pierre Du Fresne.

"Good evening, Mr. Mason. Hello again, Pierre."

George Mason, candidate of the Conservative Party for the

governorship of the state of New York, smiled languidly. "I was beginning to feel lonely, Paul. I'm glad that you've come. It has not been lost upon me that there was a fair mob for Governor O'Neil, and even a rush at Chris Greene in this hostile atmosphere, but save for a few polite questions, I have been left largely alone except for this dissolute old gossiper, whom I count a friend."

"Are you suggesting that you aren't being taken seriously, George?"

"No, Paul. But just for the record, do you remember what Bill Buckley said when he was running for mayor?"

"I do. If he won, he'd demand a recount."

"I wouldn't."

"I've been witness to the remarks of both the governor and the mayor. I'm afraid to report that neither of them shook the earth. So far as I can tell, the governor has been out kissing babies and is sure he will be reelected. Oh, yes, and he likes Sloan-Kettering and is against cancer. Chris is for jobs and job training and the dignity of man."

"Amen, and you can quote me."

Paul laughed and looked frankly at George Mason. He didn't think much of his politics, but he found him personally charming. He hesitated, then on a hunch asked, "You feeling quotable?"

The wrinkles at the corners of Mason's eyes deepened as he smiled. "A politician should always be prepared to be quoted, and to pray that he is in the hands of either friends or honest men. Shoot."

"How about Uhuru Towers?"

Mason responded easily. "In brief, circuses without bread. Take all of that money and rehabilitate the countless small properties that the city has taken over because of rent control and resultant tax defaults, all those solid little brownstones and brick buildings. The city and the state don't belong in the real estate business, but since they're there, then let them make the best of it by producing affordable dwelling units instead of theater."

"Then you don't buy the idea that Uhuru Towers is going to be an impetus for building in Harlem by the private sector?"

"You can't encourage others by making a bad example, People in the building industry know what it costs to put up so-

and-so many floors. They know, based on the assessments of similar buildings what the real estate tax would be. They know operating costs. Given those numbers, and financing costs, you know what it costs to carry the building and—including a reasonable profit for the landlord—what the rents will be. Even with a fat tax abatement, there's no way that on a straight business basis Uhuru Towers can serve a low-income community."

Paul looked up from his pad and said, "Throw out the poor and jack up the rents?"

"No, just build for their comfort and security instead of their egos."

Paul jotted in the pad, then pocketed it. "Congratulations, Congressman. That's the first decent one-liner of the evening."

"Anytime, Paul. You ought to come more often to our modest little gatherings."

"Good night, George. Good night, Pierre."

Paul dropped down to the floor level and returned to Maryanne and Eleanor Mason. "Well, have you finished being instructed by my husband?"

"Absolutely, Dr. Mason, and I'm a better man for it."

"Good, then maybe there's some hope for this charming lady. She seems to be stuck with you. I want you to know that she's done a terrific job for the dinner committee of the institute and that we're very grateful. It's hell on wheels organizing charity functions this size, especially if the charity is to end up with any of the money." She extended her hand and bid them good night.

Paul watched her as she walked toward her husband, saying, "I don't think of myself as sexist, but it's hard to conceive of a pretty oncologist."

"Nonetheless, there she goes. Great lady. Two big things in her life, George Mason and cancer research. That ought to be enough fulfillment for anybody."

He shrugged, glum again. "I'm glad somebody feels like she's getting somewhere." The small orchestra that had been playing at the far end of the hall the whole evening, opposite the pool at the foot of the temple's platform, increased its volume above the subliminal with a rattle of drums and a fanfare of brass. "Let's go see the show. The committee snared Sammy Davis this year."

It had been past midnight when the last of the lush furs had been reclaimed from the cloakroom, and their owners had swept down the marble steps into the cold evening to be whisked away in cabs or limousines to the Greene Street Cafe, or Elaine's, or to the Carlyle to listen to Bobby Short.

Earlier the long black Cadillac with the license plate New York I had picked up Governor O'Neil and Allison Vance Forrestiere and started down Fifth Avenue. "Where to, sir?" the chauffeur asked, driving slowly to give the unmarked car with the governor's bodyguards a chance to catch up.

"I've got a tough day tomorrow, Allie."

"I've had enough of the public image for the evening anyway." She put her hand in his lap suggestively. "Do you think you could conjure up the energy for a nightcap? Or do you want to just drop me off?"

Frank O'Neil slipped his hand into the front of Allison's dress and cupped her breast, rolling the nipple gently between his thumb and forefinger. "Just one drink then." He straightened himself in the seat and, turning to the driver, said, "Phil, take us to Mrs. Forrestiere's apartment please."

3

It was half past one when the limousine dropped the governor off in front of his house on Fifth Avenue. He went upstairs and without removing his outerwear, stepped into the guest bath and washed his hands and splashed water on his face and dried himself to be rid of the pungent woman smell of her. He checked in the mirror, running a comb through his hair, replaced his hat, and rang for the elevator.

He strode out of the front door of the apartment house like a king. "We were kings in the Old Country, you know," he liked to say, "the O'Neils, that is," when he was playing at Auld Sod at Hibernian Society breakfasts, or at the hurling matches at Gaelic Park up on 240th Street and Broadway.

Still in his tuxedo, but wrapped in a dark cloth overcoat against the night chill, O'Neil nodded and smiled at the doorman, who said, "A little late for the nightly constitutional, Governor."

"Never miss one, Pete. You know that." As he strode across the street to Central Park, the plainclothesmen in the car at the curb put down their newspapers and began to get out to follow him. Seeing them, he waved them back inside as he often did in the late hours when he would not be bothered by his fellow citizens.

He walked briskly for a couple of hundred yards past the zoo, then down the footpath toward Fifty-ninth Street where the park ends. He checked his watch and slowed his pace, then sat on a bench.

O'Neil watched the steam made by his breath float away in the night air, staring after it at the dim garland of lights that traced the footpaths in the mist, trying to justify his midnight errand.

He was a man suited by personality and instinct to a position of power, though it was not until his late twenties that the idea of politics was thrust upon him.

He was the son of Thomas Sean O'Neil, who had been himself the fifth generation to direct the family business since its humble beginnings in the eighteenth century. O'Neil Maritime and Fuel ran half the tugboats in New York harbor and delivered a fair share of the coal and oil sold in the metropolitan area. Dennis O'Neil, Frank's only brother, was the elder, and in keeping with family tradition had been groomed to follow in his father's footsteps.

Frank had attended St. Paul's School and Harvard and had graduated from Harvard Law in 1942. Like many younger O'Neils of earlier generations, he had planned to join the firm of O'Neil, O'Neil, and McCarthy, whose senior partner was his uncle, and whose success was guaranteed by the sizable retainer paid by its largest client, O'Neil Maritime and Fuel. Instead, he enlisted in the United States Army. After training, he was sent to join the 37th Infantry Division, and served with distinction at Vella Lavella and Bougainville, attaining the rank of captain. When the 37th was withdrawn from the line, O'Neil contrived to have himself transferred to the forward-moving 27th Division.

On June 15, 1944, amphibious-tracked vehicles brought thousands of marines ashore on the island of Saipan in the Central Pacific. There was little initial resistance and the Charan Kanoa airfield fell within a half hour. By nightfall twenty thousand marines had been landed, and there the advance stopped.

From the heights of Mount Topatchau, which dominated the island, the fanatic tactical genius General Saito opened fire with brilliantly organized artillery cover that pinned the American forces in place. With his logistical capability thus tied to the holding action on Saipan, General "Howling Mad" Smith was unable to proceed with attacks on Tinian and Guam.

Four days later the power of the Japanese Fleet was broken during the Battle of the Philippine Sea, and Smith, without concern for aircover, was able to land his reserves, the 27th Infantry Division, as suddenly available warships provided cover with a massive naval bombardment.

On June 27, the day that the American flag was raised over Mount Topatchau, a marine captain named Luigi Andretti lay screaming in a ditch. A Japanese infantryman dressed in a loincloth and a torn shirt, bleeding from wounds of his own, had pinned Andretti's hand to the ground with his bayonet as a companion kicked the prostrate American in the groin.

Andretti, half-conscious from shrapnel wounds that had rendered his free arm useless, had stumbled into the hole where the Japanese had huddled in their own excrement, shivering in fright, waiting for death to overtake them.

Frank O'Neil was leading a cleanup patrol to the yet uncaptured back side of Topatchau. He crawled on his belly to the source of the noise, and as the Japanese with the bayonet was about to administer the fatal stroke, O'Neil shot both him and his companion.

According to his citation for the Distinguished Service Cross, O'Neil's shots alerted a large group of Japs further down the hillside. O'Neil's patrol suffered heavy casualties and withdrew under fire. At great risk, O'Neil hefted the wounded Andretti over his shoulder and retreated to a cave, collecting bandoliers of ammunition from his own dead as he went. They were stuck in the cave for four hours, till a wave of soldiers from the 27th came to their rescue. During that time, Frank O'Neil had shielded Andretti from enemy fire with his own body. When found, his grenades exhausted and his ammunition almost gone, he was surrounded by forty-three dead Japanese soldiers. He had seven separate wounds, including a gaping hole in his chest.

Convalescence gave the two men an eternity to talk. O'Neil learned that Andretti came from a family of Italian importers. The business was run by his father, Silvio Andretti, who was also interested in local politics.

When they were granted leave, Luigi brought Frank O'Neil to his home behind the guarded walls of the Sea Gate compound at the end of Coney Island. His father kissed Frank and wept unashamedly. "There is nothing that is in the power of the Andretti family to give that is not yours for the asking. We owe you a life, Mr. O'Neil. We are Italians, and we take such obligations very seriously."

"Thank you, Mr. Andretti," Frank replied. "But this is wartime. Men are forever saving other men's lives. It's the times."

After a mammoth Italian dinner the men of the Andretti family retired with O'Neil to the living room to enjoy cigars and brandy. The conversation turned to politics in short order.

"Since the Roman Empire," Silvio Andretti said, "there has been no change in big city politics. To secure your political position, when you become unsure of the fidelity of the electorate, you change it, gerrymandering districts, inviting new voters. The Italians and the Irish who have always lived on the Upper East Side are no longer to be counted on by the Democrats. That's how my friend La Guardia became the mayor. Are you a Democrat, Frank?"

"Not I, sir. We're black sheep, several generations of Irish Republicans."

Andretti studied his cigar ash for a moment, then continued. "There are new generations of educated people—no longer poor immigrants. They have jobs and property. They are swayed less by tradition than self-interest. The boys who come back from the service will be still more independent. As a result, the city is being changed. These people are heading to the outskirts. In part, they are being driven. One of my *paisanos*, Vito Marcantonio, is making sure that his district is kept safe for the Democratic Party. He is encouraging thousands of Puerto Ricans to move to the city of New York, especially to his district. I'll bet you didn't even know that they were American citizens: Well, they are. And after thirty days' residence, they can vote and go on the dole.

"First the others, Irish, Italian, whatever, fight to keep them out. Then they give up and move away. You'll see. In ten years, Spanish will be the only language that you'll hear on the street." Andretti tapped the ask from his cigar and looked across at O'Neil. "Frank, have you ever thought about going into politics?"

"No, sir."

"How old are you?"

"Twenty-five."

"Let's talk some more. You might want to give it a try. There's going to be a premium on war heroes."

Brought back from his reverie by an involuntary shudder, Governor Frank O'Neil glanced at his watch and walked back up the footpath in the direction of his apartment house. When he reached the mall, he saw a man sitting on a bench equidistant between two streetlamps, yet illuminated by neither. O'Neil looked over his shoulder to be sure they were alone, then approached him. "I was expecting to hear from you, Mr. Hawkes. In fact, I was expecting a communication—a package to be exact."

"I'm sorry, Governor. There was a problem with the messenger."

"I don't like interruptions in my schedules. When you are supposed to deliver something, Mr. Hawkes, deliver it."

"I am aware, Governor. I'll do my best to see that it doesn't happen again. The delivery should be made tomorrow."

"I will be . . . disappointed . . . if it isn't. I was called by one of my people at police headquarters just before I left for dinner. There was a death at Uhuru Towers late this afternoon. The man at headquarters is aware of my deep interest in the project. Who was the man who was killed?"

"His name was Lloyd Gibbons."

"That much I know," the governor said acidly. "Was he an important part of the crew?"

"No, just a supervisor in masonry and bricks."

"Then there was no . . ." he hesitated, ". . . political significance."

"Just a regrettable accident to a poor working man."

"I'm sorry, of course. Is this going to cause any delay?"

"No, I think not."

"What does that mean?" the governor said with ill-disguised bad humor.

"We are a little behind."

"I hope that you will be finished by early fall as scheduled."

"Before the election."

"Well before the election. Our agreement envisioned full tenancy before the election."

"A lot of smiling happy black faces."

"Eating watermelon if you like. Just see that the building is finished. It wouldn't help either of us if it weren't."

"Yes, sir." Marcus Garvey Hawkes stood and extended his hand. The governor shook it briefly.

"I assume that I'll be notified of your progress through regular channels."

"Of course." Hawkes turned and began to walk away.

"Oh, Mr. Hawkes. Don't let there be any more accidents."

The governor sat on the bench for a few minutes, watching him disappear down the street. When he was sure that Hawkes was gone, he walked home.

4

The draperies in Paul Curtin's bedroom were parted halfway and light from the streetlamps cast irregular linear shadows on the white wall of his bedroom. Maryanne Middleton turned her head toward him from where she lay in the crook of his arm. She reached up and brushed at a lone bead of perspiration that trickled down his forehead. With her ear against his chest, she could hear the rapid pounding of his heart, still abnormal from the exertion of their lovemaking. He lay back against the headboard, looking unblinkingly at the ceiling. After a moment, he turned to her and traced the tip of his finger over the slight discolored mark on her breast where her skin had stretched when she had been pregnant with Petey and then Alexandra.

"Is it awful?"

"Huh?"

"The stretch mark. Is it . . . well, unappealing?"

He sighed. "Yeah. I could hardly manage. You can't imagine how hard it is." He brushed her lips with his fingertips. "I'm thinking of hanging around the girl's entrance of the junior high school. Now that's where you get firm tits."

She sat up cross-legged and turned toward him. "They're not really bad."

He caressed her gently. "No. They're not really bad. For a thirty-four-year-old lady with two children. As a matter of fact, I wanted to tell you how good you looked tonight."

"Even with the dress on?" she asked. He nodded. "God, it's two-thirty. Come, take me home."

"You don't want to stay?" he asked softly.

"Of course I do. But let's not start that again. You know that rain or shine, bloodshot eyes notwithstanding, Mama is there to give breakfast and send the troops to school each and every morning."

"I know." He swung his feet onto the floor and stood. "Can I treat you to a shower?"

They stood with their arms around each other in the warm, falling water, her head tucked beneath his chin, her breasts flattened against the blond curls on his chest. She rubbed softly at the base of his spine with her fingertips.

"Mmmm. That feels good."

"Then I'll do it some more." She was silent for a moment. "What's the matter, Paulie?"

He tightened his hug involuntarily. "How do you mean, babe?"

"It's more than just a lousy day, isn't it? This Valenzuela thing, it's just another story."

"Maybe one too many."

She pushed herself away from him a little and looked up into his face. "You half meant what you said at the museum, didn't you? I mean the part about going away."

"I'm not really sure. It's the first time I've ever put it into words. What can I say? I guess I'm just frustrated. What the hell am I accomplishing?" He took a loofa sponge from the tray on the wall, soaped it, and began to massage her back with a circular motion. "Maybe it's early male menopause, the great crisis of self-doubt. But it's not supposed to come till I'm past forty. That's New York for you. The pressure and the heat accelerate everything. It makes geriatric changes at the kindergarten level."

"But isn't that the big test? Isn't that what brought you up from Washington?"

He nodded in agreement. "That, and the money and the exposure. All of the things that you are supposed to want if you are a journalist; an interesting canvas to work on, and an appreciative, or at least a large audience. But you want to feel that you are more than a voice crying out in the wilderness."

She turned slowly under the water till the soap had run off her body, then stepped out of the tub and dried herself, allowing him to finish bathing. "That doesn't sound much like you, Paul. You're always said that the pleasure of the game was in the playing."

He turned off the water and climbed out. She rubbed him with the towel, turning him like a little boy, doing his back and chest, then bending to dry his legs and pat his genitals. He stood passively. "I believe that Artur Rubinstein could sit on the stage of Carnegie Hall and play Liszt's *Transcendental Etudes* without anyone listening and experience perfect satisfaction because he was expressing something universal—his art has meaning, the music has meaning—even if he's alone. Today, I wrote another story about the criminal stupidity which occurs at every level in the public and private sectors of this city and this state every single day of the year. So what? The public may be aware, but I see no sign that it gives a shit. The only people who are interested in what I do are the circulation manager—am I selling papers, and therefore advertising space—and the publisher—am I venting her wrath on Frank O'Neil and selling her personal political philosophy."

Maryanne stood in front of the mirror and brushed her hair out, the dryer humming. Paul pulled on his clothes, then sat at the edge of the bed and watched her as she dressed. "You sound like you feel sorry for yourself, honey," she said. "I'm not used to it."

"I'm not used to it, either. Its's more than that. I'm disgusted. I am at the top of my profession, and I feel like a flop. I'm just asking myself whether or not I'm in the right place."

They didn't talk for a few minutes while she finished. Her eyes shifted to the picture on the wall, then back to Paul. "It's

That Thursday this week." She tried to sound casual. He nodded. She walked to him and touched his cheek. "I want to go with you this time." He shook his head. "I have to, Paul, sooner or later. I want to. Can't you see that I want to?"

Paul walked to the closet in the hall and took out their coats without replying.

"Look, Paul, if I can take the responsibility for raising my children with damn little help from their indifferent father, run a household, see that everybody gets fed, and work a full-time job that supports us in this burg, then why can't I have the strength of character to deal with Jerry as a reality?"

"Jerry isn't your reality. Only mine. Petey and Alex are your realities."

"Are they your realities, too?" she said with a catch in her voice.

He reached out to her. "Ours. I mean that because I can help. I can share."

"I can help and share, too."

"Not with someone who doesn't even know that you're there."

"But you'll know. Why do you go, if it doesn't matter?"

"He's my baby."

She turned away as she put on her coat so that he couldn't see her face. "I'm going," she said. "I have already told the office that I won't be in. I've already told Loretta that she is to pick up the kids, fix them dinner, and put them to bed. I've even told Petey. So I'm going. Okay?"

When they walked out into the street, he squeezed her hand. "We can talk about it tomorrow. I'm bushed." They were lucky and caught a cab on the corner of Fifth. The driver took them to her apartment on Seventy-ninth between Second and Third. He kissed her, opened the door, and let her out. When she was safely inside, he had the cab drop him home. Too tired to think, he went upstairs, threw his clothes on the floor, and fell into a dead sleep.

He awoke with the alarm in a fog that rapidly became a foul mood. This morning he was scheduled to meet with Melanie Parsons, the publisher of the *New York Advocate,* to discuss the progress of the political campaign for the governorship, and the effect that the *Advocate* and its news and editorial departments were having on it.

Shit, he thought. What he ought to do is chuck the whole

damn thing and take his typewriter and his books, go find himself a hole up in Connecticut, where Jerry was, and write books, or magazine articles, or just chop wood, and be his own goddamn man. He shook his head in disgust. Fucking daydreamer, Curtin! Two thousand bucks in the bank. It's that fat salary that keeps Jerry in Stamford. He cut himself twice shaving.

5

At precisely 10:00 A.M. a black Cadillac limousine pulled to the front entrance of the *Advocate*. The driver, in black livery, let himself out and scurried to open the back door. Melanie Parsons emerged, holding her sable coat closed, and strode through the glass door with an aura of possession, both of herself and of the premises. As she entered the hall, a pressman with a square folded paper hat pushed the button on her private elevator and simultaneously held out a fresh-from-the-press *Advocate*. She continued to walk forward as though the door to the elevator did not exist. And indeed, it ceased to bar her way, opening in tempo with her progress. She turned, her copy of the *Advocate* in one hand and a brown paper bag containing her lunch in the other, and said, "Good morning, Morris, and thank you." Then the door closed.

It opened again on the sixth floor of the tower. As she stepped off the elevator, Madeleine Shurtleff, her secretary, took the lunch bag and the newspaper from her hand, said "Good morning, Mrs. Parsons," and retreated to her desk.

As Madeleine watched her employer drape her coat on the pink padded hanger, she mused on the fact that no one ever called her Mrs. Koenigsberg, the name of her first husband, or Mrs. Kingsriter, the name of her second husband. Nor, Madeleine thought spitefully, did anyone ever call her Parchinsky, the name her Russian-Jewish immigrant father had changed to Parsons when he had made the first of his millions in the rag trade. And, of course, they were dead. She'd survived them all.

After thirty years of bonded servitude—however well paid—Madeleine thought she could permit herself an occasional secret irreverence.

"Have we fresh flowers this morning, Madeleine? I thought that the office looked a little drab yesterday."

"Yes, Mrs. Parsons. And there was a delivery from Tiffany's."

"Good," she said, smiling. "Good." Then she disappeared through her office door.

Melanie Parsons impatiently tore apart the beribboned blue box and stuffed it and the tissue paper packing it contained into her wastebasket. She took two eight-by-ten photos from her desk drawer and inserted them in the monogrammed sterling silver frames, then set them on the desk.

"Madeleine," she called out.

"Coming." Madeleine presented herself at the desk.

"Well, what do you think?"

"Lovely," she replied. Lovely indeed, she thought. Something else to polish and dust. Melanie moved the Bachrach photos she had recently commissioned from one side of her desk to the other.

"How do they look?"

"They're excellent, Mrs. Parsons." Madeleine smiled. Like everyone else she knew, she was fond of Buddy Koenigsberg, Mrs. Parsons's fifty-two-year-old son, who also worked at the paper, and loathed her daughter, Andrea Koenigsberg Beldon, who was seven years younger. Even expert camera work could not eliminate the meanness in the narrow face, the high cheekbones, and almost Oriental eyes beneath the soft blond hair.

"Do you really think so?" Melanie asked.

"Yes, Ma'am."

"Good." She looked at her pile of mail. "Let's get at it."

An hour later, Paul Curtin appeared at the door of the private elevator and stepped forward to Madeleine's desk. She picked up a red phone and murmured into it. Paul was directed to take his place on a leather and chrome Danish settee in the corner opposite the desk. The doors of the elevator, when closed, revealed the same rosewood veneer as the walls of the foyer. Floor-length draperies covered the windows behind Made-

leine's desk shutting out the depressing view of the underside
of the highway and the disrepair of Brooklyn's waterfront to
which the gaping windows on lower floors treated the rest of
the staff.

The absence of natural light was offset by a spectacular
Georgian silver chandelier which cast a glow on the medium-
blue carpet that covered the floor. On the right wall was a
closed door that Paul knew led to the boardroom. To the left,
where Madeleine waited like Cerberus, was the door to
Melanie Parsons's private office.

The red phone rang with a soft chime. Madeleine motioned
Paul in. He picked up his pad, turned the handle, and strode
through the door.

"Come in, Paul," she asked. Her private office was
decorated in the same way as the foyer, save that it was larger
and contained built-in bookcases. A round Empire conference
table of teak footed with bronze winged sphinxes stood at one
side of the room surrounded by six damasked armchairs in pale
blue.

Melanie Parsons sat behind a Louis XV *bureau plat* that
served as a desk. On it were an elaborate sterling and crystal
encrier, the two framed photos, and a leather-bound correspondence file swollen with the day's mail. She motioned Paul
to a cane-seated chair opposite her. Her auburn-dyed hair, cut
rather short, needed renewing, the gray roots quite evident.
Her eyebrows were plucked to invisibility and replaced by
penciled lines. Her mouth was wide and thin, and turned
downward in repose. Wrinkles between the corners of her
mouth and her chin gave her a menacing air. She looked down
and brushed a bit of powder from the front of her black dress,
flat as a result of a double mastectomy done before the Second
World War. Amputations, they had called them then. They
hadn't taken the lymph nodes or underlying muscles, just the
breasts. She was well past seventy and had lived forty years
without recurrence.

"How goes the battle, Paul? I thought the Valenzuela piece
yesterday was good, carefully crafted." She turned away from
him and pulled aside the drapes a bit, looking out across the
highway and the river. "But not really what we're expecting
from you." She looked back at him. "There are two dozen
staff from juniors on up who could have done it. Not with your
elegant prose, perhaps, but sufficient for our needs."

She hesitated, gathering her thoughts. Paul saw that she was looking over his shoulder at the portrait of her father on the wall above the table, something she seemed to be doing more and more these days. He shrugged. Either she's looking for advice or asking him to smooth her way on the other side.

"I thought it was newsworthy, and important," Paul said, breaking the silence.

"I thought it was newsworthy, too. I also thought that it was self-indulgent of you to spend your time telling an oft-told tale. I do not object to the story being in the paper. I object to the waste of your focus that it represents. You have privileges and position here because your work is supposed to have special impact."

"You don't feel that one dead and two maimed are a high-enough score to generate interest?"

"This conference was called to discuss our results to date in channeling public opinion in the gubernatorial election. Bad medicine is a bad thing. I am not unsympathetic to the story. It's just not an issue we want from you. Count the phone calls that the story drew. Under the best of circumstances, O'Neil will appear on television and make a speech about misplaced trust. By the time he's through, he'll seem more of a victim than the dead and maimed.

"I'd like to know what you're going to do that will give our readers issues that touch on them. They don't care about a crooked doctor who kills a couple of tramps. They forget sensational stories. They're numb to them. We need issues that affect their pocketbooks and their everyday lives."

"How about an in-depth investigation of Howard Feldstein? A long-time friend and business associate of Chris Green's father was named taxi commissioner where he can dispense patronage and largesse to Mr. Greenberg's buddies in the taxi industry. Now there's a real day-to-day rip-off. Don't let the taxi inspectors come down too hard on the fleet cabs. The hell with public safety."

Her nostrils flared as she drew in a breath. Her lips compressed in a downward arc of rage. "When you buy your own newspaper, you can make your own editorial policy. I don't want to discuss this subject again." Her voice was a hiss.

"You mean I can't choose my subjects, and I have to watch

my words," Paul said angrily. He wasn't interested in a fight, but was in no mood to be pushed around.

"I didn't call you in here for a lecture on the probity of the press. I want to know what you are planning to do in the examination of the record of the governor with an eye toward throwing him out of office. The candidate of this paper is Christopher Greene. We already have two Conservative columnists to present the other side. You are supposed to be on my side. You are in the wrong city for naive idealism. And certainly in the wrong job. Now, are you prepared to discuss the campaign, and how we can get at O'Neil, or are you not?"

"How about if his skirts are clean and Greene's aren't?"

"Goddamn. I told you that I'm going to be the judge of evenhandedness here. If you don't like it," she slammed her hand on the desk, her voice shrill, "you can always get out. Are you telling me you can't find anything in O'Neil's administration that doesn't offend your priestly eye?"

Paul's eyes flickered, his mouth a scant line. His mind flitted from Jerry to Maryanne, and judgment overcame bad temper.

"Well?"

There was a moment of angry eye contact. Without looking away, Paul said evenly, "I have a couple of ideas."

Still white with anger, Melanie said, "Then let's share them so that we can get on with our day."

"One thought has to do with civil rights. It's certainly not the strong point of the O'Neil program. I think the Law Enforcement Aid Bill is a can of worms for him. What is it in aid of? The cops? The average citizen? I don't think that a lot of ballyhoo about making body search easier is going to help a bit. I don't think that the law has an even chance of passing its first test of constitutionality. And besides, it's just going to exacerbate community relations every time some cop gets overenthusiastic tossing a black kid outside a candy store."

She nodded in agreement, and relaxed in her chair making a note on her pad. "All right. But that's not your field. I'd rather see someone on the police beat handle it."

She was right, he thought. He remembered a favor owed. "Would Phil Seelig be the right man?" Let it be her idea.

She tapped the pencil on the desk. The air of hostility diminished. "You talk to him about it. If he has any interest, have him call me. I'll clear it with Fabrikant. What else?"

Paul looked at the notes scratched on the sheet in front of him. Based on Phil's hunch, he'd done a little snooping into the Hawkes Building Company. They were partners with Kurt Englander's giant forest products conglomerate, the Burton Corporation. He was unsure how it would strike Melanie. "I have an idea we might be able to find something in the state construction program."

"We've beaten it to death. O'Neil only hatches projects when elections are in sight, then drags them through the next three years of his term of office. Besides," she said, "he can't be blamed for interest rates and the decline in the housing stock."

"I think there may be some kind of fraud at Uhuru Towers."

She cocked her head and leaned back in the chair. "I don't know if that's an issue we want."

"Whose toes am I stepping on this time?" Paul was angry again.

"Don't get shirty," Melanie said coolly. "I'm thinking politics. If Chris Greene is going to be the governor of New York, he's going to have to leave the city with a million-vote margin to offset O'Neil's plurality upstate. That margin is going to come from the minority voter. Uhuru Towers is a very popular program. Greene's been manuevering to supplant O'Neil as its biggest supporter."

"So much the better. If we do find something, we can illustrate how even Greene was hoodwinked by the governor and his crooked accomplices. It's a no-lose proposition. And if there's nothing there, we just don't go to print."

"We just waste your expensive time unproductively. But it's my money, so that's my problem, isn't it?"

"Whatever you say."

"All right. Look at Uhuru Towers. It's better than nothing." She slipped on her glasses and turned her attention to the leather binder. "Just keep in mind the fact that I'm very disappointed with the work on the O'Neil campaign thus far. I'm reviewing my options."

He sat and watched her for a moment, then realizing that the audience was at an end, he rose and walked to the door.

She looked up and called out as he left, "Call me when you have something concrete on Uhuru Towers."

Paul seethed as he descended to the ground floor. Reviewing

her options, is she? How'd she like to stick her options up her keester? He stomped across the lobby to the public elevator and ground his teeth as he rode back up to the fourth floor.

Back at his desk he flopped down in his chair and put his feet up on the edge of his wastebasket. After a moment of scowling at his shoes, a smile crept across his face. The old bitch. He hadn't had a temper tantrum since he was seven.

Paul drew a breath, straightened up and looked at the pad he had thrown on his desk. He reclaimed a manila folder from a drawer and looked over the page and a half of notes he'd garnered about Hawkes Building from a couple of phone calls. He snapped his fingers. Damn. He wanted to get ahold of Phil Seelig to tip him off on the possible byline series on the Law Enforcement Aid Bill.

Paul dialed the direct number to the *Advocate*'s Police Plaza bureau.

"Seelig."

"Phil, Paul Curtin. I have a little something that might interest you."

"I was just on my way out the door," Seelig said.

"It'll keep."

"I've been trying to get you all morning. I thought you were returning the call. You want to go to a funeral?" Seelig offered.

"I just spent an hour with Mrs. Parsons. Will this be more fun?"

"Possibly. It's old Lloyd Gibbons. They're going to put him in the cold, cold ground."

"Where are the festivities?" Curtin asked.

"Old Sam Smith's African Methodist in Woodhaven. I saw him bury a cop two years ago. I thought we'd skip the church and go straight to Mount Zion."

"That's the marble orchard on the way to the airport. You'll pick me up?"

"That's the place. I'll be in front of the door in ten minutes."

Seelig flicked off the radio and joined Paul as he walked between the rows of stones toward the mound of earth that marked the newly dug grave. A caravan of fifteen cars followed a gleaming old Cadillac hearse draped with swagged black curtains.

A tall young man in a dark raincoat was the first to emerge from the limousine parked behind the hearse. He reached inside with one hand, while holding an umbrella with the other, and helped a woman in a black coat and a hat with a veil through the door.

"The widow," Paul guessed.

Within a few minutes all of the cars had been emptied and their occupants stood in a semicircle around the foot of the grave site. Paul and Phil edged closer and mingled at the edge of the crowd. Paul saw only two other whites in the sea of fifty or sixty black faces.

"That's Hawkes, over there with that big guy," Phil said under his breath, nudging Paul with his elbow and looking across the group to the slight elevation on which the clergyman had stepped.

Paul nodded. "I recognized him from a picture in a brochure I got from a guy in the real estate business."

At the same time, Hawkes cleared his throat to catch George Gaines's attention. "That's Seelig, the reporter from the *Advocate* who came up to Uhuru the night that Lloyd died."

"Which one?"

"The smaller one. Older."

"Who's the other one, Marcus?"

"I don't know."

"We ought to know." The voice was a rumble in his chest.

"Dearly beloved," the Reverend Samuel Kip Smith intoned, "we are gathered here in the sight of God to lay to rest our departed brother Lloyd Gibbons." Smith turned to his right. "He was a devoted father and husband." The young man who had emerged from the car looked stoically at the gaping grave and wrapped a long arm around his mother, her face hidden by the veil. "He was a man of kindness and charity, of skill and decency."

"Amen," a half dozen voices chorused.

As the reverend droned on, his voice rising and falling like water over the words of condolence, Paul's eyes played over the crowd, systematically. Almost all clasped their hands before them and bowed their heads studying the ground at their feet which would some day claim them, too. At the rear, nearer the cars, three younger men stood apart, their shoulders touching. They wore caps from which tightly wound curls crept. Paul's eyes stopped for a moment then continued on, going from hat to hat blocked here and there by an umbrella. Suddenly, he froze, his eyes locked in contact with another's. He recoiled slightly, then shifted his focus to take in the whole face. It was the tall man standing next to Hawkes, his face partly shaded by a snap brim hat, hands stuffed into the pockets of a leather trench coat. Paul had never seen him before, but knew he would never forget him. He shivered and looked away.

"Ashes to ashes. Dust to dust. So it is that we return the body of our departed brother Lloyd Gibbons to the earth from which he sprang in the sure knowledge of the Resurrection and of Life Everlasting. Amen."

"Amen," the congregation responded.

Reverend Smith took Mrs. Gibbons's left arm, her son the right, and led her past the mourners. They stopped at each small group and said a word or two. Paul and Phil stationed themselves almost at the end of the queue.

Paul saw the beginnings of a man's face peering out through the still youthful round cheeks of Lloyd Gibbons's twenty-three-year-old son. Cheeks stung by hot bitter tears. Mrs. Gibbons was a handsome woman in her late forties. Her large eyes were misted over, but her grief was masked by dignity.

"Thank you for coming, gentlemen," she said in a firm voice. "I'm sure that Lloyd would have been grateful."

Paul felt a twinge of discomfort. He nodded at her silently and watched as she finished her walk of bereavement and disappeared into the rear of the limousine.

As Paul and Phil turned to walk to their car a voice cried out, "Oh, Mr. Seelig. Mr. Seelig. Wait. I'd like to say hello. It's me, Mr. Seelig. Marcus Hawkes."

Phil stopped next to Paul as the rotund figure moved across the wet path toward them. The tall man in the leather walked by Hawkes's side with feline grace.

Hawkes stuck out his stubby hand. "It was very thoughtful

of you to come to the funeral. I'm sure that Mrs. Gibbons was touched, Mr. Seelig. Have you been to visit with her?''

"No," Phil replied. "No, I haven't."

Hawkes turned to his companion. "I'd like you to meet a business associate of mine. This is George Gaines. Perhaps you're already familiar with Gaines Masonry. He's our subcontractor on Uhuru Towers," he added with pride.

Gaines stuck out a hard hand and enveloped Seelig's. "Nice to meet you." Then he turned and looked pointedly at Paul.

"Excuse me," said Paul, offering his hand. "I'm Paul Curtin." He found Gaines's touch cool and dry, almost reptilian. He resisted a slight pressure.

"I know who you are," Hawkes said with boyish delight. "I've read your pieces often."

"It's nice to know that someone does."

"Oh, I know that I have lots of company," Hawkes gushed. "What brings you out here?"

Paul said without hesitating, "Phil hates this kind of thing. I didn't have anything to do, so I thought I'd keep him company."

"How nice."

"We're old friends. Interesting project you have there up on 125th Street."

"Are you familiar with it, Mr. Curtin?"

"Just in passing. Perhaps I could drop by one of these days and take a good look. Maybe ask a few questions, too."

"Please. You'd be our honored guest. Just call my office. We're on the Avenue of the Americas, you know. I'll be glad to be your guide."

"Nice meeting you, Mr. Hawkes." Paul shook hands again. "You, too, Mr. Gaines."

Gaines nodded, looking up from under the brim of his hat.

Seelig and Curtin walked to their car and drove away down the solemn alleys. Neither spoke till they got onto the parkway.

"Hawkes makes me uncomfortable," Seelig said. "It's like watching a stuffed doll or a puppet."

Paul nodded, gnawing at a nail. "I'll tell you what, Phil, looking into Gaines's eyes just scares the shit out of me. What a mean-looking cuss."

"Just your everyday businessman. You learn anything? I didn't."

Paul shrugged. "Maybe I should talk to the widow."

"Old Hawkes was certainly anxious to know if I had."

"That's why maybe I should. I'll do a little more reading up on Mr. Hawkes and Mr. Gaines, I think." He looked over his shoulder at the receding graveyard.

Marcus Hawkes sat in his brown Lincoln waiting for Gaines to join him. He was talking to three young men who had driven out with him in his own car. Hawkes fidgeted uncomfortably. Gaines had his back to him, and he could neither hear him nor read his lips.

"You would recognize the tall honky, then?" Gaines asked of the three men.

They shook their heads.

"I may want him watched. All right, go back to the job. I'll drive in with Hawkes. Don't scratch my car."

When he sat down in Hawkes's car and slammed the door, Hawkes said, "What was that all about?"

"I just wanted to know if the boys had a fix on Mr. Curtin and Mr. Seelig."

"For what?"

"You never know when you might want to look someone up."

Hawkes started the motor, then gunned it. "Don't you even think about approaching the press. You don't fool with them, George."

"You didn't seem to mind asking them if they'd been to see Claudine Gibbons. You wouldn't have been happy if they had."

"No, I wouldn't, George." He shifted into drive. "But, there isn't a hell of a lot I can do about it if they did."

Gaines sat silently and looked out of the window across the East River at the gaunt skeleton of Uhuru Towers, thinking to himself that he felt no such constraints.

Jefferson Jackson looked in the mirror over the sink. His eyes were bloodshot. He stepped back a pace, and while his eyes seemed just as red, his image was clearer. "Gonna have to wear glasses to shave soon. Either that or switch to an electric razor before I cut my throat."

Jeff ran his hand over the stubble on his dark brown cheek. He stuck out his tongue, and then pulled it back, and said, "Fuzz."

Unlike many men in their mid-fifties, Jeff Jackson had experienced no middle-aged spread. At five foot four, he still weighed one twenty-eight. His body was lanky and loose. Ropy blue veins stood out in relief through his skin against well-defined muscles.

Trying to overcome the aftereffects of the previous evening's drinking, Jeff brushed his teeth and managed to shave with a minimum of scraping and no blood. He dressed in a brown suit with a white shirt and a somber tie. He ran a brush over the tight black curls on his head, cut very short and beginning to gray. He put down the brush and straightened the tie in the mirror, leaning away to get a clearer picture. Giving up, he sighed and took a pair of tortoiseshell glasses from the breast pocket of his jacket and put them on the bridge of his narrow, crooked nose.

Jeff's three-room apartment on Second Avenue at Seventy-sixth Street was sparsely and simply furnished. A small bedroom with a bed and dresser. A living room with a dining alcove, some tables and chairs, a stereo and a TV set. He went to the closet and took out his fur-collared wool coat, then turned out the lights. As he was about to open the door, the telephone rang. Dropping the coat over a chair, he went to the table at the side of the couch and took the receiver from the hook. "Jeff Jackson."

"Jeff Jackson, that you?"

"Yes, this is he."

"This is Malcolm Woodruff."

Jeff hesitated for a split second, searching, then said, "Yeah, Malcolm. How are you? How do you like life in the private sector? Things hopping over at Hawkes Building?"

There was a pause. "It's okay. Listen, can you meet me for lunch?" When Jeff didn't respond immediately, he continued, "On me. You're my guest."

"That's nice of you, Malcolm," Jeff said, uncertain. "What day? Where would you like to meet?"

"It's got to be today."

"Today? I don't know, Malcolm."

"I got to talk to you man," Woodruff said in an urgent whisper.

"Well, okay. Where? Uptown?—the Red Rooster, maybe? I'd go for some ribs and greens."

"No," he replied in a hush. "Downtown. You know a bar called Martell's? It's on Third Avenue and Eighty-third."

"Yeah. I know it."

"Twelve. I'll make a reservation in your name."

"I'll be there," Jeff said, but Woodruff had already hung up.

Jeff checked his watch. It was ten past ten. The rest of the regular editorial and news staff had filed in for their day's work at the *New York Advocate*. Copy boys had trimmed the wires, taking the continuously fed sheets of paper from the wire service telex machines, cut them into manageable lengths, and distributed them to the appropriate desks—metropolitan, national, or international. News was being gathered, assimilated, and reported for a new day at New York's oldest evening newspaper.

It would take a good half hour to get to the office on South Street, and the same time to come back. Jeff picked up the phone and called through to Amadeo Conforti, the assistant metropolitan editor.

"This is Matt Conforti."

"Morning, Matt, this is Jeff."

"Where are you? Hung over?"

"Yes. But my legs is still movin'. Hey, I got a funny phone call. Okay if I don't come in till after lunch—around two, two-thirty?"

"Sure. What kind of funny?"

"A guy I know, casually only. Works for a big black construction company. He asked me out to lunch. Very odd. He used to be a semi-big man in the State Housing Authority. Took his retirement about a year ago. Hell, he must be sixty-two or three. Then he started to work for Hawkes Building."

"Sounds like the last guy in the world who'd pay for somebody's lunch," Matt admitted.

"Newspaper people excepted, of course."

"Of course. Okay. I'll keep one of the guys over lunch hour, then let him go at two if you can get back by then. Then you can either handle the late stuff for the 2:30 late edition deadline, or you can clean up for the Sixth Race Final."

"Suits me. See you."

Jeff hung his coat and jacket in the closet and fetched the *Times* from outside the front door. He did a quick scan of the front page. Nothing remarkable. He turned to the sports page. Both the Knicks and the Rangers lost. He checked the obits. There was no one he knew. Lean pickings. The *Advocate* always lifted its obits from the *Times*—just two or three a day. After all, why duplicate the effort? The *Times* is a morning paper, with the biggest prewritten obituary file in the world, forty thousand names. Famous or infamous, anyone of notoriety walks around with a passport to the beyond, compliments of the *New York Times*.

Jeff settled into the couch and looked at the paper more thoroughly. It was an important source of news for the *Advocate*. Yesterday, it had been Jeff's turn to be the "reader" who clips the stories from the *Times* and sends them on to the appropriate editor. It saved a lot of legwork. Either somebody was assigned to cover the story, or they were simply lifted and rewritten.

Jeff hefted the paper in disgust. It seemed to be seventy or eighty pages—light for the *Times*. On the day he had been the reader, they'd come out with four sections totalling a hundred forty-four pages. He looked over the synopsis on the front page of the second section; wildcat strike at Kennedy, charity ball at the Met. He went back to scanning the paper. On page twenty-seven of the second section there was a short blurb on the accident at Uhuru Towers.

He read it through, then went on.

When he finished the first section, he walked to the kitchen to make himself a cup of coffee. Maybe Woodruff's call had something to do with the accident. As he watched the pot, he tried to remember what he knew about Woodruff. Member in good standing of St. Phillip's Episcopal on 134th Street. A conservative parish. None of that "Amen, Brother" shit. Old Fashioned Nigra Gentleman. Up from the rural South in the thirties to better himself in the Big City. Just in time for the Depression. Six or eight years of waiting tables and washing floors to stay alive and manage NYU at night. Then the degree. A hollow triumph. Wrong time. Wrong color.

Then a small piece of luck. Through a connection with a Harlem politician, a civil service job. Not your American Dream, maybe. Low pay, but steady work and respectable. The rest of the story would be a cliché. The war ended the Depression. Four years in the army counts as seniority and pension time. By the time you're discharged you've got ten, eleven years of good time. You have to be crazy to give that up. Patience and perseverance give way to monotony. Age and family responsibility eat up ambition, and give birth first to insecurity and then to fear.

Jeff understood how things like that happen. He was just about out of aspirations himself. He walked out of the building with a nod to the doorman. He was the oldest tenant. The rest were all single, too. Stewardesses and young men on the rise, two to four in an apartment to stretch the money. Twenty-six apartments on each of seventeen floors, the biggest with two bedrooms.

As he walked west to Third Avenue he recalled last meeting Woodruff. It had been at a fund raiser for United Negro Colleges. There had been push and shove to get in because Shirley MacLaine was there and Leonard Bernstein was the host. Jeff had been covering it for the *Advocate,* and Woodruff had been invited as a representative of the state government. They'd talked a little. Woodruff had a kid, a girl just married. It must have been six or seven years ago.

Jeff was frozen and damp from intermittent drizzle when he got to Martell's. The inside was dark and crowded for lunch, decorated in phony barroom 1890's style. It was hard to see anything among the mahogany booths and the frosted glass dividers.

"May I help you, sir?" said a young man in a blue suit.

"Mr. Jackson, party of two. We have reservations."

"Yes, sir. The gentleman is waiting for you. Follow me, please."

They walked through the main room and past the bar into a smaller but equally crowded area. "He's over there, with his back to us."

Jeff wrestled off his coat and stuffed his cap into the pocket, and hung it on a hook, patting his suit pocket to make sure that he had his steno pad with him. He walked over to Malcolm and tapped him on the shoulder. He half rose, startled, and spilled some of his drink on the table.

"Hey, Malcolm, I'm sorry I scared you. How you doin'?"

Malcolm waited till Jeff came around to the other side of the table and sat down before he extended his hand. "Hello, Jeff. I guess I'm all right. Thanks for coming."

"Long time no see. It's got to be six or seven years. You have a daughter, right? She was just married when I saw you."

"Right. She's been married a little over five years. She's got a boy now. Two years old. I guess I never thanked you for your note of congratulations, either. I got so many."

Jeff was puzzled, then remembered scratching a few words on a memo pad when he'd seen the announcement of Malcolm's appointment at Hawkes Building in the *Times*. "How long is it since you joined Hawkes, Malcolm?"

"Not quite two years."

Jeff shook his head. "I'm getting old. Look at this. Bifocals. My arms are getting shorter by the month. The truth is, I didn't even remember sending you the note."

The waiter pushed his way to them and said, "What can I get you to eat, gents? See the menu? It's over there on the wall in chalk."

"I'd like a Bloody Mary," Jeff said, adjusting his glasses and looking over Malcolm's shoulder. "And I'll have a bowl of chili and an Englishburger with cheese, rare."

Both Jeff and the waiter turned to Malcolm. He hadn't looked at the menu, fleshy lips compressed in a tight line, as though he were concentrating.

"Malcolm, what're you going to have? The menu's on the wall behind you," Jeff said.

Without turning, he asked, "They got fish?"

"Filet of sole and striped bass," Jeff replied.

"I'll have a bowl of that chili, too, and some of that sole. And bring me another beer, too."

The waiter looked at him oddly and walked away.

Despite classic Negroid features, Malcolm was very light-skinned, with several dark moles on his cheeks and liver spots on his hands, which trembled slightly as he passed his glass back and forth nervously between them. His chin receded slightly, giving him a peeved expression. Jeff wondered whether forty years in the civil service had made him look that way.

Jeff waited, not wanting to interrupt a train of thought. When the silence became indecent, he said, "Are things okay at the job? You still going regularly to St. Phillip's?"

Malcolm looked up. "I'm still going to St. Phillip's. There's some talk of making me a deacon next year. Rose would like that."

"How's she getting along?"

"She's fine. Occupied with her grandchild and her hard work." He paused. Jeff sat very still, as though afraid to spook an animal.

Finally, Malcolm said, "The job." Then he paused again. "The job is why I asked you here." He leaned his head toward the table.

"I don't understand," Jeff said.

"It's this Black Capitalism business. There's something wrong with it."

"Philosophically? Or it isn't working out? Or it isn't making money? Trouble with the parent company?"

"It's a real nigger mess."

"And you think it ought to be in the papers. The public should know. That's why you called me."

Malcolm shivered. "I don't know where it belongs. I didn't know anybody else I could call. I don't know no newspaper people." He leaned forward conspiratorially. "Is it true that you people never give up your sources, or is that bullshit?"

"Personally, I never had anything to give up. But, yeah, it's true. Reporters have gone to jail to protect their sources. Editors, too. In defense of the First Amendment."

Warming a little, Malcolm hunched over still further. "Yeah, but is it just for big stuff? For Watergate? For shit like that?"

"No. So far as I know, it's universal. I never heard of a reporter ratting on a source of information, if that's what you mean."

"How do you feel about it yourself?"

"I'm not really a reporter," Jeff said. "But I think that's the way it should be. Otherwise no one would talk to the press, and a lot of bad stuff would never come out."

"A lot still doesn't." He reached out and took Jeff's hand. His touch was clammy. "Can I talk to you?"

"Privately, you mean?"

"Confidentially."

Jeff hesitated a moment then said, "Look, I won't repeat anything you say unless I clear it with you first. And I won't tell anybody who you are."

"No hints. No telling them where I work or anything like that, so that they can figure it out." Malcolm's voice was strained and guttural.

Jeff took his hand back and sat up straight in the chair, looking into Malcolm's face. "What is it, man? You're scared."

In a raw whisper, Malcolm said, "You bet your ass I'm scared." He clamped his lips and sat up abruptly as the waiter came with their food.

"Two chilies, right?"

"Right," Jeff said, "and can you get me another Bloody Mary? How about you, Mal . . ." Woodruff looked up. Jeff finished, "How about you?" Malcolm nodded. "And another beer, please," Jeff said.

The chili was steaming hot and heavily spiced. As Jeff started to eat, the vapor made his eyes water, and bit the stuffiness from his nostrils. As he ate in silence, he glanced at Malcolm over the top of his glasses. The more that he had talked, the more nervous he had become. He was concentrating on his bowl, taking measured bites and chewing in cadence, occupying his mind with a small mechanical task. Halfway through the bowl, he stopped eating and looked up. "You write for the paper, don't you, Jeff? I mean really. It's a real job. You're not just a . . ."

"No, Malcolm. I'm not a clerk. I don't do floors. I work on the metropolitan desk. I rewrite and edit stories sent in by reporters, and I write headlines. It's a real job."

"I know you did that kind of thing when you were with the *Amsterdam News*."

"God. Do I know you that long? That's twenty years or more. That's what I did there, and then on the *Mirror* and the *Tribune*. After that, I came over to the *Advocate*. That's more than ten years now."

"Yeah. I remember where I met you. It was a basement dance at the church. You were with some cute gal. She was a Geechee. Did you know I was from Charleston, too? That's how come I remember." He seemed to relax a little. The waiter cleared the table and brought the main courses and drinks. Jeff didn't push any further.

Halfway through the fish, Malcolm put down his knife and fork, took a pull on his beer, and leaned forward again. "Are you sure you won't say who I am?"

"Hey, listen, I told you. I'll swear if you like."

"I just don't want to get killed."

Jeff lowered his own voice to a whisper, and said in consternation, "Hey, listen, if this has to do with killing, you should be talking to the police."

"I wouldn't get to say it but once. There wouldn't be no twice."

"Hey, Malcolm, you're not a Bowery bum, man. You're a vice-president in a big company. You were an official of the state government. People just can't dispose of you. That's what the cops are for, to protect people."

"Not who know what I know. It goes too high. I tell my story to the cops, I don't see the next sunrise." Jeff sat back in his chair. Malcolm returned to his fish.

Martell's was starting to empty out. The protective crush of the crowd and the babble of conversation reverberating from the walls and masking their words were diminished. "You want to go to my place?" Jeff asked. "I only live on Seventy-sixth Street."

Malcolm shook his head. "I don't want to be seen with you. I don't want anybody seeing me going up to your place."

"Where do you want to go? And when?"

"The john. Here. Now."

The men's room was at the back of the dining area. It was small and dingy. Jeff walked in first. Malcolm followed and locked the door. There was one commode and a sink, neither very clean, and a stale odor of urine and cheap disinfectant.

"I'm quitting my job," Malcolm said, his eyes darting about. "I got to get out. There's money being spread around. There's stealing going on. I'm talking big numbers."

"What's the big deal? Isn't that standard in the building business in New York? So it goes up a little higher this time. Who is it? The president of the Building Trades Council? Maybe even the commissioner? It wouldn't be the first time."

"What do you take me fo', some kinda fuckin' amateur? I ain't no lilly. I know how this business works. I ain't on the inside, but I can see what's goin' down. They're stealing materials, man. This is a big project. We're talking millions. But they're smart. To prove it, you got to dig. Somebody's got to talk."

"Who is on the inside?"

"Hawkes. His brother, Charles, maybe. He's the chief estimator. And George Gaines, he's the masonry contractor." He shuddered. "He's a bad dude."

Jeff looked at him, puzzled. "I don't get it. In the first place, you're on the board of directors, aren't you? How can they pull off some big scam without you noticing it. In the second place, you're not alone. You're in partnership with a big company. Burton Industries is listed on the New York Stock Exchange."

"That's right," Malcolm hissed. "With two billion dollars in sales and building materials plants and sawmills and forests all over the fuckin' world, and they're just another bunch of honkies being had by a couple of street smart niggers. You think that Hawkes and Gaines bring up a monthly plan for how much they're going to steal at the board meetings? And me? I do paperwork. I do all the filing of applications with the federal government and the state. I take care of the requests for bonding and insurance. I don't have nothing to do with the building itself—on Uhuru or any other job. But I been looking at paperwork in the building business for forty years, and I know when there's a nigger in the woodpile."

There was a knock at the door. Malcolm jumped a foot. "Be right out," he said. He turned to Jeff. "Listen, we got to go."

Malcolm moved close enough for Jeff to feel his breath on his cheek. "I'm going to try to get out. I haven't been getting along with Hawkes. He don't like me worth a shit, neither. I'm just going to say that I'm not happy, and I want out. But if a word gets out that I talked to you, or I get connected with anything that happens up at Uhuru, I'm going to wind up dead. If you nose around and find out something on your own, that's fine. Ain't nothin' says you can't find out things independently. You blow the whistle and get a big story, and I get to live to be a deacon, and collect my pension."

"It's too vague, Malcolm."

"I can't give you no more. Bills are being kited. Materials are being stolen. The way it's being done, Christ knows how high it goes." There was another insistent knock, and Malcolm opened the door.

They walked out together under the odd stare of a young man in a pin-striped suit who had been waiting to use the facilities. They returned to find that their table had been cleared. The waiter gave them the fish eye from the corner. He walked over and said, "You want some coffee? I thought maybe you'd skipped out on me."

"No coffee," Malcolm said. "Just the check."

When the waiter left, Jeff asked, "When can I call you?"

"You can't. Don't call me at home. Somebody may be listening, and I don't want Rose involved. And for God's sake, don't call me at the office. If I have something to say, I'll call you."

"But how do we get more information? Where do we start?"

Malcolm looked very frightened. "I thought you knew how to do this."

"We need a starting point. Listen, does this have anything to do with that accident yesterday."

Malcolm's voice was like a fingernail on a blackboard. "Accident. That wasn't no fuckin' accident. I knew Lloyd Gibbons. He stuck his nose in where he shouldn't have, and they cut it off. I don't want to end up the same way. You think I came to you cause I give a shit about the public? Fuck 'em. I'm worried for my old bones. I figure if you get something on these folks and get them put away, my chances improve. Talk is cheap, proving it is something else again."

The waiter brought the check. Malcolm looked it over quickly and threw some money on the small plastic tray. The waiter grunted thanks, then walked away.

"You go first," Malcolm said. "I'm just going to sit here for a while." He reached out his hand. It was trembling. Jeff shook it.

"I'll see what I can do, Malcolm. Call me if you want." He handed him a card with his direct line at the office. "And don't worry. I won't mention your name."

Jeff took his coat from the hook and exited with one quick backward glance. Malcolm was staring fixedly at the table.

8

Melanie Parsons closed the folder in front of her and looked down the long table. "Thank you, gentlemen," she said. The three editors in charge of the paper's major areas of coverage rose and left with the heads of the sports and financial departments and the advertising manager. They'd toted up the advertising lineage, established the size of the news hole, and filled it, parcelling space to the various departments.

Max Fabrikant, the managing editor, stood sour-faced at his end of the table stuffing the layouts and reporters' assignments into a swollen brief bag. "That's it for the day, Mrs. Parsons?"

"Yes, Max. Please see that the columns and the lead story are at my house by 10:00 tonight. Rough copy will do." She turned to the papers in front of her.

Having been dismissed, Fabrikant would normally have closed his bag and been on his way. But he stood his ground and continued to look her way.

After a moment, she felt his gaze and looked up. "Is there something you want to discuss, Max?"

He cleared his throat. "What are we going to do with Paul Curtin?"

Her mouth dropped into the inverted arc of displeasure. "I thought," she emphasized, "that we had been over that. It was my understanding that he was on special assignment and would report to me till further notice."

Fabrikant ground his teeth, squared his jaw, and went on. "I heard what you said, Mrs. Parsons. I just want to point out that you have a man who's earning fifty percent over guild scale dawdling around. It doesn't make much of an impression on the members."

"Are you giving up your managerial position to become a shop steward? If he's on special assignment to me, how can he be dawdling? He's trying to put together a telling series on O'Neil. Something that's going to drive him out of the governor's mansion. And that's," her voice rose an octave, "what I want him to do. Now, if you can find a better way to do it, or tell me how someone else can do it, I'm willing to listen. Until then, or until I am convinced that Curtin has no more potential, my interest in jealousy over his salary will remain limited. Do you understand that?"

Fabrikant snapped the catch closed and picked up the bag. "I do. Good day, Mrs. Parsons." He stalked out of the room fuming.

Melanie was left alone in the room with Oscar Bornstein, the executive editor. As was his custom, he sat at the opposite end of the long walnut table, one foot resting against an ornate carved leg, balancing in his chair. When Fabrikant left, he rose, tall and elegant in a blue serge suit from Savile Row, and walked past the dozen chairs that separated him from Melanie Parsons. She looked up at his patrician face, a long curved narrow nose above a tight small mouth. His eyes were wide set and dark, his hair—black, straight, and slicked back from a high forehead—was streaked with silver. He ran the business of the *New York Advocate*. When she had bought the paper more than twenty-five years before, she had gone to him and said, "Go to the Bankers Trust and find out how much I can afford to lose each year, then run the paper so that it does no worse." He had. And better.

"I don't know what to do with Curtin. He's disappointing." She waited, then said, "Well, aren't you going to offer an opinion?"

"He's stale. He's too close to O'Neil to be an effective critic anymore. And besides, it's not the same passion with him that it is with you. You want the poor man's blood. Maybe Curtin shares some of his passion with a girl friend."

"It's better than a taste for young men," she snapped.

Despite his self-possession, he blushed a little. "Low blow, Mel."

"Well, to each his own, Oscar, dear."

Bornstein straightened his tie and sat down. At sixty, his skin remained taut, his body slender from squash and tennis. "Have you ever thought about freshening his point of view by giving him a leave of absence from O'Neil? Let him chase after Greene for a while."

"I hope that this is just temporary. I don't think that will serve a purpose, and that's not what I pay him for. If he can't do O'Neil right, then he can't do anything."

Bornstein drew a cigarette from a gold case and lit it with long delicate fingers. "But, as you say, Mel, he seems to have struck a dry spot. He's been nonproductive or at least dull for several months. He needs a new perspective."

She pulled off her glasses and pursed her lips. "Don't worry about that. I'm going to give him a little motivation. No one is indispensable, you know. Oscar, be a dear and have Madeleine call Curtin for me."

She watched him exit from the windowless boardroom, still lithe in middle age. He had been slinky when he was young. He'd been a star tennis player at the Century Country Club in Purchase. The son of a respected banker who'd managed to hold on to some money in the thirties and still belonged. The poor man had all but killed himself when his son Oscar was found cuddling in the shower with an assistant golf pro. She remembered how her own father, almost alone among the members, had defended him.

Oscar had gone to work for the rest of that summer at Royal Mills, Sam Parsons's textile enterprise in the decaying mill town of Woonsocket, Rhode Island, and the matter had been hushed up. He had stayed weekends with the family in the great seashore house opposite Newport Island. When Oscar graduated from Yale, he became a part of the Parsons empire—textiles, rubber products, beer, soft drinks.

When diabetes had felled Sam Parsons, stopping his circulation and costing him his legs, he had called Oscar to him. "You are young," he had said in his thick Russian accent, "too young to turn things over to. I have made arrangements that everything will be sold. Only money will be left. The Bankers Trust will run it all. Rachel will need for nothing. My four girls, I have put all of the money in trust. Only Sandra is unmarried, and she is very young. The others are married to schlemiels. You will watch out. I leave you some reasonable money for your comfort. Much more important, I leave you responsibility. God has seen fit that you will not raise a family of your own. That is His will, and your preference. I make you the gift of something to nurture besides your beauty, your appetites, and your vanity. I wish you had been my son." In a few months, Sam Parsons was dead.

Oscar had gone into the air force and served with distinction in the Pacific. He went to work in Wall Street when he came out. Competence and discretion carried him quickly upward. The nest egg that Sam Parsons had left him, together with a small inheritance from his parents, became a modest fortune. The Parsons girls often called upon him as the brother they never had, and the earthly representative of Sam Parsons's shade. He offered a word of advice here and there, provided a shoulder to cry on, and did the occasional chore.

Suddenly, Melanie, the brightest and most serious of the Parsons girls, exploded in a frenzy of activity. An object of whispered pity and concern since her mastectomy, further burdened by the grievous wounds of her son, all but killed in the last days of World War II, she had suddenly thrown off her shroud. She cast off her bumbling husband without a farthing and attracted and married an athletic and modesty successful, if fundamentally weak, businessman, and devoured him and his children. Having reestablished her femininity, she bought the *Advocate* as an outward manifestation of her wealth and power, and her determination to use them to cast her shadow beyond her personal life. When she decided to buy the paper, Oscar was the first person she had called. He had agreed to join her as a matter of course.

Oscar returned to the room with a wry smile. "Madeleine was out. I called him myself. I sounded very grim."

Melanie smiled and ran her hands through her thin hair. Oscar could always make the anger fade, even if only for an instant. "What did he say?"

"He's on his way."

Oscar had just had time to sit down when there was a knock at the door. "Come in," Melanie called.

Curtin entered and stood at the end of the table. "You wanted me, Mrs. Parsons?"

"Please sit down. I realize that I said I would wait for your call, but after discussing the matter with Mr. Bornstein, I thought it would be better if we had this chat now." She hesitated, watching his face. He was impassive. Annoyed, she went on. "There's a certain amount of—I don't want to use the word dissatisfaction—concern about your work on the part of members of the editorial board. As we discussed earlier today, there seems to be a lack of direction, and more importantly, of results. We're beginning to feel a bit like patrons of the arts, where you're concerned."

Bornstein leaned forward and said, "I was thinking that perhaps a change of atmosphere might do you some good. Do you think a change in your beat, or some fresh subject matter might get you untracked?"

Curtin's eyelids lowered. His hands were flat on the table before him. "Listen, Mr. Bornstein, I just went over this with Mrs. Parsons. I'm not even a guild member. I have a year left on my contract. You don't have to hassle with the union to get rid of me. You can assign me to do anything you want. But don't ask me if I need to get untracked. I don't. What do you want me to do? Frame O'Neil? Fabricate something out of thin air?"

"I think that's impertinent, young man," Melanie said.

"I think it wanders close to the truth. Didn't we just finish with the probity of the press? Either I'm inept, or he's clean. You can point out his failings, but everybody has them. If Greene is elected, he'll have them. All we can do is point them out and hope that the electorate chooses to throw O'Neil out and elect your boy."

Melanie controlled her voice, though her face was taut with anger. "Have you no conviction? How can you do your job if you don't believe in what you're doing?"

"I do believe in what I'm doing. I'm dealing with realities. O'Neil has flaws. I try to expose them, even to put them in a bad light, because I know that's what you want. And I know which side my bread is buttered on. I thought we'd already decided on what I was going to do."

"That was before today's editorial meeting." She looked at him over the length of the table. "Now I'm not sure what I will do. I would be sorry if either of us came to a conclusion without proper reflection." She paused, ruminating, then said,

"Why don't you take a few days off? Today is Wednesday. Why don't we meet again on Monday? I'll tell Mr. Fabrikant that you're—shall we say—contemplating your future."

"Fine," Paul said. "You do that. When do you want me Monday?"

"Shall we say eleven?" She watched him as he turned on his heel with a perfunctory nod in Bornstein's direction and closed the door firmly behind him. The silence lasted a full minute. "Well," she said in exasperation, "aren't you going to say anything?"

"Do you want to fire him?"

She shrugged. "No. Why would I want to do that? He's a good reporter. I think he's getting a bit lazy."

"He's a sophisticated and intelligent man. It's possible that he's been oversaturated. It's possible that he feels as frustrated with his lack of results as you do." Oscar studied his nails. "I wouldn't want him to resign."

"If I thought it would come to that, I would rather fire him."

"Then I think that you'd better spend some of the time that you gave him to think thinking about it yourself. If you push him any further, he's liable to walk. He didn't seem at all intimidated to me."

9

When Jeff Jackson returned from his lunch and walked out of the elevator on the fourth floor, where the news department of the *Advocate* was located, his eye lit upon the derelict Linotype machine which had been wrenched from its place in the typesetting department when the paper had gone electronic.

The atmosphere was very different from the one that would have greeted him in another age. Even though the afternoon deadline would have passed, the room would have been a-bustle with copy boys scurrying about, carrying masses of paper from desk to desk and to the production departments.

Instead, the floor was hushed. Even the clack of typewriters had been submerged in the silence of the bulky televisionlike word processors that sat on almost every desk.

The desks were grouped according to their area of interest, metro, national, or international, or by department, sports or finance, spaced across the floor to the back wall where the senior editors' offices were located, on the opposite side from the elevators.

Jeff looked across his desk at the big square face of Matt Conforti, his blue eyes perfectly balanced between his rugged chin and his great bald dome. His eyebrows, like the fringe of hair on his head, were light brown, turning to gray. His nose was large and a bit thick at the end. He bristled in repose.

When Jeff had been pulled into the army in 1944, through a series of flukes which after thirty-five years were still not wholly clear, he'd become a copy boy for Matt Conforti at *Stars and Stripes,* and spent a year on the Champs Élysées.

When he'd been mustered out, he'd come back to New York and tried to get a job on every paper in town. He was black. And then came the great newspaper strike of 1946, and the beginning of the end of the printing industry in the city.

He mooched around till he got a job running copy for the *New York Amsterdam News,* the Harlem paper. He was still running around in circles when Matt Conforti moved in from Chicago to become a desk man for the *Mirror.* He brought Jeff in to run copy, and then fit him in at the desk a little bit at a time.

Shortly after Matt moved to town, there had been another newspaper strike. The unions won another Pyrrhic victory. A few steps ahead of the sheriff, he and Jeff had moved to the *Tribune.* Then it was merged with the *Journal-American.* Matt smelled further trouble. He wangled an assistant editorship at the *Advocate,* a crummy rag then, held together only by Melanie Parsons's money.

Jeff wound up doing rewrite and headlines on Matt's metropolitan desk. There were a lot of shaky moments, but when the *Trib* went under, the *Advocate* was among the three papers out of thirteen left in America's largest city, and the only one printed after noon.

As the introduction of electronics had eroded human contact, the reporters, all members of the Newspaper Guild union, began to refer to their editors as management, and common interests drowned in a sea of rules represented by the bound copy of the 200-page Collective Bargaining Agreement chained to the center post in the giant room, available for the arbitration of all disputes.

Matt scowled behind his desk, then looked surreptitiously in the dog-eared operating manual next to his word processor, and pushed a button, and then another. "Look what I have for you," he said, smiling broadly. He handed Jeff a three-by-five card with a dozen four-digit numbers on it.

Jeff nodded and took the card. The paper was being assembled for its final edition, which would contain the Wall Street closings and the last fresh stories of the day. He hit the switch on his word processor and watched as the green dot spread to fill the screen. When he'd edited all of the stories on the card, he looked up and said, "It's a wrap."

"Okay," Matt said. He typed in a code which released the block of stories from the fifth-floor memory bank into the teleprinters in makeup on the third floor, where they'd be cut, pasted, photographed, and made into printing plates for the presses, almost without the benefit of human hands.

Matt hit the off button of his machine, and the screen dwindled to the inevitable dot and winked out. No more "–30–" typed at the bottom of cheap yellow paper. No more press badges on the bands of snap brim fedoras. "Casey, Crime Photographer, where are you now?" he asked wistfully.

While Matt and Jeff conjured with their machines, and the Wall Street edition of the *Advocate* passed invisible and silent along coaxial cables that connected the mainframe computer with its satellites, a child of another era sat across the room.

Paul Curtin tapped the keys of his console with casual familiarity. He had just spent an hour at the desk of Abe Schneider, the only member of the chronically weak financial department whom he held in esteem. He was booking his notes into the memory bank for further reference.

"Y'know, Paul," Abe had said, "this material you have about the Superdome," gesturing at the folder on the desk between them, "doesn't really apply to New York. When did you write it?"

"Must have been the end of seventy-two or the beginning of seventy-three. This is the story that moved me up from the *Times-Picayune* to the *Washington Post*."

"Well, times change, old buddy. And New Orleans isn't New York. And the Superdome isn't the same kind of scam you find in the real estate game here."

"Courses for horses, and horses for courses?"

"You got it. New Orleans crooks have different techniques than New York crooks. Likewise, the property outlook in New Orleans requires different kinds of swindlers." He laughed a rumbling laugh that turned into violent coughing in a cloud of blue cigar smoke. Abe Schneider had been covering real estate for the financial department of the *Advocate* since 1948.

Paul rose, picked up the folder, and said, "Thanks Abe, you're a peach."

Try tax abatement swindles, Abe had said. A party wants to get rich, he gets a big abatement. No tax for twenty years. Builds what is supposed to be a middle income building. By the time he's finished, with inflation and all, it's a luxury building. Even with the abatement, the rents have to be fifteen hundred a month for two bedrooms for the building to break even. At fifteen hundred a month, it's hard to encourage the middle class to stay in the city. The reason for the tax abatement is submerged in a lot of hand wringing over rising costs. The builder makes a ton. Paul put the folder on the desk.

He'd already studied the larger issues. In ten years the population of New York City had dropped from 7.8 million to 6.9 million. The white population had gone from 6 million to 4.2 million, while the black and Hispanic had risen from 1.6 to 2.7 million. The well-to-do neighborhoods had become enclaves of white in an ethnic sea. On the other hand, the rich Europeans who were buying the townhouses and co-ops didn't really give much of a shit about the South Bronx or Crown Heights.

Paul rubbed the bridge of his nose and squeezed his eyes shut. The late night and the early morning were catching up with him. Uhuru Towers, he thought, was supposed to be a beacon in that sea of poor people, to give them something to look up to.

Based on what he'd dredged up since Phil Seelig had called him to tell him about Lloyd Gibbons's death, and his brief encounter with Hawkes and Gaines at the funeral, he was not sanguine about the quality of the light.

He kicked the drawer shut. Maybe he was so anxious to have a story to feed Melanie Parsons, and so sick of the city that he was getting carried away. He leaned forward on his elbows and began to go through the file again.

With the closing of the final edition and the ending of the shift, the floor of the newsroom emptied quickly. In the metropolitan section, only Jeff Jackson and Matt Conforti sat at the group of scratched and ill-assorted desks, drinking coffee from Styrofoam cups.

Matt crushed his cup and threw it in the basket as a young reporter hurried out, looking at his watch. Of the sixty or seventy people on the news floor, more than three quarters were between twenty-five and forty. They never had to look at the instructions for the computer terminals. And they came and went according to the schedules in the big book at the end of the chain, with two coffee breaks and an hour for lunch.

Matt turned his chair and looked across at Jeff. "Okay, Midnight, what's on your mind?"

Jeff debated with himself before he spoke. He wasn't sure that he had enough to go on, but unless Woodruff had become a complete crackpot, there was something worth looking into. At the same time, Woodruff's fear for his safety thrust a responsibility upon Jeff from which he shrank.

"A man I know told me that the accident at Uhuru Towers—you remember?"

"Vaguely."

"A man named Gibbons was killed. My man says it was no accident."

Matt raised an eyebrow. "So why doesn't he go to the cops?"

"The implication was that he'd be dead in a day if he did. He says there would be a leak, and they—whoever—would waste him."

"What does he want from us?"

"He wants me to keep this strictly quiet, but to have the story broken. That way, the bad guys get caught before my man has a chance to read his own obituary."

"He's not a nut case, is he?"

"Strictly reliable."

"No ax to grind? No sour grapes?"

"Not likely. He could be mistaken, but not crazy."

"Well, I sure can't do it," Matt said, "and you can't. If I find somebody that I trust and assign it to him, it'll end up in front of the editorial board. Three is already not a secret. . . . ."

"Can't we get someone to take a look without giving too many details, or names?"

"Forget it. Our police beat people aren't going to let you play them like a puppet on a string. Why should they bust their ass for you if you can't trust them?" Matt chewed a nail and cast about aimlessly for a thought and looked across the floor.

Paul Curtin pawed through the files in the drawer of the desk he used. *The old bitch is right. Who knows? Maybe I need a shove, if I can't make up my mind to jump. I'll give it the weekend. If worse comes to worse, I can take a loan from the bank before I quit, and sweat till I can sell something. As for Jerry, I'll swallow my pride and put the bite on Thurlow Proctor. A grandfather ought to be good for a year's tuition, anyway.*

He shook a box of papers. *Either I'm going to dig something out of here,* he thought, *or I'm going to throw it all in the garbage.* He kicked the drawer shut, closed the hasp, then clicked the padlock. *If you don't nail everything down around here, it's gone by morning.*

Paul pushed himself to his feet and picked up the box. There was no one left on the floor except Matt and Jeff. He'd had little to do with the older men. He knew they were pros and admired their work, even though he knew they were just marking time.

Jeff eyed Paul, and asked, "Is he packing up his desk?"

"I don't know," Matt said. "It looks that way. The word is that he's having a tough time with the old lady. Fabrikant walked right past him without saying good night when he left. That's a bad sign. I hear they think he's stale."

"If he's out of material, maybe he'd be interested in a new beat."

"Which leaves us facing your problem, old fella."

"How do we get him interested without spilling the source?"

"Matt, what would happen if we just told him the truth?"

"A novel approach. You want to trust what's-his-name's life to Paul Curtin?"

"He writes well."

"One of the best." Matt looked across at Paul again. "He's got a pretty free hand. Maybe he can get by the editorial board without giving away too much." Curtin had just sat down in his chair and picked up the phone. "Wait'll he gets off, then invite him out for a drink."

Jeff motioned toward the coffee machines. "What about them? They'll wonder, no?"

"Invite him up to your place later. Of course, you'll have to swear to him that you're straight."

"Fuck off, Baldy."

Paul closed his eyes and listened to the phone buzz in his ear. After a half dozen rings, there was a click. "Hello, who is this please?"

"It's me, Petey."

"Hi, Paul." The response was full of cheer and welcome.

"Can I speak to Mom?"

"I'll get her. Say, are you coming for dinner?"

"I am."

"Bring Scotch tape, please." The phone thudded to the floor as Petey Middleton ran off to call his mother.

After a moment, she picked up the phone. "I'm wet and naked."

"Sounds wonderful. Have you cooked anything?"

"I was going to broil a steak."

"Don't. I'll bring Chinese."

"Yum. Hot stuff for me . . ."

"And chicken and walnuts for the kids. I know."

"Seven?"

"Seven-thirty."

Paul hunted up a piece of string and tied it around the box, and walked toward the elevator. As he passed the metro desk, he smiled and said "Night, Matt, Jeff."

"Got a second, Paul?" Jeff asked.

He was half a step beyond the desk before he realized that he'd been spoken to. "Huh? Sure." He put the box on the desk.

"I'd like to go over something with you," Jeff said. Paul waited politely. "I can't do it here. Could you come up to my apartment later? It won't take long." He watched Paul's face. "It's important. It's got to stay just between us."

"What time would you want me? I have a dinner date."

"Whatever suits you. Ten, eleven."

"Let me have your address." Paul stuffed the piece of paper in his pocket, and walked on, curious as hell.

10

Marcus Garvey Hawkes glanced at his desk clock, then at his phone. It was almost eight, and it would be five o'clock in San Francisco. In a minute or two, the phone would ring. Kurt Englander, the president of Burton Industries, was on his way to look at a plywood plant in the Philippines. He had promised to call before he left. He wanted to talk about Uhuru Towers.

Hawkes had a large office on the corner of a new building. Two of the walls were floor-to-ceiling windows, looking out on Rockefeller Plaza across the Avenue of the Americas to the east. When Marcus walked to the window and looked down, he had the sensation of isolation and flight, hovering motionless above the streams of light. God must feel like this, he thought.

The floor in Marcus Hawkes's office gleamed with wax, bringing up the natural highlights in the wood. The furniture was functional Scandinavian in chrome and tan leather. The accessories were coordinated.

Hawkes turned away from the windows and toward the wall opposite his desk. He stretched out his arm and straightened one of the numerous hanging plaques. It was imprinted in bold black letters on brass: "In Appreciation for his Concern and Contributions to Our Cause. To Marcus Garvey Hawkes. From the League of Harlem Mothers."

He appraised his handiwork, grunted approval, and returned to his desk chair. The wall was a monument to Marcus

Hawkes's stature in the black community. He had always been available for dinners, fairs, and the like, but too involved in the broader aspects to make a commitment to any one group—or to risk overexposure. And his efforts had borne fruit. These grass roots organizations became major conduits for millions of construction dollars from federal and state governments to the crumbling inner cities of America. Local group sponsorship was the requirement for participation in the nonprofit housing projects which had been conceived as a cure for urban blight.

At ten past eight, the phone rang. He waited for a second ring, then picked it up. "Marcus Hawkes," he said.

"Marcus, Kurt Englander. How are you?" The voice was deep and devoid of emotion.

"Well, thank you. You're on your way?"

"Yes, I am, Marcus. I haven't a great deal of time. I wanted to ask you about the Uhuru Towers project."

"What in particular, Kurt?"

"We're getting a lot of questions from the insurance company, Marcus. That building is supposed to be habitable by early autumn. John Holderness tells me that he is unable to ascertain from your organization just exactly where you stand from a percentage completion point of view. I'd like a brief word from you on the subject now, and a complete analysis when I get back."

"I can't understand what trouble Jack is having, frankly. The entire job is on the computer. Everything is scheduled. The schedule, give or take a bit, is being kept. You'll have what you want, of course."

There was a stillness, then Englander said, "Of course." After another pause, he continued, "You must understand, Marcus, that having guaranteed the bond for the building's completion—that's some sixty million dolalrs—Burton Industries is damn concerned."

"We're partners in this, Kurt. I'm every bit as concerned as you. My reputation hangs on it. We've got good people here. You've got nothing to worry about."

"I certainly hope not. Please keep John informed on Uhuru. How are the other projects doing?"

"Fine, Kurt, just fine," Marcus said, relieved that the subject had been changed.

"Good. I'm glad to hear it. Remember though, Uhuru is

bonded for the same money as all the rest combined. I've got to go, Marcus. See you in a couple of weeks."

"Good night, Kurt. Good flight."

Marcus waited for the click, then slammed his own receiver on the hook. Cold bastard. What are your motivations, honky? Was it compassion that made you lead a two-billion-dollar building products company into a partnership with a penniless black builder? Was it trying to preserve the system? Too noble, either one. Political ambition? A lot of people think that you'd made a good ambassador. You and your Protestant work ethic. You're in it for yourself. Just like me, honky. You smell a buck. You're not better—just whiter!

"Charles," Marcus yelled, "you out there?"

Charles Hawkes opened the door tentatively and looked around its edge like a small child. "Did you want me, Marcus?"

"No, Charles," he said venomously, "I always yell like that. It's good for my lungs. Is Mack Bell still around, do you know?"

Charles insinuated himself into the room. The British planters in his background were apparent in his features and in his Caribbean twang. He was shorter than Marcus, heavy, but not as broad as his brother, and, at sixty, four years older.

"I think maybe he's gone home."

Marcus mimicked him nastily, then said, "Well, get off your ass and trot down to his office and find out."

"Why don't you use the intercom?"

"Because it cuts off when the switchboard is shut down."

"Okay. Okay, I'll go. Listen, did Kurt call?"

"Yes, he called. Why do you want to know?"

"I saw he left a message that he'd call. Is everything all right? We don't have any problems, do we?"

"With you estimating the costs of our construction jobs, how could we?" Marcus curled his lip in contempt. "Why don't you go on home to Clarice and have her fix you some hog maws and greens?"

"You have no call to talk about Clarice like that."

"You should have married one of your own, Charles. You're even beginning to sound like a field nigger. Now why don't you just see if Mack is around, and go?"

As he left, Marcus turned his eyes to heaven—to marry an Alabama field hand!

Mack Bell strode into the room without hesitation. "You want me, Marcus? I was just trying to get out of here." Bell was a massive figure, much taller than Hawkes, over six feet four, and equally broad, though there was little fat on him. His shoulders were wide and square. His face was an African mask, flat and shiny with high cheekbones, adorned by a thin moustache.

"I had a call from Kurt Englander," Marcus said casually, reclining in his chair. Bell stood stone-faced. Marcus continued, "He'd like to know how things are going."

Bell snorted derisively. "You sure of that?"

"What does that mean? What does the computer say?"

Bell dropped into the side chair and smiled across at Hawkes, his teeth gleaming. "You're terrific, Marcus. It's a machine, Marcus. That's all. Just a machine. It can't build no building for you. Marcus, don't you know by now, you can't bullshit up a building? You have to build the sucker." He laughed aloud. "The computer knows what we tell it. It knows what the schedule for the building elements are. It's a kind of alarm clock. We've overslept, Marcus. Why do you bullshit yourself?"

"What seems to be the problem?" Hawkes asked pompously.

Bell rose and looked down at Hawkes, the smile gone. "The same problem that we had yesterday, and all the other yesterdays. More than we can chew. Incompetence. Tinker and Gaines."

"Tinker is the only black licensed union plumber in the city of New York. Gaines is the only black masonry subcontractor. This is a black job, in a black neighborhood, sponsored by a black organization. We're supposed to be training minority subcontractors, developing their skills."

Backstage at a disaster. "We're supposed to be building a fifty-story building. You can't do no on-the-job training on a project the size of Uhuru Towers. Not if you want to finish it. Tinker don't know more about plumbing than to flush the john. And Gaines is that much worse, besides being a part-time pimp, a hood, and a religious freak. Neither of them has ever done anything but a few little local rehab jobs on tenements."

Hawkes waved his hand expansively, and said, "Still and all, Mack," his voice ingratiating, "you have to keep in mind what Uhuru Towers represents. It's a great experiment in cooperation. We have a mission. We're burying the aftermath of three centuries of slavery."

Bell wiped his palms on his thighs. "Right. Well, I got to go, Marcus." He turned to leave.

"You didn't tell me about Uhuru. Are we really behind?"

Bell turned to him wearily. "By at least nine weeks. It's much worse in masonry and plumbing. And I got to go slow because we're in the middle of a shitty winter, and I got lousy subcontractors, and there ain't no sense in trying to go faster, otherwise we're going to kill some more people, and still not get it finished on time."

Hawkes looked at him contritely. "That was terrible about Gibbons's accident. He was a good man."

"Yes, he was," Bell said, then turned and walked to the door. He looked back over his shoulder. "Good night, Marcus."

11

"I'm freezing," Paul said to God as he struggled across South Street, through partly jelled puddles invisible in the broken black pavement, to the parking lot under the elevated highway where he kept his car. He had bought the Corvette when he had signed the contract with the *Advocate* four years before. New York weather notwithstanding, it still was shiny red, with only minor dents. He opened the trunk and stuffed the cardboard box into the space available next to the spare, let himself in, and started the engine. There was a moment of tension when the power of the battery began to decline, struggling with the cold motor, but finally it caught.

He drove up into Chinatown and wove through the narrow alleys till he found Division Street. He flipped down his press card and double-parked in front of Canton. Ten minutes later, clutching his coat with one hand and a brown paper bag with the other, he said, "Good night, Irene. Thanks," and pushed his way out of the door.

It was just seven when he arrived at Maryanne's building. Incredibly, there was a space and it was legal till eight in the morning. Sometimes the press card worked, sometimes not. At thirty-five bucks a pop, he thought, shutting the car door, who can afford to take chances?

As he emerged from the elevator, the apartment door flung open and Petey tackled him at knee level, almost bringing him down.

"Hey, watch it, Yoyo."

"Watcha got, huh? Watcha got?"

"Worms."

"Yecchhh."

Paul took the bag into the kitchen and dropped it on the table, then walked back through the dining room to the living room, where Maryanne waited with a long scotch and soda. He kissed her soundly. "Thank you." He looked down. "Ah, here we are."

Alexandra Middleton was wearing her pink party dress and patent leather Mary Janes. As he bent to kiss her, she said, "I'm hungry and you're late."

"I was working."

"Work stinks."

Paul picked her up and squeezed her. "You look very pretty. Was school fun today?"

"School stinks."

"Not as much as work."

By eight-thirty dinner was finished and the children had been bullied into their pajamas and nominally, at least, into bed. Paul had been pleasantly noncommittal and Maryanne was ravening with curiosity. She made each of them a brandy and sat at the other end of the couch regarding him speculatively. "So?"

He had debated with himself throughout the dinner as to how to tell her about his confrontation with Melanie Parsons. When the subject of his quitting had come up the previous evening, she'd seemed genuinely apprehensive. Well, so was he. The whole idea was in such a nebulous state that he preferred not to hash it out.

"Not much to say, really. She ragged my ass fearfully about not being productive enough to suit her taste. I procrastinated because I had very little to say."

Maryanne took a sip from her glass and rolled it in her palms. "That sounds very inconclusive."

"Well, it was," he said defensively. He brightened. "Something did come out of it, though." She turned in her seat to face him squarely. "I'm off till Monday."

Maryanne finished the brandy and put the glass down on the table, studied it for a moment, then rose and walked across the room to the desk and took the phone. She dialed and waited. Paul started to ask her a question, but she put her fingers to her lips.

"Forrest," she said in a firm, clear voice. "You're going to do me a favor." There was a pause. "No, Forrest, I'm sure it was an oversight. You don't even have to tell me you'll drop it in the mail. No, not even last month's. When you get around to it. I'm sure that the Morgan Guaranty is very slow paying its vice-presidents. You just take your time." Paul put his hands over his face. "Forrest, you're going to take your children this weekend. You're going to have your mother pick them up at school on Friday afternoon at three o'clock. They will have little suitcases with them. You will deliver them back at your leisure after six o'clock on Sunday night."

She listened for what seemed to be a full minute, then said, "I'm not asking you, Forrest, dear. I'm telling you. And they'd better have a good time, or I'll stop being forbearing about your being so slow with the damn child support payments." She listened patiently, then said, "I'm sure that you do as well as you can being a father. I know how tough the banking business is just now, what with interest rates and all. I'm sure it keeps you up nights." She listened again. "Take them swimming at the club. They love that. All right, Forrest. Thanks. Good night."

"I hope I never get on your bad side, Maryanne."

"I hope you never turn out to care so little about anything but yourself. You know, he really things he's doing me a favor to take his own children."

"He's not so bad."

She smiled sweetly. "He's a shithead." She walked back to the bar and poured herself another dollop.

"What was that all about?"

"I thought since you were taking me to meet your family tomorrow, I might as well take Friday off, too, and we could enjoy a rare weekend of solitude."

Paul put his glass down carefully. "I did not agree to take you tomorrow."

"Nonetheless, you shall." He looked up. There was a stubborn set to her jaw that Paul could not remember seeing before. "I told you. It's set. When do we leave?"

He weighed the value of protest, then thought to himself, what am I fighting for? "Nine. I'll pick you up at nine."

"That's better."

"Did you push poor old Forrest around like that?"

She sat on his lap. "To push there has to be some resistance. You cannot push the man who is not there."

He looked at his watch. "Speaking of which, I gotta go."

She stood up and touched his face. "Hey, you're not mad, are you?"

He got to his feet and stretched and took her in his arms. "A guy at the office asked me to stop over and see him around ten or eleven. I want to get it over with."

"Come back."

"If I can. I'll call you if it isn't past eleven. Otherwise, I'll see you in the morning." He put on his coat, but stopped at the door. "Listen, thank you for calling Forrest. I'm sure it wasn't easy. See you."

When the door was shut behind him, she said, "I love you, Paul. Don't run away."

12

Marcus Hawkes waited a decent interval after Mack Bell had left, then walked down the hall till he reached a door marked "Vice-President—Construction." He turned on the light and entered the room, which was less than half the size of his own office. The furnishings were spartan. The walls were corkboard, with blueprints and diagrams pinned in a random array from waist level to eye level on all sides. The desk top was buried in a heap of papers. On a table directly behind the desk, lay a large pile of computer printouts, still linked together at the edges like a two dimensional serpent. The top sheet was marked in red: Critical Path Analysis.

Marcus removed the sheets and looked at the bar charts, one dark indicating the projected level, one light indicating fulfillment. In each category, plumbing, concrete, and the rest, the dark towered above the light. He flicked off the switch and returned to his office, checked the time, and reached for the phone.

The number rang, then answered. "George Gaines."

Despite his long familiarity with Gaines, Hawkes still felt uneasiness at the current of violence which he perceived in the bass drum voice. "It's Marcus," he replied.

"Can you meet me?"

"You have our friend?"

"Oh, yes." There was relish in his voice. "Indeed I do. What would be convenient?"

"The market by the river. It's quiet and on my way home. Near the coal pier."

"Half an hour?" Gaines asked.

"Fine."

As Hawkes descended to the basement to retrieve his brown Lincoln from the garage, he considered that even if he did not have need of Gaines, it would be difficult to break the ties that bound them. They reached into the eighteenth century, and two thousand miles across the sea.

Their forebears had been Yorubas, sold away in chains to Arab slave traders by their greedy chiefs. They were among the fortunate who survived the forced march, yoked like oxen, through the jungles of Benin to the stone fort and pier at Warri where the Yankee buyers came, laden with Bibles and rum.

When next they saw the sun, they were dragged, reeking of their own filth, by ropes from the hold of a ship. To make them presentable at dockside, the captain had them hauled from a boom through the tropical water as he tacked across the entrance to the harbor of Kingston, Jamaica.

Thirty-five years later, in 1739, a muscular slave named Gaines led a revolt against the planters of the island. His band, known as Maroons, broke into a store of arms on the plantation owned by his master, and after slaughtering the entire family, men, women and children, like suckling pigs at the Feast of Saint John, went on to wreak havoc across the island.

At the end of the first week, the army moved out of Kingston's forts to contain the rebellion. Slaves known to have given refuge to any member of the roving band known as Maroons were mutilated. Testicles, breasts, and limbs littered the clearing of small villages all over the island.

The slaves began to take ears.

All trapped rebels were drawn and their entrails thrown into a fire.

After six months, sanity prevailed.

The royal governor decreed that the slave army called Maroons was a band of free men. They were separated forever from their masters—and all they had left behind them. They had won.

Stripped of all of their possessions, condemned to starvation and poverty, the Maroons retreated to the jungle hills and subsisted there until a century passed, and the rest of Jamaica's slaves were manumitted under less dramatic circumstances.

As the rebellion receded into history, the Maroons were reintegrated into Jamaican society. But into the twentieth century a man who could show that he was the descendant of a Maroon bore a special cachet, like a member of the Daughters of the American Revolution.

As Marcus Hawkes drove from his garage to meet George Gaines, it occurred to him that it was not their first historical connection that bound them, as much as the second.

Their fathers had followed Marcus Moziah Garvey from his home at St. Ann's Bay just before the First World War to the height of his power as the head of the Universal Negro Improvement Association. Delegates from twenty-five countries attended his Black Congress in Philadelphia in 1920. Until Martin Luther King, Jr., no greater mass movement of black people existed in the history of the world.

They had followed him through the calvary of his madness—he named himself Emperor of Africa in 1921—and through the disgrace of his conviction for securities fraud in 1922 and his imprisonment.

With the end of the dream, Garvey's followers were left to founder. Hawkes's father got a job as a bookkeeper in New York. When his wife became pregnant, he sent her home to Jamaica to have her baby. They called him Marcus Garvey Hawkes.

George Gaines's father took a job as a garbage man and used his brute strength to good advantage as an enforcer for a numbers runner. Time and frustration took a toll on his mind. When Garvey prophesied the coming of a Black King on Earth, the elder Gaines became a Rastafarian, and worshiped the divinity of Haile Selassie, the Emperor of Ethiopia. He became a dealer in ganja—marijuana—the ceremonial herb, and escaped New York after a gun battle with the police. The day he jumped ship in Jamaica in 1940, Marcus Garvey died in penniless oblivion in London.

Forty years later, as Marcus Garvey Hawkes exited from the Harlem River Drive, he reflected that while George Gaines had lost much of his father's religious zeal, he had maintained the same penchant for violence. Old Jeremy Gaines, Marcus thought to himself, shot dead by the police in Jamaica almost thirty years ago, his pupils contracted to pinpoints by drugs and the name of God on his lips.

The Bronx Terminal Market is dank and smelly beneath the expressway. Though in the early morning it bustles with wholesalers and retailers in the grocery trade, at ten o'clock at night it is as deserted and cheerless as a tomb. Hawkes cut through the parking lot to the riverside and continued a hundred yards to an adjacent coal storage and loading facility. A car and a truck stood silently parked in front of the tall silhouette of a coal crusher at dockside. He drew up next to them and stepped out, pulling his hat firmly on his head because of the gusty wind.

In the shadow of the angular machine housing, which rose a hundred feet in the air, two men in work clothes held a third prisoner between them. George Gaines stood to one side, smart in a leather overcoat and a snap brim hat.

"Mr. Hawkes," he said. "I want you to meet Al Jenks. He's an ace bricklayer. I believe him to be a smart nigger. I think he has a lot of things to tell you." Gaines walked over to him. "I don't think he's going to be laying any bricks for a while, though." Gaines reached out and squeezed Jenks's hand. He screamed, then vomited, choking. "He didn't want to come with us. And in the discussion," he squeezed again, and the man fell limp between his captors, "his fingers got broken— one at a time."

Hawkes moved closer, his bulk casting a shadow on the man with the broken hands. Jenks was sobbing softly. "You know, Mr. Jenks, there is nothing that I appreciate more than a fine craftsman. A skilled man is a valuable tool. But in addition to his talents, he must know his place, even as he strives to better himself. Do we understand each other?"

Jenks hung on the two men, his head down.

"I can't hear you," Hawkes said softly. The two men shook Jenks's arms roughly.

"Yesyesyesyesyesyesyes."

Hawkes put a gloved hand over Jenks's mouth. "No need to carry on like that, Mr. Jenks." He removed his hand. "I understand that you were trying to raise a little cash. You have a little information to sell. That's what we'd heard. We might be a ready market. We'd want to be exclusive, of course."

"I don't know nothin'," he whined. "Nothin'."

"I understand quite differently from Mr. Gaines. I hear you indicated to one of your fellow workers that there might be something wrong with the brick count at Uhuru Towers. Do you recall saying that? Did you tell anyone else?"

"I don't know nothin'. I swear to sweet Jesus. I didn't say nothin' and I don't know nothin'."

Hawkes turned to Gaines and said, "George, I am beginning

to doubt your judgment. You told me that this was a smart nigger. He seems pretty dumb to me."

"Jenks," Gaines said, "have you ever seen a chicken eat?"

In shock from the pain of his ruined hands, Jenks looked at him dully without replying.

"Often, you'll see a bird peck a stone or two. It's an aid to their digestion." Gaines started to walk away. The men holding Jenks dragged him along behind. "They don't secrete acid, as humans do. The strong muscles of their stomach crush their food against the stones till it is digestible." Gaines came to a halt before a platform with a portable cement mixer about shoulder height fixed to it. He nodded.

The two men lifted Jenks bodily from the ground. He didn't begin to struggle until they had lifted him almost into the mouth of the mixer, and then it was too late. He shrieked as his destroyed hands struck the metal. It made an odd hollow sound inside the oval chamber.

Gaines walked to the mixer and peered over the edge. "Are you still with us?" Jenks scrambled to his feet, leaning against the angle wall of the vessel. His chin was even with its lip.

"Please don't fuck with me no more, mister. I don't know nothin'. Just that there was something wrong with the brick count."

"What was wrong? Who knew?"

Jenks looked at him blankly. Gaines threw a lever. With a clanking sound, the gears of the motor engaged with the sprocket at the base of the mixer well, turning it slowly. Jenks started to fall, then regained his balance, and began to move in the direction opposite the machine's motion like a rat on a treadmill. Gaines increased the speed, then raised his voice, "Well, Jenks?" When there was no answer, he bent and threw a rock into the opening. It rattled about with a clanging noise. Jenks drew a sharp breath as the rock ricocheted from the metal, gashing his leg. Gaines smiled and threw in a larger fragment.

"Lemme out. Lemme out, God, please." Gaines stopped the machine.

"Talk to me," Hawkes said.

"He gonna kill me," Jenks said, looking wildly at Gaines.

"Maybe not. It depends on whether I think you're telling the truth. Talk to me."

Jenks swallowed. "I saw Gibbons leave his toolbox open the day before he was killed. He went off to lunch, and I took a look."

"You mean you went to see what you could snitch. What did you take?"

"I swear to Jesus God Almighty. I didn't take nothin'."

"What did you see?"

"I saw the shipping manifests."

"Go on," Hawkes urged gently.

"It said that sixty skids of brick totalling 120,000 bricks had been delivered."

"So?"

"They ain't but one thousand brick on them skids. Somebody is takin' delivery of the rest of them bricks and puttin' the money he sells 'em for in his pocket."

"Please continue."

"If it takes three million bricks to build the building, and somebody orders six million and sells half for his own account, he's makin' a lot of money."

"Who knew about this?"

"Nobody. We ain't supposed to get these manifests. It must of been stuck on a skid by mistake."

Hawkes laughed mirthlessly. "I suppose you could say that. Then what did you do?"

Jenks started to fall. "My hands. I can't stand the pain no more."

"Do you want the machine turned on again?" Gaines asked.

"No. Don't do that. I wrote a note. A note to Mr. Gaines. I knew he was cool. He's ripped contractors off before. I said I knew about the scam and wanted a cut, and to put the money in a mailbox for me, or I'd squawk."

"Go on," Hawkes said. "You said you had some papers. Where are they?"

Jenks swallowed. "They're in a model airplane in my kid's room. A Japanese Zero. It's a couple of those manifest sheets."

"Does anybody know about this big scam of yours? You told anybody that you're going to hit it big?"

"I told my wife that maybe I'd run into some money soon, but I didn't tell her no details."

"That's it?"

"I swear to Jesus God Almighty on my mother."

"Thanks," Hawkes said. He turned and walked away. Gaines reached out and threw the lever on the machine all the way forward. It began to spin rapidly, knocking Jenks from his feet. Gaines casually threw a half dozen jagged rocks into the mixer.

"Just let it run for a while," he said to one of the men who had held Jenks. "Then just fill it with water from the standpipe and empty it into the river. About five minutes should do."

The man tugged at his tightly coiled Rastafarian forelock.

Gaines caught up with Hawkes and took his arm, walking beside him. "While you're dropping me off at home, Marcus, we can discuss the rest of the Jenks family. I hope you don't mind, but my car's getting a tune-up."

13

Paul pulled the crumpled slip of paper out of his jacket pocket as he left the hall of Maryanne's building. Realizing that he was only three blocks away from Jeff Jackson's apartment, he left his car where it was parked, and walked.

A seedy-looking doorman asked him where he was going, then passed him on to the lobby. The elevator took an eternity. Paul, preoccupied with his personal problems, had no thought of what Jeff might want even as he strolled down the long hall looking for 4L.

He rang once and the door popped open. "Come in. Let me take your coat," Jeff said. "Still dripping?" he asked as he hung it in the closet.

"Half snow. Crummy." Paul looked around. "A regular newspaperman's den of iniquity."

"The poor we have always with us," Jeff quoted, ushering him into the living room. Jeff remained standing while Paul sat on the couch. "What can I get you to drink?"

"Let's see. I started with scotch then switched to brandy. How about going back to scotch?"

"That's what I'm drinking myself." Jeff returned from the kitchen, handed Paul his glass and sat down in a chair opposite him. "Cheers. Welcome."

Paul raised his glass and took a swallow. "You know, I don't think we've ever sat down and talked for more than five minutes in the four years that I've been on the paper."

Jeff smiled wryly and took a sip. "Could it be that we travel in different social circles?"

"I'm a snob?"

"Oh, no. It's just that I don't get called up to talk to the publisher as often as you do. No offense intended."

"A certain amount taken. But you're right. I guess we just haven't really had the occasion. This being said, what brings me to your door?"

There was a lengthy pause as Jeff looked first into his glass, then very intently into Paul's face, trying to find something there that was not really visible. "I talked this over with Matt Conforti."

"You're always talking to Matt. You were at the press table at the Last Supper together, the way I hear it."

"Close. *Stars and Stripes*, the *Mirror*, the *Trib*."

"*Requiescat in Pace*."

"Amen. More than thirty years, we've been friends. He's a very straight guy."

"And a top slot man. A good editor."

"He thinks you're a pretty good reporter, and guesses that you're not a bad guy. Me, too. That's why you're here. We have a very touchy story. It will probably require a lot of digging, a lot of connections, and most important a lot of discretion."

"And I don't kiss and tell?"

"More than that. We think that because of your—shall we say social position—maybe you don't have to answer as many questions about what you're doing with your time as some other people might."

Paul finished his drink and held out the glass. "At the risk of being a pushy guest. . . ." As Jeff rose to take his glass, he continued, "You shouldn't count too much on my clout. I suppose I can trust you, too. I think I came within two or three ill-chosen words of getting the sack this afternoon."

Jeff came back with the refills. "We saw Fabrikant didn't kiss you good night as usual. We thought you might be in the market for a lead." He leaned toward Paul. "Are you still in a position to pick your own assignments?"

"Between us?"

"For sure."

"I'm not sure I'm going to survive Monday morning. We've decided together—in quotes—that I have the weekend to get my shit together and bring her a new perspective on the gubernatorial campaign, something with teeth."

"What does she want?"

"Nothing elaborate. Salome dancing into her office with a silver tray bearing the head of Frank O'Neil. Maybe a roll of clear color pictures of him in a pink tutu cavorting with the eleven-year-old catamites in his basement."

Jeff jiggled the cubes of ice in his glass. "If this story is handled wrong, my source is going to end up dead," he said calmly.

Paul sputtered on a mouthful of scotch. "A little heavy for my regular beat."

"It has to do with state government."

"My boys don't normally get violent. They just cheat and swindle."

"My man says this is in the millions and reaches all the way to the top."

"O'Neil?"

"Maybe."

"But where does the violence come in?"

"Somebody got killed. It was supposed to be an accident. But my man says it wasn't."

"Let's say he's right. Where do we start? Assuming I'm interested."

"What do you know about Uhuru Towers?"

The color drained from Paul's face. "Huh?"

"You know something?"

"I went to the funeral. A guy named Gibbons. Is that what you're talking about?"

"Yes. I don't understand. . . ."

"Phil Seelig called me the other day. Just a shot in the dark. He heard that Gibbons got walloped with a skid of bricks. He checked it out on his way home. He called because he knows it's O'Neil's pet project." He took a swig from the glass. "The guy says it was no accident?"

"He says it was murder. Shit, it never even made our paper."

"The *Times* had it. I saw it."

"Yeah, but no TV."

"Phil called me on a hunch." Paul brushed the lanky hair off of his forehead. "I took a quick look—made a few calls—because I didn't have anything better to do. It looks like another industrial accident. The only thing that doesn't ring true is this guy Hawkes who runs the construction company. A real sleaze for my dough. More concerned about his press notices than the death of his employee. But what the hell, welcome to the Big Apple. Why doesn't your guy go to the cops?"

"Panic-stricken. He says they'll kill him. You haven't discussed this with anyone, have you?"

"The only person I've talked to is Melanie Parsons. Maybe Bornstein heard a word or two, but I don't think so. That's it."

"Christ. She'll bring it to the editorial board."

"No, she won't. For the moment this is between us. If I tell her what's going on, six gets you five she'll shut up. She loves this kind of stuff. But it can't take too long. She's short on patience. She likes concrete results—right now!"

"What about bringing Phil Seelig into this?"

"A very good reporter. But all his connections are through NYPD. If he starts to look, and your source is right about his vulnerability, it'll be fatal."

"So where do we start? If we start."

"If we start? How can we not start?" Paul rocked back and forth in his seat, looking at Jeff with frank appraisal. A good man. Conforti's a good man, too. Maybe their source is just another angry disappointed person. Maybe he's full of shit. On the other hand, given my alternatives, it's irresistible. I'm going to get fired or quit anyway. What do I have to lose?"

"Look, Jeff, I'm already committed to bringing something on Uhuru to Melanie on Monday. I've suggested that it's likely there's a scam there that we can use on O'Neil. I can probably buy myself a couple of weeks without telling all. If Gibbons's death was no accident, and there is a cover-up, I ought to be able to make the connection fast enough. I'll give it my best shot."

Jeff stood and extended his hand. "Thanks. And, be careful."

Rising, Paul took it, and replied, "Not to worry. I don't want to look you in the eye after reading your friend's obituary."

"I mean be careful yourself."

"I don't want to read my obituary, either."

It was almost midnight when he reached his car. He looked up at Maryanne's building, then changed his mind and drove home.

14

The sky had brightened, and though it was a bit breezy, the temperature had risen, and there seemed to be the slightest suspicion of spring in the air. The governor looked up over the steeples of St. Patrick's Cathedral as he stepped out of the limousine and crossed the sidewalk to the broad steps. Three Japanese tourists twittered to one another and compared settings as they took pictures of the church and of the statue of Atlas supporting the world across the avenue. Before he entered the bronze doors, sculpted with saints in high relief, he removed his homburg and smoothed his hair. He looked over his shoulder to see that his driver had followed his instructions and driven away. He did not want his official car to call attention to his presence.

Frank O'Neil strode up the aisle with the confidence of a man intimate with the house of God. He stopped at a pew a half dozen rows from the front. The brass plate on the back of the bench glowed with the patina of time and polish. In Memory of Thomas Xavier O'Neil. Frank O'Neil had served as an acolyte while his parents had sat there, fifty years gone by.

Ten o'clock mass was celebrated by one of the younger priests on the staff of the Episcopal See of the Diocese of New York. It being a Thursday, the homily was thankfully brief. A

queue formed before the main altar as worshipers stepped forth
from their pews to accept Communion. Frank O'Neil twisted
wretchedly on the bench, suddenly hard and punishing to his
flesh. As the parishioners filed out through the lofty cathedral,
he rose, stepped into the aisle and knelt again before the Cross.
He had not taken Communion in two years. Nor had he been
confessed and shriven of his sins.

He stood and walked to the private door, hidden by curtains
to the left rear of the altar which led to the chancellery.
Stepping through, he knocked firmly. A young Irish priest in a
cassock and wearing thick glasses peered up at him. "Yes,
sir," he asked. "How may I help you?"

"I'm Frank O'Neil, Father. I have an appointment with
Monsignor Connelly."

"Yes, sir, Governor. I didn't recognize you," the priest said,
embarrassed. "I don't see terribly well. Won't you come with
me?" O'Neil followed the priest, who was skin and bone with
a bobbing patch of red hair, across the hall, and up wide red
carpeted steps to the second floor. He knocked diffidently at an
oaken door. A military voice rang out, "Come in."

"Monsignor, it's the governor to see you."

"Thank you, Father." Monsignor Connelly walked to the
door and pulled it fully open to admit his guest. The priest
bowed and scurried away. "Please come in," the monsignor
said, closing the door behind O'Neil.

Once alone, the two men smiled at each other with an easy
familiarity. Boyhood friends, as one had gone to Yale, so the
other had gone to the North American College in Rome. As
one served the state, so did the other serve the Church. "Sit
down, Frank. Would you like a cup of coffee?"

"Thank you, John. I'd love one."

O'Neil watched as Monsignor Connelly called through on
the intercom on his desk to pass on the request. He had grayed
and his hair was quite thin on top, otherwise he seemed to be
the same boy who had been his company commander in the
Knickerbocker Greys a thousand years ago. Red cheeks,
straight nose, steely blue eyes. He had always seemed destined
for the army, but at that crucial moment had found his calling.
He had a bit of a paunch, but still kept himself fit.

The coffee came on a silver tray and was left on the desk

between them. The monsignor poured. O'Neil searched his face for a hint of what was to come. He was without emotion.

"How are the children, Frank? Isn't Teddy to graduate this year?"

The governor took a sip. Was this to be a waiting game? he asked himself. "Ted comes down from Yale, prayerfully with honors this June. That's the last of them, John."

"Have I not baptized all eight? A first-class Irish family. Would to God that dear Mary were here alive to see them. She would be justifiably proud. Heaven knows it would be hard to believe her five times a grandmother. I must say, it isn't even easy to think of you that way, Grandpa."

O'Neil drained his cup and put it on the tray. If this wants patience, then patience it shall have. What is he stalling for? "I don't feel like a grandfather. I feel like a man in the early afternoon of life, John. I'm ready to deal with another eight, should they come along."

"I'd be proud to dip them in the font as well, Frank, as the product of a happy marriage."

"That would please me no end."

"It'd have to be a marriage sanctioned by the Church."

"How else then?"

Monsignor Connelly pinched his nose between the thumb and forefinger of his right hand and closed his eyes. "Let's stop sparring, Frank. I feel bad enough as it is."

"You've talked to His Eminence, then?"

"I did as you asked."

"It was your idea, John."

"I said that if you came to him and asked him directly, you would give him neither time for reflection nor a chance to give you the benefit of the doubt. You can get an appointment with the cardinal as readily as I can."

"I'm not the secretary of the Episcopal purse."

"That's my job, Frank. It's like being in armor, rather than the airborne. I'm still just a soldier of God and I follow the chain of command. I don't think it would be to your benefit to bring this subject directly before the cardinal."

O'Neil's face clouded over. "I can't believe this, John. The Church will not look favorably upon my petition to marry Allison Vance?"

"Forrestiere," he replied pointedly. "Allison Vance Forrestiere. I don't want to preach at you, but there is one Church, and one set of rules. She married in the Cathedral of Sienna before a thousand onlookers. Were that not sufficient, she was joined in matrimony with Count Forrestiere by the Bishop of Florence, His Eminence Cardinal Durazzo. She bore him two children, baptized in the Church, then left him and obtained a civil divorce in Haiti. That divorce is not sanctioned or recognized by the Church."

"John, Armando Forrestiere is an outrageous wastrel and a fool. He made an ass of himself, and of Allison and their children, in every public place from Palm Beach to Monte Carlo. He was an impossible husband. He stole. He lied. He was an overt and persistent adulterer."

Monsignor Connelly looked sternly at his old friend. "His sins do not change the nature of the laws of the Church. If there were prior cause for excommunication—some evidence that she had not given her vows freely—then perhaps there would be room for further discussion." He sat straight in his chair, his eyes unflinching, his voice rolling like a drum. "I must tell you that in the absence of circumstances warranting annulment, it is the viewpoint of His Eminence that in the eyes of the Church, Allison Forrestiere is still a married woman. Were she to marry you, the Church would look upon her as a bigamist. She could not be married in the Church. Were you to marry her outside of the Church, you would yourself be denied the Blessed Sacraments."

"John," O'Neil leaned forward in the chair and put his hand on the desk. "This means a great deal to me. I suppose you could say that I . . . I need this marriage. . . ."

Monsignor Connelly's expression softened. "I wish I could help you, Frank. Your old friend John, that played in the mud with you, and that staggered home at three in the morning with you, and that baptized your children, wants to help you in any way that he possibly can." He stood behind the desk and walked around it, putting his hand on the governor's shoulder. "But Monsignor Connelly, the son and servant of Holy Mother Church, is bound to tell you that that help cannot be in this matter."

O'Neil looked up at him. "That's it?"

The Monsignor shrugged. "You can petition Rome. You can seek canonical counsel to present a case. It is possible that Allison could be granted an annulment."

"What are the chances?"

"If you are asking me as a businessman, I don't think they are great. If you are asking me as a friend, I think that you are making a mistake, for you will surely displease the cardinal. And for reasons personal and political, that could be grave. If you are asking me as a priest, I will tell you that it is wrong. I'm sorry."

O'Neil sighed and rose from the chair. He extended his hand. "Thank you, Monsignor, for all you have done. I'll think about what you've said carefully."

In the two hours he had passed in the gray stone fortress, clouds had pushed in from the west, and the blue sky and sun had disappeared from view. The governor crossed to the garage in the sidestreet where he had told his chauffeur to await him.

"Where to, sir?"

"I want to pick up a pair of shoes, and I could use a shine."

"Chester's?"

"Right, Phil."

On Fifty-first Street, just past Eighth Avenue, where small restaurants line the block, there is a little shoeshine stand built against the wall of a tenement. The governor got out of his car and stepped up onto one of the two worn seats and planted his shoe on the brass pedestal.

"Good mawnin', Gunnah," Chester wheezed. O'Neil found it increasingly difficult to understand what he said as the years went by. He was fat and short, his bulk wrapped in a polish-stained gray cotton jacket. Underneath it, to protect him from the elements, were an assortment of sweaters of different shades and lengths, some of which had belonged to the governor, with holes in varying places. He bent over his substantial stomach, picked out the tools of his trade to suit the occasion, and sat on a tiny stool.

Chester seemed to possess a sixth sense about the governor's moods. This morning he didn't want to talk. He worked rapidly, and finished with a flourish, tipping his hat as he always did. The governor gave him two dollars.

"Thank you, Gunnah. Doan fogits you shoes. Them just come back from de fixer."

"Thank you, Chester." The governor took the brown, wrapped parcel and stepped back into the car. He told Phil that he wanted to go home. Surreptitiously, he pulled the wrapping paper aside and slipped the shoebox out partway. He bent the cardboard cover back. Keeping the box well out of sight in his lap, he looked down at the rubber-banded stacks of old bills. He stuck in his finger and tested. It was full from top to bottom. Feeling better, he closed the package again, sat back, and tuned the radio to the news.

15

"You look very pretty," Paul said, holding the door aside for Maryanne. She smiled at him affectionately and slid into the low seat of the sports car.

"We're off," she said as he started the engine and pulled out into the street. "You're right on time. Nine to the second. How come you didn't call last night? I waited."

"I'm sorry. I thought about it. But I didn't get back here till nearly midnight. I just went home."

She waited for him to talk some more. But, when he was quiet, both hands on the wheel, staring over the hood, she just unfolded the copy of the *Times* that she had brought and left him to his thoughts.

After a half hour of weaving through traffic, they entered the Hutchinson River Parkway, and in a few minutes were in Connecticut. "I read the sports section." Paul squinted a bit, but seemed not to have heard.

"Yoo hoo, Mr. Curtin. I'm here. It's little me."

"Huh?"

"I said that I'd read the sports section."

"Oh." He glanced at her, then turned back to the road. "I guess I'm not very good company this morning."

"Good guess. What's going on in there?" she asked patting the top of his head.

"I don't know. I wish I had a name for it."

"More general malaise? Did last night turn out to be of any

interest? Is it that you're concerned that I've come along to see Jerry?''

"I have to admit that That Thursday is never a stellar day. It's like a broken record. I just keep going over and over the same little musical phrase. It's my big guilt trip. Who's to blame? Does there always have to be someone to blame? My old man used to tell me that ineptitude and indecision were their own rewards. I therefore strive, in all things, to be adept and decisive.''

"Delightful traits in the male animal.''

"You agree with my father. But, not everything runs smoothly all of the time.''

She reached to squeeze his arm. "I notice that on That Thursday you are rarely a ball of fire. I feel that way once a month. Not every two months.''

"Does menopause bring peace?''

"I suspect that its onset is the most frightening thing that ever happens to a woman. I would feel that way if it happened to me now. If you mean is there a certain relief at the reduction of responsibility for your body—I guess.''

"The greatest pleasure and the most intense pain arise from acts of creation. Is there something more joyful than the act of love? If there are things which can be compared, are they not also climactic in nature? You paint, you sculpt, you make a baby. And then the work is criticized. Or the baby is imperfect. Is your eye imperfect? If your art is imperfect, is it a matter of your perception, or execution? If the baby is imperfect, is the flaw inherent? To whose genetic credit is the flaw?''

"Is that important?''

"If you ever want to paint another picture, write another story, or have another baby, it is paramount.'' He turned off of the parkway onto a service road. "Look, we're almost there. It's a few hundred yards.''

At the end of the road a signpost stood before a drive. A discreet wooden panel said Stonybrook. Paul turned in and followed the wide path between rows of dogwood trees which in the spring would burst into a riot of tulip-shaped, pink-fringed white blossoms. In the winter their branches are naked and seem twisted, silhouetted against the sky.

The house was of a rambling colonial style, white clapboard with blue shutters. "It used to belong to a couple of gangsters," Paul said, helping Maryanne out of the car. "Now it belongs to kindly old Dr. Jekyll and his dear nurse, Miss Hyde." They climbed the porch steps and rang the bell.

Florence Greenthal opened the door and said, "Welcome, Mr. Curtin. Come on in." She was short and fortyish, with dark hair in a short cut around a heart-shaped face. One would have said she was pretty, though her mouth was over-large. Her brown eyes were hard as flint under heavy brows.

"This is Maryanne Middleton, Dr. Greenthal. Maryanne, this is the keeper of the keys. How are we doing, Doc?"

"It's nice to know you, Mrs. Middleton—it is Mrs.? These days one never knows whom one is offending."

"It's Mrs., Doctor, but you can call me Ms. if it suits me better."

Dr. Greenthal laughed politely and led them across the spacious foyer to a small, paneled room on the left, whose walls were lined with bookcases. Myriad diplomas hung in the spaces separating them. "Sit down, won't you." She indicated an overstuffed leather couch. She sat in an armless straight-backed chair to the side of a massive desk. "Jerry is very well, Mr. Curtin." She paused. "Though there has been no material change in his behavior pattern. But, it is hard to see developmental changes when one is as close to him as I am." She looked directly at Maryanne and said brightly, "We've had Jerry here with us at Stonybrook for four years. He's made quite remarkable progress. He's unusual for a Down's child." She looked back to Paul. "Have you any specific questions?"

Paul had been afraid that he would be inhibited by Maryanne's presence, but rather found himself comforted by it. "I ask the same questions every time I come. I feel a little foolish."

"You should not feel at all that way. It's simply part of the process of becoming inured to the reality."

"Is there any sign of . . . well . . . contact?"

"No, Mr. Curtin. Jerry doesn't respond in the sense that you mean. As I say, he's unusual for a child with Down's syndrome. His physical appearance is different, in that it's less pronounced. But at the same time, the open and affectionate behavior common to Down's children is absent."

"Is there any sign of the other physical symptoms?"

Dr. Greenthal smiled. "Mrs. Middleton, Mr. Curtin has

developed that fearful defense mechanism of buzzword-itus. Most Down's kids don't live far past puberty because they have congenital heart defects together with the rest of the symptomology. Jerry doesn't. And he won't, all other things being equal. There is nothing wrong with his heart."

There was an awkward silence. There always was, Paul thought. But the good doctor just sits there with that frozen smile. She'll sit there all day if she has to. It's part of my therapy. For twenty-five thousand dollars a year, she will take care of my retarded, withdrawn child, and every two months, she will suffer my foolish questions, both of us recognizing that the answers will never change. Each time I am prone to ask fewer and fewer questions as hopelessness becomes a fact and not an emotion. Eventually, I will come less often. And perhaps, then, not at all. My parenthood signified only by the arrival of my monthly checks. God.

"Why don't we see Jerry now, Doctor," Paul said, getting to his feet.

"That's a good idea." Florence Greenthal led the way through the foyer to a set of heavy wooden doors that separated the entry from the rest of the house. She opened the door with a key affixed to her wrist by an elastic band.

The other side of the door was a different world. As it closed behind Maryanne with a firm click, a thrill of apprehension ran up her spine. She caught herself reaching for Paul's hand, and determined to stand on her own, edged away from him.

Two children confronted them, each in a different way. A boy, who so far as Maryanne could tell was in his early teens, stood immobile in the middle of the rectangular room. His hair was straight and fell forward over a narrow forehead. His nose was tiny and angled severely upward. His eyes bulged, but at the same time, had the Oriental slant from which the common name for Down's syndrome—Mongolism—is derived. His expression was one of infinite patience. Dr. Greenthal walked around him, patting him on the shoulder. "Hello, Jimmy."

Maryanne stood her ground as the other child raced across the floor, her legs partially bent, occasionally touching the ground with one hand for balance. She seemed to be about seven, and her arms and legs were spindly as sticks. She wore a short pink dress under which was pinned a double thickness of diapers. She climbed Maryanne's body as a spider monkey swings through a tree. When she had wrapped her arms about her neck, she looked at her with enormous liquid brown eyes and with absolute conviction crooned, "Mommy?" There was only a moment's hesitation before Maryanne closed her arms about the slender body and hugged her.

"Susan calls all women Mommy," Dr. Greenthal said. "She is an artifact of the American movie generation. Susan is in love with love. If you tell her to sit in that chair over there, she will do so without taking offense. If you wish, she will hang around your neck like a feather boa all the day long and give and take as much affection as your nervous system can stand."

"I think I'd like to hold her for a while." She walked to the armchair the doctor had indicated and sat down. "It must be very difficult to give up someone who gives so much love in a hard world."

Doctor Greenthal looked into her eyes, her brows beetling. "Yes," she said, bemused. "But it is not nearly as difficult as spending perhaps fifteen years, or twenty, or more chained day and night to someone who has the size and mobility of a growing being, and the mentality of a three-year-old. And were that not sufficient motivation, Susan is among those with congenital heart problems. We almost lost her twice this winter. It is a sword that truly has two edges. On the one hand, to give the child's care into strange hands is a torment, and a source of guilt. On the other hand, to resist is also an abnegation of life—one's own."

"How do you manage?" Maryanne asked.

Dr. Greenthal weighed the question, and the intonation, and decided that it was sincere. "It is my job. And sometimes, I don't manage." She turned away and pointed. "Here comes Jerry."

Maryanne was glad that she was seated and had Susan to hold onto. Paul walked halfway across the room, past the statuary form of Jimmy. An attendant in a tee shirt, slacks, and sneakers was leading his child across the floor. Maryanne squeezed Susan against herself. Jerry seemed like a normal nine-year-old-boy. His hair was cut short and made an ash blond fringe above a high white forehead. His eyes were as blue as they seemed in the photograph in Paul's bedroom. He was dressed in Saks Fifth Avenue's best. His white shirt boasted a tiny green crocodile. He was a bit short for his age, but stocky and healthy-looking. But unlike Jimmy, whose eyes bespoke bovine contentment, Jerry's eyes were like those of the blind.

Paul knelt on one knee and opened his arms to him. The attendant led Jerry forward, but when he dropped his hand, the child stopped dead in his tracks. Paul reached out with the strong hands that Maryanne knew so well and pulled Jerry to his chest and hugged him. The boy stared numbly over his father's shoulder. Paul stood and said, "I'd like to take him for a walk."

"Of course," Dr. Greenthal said. "You may take him back to the playroom, if you'd like. You can give Susan to me, Mrs. Middleton."

"I think that perhaps Mr. Curtin would like a few minutes alone with Jerry," Maryanne said. "I'll just stay here."

Paul looked at her with gratitude and walked off down the hall holding Jerry's hand, the child following like an automaton.

They came back in ten minutes. Susan had gone to play in a corner, and Maryanne awaited them. She talked to Jerry for a few moments, then held him and kissed him. It was clear that he was unable or unwilling to respond. She extricated herself as gracefully as she could and waited for Paul's instructions.

"There's no point in taking him out for lunch, is there?"

"Honestly, Mr. Curtin, no. Jerry will sit. He will allow you to feed him. He will create no disturbance. But for all intents and purposes, he will not be there, not in the sense that you will be."

Paul nodded in agreement. "You're right, of course. Thank you very much for your time, Doctor."

"That's what we're here for. Till next time, then."

"Good-bye, Doctor. Good-bye, Skipper." The boy stood immobile.

Once they were out of the driveway Maryanne said, "I'm hungry. I want a big lunch. Come on Curtin, where are you going to feed me?"

"I don't know. There's a pretty good place over in Pound Ridge called Emily Shaw's."

"Sounds delicious. I had an aunt named Emily."

Rather than returning to the parkway, Paul wound through the narrow, back country lanes past the wide gates of lush estates, their roofs hinting at their presence atop forested hills. "Well?"

Maryanne turned to him and replied. "He is a beautiful child. He is very like you, physically, except that he seems a bit smaller-boned."

"His mother seemed a fragile woman. Tough really, but small-boned."

She waited for him to go on. But he did not. In the two years that they had kept company, the subject of his wife had come up twice. She had died when the boy was a year or two old. Maryanne had never pressed what seemed to be a very private matter. "He doesn't seem at all like the others."

"I guess," Paul said with a weary voice, "that within the limited realm of their own competence, they are as variegated as normal people. We probably don't notice it."

"It would be easier if he responded to affection," she said tentatively.

A small smile crept onto Paul's face. "That was as delicate an appreciation of the problem of autism as I have ever heard. Yes. It would be easier if, like little Susan, he would hug and kiss, and even wet your lap from the sheer ignorant joy of being recognized and offered some human warmth. But, he rejects that. I often think, when I leave here, that Jerry is a kind of savant, that he's taken a quick fix on the world, recognized it for what it is, and withdrawn into a shell. When I'm low I say to myself that the withdrawal is prompted by fear and cowardice. When I am feeling good, I think that it was a conscious decision prompted by good taste. Of course, it's neither. Jerry has a birth defect. Choice had nothing to do with it."

"You have to continue to regard him with some hope. He is, at least, superbly well taken care of. She is a very tough and competent lady, our Dr. Greenthal. You have done as much for him as you can. You can hope that he will live his life in the best circumstances that he can. If it is true that he doesn't know it, then the pleasure can be derived from the fact that you do, yourself."

Paul pulled to the side of the road on top of a rise that fell away to the left into a small valley. A stream, already full with the runoff of snow, splashed over rocks in the midst of the meadow. Three mares full to bursting with their spring colts stood passively, nodding in the breeze across a split-rail fence.

"Hope is what it's all about. My midlife crisis. I decided that last night. I passed your door at midnight, and I wanted to go in, but I deprived myself. You are the representative of hope in my world. And I love you for it. I love Jerry, too. But he represents the dark side of my universe. You're right, there is satisfaction in knowing that at least materially, he is cared for. That is a triumph of my skills—and my ability to cash in on them—over my environment. But on the other hand, I can't ever expect to know a smile. I don't want to hear him say thank you. I just want to know that in his universe-in-the-head that he is happy.

"I see the same dichotomy in the world I work in. I am a believer in my profession. Or at least, I have been a believer. Little by little, the cynicism and the—is it superreality? or total falsity?—of the city have chipped away till I want to run. If I run, as in my two views of Jerry, am I escaping what I can't handle? or am I running toward myself?

"I got a lead last night about a murder. Maybe it'll tie in to the gubernatorial campaign. It's an interesting possibility. The most enthusiasm I could raise from myself on the subject, lying on my back in bed last night with an ache in my groin wishing I had gone up to your place, was that maybe it would save a job that I'm not sure that I want anymore. That's not the kind of thinking from which self-esteem is made. I'm better than that. Shit on it. Either I should get out, or do the job right."

"Do you see that copse up there on the hill?" Maryanne asked.

"Over on the right, up the dirt road?"

"Yes. I want to go there."

Paul started the car again and wound up the slippery path slowly. When he was under the trees, he stopped. The mares, spooked by the movement, had ambled away from the fence and down into the valley, to poke aimlessly with their muzzles at the stubble in the ground.

"You are better than most, Paul. But you have a dark side, too. You have to learn to share. In some ways, you're just like Jerry. You show a stone face and a deaf ear. I'm better than that. Don't you treat me like my fatheaded ex-husband did. Let me in to your pain. I want to share and to participate. I'm tough, too. And I think, and I decide. I do it for me and my children. And I want to do it for you. It's about time I got to see Jerry."

Paul turned in the seat. "What shall I offer you? That Thursday represents twenty-five thousand of the sixty thousand dollars I earn every year. And my financial prospects are behind me. I am already overpaid by Newspaper Guild standards. I make the same money as the managing editor. He hates my guts for it. And life in the Big City isn't getting any cheaper."

"I'm rent controlled and I work. Move in with me."

"I can't. I'm not sure."

"Of me? Of us?"

"Of me. I've lost my way a bit. I don't like it. I want to know what I'm all about before I inflict myself on your lives. How the hell do I know what kind of a father I'm going to make? The only child I have doesn't even know I'm there."

"Jesus, my kids are crazy about you."

"Sure, as the Good Humor man, I'm great. But what kind of a father am I going to make for them if I can't decide what I want to be? Goddamn it!" He pounded his fist against the dash. "I want to assert myself. I'm sick to death of swirling around in the current."

"Then do what you do with conviction. Do the fucking story." Maryanne's voice was shrill with emotion. "Believe that it matters if you find out that somebody murdered that man. Or find out that Uhuru is a fraud. Or find out that there was no murder. But believe that whatever you find out, you will be performing a service and living up to your capabilities instead of finding a way to hang on to a fat salary. And stop playing with yourself and with me. Jerry's autism is no excuse for demeaning yourself as a father. New York is a tough place to live. It's a cruel world. That's no reason to drown in self-doubt. And it's no reason to doubt the people who love you. You are a man." She leaned across the seat and locked her fingers in the curly hair at the back of his head and pulled herself toward him, kissing him fiercely on the mouth, her tongue darting and moving like a hummingbird. She slipped her free hand between his legs and touched him lightly, rhythmically. He responded instantly.

As Paul wrapped his arms around her, she took her hands away from him and unfastened her pants.

"Are you nuts?" he said.

She wriggled them and her bikini to the floorboard. "Move under me," she said, her voice almost angry. She arched her back against the low top of the car as he awkwardly edged over the shift. She reached down and undid his zipper as he slipped into the seat. She liberated him from his pants, touched him gently, and then, kneeling above him, impaled herself. "Oh, God, I love you." She held his face between her hands and looked at him intently, the breath escaping in whistles from between her clenched teeth as she rocked back and forth slowly. "I want you to sit there and hold me and let me do you. I want to be a full half of this relationship. I want to bring some of the pleasure and some of the pain, and I want to participate in the good and the bad. If you want to go to Wyoming, we'll do that. But make it something positive, Curtin. Make it something more than trial by failure." She leaned forward and kissed his lips. "Slowly. I want it to last." She leaned back again and pulled up her sweater. "Paul, touch my breasts."

The restaurant was closed for lunch when they finally arrived. They stopped at Kentucky Fried Chicken and ate from a cardboard bucket perched between them as they drove back to town.

16

In the summer, there is life in the streets of the South Bronx. But, when it is cold, in the dead of winter, there is no one to keep the stray cats and the garbage company. Tenants huddle in their fear of the cold, and of each other, behind the ill-kempt walls of frail buildings, amidst cracked pipes and insufficient heat, their fate bewailed in newspapers they don't read and on television programs that they don't watch that compete with reruns of "I Love Lucy" on sets that are being paid off on time, or stolen.

There are whole blocks of the South Bronx, dozens of them, that resemble the Germany of 1945. Increasing costs of operation, heating fuel, and the merciless and inexorable rise of real estate taxes have combined with rent control, landlord greed, and the aboriginal living habits and indifference to property of the urban poor to turn old neighborhoods into great wastelands of abandoned tenements. Occasionally, such an eyesore is erased by fire, either spontaneous or willful, so that its gutted skeleton stands as a precursor of things to come in the evolutionary chain of decay, and the return of man to dust.

In a building not far from the Third Avenue Bridge, around the corner from Willis Avenue, the southernmost street of the borough of the Bronx, several men sat around a card table in an apartment on the ground floor. The door to the kitchen was open, as was the door to the oven, which was going full blast to provide a supplement to the overworked, substandard boiler in the basement and the pitiful wisps of steam it forced through radiators corroded by rust and time.

On each of the three floors above, two apartments, called railroad flats because the rooms were in a straight line from the front of the building to the rear, straddled a central staircase, littered with papers and smelling of urine.

In one of these apartments on the third floor, raucous laughter could be heard. Two families shared the apartment, which consisted of four rooms and a kitchen. Between them, there were nine children, all related, as the two men of the families were brothers.

On the top floor, Sarah Jenks lay huddled under the covers next to her ten-year-old daughter, Jenny, who slept fitfully, occasionally coughing. The light from the lamps on the roadway shone through the holes in the worn shades covering the window in this the front room. She wondered where her husband Al had gone. On more than one occasion he had come home at three or four in the morning, or even stayed out the whole night, but she hadn't seen him in thirty-six hours, and she was beginning to feel the stirrings of real worry. She huddled closer to her child. Drinking aside, he was not a bad man. There were four children in all, sleeping in the sparsely furnished but scrupulously clean apartment. The filth of the tenement stopped abruptly at Sarah Jenks's door. Al wasn't a union member, of course, being black, so he didn't make big money. But everybody ate good, and there was a big color television in the living room.

In his room at the back of the building, Willie Jenks put down his math book with some satisfaction. He was just fifteen and already in the tenth grade, and he was doing pretty well. There was some talk of scholarships and colleges, even. Mr. Greenstein, the principal, had said so himself. He understood mathematics. His teacher said that he had a gift.

He looked up at the assortment of model planes dangling in fanciful attitudes of flight from wires on his ceiling. In the position of honor was a Japanese Zero, each detail crafted to perfection over many weekends and many coats of paint. He pulled off his clothes and turned out the bedside lamp. He started to reach for the worn girlie magazine stuffed under his mattress, but thought better of it, and dropped off to sleep.

In the basement, skilled hands disconnected the shunt that forces natural gas from the main in the street to the hot water boiler. The gas hissed noisily into the closet-sized room. A second set of hands shut off the pilot light, which had flared momentarily. The door of the boiler room was firmly closed, and the escape valve for the interior line which fed the building's stove was partially opened. On the first floor above, the card players were too absorbed in their game to notice the diminution in the flame.

One of the men in the basement taped a Mickey Mouse watch and a nine-volt transistor battery to a quarter stick of dynamite, then wired the assembly to a blasting cap. He rested the package against the door of the boiler room, left with his companion as they had come, through the cast-iron security gate whose hasps had rusted through a generation ago.

The men walked several blocks to where they had left their car in a darkened lot between two tenements. They went unnoticed in the empty streets in a neighborhood which was rarely patrolled by police. Only the brown Lincoln might have betrayed their presence had it been left in the open in so unlikely an area.

In a half hour, the concentration of gas in the little boiler room had become so high that it had begun to seep through the interfloor space and the floorboards. The law requires that natural gas, an odorless material, be perfumed with a strong and unpleasant sulfur smell, so that leaks will not go undetected, risking asphyxiation. Despite the cover of cigar and cigarette smoke, and their concentration, the smell of gas had begun to tinge the air, and the card players began to sniff suspiciously. At first, they ignored it as still another eccentricity of the dilapidated building. Then, as it persisted and became stronger, one of them rose and walked into the kitchen to check on the stove. He turned up the flame as far as it would go, remarking aloud about its small size.

At precisely that moment, the movement of the little watch touched the wire strung from the battery to the blasting cap. The fulminate of mercury which it contained vaporized in a flash of heat, exploding the dynamite. The second explosion followed so closely on the heels of the first that, even had there been a survivor left to tell, he would have been hard pressed to make the distinction.

With a burst of energy, the ceiling above the boiler room erupted. Such were the heat and the pressure that the head of the man at the stove, which was torn from his body by the explosion, was lifted through succeeding floors as each succumbed in its turn, to be spilled onto the roof.

The shock wave cracked each of the supporting wooden beams that held the flooring of the building together. The staircase collapsed, as did the center of the roof. All windows front and rear were shattered. The change in the air pressure sucked the flames from the center of the building across the miserable possessions of its inhabitants, setting them ablaze.

The men at the card table were killed immediately by the blast, victims of concussion and flying debris. The people in one second-floor apartment died in the initial burst of flame. Those from the other apartment on that floor rushed into the smoke-filled hall, and dashing madly for the staircase, fell into the hole which it had lately occupied, and into the maelstrom of fire which it had become.

The Hernandez brothers and their wives, addled by drink, and exhausted by lovemaking, barely stirred and died in the smoke and flames, as did the younger children. The two eldest, Almeda and her eleven-year-old sister, jumped from their bed and ran to the door. The younger girl stumbled and fell to the floor to die of smoke inhalation with her family. Almeda, unheeding, ran on to the staircase and pitched screaming to her death.

Sarah Jenks and all of her children, save one, died in seconds when the supports of the fourth floor cracked and dropped the front half of the apartment several floors, with tons of debris cascading after them.

Willie Jenks, alert and agile, sprang from his bed. With presence of mind, he quickly grabbed his bathrobe and slippers and put them on. He started toward the door, then turned back and took his math workbook from the table and the Zero from its wire. Satisfied, he opened the door and stepped out through the smoke into nothingness.

The fire truck arrived at the scene less than ten minutes after the explosion. The men went through the motions of hooking the pumpers to hydrants. The assistant chief surveyed the scene with an experienced eye to assess the conditions, and the possibility that the blaze might spread. He deployed his forces accordingly. An ambulance, siren blaring in the freezing night air, pulled in next to the pumper.

A veteran of twenty years in the department turned to the chief and said, "A fool's errand."

The building roared like a giant Roman candle, sending flames and sparks high into the sky. In ten minutes more, all combustible material ablaze, two walls collapsed. Some of the victims were totally incinerated. An accurate count would never be made.

17

"I think that you will find the Schramsberg a reasonable equivalent to a middle-range Epernay bottled wine."

Frank O'Neil watched the tasting ritual with interest. In the choosing of wines he had long ceded the traditionally masculine honor to Allison's more cultivated palate.

The sommelier of La Côte Basque hovered over Allison's shoulder as she lifted the crystal flute to her lips. She tilted her head slightly and mouthed the pale liquid. She swallowed and smiled. "They're getting there, Paolo. Definitely, they are. You'll see that in a few seasons, weather permitting, they'll be indistinguishable from the moderate French champagnes."

The consul general of France broke a piece of bread from the small baguette on his plate and cut a morsel of pâté de foie gras. "The nectar from the ambrosia. I suppose you are going to tell me that you are planning to supplant our food industry, as well as our wines."

"I can tell you with full authority," O'Neil said, "that the Hungarian geese who gave up their livers for our pleasure were processed in Strasbourg, and the truffles are from the Périgord."

"In that case, I feel less a traitor drinking California champagne." He took a sip and raised an eyebrow.

Allison raised her glass. "À nos amis."

"I'll drink to that, even though not a word has been mentioned about New York State champagnes," the governor said.

"You ought to be grateful, Frank," Allison said with a smile.

He took a sip and replied, "Can't a man be a partisan in his own state?"

"No man is a prophet in his own land, Frank," Michel de Montignac said.

"Where the wines of New York are concerned," Allison said in his defense, "I can hardly blame the governor. It's the grapes."

O'Neil shrugged helplessly. "Either way, I lose."

The limousine picked them up promptly at half past ten, delivering the de Montignacs to their residence, and then taking them to Allison's apartment on Park Avenue.

"Good evening, Mrs. Forrestiere. Good evening, Governor O'Neil."

Allison allowed the sable coat to fall from her shoulders into her butler's outstretched hands. "Good evening, Wardwell. Were there any calls?"

"Your father called at eight, madam. And Count Forrestiere at ten. He insisted that I wake the boys so that he could speak to them."

"And you did, I suppose?" Her voice rose half an octave.

"I felt that I had no choice, madam," he replied in his precise English accent.

"How long did he stay on?" she asked between clenched teeth.

"About fifteen minutes. They went right back to sleep."

"Do you know where he called from?" she asked.

"He didn't say, madam. But, I believe he was abroad."

Steaming, Allison walked down the fifty-foot gallery, its walls lined with small canvases of the Dutch School, a Van Eyck, a Rubens, and said over her shoulder, "We'd like coffee in the library, please, Wardwell. Then you can go to bed. I'm going to call my father."

The library was dark and empty when O'Neil arrived. Allison had chosen to make her call from her bedroom. O'Neil flicked on the light and sat down on the sofa, which occupied a niche in the mahogany paneling and shelving which lined the room. He opened the wooden box on the table beside him and pressed a button. With a whirring sound, the panel above the fireplace rose into the niche created for it in the ceiling, exposing a rear projection television screen with a five-foot diagonal. Another button turned on the set. In a moment a familiar face appeared.

". . . and it is not apparent what caused the blaze. It only is certain, according to Fire Department sources, that an explosion was heard shortly before the alarm was sounded." The face was erased from the screen and replaced by a live picture of a half-collapsed building burning like a bonfire, flames whipping like pennants in the wind. "This is Peter Bannon on Willis Avenue in the South Bronx. An explosion of unknown origin began a blaze in this tenement building on a block with one other burned-out tenement and two abandoned buildings about an hour ago. Four fire trucks responded to the alarm. Wait, please. . . . Chief. Chief, could you step over here for a moment? Thank you. Chief Aiello, have you been able to bring anyone out of the building?"

"There isn't a hope. Unless someone escaped before we came, and we have no reason to believe so, according to people who came out into the street when they heard the blast. There was no survivors."

"Does anyone know how many people were in the building?"

"No, Peter, I'm afraid we don't have any information. I'm sorry. You'll have to excuse me." The chief walked away shouting directions to another uniformed officer. A siren could be heard in the background as more equipment rushed to the scene. "Now switching back to the studio and Dave Marash."

"Thanks, Peter. Another grim tenement tragedy. From people in the neighborhood, it seems that the buildings was heavily populated, and several dozen people may be victims of this disaster. We've been informed that Mayor Greene has been called at Gracie Mansion and is on his way to the scene at this time."

O'Neil shut the set off and shuddered. Probably a gas line. Jesus, he thought, a whole houseful of people. He toyed with the idea of going himself to make a statement. There was Allison to consider.

He pulled himself to his feet from the enveloping cushions and walked to the desk. None of the buttons on the phone were lit. She must be talking on the private line, he thought. He picked up the phone and dialed a number.

"Ken Miller." The voice was crisp and clear.

"It's me. Have you been watching the tube?"

"Yes, sir," the governor's chief of staff answered. "It's a bitch. A lot of dead people in there. I hear Greene's on his way. I've taken the liberty of getting Senator Carney out of bed and asking him to go up there on behalf of the party and the governor's office to show our interest."

Despite his real concern for the victims, the governor was prompted to smile at Miller's crisp efficiency. "Covering all of the bases?"

"Yes, sir. That's what you pay me for. I thought that the Republican Leader of the State Senate was weighty enough a personality to throw into the fray. I wasn't sure where you were going, or whether you'd want to be disturbed."

"Well played, Ken. Thanks. If there's anything that ought to be done, do it. I'll be home in a couple of hours. Don't hesitate to call then."

"There ought to be a strong statement, Governor."

"Draft it. I'll call you when I get in."

Wardwell knocked diffidently at the door, then entered bearing a silver tray with an antique Meissen coffee service, a bottle of Courvoisier Napoleon cognac, and two large balloon snifters. He placed the tray on the table in front of the couch and lit the small silver spirit lamp with which the snifters could be heated.

"May I pour for you, sir?"

"Yes, thank you, Wardwell. Mrs. Forrestiere should be along in a short while. She'll deal with the rest. You go to bed."

"Thank you, Governor. Good night."

A moment later, Allison Forrestiere opened the door and slammed it behind her. She had taken off the broad-shouldered black-sequined Valentino jacket and dress. Her hair had been let down and combed out. She wore a blue moire dressing gown, its breast pocket embroidered with a seven-tined crown of gold thread. She sat at the edge of the couch and poured a cup of coffee, then delicately filled the bottom of the remaining snifter with brandy. She slipped the glass into the holder above the flame and turned it slowly as the heat released the fumes, so that she might better appreciate the bouquet of the amber liquid. At the proper moment, she lifted the glass, breathed deeply from the globe, and sipped. "Can you imagine that Guinea bastard waking the kids up in the middle of the night?" she asked. She took another sip and placed the glass on the table.

As she brushed the hair out of her eyes, the front of her robe opened, exposing jutting conical breasts augmented and reshaped by cosmetic surgery. "I mean it, Frank. I wish I could think of a way to really fix his wagon. You know that?" She picked up the glass again. "I asked Dad what we can do. Since we had to settle him out to get rid of him, he has money of his own, so we can't cut off his water. Shit." She took another drink.

O'Neil was half amused. He had heard the tirade before. Allison did not care to be trifled with, and Il Conde di Forrestiere knew exactly which buttons to push. O'Neil felt a sneaking admiration for him, lying on his silk sheets with a malleable young lady, his handsome mustachioed face wreathed in a smile, as he contemplated Allison's irritation.

She looked up suddenly from the brandy glass and said, "Frank, weren't you supposed to talk to the cardinal today? Wasn't it today?"

"He simply wasn't available," he lied smoothly.

She arched an eyebrow at him. "Not available to the governor of New York? Not to His Catholic Majesty Francis Xavier the Umpteenth?"

"He does have other worries, you know."

"Well, unfortunately, I have only one. So it preoccupies my mind. Frank, when I was a young and impressionable girl," she pulled the lapels of her robe together fastidiously, "I met a dashing Italian Count."

O'Neil smiled. "Isn't this where I came in?"

"Before, actually. Damn it, Frank. It's not funny. The only real pleasure I finally got out of being married to the bastard, the children excepted, was having people call me Mrs. Forrestiere when he or his mother was around instead of Contessa because it annoyed them so much." She smiled brightly at the memory. "I've been a contessa. If I wanted to be somebody's girl friend, I'd go camp on Warren Beatty's doorstep. I have the money," she let the robe fall open again, "the looks, and the talent. I like being the governor's lady. I thought we might even take a crack at the White House together. But no president can live in the White House with his mistress. I have to be Mrs. O'Neil."

O'Neil's temples began to throb with the onset of a headache. They had covered the same ground with increasing frequency for the past six months. It was hardly reluctance on his part. In fact, she had no idea how desperately he wanted the marriage. "Marrying you is my first priority. You know that, Allison."

She stood up and flounced across the room in anger and frustration, then turned and said, "Oh, for God's sake, Frank, at least be honest with yourself. Your first allegiance is to your office, which I think I understand well enough. But after that, it's your Mary's memory, the eight children she bore you, Holy Mother Church, and the Pope!" She picked up volume and velocity as she went along.

"Why do you kid me along with this business with the cardinal? What is it that prevents you from doing what everybody else does?" She swept the hair out of her eyes, thrusting her chin in the air. "I've read up on the subject, Frank. What's the matter with the American Norms, Frank? All you have to do is get three priests trained in Canon Law to form a tribunal. Nine times out of ten, after they've gone through the mumbo jumbo of reading the application and the psychological examinations, they conclude that the parties were psychologically immature and that no true marriage existed. Poof! There never was a marriage. Then you and I can get married by the cardinal in the cathedral, if that's what would please you. And I'll wear white while my children watch me walk down the aisle. You must have three priests in your pocket, Frank. Pull some strings. And if that doesn't work, you must know at least one priest, anyway. We'll get married in City Hall, then we'll go to him, and he'll tell you that in good conscience you can still take Communion.''

"That's no satisfactory answer for my conscience," he snapped, "nor is it recognized by the Church."

"Well, I don't give a damn. I want to be legitimized, Frank. You pull some strings. You've got friends in the Church. Or find a tribunal or a priest with an open mind. But, if that goes against your grain, Frank, you're just going to have to make a choice somewhere along the line—real soon."

"Are you finished?" he asked her, looking out from the midst of a dark frown. "Have you blown off enough steam at my expense?"

"Stuff it," she replied angrily.

O'Neil rose to his feet and crossed the room, grasping the lapels of her robe and jerking her toward him with such force that her head snapped back. "That's enough, Allie. I'm working on the annulment. I don't want to discuss it anymore. I'm doing as much as I can, and as fast." He jerked again and the robe fell open.

He pushed her out to arm's length, his fingers digging into the soft white flesh of her shoulder. Her eyes were round and moist, and her breath was shallow. She was afraid.

He could feel the pulse throbbing in the artery under his jaw. He glanced down at her body, the weight of which was supported almost entirely by his grasping hands. He stared with fascination at her smooth stomach, where a childhood operation had excised her navel, leaving an unbroken stretch from her breasts to the welter of light brown curls between her legs. Perspiration trickled from his hairline. He lifted her like a doll and placed her on the couch, then shedding his years as he did his clothes, took her as a boy would a girl in a spring meadow.

After they had made love, he lay naked on the couch. She knelt beside him on the floor, her head on his chest. She sighed, and said, "Frank, do we have to marry in the Church? Can't we just find a justice of the peace?"

"Jesus, Allie. One more time? Politically, leaving the Church would be suicide. And I would have a hard time turning my back on the habits of a lifetime. I want to marry you more than you know. I'll work it out." He wanted to shout at her that he was Irish Catholic born and bred, and that a few generations of gentility won't wash off ten centuries of hedge school teaching by wild-eyed priests. He even thought sometimes about his immortal soul. But in the end, he was himself not sure what he would do, as he faced the reality of his declining income from the family business, his enormous expenses, and his advancing years. Allison was a tonic for them all.

18

The brown Lincoln Continental carrying George Gaines and Marcus Hawkes crossed the George Washington Bridge to New Jersey and angled off to the right to enter Route 4.

Gaines looked at his watch. "Just about now, I'd guess."

Hawkes, who was driving, nodded in agreement, keeping his eyes on the foggy road. "Turn on the radio, 1010. It's all news."

Above the low chatter of the announcer's voice, Gaines said, "Marcus, you don't suppose Jenks could have told anyone else, do you?"

"It's possible, George. But it doesn't seem likely to me."

"I'd like to make sure that all the doors are properly shut."

Hawkes licked his lips. "I think you've made that clear."

"But you understand. It had to be done. It was clear that a

man like Jenks would be close to his children and his wife. You see that we had no choice. We couldn't take the risk.''

"Yes, George. Yes, of course. No choice." Hawkes turned off into Hackensack, up the hill to the residential district, and into the driveway of George Gaines's house.

"You want to come in for a drink, Marcus?"

"No. Let's just talk here for a minute. Thank you anyway." Gaines turned in his seat and looked at Hawkes. The announcer said, "We've just received a bulletin that a major explosion and subsequent fire have consumed a building in the South Bronx. While no confirmed reports are available, the speed with which the blaze spread has cast doubts on the possibility of survivors.''

Hawkes reached out to shut off the radio, but Gaines held his hand. "Leave it. It could be any building in the South Bronx."

"Half a dozen units, including a superpumper are being called to the address on Willis Avenue to prevent a strong wind from spreading the flames to other—''

"Satisfied?" Hawkes asked, flicking the switch.

"Now, I am."

"Well, it's all over for the moment. But that's not to say that it can't happen again. Do you have any idea how that damn manifest got into Gibbons's hands?''

"It can't be anything but what Jenks said," Gaines replied. "I've covered all the bases. It was an oversight by the damn fool who packed the bricks. I'll see to it.''

"I'm sure it wasn't your fault, George," Hawkes mopped his brow. "It's February. In another three or four months we'll be home free.''

"It seems like eternity to me. It's like juggling; the damn Housing Authority, the sponsors, the people from Burton Industries, our own employees . . .''

Hawkes put his hand on Gaines's arm. "We're aiming high. If we don't lose our self-control, we'll make it. The hard part is behind us. When do you leave the country?''

"I'm supposed to go on Sunday. I'm flying to St. Petersburg and then into Grand Cayman. When will I have the money?''

"I'll see that you have it by tomorrow night. You'll carry it in a suitcase and check it through.''

"Jesus, Marcus, what happens if they lose the damn bag? It happens.''

Hawkes shook his head. "Statistics are on our side."

"What do I do if it does happen, Marcus? Make a claim for a suitcase with two million dollars in small unmarked bills?"

Hawkes leaned across the seat. "Now, listen to me, George. We have spent two years setting this up. We have performed a miracle, you and I. We have the support—and the blind eyes— of the governor of New York and the mayor of the city. We are public spirited and admirable. We are a credit to our race." He paused, his eyes twinkling in a smile. "And we have their money. We have a million dollars in the bank in Grand Cayman, and another two million to be delivered in that suitcase on Sunday. In three months, we'll have seven million dollars. We will be in Jamaica with other passports and other names and a lot of untouchable money in a numbered account in a tax-free haven with no extradition. Isn't that enough to cool your frazzled nerves?"

"What about Kurt Englander? What about Burton Industries?"

"By the time they know, we'll be checking out the best-looking string of girls in the Caribbean and smoking long cigars."

Gaines relaxed and returned the smile. "You make it sound easy, Marcus."

"Just stick to the plan. You're taking a well-deserved, ten-day rest. You get off of the plane in Grand Cayman, walk to the special customs desk, and meet Mr. Watley. From there on in, it's all downhill."

Gaines shook Marcus's hand, got out of the car and walked briskly up the drive to his front steps. Marcus watched him disappear through the door, then took a deep breath and exhaled. The car felt close and stuffy. He lowered the window and loosened his tie, then backed out and headed toward his home in Teaneck, to the north.

He slammed on the brakes abruptly, almost passing a light. He looked up at the light, tapping his fingers on the wheel, thinking about his father. Damn old fool. He thought that because he didn't talk like a nigger, people didn't think he was a nigger. He read books. He made Marcus and Charles read books, but he earned the same nothing a week tending the books in that miserable store as other niggers did carting trash—sometimes less. He'd made Marcus stick to the books.

Be a practical man, he'd always said. Don't ever be tempted by other people's beliefs. Don't be seduced, he'd said, by strange gods.

Marcus sneered and stepped on the gas. He'd meant, don't be a damn fool like I was and follow some crazy in a fake general's uniform all your life and end up spouting philosophy in a third-floor cold-water walk up.

Marcus, dressed in clothes cleaned till they were threadbare, had gone to school until the beginning of the war. The old man had begged him to go to college. To Marcus the war had been an escape route from the preaching. Those who can, Marcus thought, make out, those who can't preach. And whimper. And draw welfare. And die when they are in their fifties of disappointment and unfulfilled dreams and pneumonia. Just as his father had done.

When he'd gone into the army, they put him in a maintenance battalion, cleaning latrines and washing floors. It wasn't what he'd had in mind. He had volunteered for a demolition training course, that service being one of the few integrated units in the military.

His father had died while Marcus stood shivering in the ice-cold water not far from the beach at St. Malo. Marcus didn't grieve him. All he'd left behind was a taste for Jamaican cooking and a tinge of a Caribbean accent.

Marcus got out of the army believing that his experience in demolition was going to give him a head start in the construction business when they began to rebuild New York after the war. He'd been wrong. Niggers weren't going to build anything. After a few months of listening to doors shut in his face, he'd taken his G.I. Bill money to Brooklyn Polytechnic. His mother, struggling along on her Social Security, gave him house room. He'd scraped by for two years on the remains of his separation pay. Then, his mother had died. He felt some pain about that. She'd followed the old man into perdition, and all she'd gotten for it was a consumptive death before she was sixty in a lumpy bed far away from the sun she'd always known. When she died, she'd reached out for his face. She'd said, never believe anyone who thinks he's God, or who speaks to Him personally. That was all the old man had left her. That, and the Social Security. When she died, that stopped, too.

Life had taught him the same lesson. He had never really been able to believe in anything. Why should he? he thought.

When his mother died, he had had two choices: quit college and get a job, or starve. His two years of engineering training didn't improve his reception at the big firms in New York when he approached them again. But he caught on with a short job here or there among the small contractors, both black and white, in Brooklyn and Harlem, spackling walls and installing new commodes cheaper than even a nonunion tradesman would. He quickly found that he had no taste for apprenticeship in the trades.

While his hands did not serve him well, he had an aptitude for sales. He bounced from job to job on the fringes of the building business for years. He stepped out on his own a few times. Small time. A couple of rehab jobs. A small supermarket. Two garden apartments in Queens. Thirty units in all. When a contractor is on a cash basis and has no capital, a day or two delay in delivery of a strategic material becomes a calamity. Each time, bad breaks, real or perceived, and lack of training had combined to frustrate him.

During his years working for this contractor and that, he had learned a number of the survival skills. He was adept at kiting invoices, double ordering, fee splitting with suppliers, and dealing with building inspectors from the bottom of the deck.

He had been smart enough never to give his personal guarantee, though he'd gone through three corporate bankruptcies. Then, the tide had begun to turn. He'd gone to work with A. Waldstein and Son. It was the time when it was beginning to be fashionable to have a few black faces around. He imagined that at the fund raisers, Arthur Waldstein sang "We Shall Overcome" louder than anyone else.

He'd started as a timekeeper, then was promoted to assistant superintendent, when the streets had heated up and Black was Beautiful. He kept his eyes on the superintendent, who was very competent, and kept his mouth shut. He'd learned the lingo, if not the skills.

After several years, anxious to attract some community sponsors and some federal training-program dollars, the Waldsteins had made him the construction superintendent on a thirty-story apartment house, complete with swimming pool and health club, near the Long Island Expressway. The understanding was tacit. He stood with his hands on his hips, in a business suit and tie, the improbable whole topped by a hard hat, talking to the sponsors and getting his picture in the papers. Billy Waldstein, the youngest of Arthur's sons, who had worked every summer since he was fifteen and was two years out of MIT, was his assistant.

When the job was successfully finished, he asked for and was granted a leave of absence. He bought a homburg and a tightly wrapped umbrella to go with his three-piece suit, put a Jamaican flag in his lapel to separate himself from the unwashed, sat down with a phone book, and began to make the rounds of Wall Street. After two months of going door to door, to increasingly smaller and less reputed firms, he found a young fellow at a small house who wanted desperately to do well by doing good. In five minutes, Marcus knew that he had his fish. The young man was connected with Burton Industries: trees, paper, building materials, and progressive management.

It had to be said that he had something to deliver as his part of the bargain. The local sponsors for the housing projects were proud and fearful, trying to learn the rudiments of community representation in the white man's world. Some were uneducated, others naive, but all were scarred with the effects of racial prejudice, and skeptical.

He hadn't believed in a cause. But he'd had the beginnings of belief in himself. Had he limited his role, he might have been successful. But he'd begun to believe his own inventions, and the well-intentioned but exaggerated references given by his former employers.

Once installed as chief executive of Hawkes Building Company, and past the talking stage, he found that his skills were no match for his new opportunity. He saw quickly that he would be unable to overcome his technical shortcomings without stepping down from his post, or asking for help. Either would result in loss of both face and control of the company. Immediately, he reverted to the habits of a lifetime and began to cast about for a way to tap the vast funds at his disposal, and to profit quickly and abscond before anyone was the wiser.

He sighed as he pulled his car into the garage next to his house in Teaneck. Stealing large and small, he had found, were exactly the same. He accepted his change in role from community hero to thief with equanimity. He deemed himself fortunate to have fallen upon such a great opportunity.

But, he had never counted on the violence. He had had a

moment of panic when he had realized that Gibbons had stumbled onto a shred of evidence and had agreed to his elimination. He had managed only by a slim margin to convince Gaines that disposing of Gibbons's wife and son was unnecessary. Had she known anything, he and Gaines would already be in flight or in chains. Their deaths, on the heels of Gibbons's own, would have exposed the myth of the accident.

He had agreed to Jenks's death. Then to the fire.

As he tried to sleep that night, he was haunted by the specter of George Gaines's stolid face, and the clanking of the cement mixer, and Al Jenks's voice.

19

The meeting on the evening of the Willis Avenue fire was a perfect example of the Chris Greene technique in action. Less than forty-eight hours before, he had rubbed elbows with the affluent and influential of the city, praising their charity and farsightedness in supporting cancer research.

On Thursday evening, in another element, dressed in a pair of gray slacks and a faded, tieless plaid shirt, he confronted an audience, much of which was drawn from the heart of his constituency, and wherein his hopes for the governorship lay.

The locale was as different. In contrast with the colonnaded symmetry of the museum, on Ninety-sixth Street between First and Second avenues there stands a massive building of dirty yellow brick built in an architectural style that died unlamented before the Second World War. At first glance it appeared to be a prison because of its heavily barred windows. In fact, they were meant to protect the building from the community, rather than the reverse.

In the basement of the Manhattan Technical Vocational High School, Christopher Greene stood behind a lectern. He leaned on the podium with one hand and pointed into the audience accusingly with the other.

"No," he said in his sharp voice. "You're the one who doesn't understand. You think that the color of your skin gives you a monopoly in feeling pain. Wrong! Everybody who thinks that his life doesn't amount to anything, and never can, feels the same way. If you have hope—even if you have nothing else—you are still somebody. When the hope dies, you die with it. That's what my campaign is all about. I want to be the governor of a state full of somebodies. I don't want any nobodies in my state."

He scanned the audience. He'd handpicked the area. The north side of Ninety-sixth Street is poor, black, and Hispanic. The south side is white and wealthy. Like the Berlin Wall. The minority of whites who had come had arrived early and sat isolated near the podium, awash in a sea of brown.

"Who else?" Greene asked aggressively, begging for an argument. A middle-aged man in the second row stood and raised his hand, asking to be recognized. Greene passed him over, looking deeper into the hall, but the man spoke out. "Here, Mr. Greene." He was short with a small face and a fringe of gray hair about a pink scalp. Thick wire-rimmed glasses gave him a mousy air belied by a stentorian voice.

"Yes, sir."

"I favor your social programs, Mayor Greene. I'm a lifelong progressive Democrat."

"Thank you, sir," Greene smiled and looked beyond the standing man for another raised hand.

". . . but, Mr. Mayor," the man continued, his words carrying clearly, commanding Greene's attention, "it seems to me that we have ourselves in a guns and butter bind. How do you hope to manage an increase in city-backed welfare spending without putting us back in trouble with financial institutions and the federal government?"

Greene rested his hand on his hip. "You have to order your priorities, my friend. First, you worry about the lame, the halt, and the disadvantaged. You decide how you're going to feed them, clothe them, house them, and provide medical care. Then you go about tapping the enormous resources of this state to pay for them. This city, in its most dire straits, was backed by a Democratic congress in Washington, and loan guarantees were forthcoming. The city survived. Not only did it survive, but it prospered. We are besieged by the rich of every continent, pushing and shoving to get their hooks into our limited land mass, and our limited quality housing stock, because this is the Big Apple. It is the capital of the commerce of the free world. Instead of reserving all of the benefits of New York's place in the sun for rich landlords, we ought to be able to save a small piece for our needy citizens. When you have a bright future—now an established fact here—you ought to be able to borrow against it."

As Greene turned away from him, the small man persisted. "But how can you borrow for additional programs with the current loan restrictions?"

"Now there's a question after my own heart. You elect me governor and I'll raise hell with the legislature and the banks and the federal government, and the Municipal Assistance Corporation. They haven't got their priorities straight either. New York has proved its point. It's bigger and better than ever. I'll see that the restrictions on the city are changed to deal with the current situation, both social and financial, and not with a ten-year-old nightmare. That goes for all our urban areas. They've been stepchildren long enough." The rising note in his voice brought him applause.

The man with the glasses was joined on his feet first by a quarter, then a half, then all of the audience. The man looked about himself, shook his head, and sat down, his questions unanswered.

Greene sensed the moment. When the applause died down, he stepped out in front of the lectern. "I want to thank the East Harlem Committee for Better Government for the opportunity to get out here where I belong—with you. I'll be back. Thank you. *Gracias.*"

As he finished, the back doors were opened, and a rush of cold air filled the room. The audience, still standing, offered another ovation. He acknowledged them with a wave and a smile, and watched them file out.

Larry McClanahan, leader of the West Side Democratic Club in the old Tenderloin District, closed the door and joined him. "You got to do the press. They're waiting in the hall."

"How many?"

"Four. No TV."

"No. I meant how many in the house?"

"Two fifty-eight, Chris. Not bad. Just right for this kind of meeting."

"You didn't always think so, Larry. Thousands cheering, you used to say."

McClanahan was thin and red-faced. Third-generation Tammany Irish, his kind had run the city for a hundred years. "Yes, Your Honor. Right you are. You want to talk to the proles in small groups. Then they tell their friends what a regular guy you are."

"Sour, Larry. Sour. Let's go meet the press."

McClanahan followed Greene through the door. He had been among Greene's most vociferous opponents during the mayoral primary. Larry McClanahan didn't think much of amateurs. And he didn't like rich Jewish kids. When Greene knocked the organization on its ass, he'd been the first to switch. The only thing worse than an amateur is a loser.

Greene slowed his pace deliberately to accommodate McClanahan. He knew the ropes of precinct organization like his catechism. Without that, Greene would be lost in the fall. His whole campaign rested on getting out the urban vote.

"Listen, Larry, I got to go back to the house when I get through. I've got a few things to look over. Why don't you come have a nightcap with me?" There was a silent pause.

"Why not?" McClanahan said, relaxing a bit. "A little hair of the dog never hurt anyone."

Greene turned and strode athletically toward the group of reporters, huddled with their breath steaming in the night air. "Gentlemen and one lady, what can I do for you?"

Joe Harper of the *Times* said, "I could have sworn you said that you were going to renegotiate the city's loan guarantees if you were elected."

Greene ducked his head and smiled disarmingly. "You're trying to get me into trouble, Joe. I said that I thought we ought to seek relief from some of the more restrictive elements so that we can give our disadvantaged citizens a better break. Now you go and make it sound like I want to take on the whole world—or renege on commitments."

The female reporter asked, "Aren't you afraid that by placing so much emphasis on urban problems you're conceding the rural vote?"

He turned serious again. "I guess you think that people who live in rural areas have no compassion. Not only have I not given up on them, I'm counting on their support."

After a further moment of banter, Greene excused himself and walked out into the street with McClanahan. The mayor's unmarked car was parked in the shadows down the block from the school with a police escort. The mayor paused a moment, watching the reporters move off, looked into the rear seat where Jennifer Ashton sat waiting, and gave a quick negative shake of his head. He turned to McClanahan and said, "Let's walk. I can use the air."

About three blocks down First Avenue, McClanahan said, "I hope that you don't get trapped in too much detail about loan guarantees. That's a hole with no bottom."

"I play to the audience at hand. You heard me with the reporters. I wasn't about to be pinned down. And besides, we've got people thinking that through very carefully. You worry about getting out the vote, I'll worry about the platform."

When they arrived at Gracie Mansion they were thoroughly chilled. The policeman at the gate saluted them through to the large white colonial house on Eighty-ninth Street and the East River, on the crest of a knoll behind a wrought-iron fence.

They sat in the library at the back of the first floor that looks out over the river and the lights of Queens on the other bank. Greene poured a couple of whiskies over ice and dropped into a deep chair across from his guest on the couch.

He raised his glass. "*Slainta*." McClanahan returned the Irish toast. "Well, Larry, what do you think so far?"

"All right, Mr. Mayor. Better than we ought to have expected. This isn't a campaign I'd have chosen to wage."

Greene held his glass up to the light and watched the spectrum glance off its moistened edge. "It's the territory that we have. The right is not our ground. And you can't win an election from there in New York, anyway. Watch George Mason trying to sell laissez-faire economics to a bunch of welfare mothers with children at a methadone clinic. The center has been preempted by the governor. You can't win with me-too." Greene took a sip and expanded. "I don't think we have to try to please everybody. Face it, Larry, this isn't a middle-class state. Manufacturing leaving for the Sun Belt.

Cost of living way up over the national average. We got poor and we got rich. The middle class that we do have don't care. They just want to be left alone. If you don't threaten them, if you stay out of their neighborhoods, if you soft-pedal busing, they don't care what you promise anybody else. They're tired.

"So what we continue to do is to concentrate on getting the disgruntled and disaffected to the polls. We show them how well the rich are doing, keep reminding them of the apartments that sell for three million when tenement rents are being squeezed up all the time. Show them eight-hundred-dollar bags at Gucci when they have to cut down on cigarettes to save dough. Most of the rich vote against us because they're comfortable, the rest with us because of their consciences. The poor and the people who are being pulled down by inflation will be for us if we get them to the polls. The middle class—we hope they stay home."

McClanahan took a swig. "I'm on your side, Chris. Who is to say that it can't be pulled off?" He put down his glass. He wasn't sure whether he believed that or not.

"Let's talk about something concrete. Did you get to Willy Albert in Buffalo?"

McClanahan studied his glass grimly. "I have tried. I don't know what he wants. He says he wants to talk to you directly. He says if you want the black population of Erie County out there on election day, there are some things he's going to want from you. He says he runs a big risk coming down on the other side of the fence from Big Frank." He looked up at Greene. "You don't suppose he's on the payroll?"

Greene shook his head. "I don't believe it. But he might want to be on ours."

"I asked him point-blank if he wanted a job. He said no, though there are people he'd like to have taken care of."

"That goes without saying. Patronage is the plum." Greene stood up. "I've got a bunch of papers I've got to go over before tomorrow. Thanks for coming. And keep after Albert. Tell him that we can meet here on Tuesday. I'm in all that day."

Greene phoned the gate and arranged for a patrol car to drive McClanahan back to his home in Chelsea. Jesus, he thought to himself as he watched the car drive away, you've got to kick one end and stroke the other all day long.

He rubbed his eyes, poured another small drink, and sat

down at his desk. He took a key from his pants pocket and opened the bottom drawer, removing an envelope sealed with Scotch tape. He pulled it carefully apart and drew out the half dozen sheets of paper and spread them out before him. He looked them over and reshuffled them again. He'd told McClanahan nothing more than what he believed. In New York, you can get elected by a coalition of the malcontent and the conscience-stricken. You just have to line them up right. Get the blacks and the Hispanics out to the polls, call out to the habit-bound Irish and Italians in the unions who hadn't voted Republican in four generations, appeal to the better nature of the Jews and the liberals, and you have a plurality. All you have to do is mouth the right issues, eat knishes, grits, and pizza and you can be king. Rockefeller did it for sixteen years.

But eventually, Chris Greene was discovering, you have to deliver. During the fifteen years that he had pursued his political career, his end, his target, had been the next election. But he had found that the executive and the legislative were very different. To be sure, as mayor he wielded powers he had never had before, but at the same time, he had forsaken the safety of the sidelines, where he could criticize without repercussion. He had become the dispenser of favors, but he was now required not to pose the questions, but to find answers for them.

Somewhere along the way, in manipulating and coercing, he had slipped. He had inherited a city on the rebound and had viewed it as a stepping-stone to higher office. He had studied the mayors who had gone before him—Wagner, the Tammany heir who understood politics, but whom the city outgrew; Lindsay, the limousine liberal with his eyes on the White House who turned out to be neither politican nor administrator; and Beame, the worn-out party hack who had parlayed a misplaced faith in his management capability into the brink of bankruptcy—and decided that he was smarter and better.

For the first year and a half of his term in office, he had benefited from the city's restructured debt, congressional loan guarantees, and the rebound brought about by an increase in confidence, as well as an enormous influx of foreign capital during the period of the weak dollar in the international marketplace.

Riding the crest, he'd decided that he would take on Frank

O'Neil and leapfrog to the Governor's Mansion before the city exposed his weaknesses and ruined his career as it had the others'.

When he had made his strategic decision as to his position in the political spectrum, he had cast about for people to use. He accepted Larry McClanahan into his camp without a twinge despite his prior opposition. He made his peace with the president of the city council who had been his main opponent for the mayoralty, and with the comptroller, ceding major patronage plums that should have been his to dispense in return for their public cooperation. After all, he had explained, when I run for the governorship, we all move up a slot.

He'd needed some bona fides in the black and Hispanic communities. Lip service wasn't enough. He handed out a few top jobs. He insisted publicly on a higher quota for both groups in selecting fire and police personnel from the ranks of those waiting for appointment regardless of scores or capability.

As he cast about for a better handle on the minority groups that would not overly indebt him, he attended the opening of a day care center in the East Bronx. He met a builder named Hawkes.

"You seem to have a real interest in the inner city," Hawkes had commented. "I'll bet we have a great deal in common, philosophically. I have a few ideas that might fit in very well with yours."

A week later, Greene had taken him to the Ko Shing Rice Shoppe behind City Hall for a quiet dinner.

"You can see," Hawkes said, "that I've managed to get a little White Power involved." He put the letters from Burton Corporation back into his briefcase. "And I have the sponsorship group lined up. There's going to be a monument to the community on 125th Street." He looked up at Greene archly. "The governor's behind it, you know."

Greene's smile had frozen. "Well, Mr. Hawkes," he said coolly, "then I don't suppose you'll be needing me, after all."

Greene still wondered at Hawkes's gall.

"Hell, Mr. Mayor, that doesn't mean you can't be the main beneficiary. I'm sure that there's a way that between us, we can figure out a way to arrange the bulk of the credit to fall in your lap. Let's face it, it's going to take more than a little gubernatorial clout to get the building built." Hawkes had leaned forward and looked into his face, gauging, weighing. He plunged. "We both know that there's no way this building can be built within its budget. It's going to require a lot of—let's call it sophisticated community relations—to get it built at all, what with unions that don't accept blacks, and general hard feelings in the community. There's going to have to be a certain amount of official leeway. There'll be a lot of stuff stolen—copper tubing, tools, wire—that can be turned into ready cash by the unfortunate. . . . What can I say?"

"And you're going to need a certain amount of—let's call it license," Greene had replied. "A little relaxation of scrutiny."

"Let's call it an understanding of local problems."

Greene got the drift. He would blink, and he would become the champion of the community. It was Frank O'Neil who had approved Uhuru Towers, but it would be the sensitivity and understanding of Christopher Greene that would make its completion possible. He had made up his mind in thirty seconds. Hell, it was only one project in a $14 billion budget.

By now, a year later, it had become apparent to Christopher Greene that he had made a mistake. He was on the hook. Either Marcus Hawkes was the most incompetent builder in the United States, or the biggest crook. And there they stood, Hawkes and Greene, hand in glove for all the world to see.

He glanced over the papers with a jaundiced eye. On the one hand, he had the statistics for the percentage completion of the building as reported by his personal spy at the Housing Authority—a man he could trust, his brother's continuing freedom on parole depended on it. On the other hand, from an equally worthy source in the State Comptroller's office, he had a record of payments made to Hawkes for work done. He was well ahead of himself. He had taken in more money than he had built building—a theoretical impossibility given the system of checks and balances. Of course, Greene said to himself, it wouldn't be easy to discern, and not everyone had as specialized an information network as he did. He smiled grimly. How much did O'Neil know? How far out on the same limb was he sitting? Could he really be dumb enough not to know?

Greene slipped the papers back into the envelope and locked them in his desk drawer. He put his hands to his head to check his hairpiece.

When he got to the Governor's Mansion the deficit in the accounts of Uhuru Towers would disappear in a cloud of paperwork, and no one would be the wiser. If that were not possible, he would howl that he had been duped by O'Neil and throw Hawkes to the wolves. He rose to leave. Jennifer had been cooling her heels in the car for more than an hour.

On his way, the phone rang. Cursing, he turned and took it from the hook. "Greene."

"Mr. Mayor, this is Ray Muldoon."

"Yes, Commissioner."

"We've got a very serious tenement fire. I thought you'd want to know. There are going to be a lot of deaths. It's a bitch."

"Give me the basics."

"It's on Willis Avenue, just on the other side of the bridge. Must have been a gas leak. It blew sky high. We're trying to contain it."

Greene bit his lip. "Shit. All right. I'll be there. Ten minutes." He hung up and walked rapidly out of the office.

He slammed the door of the mayoral mansion behind him. The army-green Chevy that he used as a limousine was parked at the foot of the path on East End Avenue opposite Doctor's Hospital. Jennifer sat in the backseat nodding. Gracie Mansion was the official residence, but he lived in an apartment building three blocks away. Jennifer lived on the floor below him.

As he got in, Jennifer lifted her head from her chest with a smile. "I thought we were going home."

"Fucking fire." He looked up at the driver. "Turn on the fire band, Harry. It's a pisser on Willis Avenue."

Jennifer slumped back in the seat as the driver pulled out and turned the corner. When they were on the drive, she took a black enamel and gold compact from her handbag and clicked it open. She glanced sidelong at Chris Greene. He was looking out of the window at the River and chewing a fingernail. There was a small spoon nestled on a cake of white powder. She dipped in the spoon, lifted it carefully under her nostril, and inhaled. As she replaced the spoon and closed the compact, Greene turned his head. He slapped his hand on top of her thigh resoundingly. "Dumb cunt," he said between his teeth.

Still smiling, she shrugged at the pain, and closed her eyes.

The car had arrived in advance of most of the media. The

flames had been visible from the moment that the car had entered the drive. The glow of the burning building outlined the Triboro Bridge in front of it. Greene pulled a note pad from his pocket and quickly concocted a message of grief. He pocketed it and walked out to stand next to Chief Aiello. "Jesus Christ. It's a death trap. Accidental?"

"We'll probably never know, Your Honor. You could smelt iron in there. It'd be more likely that it was arson if it was one of them two there," he said, pointing at the adjacent abandoned buildings, glistening in the heavy rain being poured upon them by the pumpers in an attempt to prevent the fire from spreading. "This one was full of people." He raised his hand to shield his eyes as something flared. "But you can count on the fact that we'll do the best we can to find out."

The mayor stayed for an hour, till all of the press had had an opportunity to photograph him and take down his statement. To his irritation, Senator Carney, the Republican majority leader, appeared shortly after he did and read a message of sympathy and dismay on behalf of the governor.

Harry, the mayor's driver, dropped Greene and Jennifer off in front of their apartment building. As they climbed toward his floor in the elevator, she slumped against the oiled wood paneling. He squeezed her bicep, and she straightened. He steered her down the hall and pulled the key from his pocket. When he opened the door, she staggered out of his grip toward the bedroom, strewing clothes as she went.

By the time that he had hung up his coat and followed her, she lay naked, arms outflung and legs spread across the bed, snoring softly. He ran his fingers across the ruff of blond hair between her legs. She mumbled something unintelligible and rolled over on her face.

He stripped, put his clothes away and brushed his teeth, then lay down beside her. His mind flitted back and forth between the burning building and the damning papers hidden in his desk drawer. He would have to get rid of them in the morning.

He rose on his elbow and slapped Jennifer sharply across the buttocks. She barely stirred. At least he would have liked to get laid. He flicked out the light and stared at the ceiling.

20

George Allen Mason wandered aimlessly from the den in his East Sixty-third Street apartment trailing ashes and sat on the chrome and leather settee in the living room in front of his wife's desk to continue his ruminations.

Eleanor Mason smiled silently without looking up from her work. She focused on the formula before her which held the promise of someday eliminating the cancer cells which destroyed uterine tissue, causing barrenness in young girls, or death. It had struck her in her sixteenth year. She had recovered and had dedicated herself to the study of the disease that had robbed her of the fulfillment of childbearing and a normal married life.

Or so she had believed at sixteen. She had shunned boys in favor of her books and succeeded brilliantly in her studies. She learned to make friends with men without becoming involved and turn away their advances without offending or estranging them.

She was in her senior year at Barnard and had already been accepted at NYU Medical School. She was fresh-faced, and raven hair trailed down the back of her pale blue sweater as she hurried across Broadway at 116th Street toward the Nicholas Murray Butler Building to a class.

Suddenly, she found herself sitting, quite surprised, in the middle of the sidewalk, listening to the stuttering apologies of a tall angular man in his mid-twenties with a pipe wobbling dangerously in the corner of his mouth. He was quite the most handsome man she had ever seen. As he helped her to her feet she smiled graciously, and walked off to her class, regretting that she would never see him again. When she came out two hours later, he was sitting on the steps with his nose in a book.

"I'm George Mason. I knocked you down. I've been waiting for you."

"You want to try again?" Her eyes twinkled at his discomfort.

"If that were necessary to get you to let me buy you a cup of coffee, I would even stoop to that."

In the end, it was not his good looks that seduced her, but his consideration, and his understanding and appreciation of her commitment to her work. Even at twenty-five, she thought, he had been profoundly thoughtful, and respectful of her individuality.

In the midst of study one day in his cluttered room in a university owned building on Cathedral Heights, he put aside his work, made up his mind, and said, "Elly, I want you to go to bed with me."

She put the book she had been reading in her lap. A single tear wended its way down her pale cheek. She had accepted the fact that this moment would come from the hour that she had sat listening intently as he spoke in the coffee shop almost a year before. Now she had to face it. And the truth. And she loved him terribly.

He had never seen her cry. He was dumbstruck and cleared his throat, searching.

"I need to talk to you. No, don't say anything till I am finished." She wiped the tear away, and straightened herself in the chair. "We have often discussed my commitment to medicine. Your patience with my schedule, and that commitment, has earned you my gratitude and my respect a thousand times.

"I have been less than honest with you, George." She shook off his quizzical look. "Yes, it is so. My motivation is more than unquenchable curiosity, or a morbid obsession with neoplastic diseases. I am not a crusader, George. I'm a cripple." She tried to modulate her voice, to throttle the emotion which threatened to make her words unintelligible.

"I had cancer," she went on. "Cancer of the cervix. When I was sixteen. I have had no recurrence in these six years. By that standard of measure, I am cured. I am also barren. I had a complete hysterectomy. I can never have a child. I'm sorry, George. But, you can see, we can't really be more than friends."

He nodded. His face relaxed into the calm studied expression that she had come to know so well. He thought for a moment before he spoke. She chewed her lip, wanting to turn away, to run, but held her gaze.

"I am truly sorry, Eleanor. I cannot imagine a pleasure greater than creating a new life in your body. But, in its absence, I will have the pleasure of absorbing all of your affection myself. Now, take off your clothes."

She had never been touched by a man before. He sat at the edge of the rumpled bed and looked at her nakedness. "And David looked upon Bathsheba, and she pleased him greatly," George quoted.

Twenty years later, George Mason sat with his feet propped up on a chrome and glass coffee table, sucking at his pipe, and squinting down at a set of statistics. He wiggled his toes in his carpet slippers and cleared his throat. Twice.

Eleanor put her pen down, stretched, and pushed away from the desk. "What's on your mind, George?"

He held out his hand without taking his eyes off of the papers. She walked across the room and sat on the floor next to him, her legs tucked up under her. She took the hand and rubbed her cheek against it.

"You heard my call for help, then?"

"I did."

"Mr. Greene and Mr. O'Neil have armies of people examining each other's records, and mine no doubt."

"The armies of the night."

"I have a few people doing the same thing, after all. I would have more if I had a bureaucracy to use."

"All officeholders have the same advantages, and the same propensity for sin."

"I like to do a lot of the digging myself. It cuts down on embarrassing errors and retractions."

"I don't think that O'Neil or Greene ever get embarrassed, George."

"These are the capital budget summary sheets, Elly." He poked at one sheaf of papers. "And these are the operating budget sheets by month with percentage attainment almost to date." He glanced over them with a practiced eye. He took the pipe out of his mouth. Eleanor took it from his hand and knocked out the dead ashes into a receptacle with expert ease.

He wanted to frame his sentence. She sat patiently. He had been a member of the Citizens Committee for Sound Fiscal

Policy during the collapse of the city under the Beame administration. He used to tell Elly that New York had drowned in overanticipation. Four billion dollars of short term debt—RANs, TANs, and BANs—revenue anticipation notes, tax anticipation notes, and finally borrowing anticipation notes. The reality had not met the anticipation.

"Elly, I am unable to put my finger directly on the problem. I have sifted through this morass twice. You are a good judge of human character. You wouldn't think, after all that has gone before this city, that Christoper Greene would resort to an old chestnut like stealing from the capital budget to make up deficits in the operating budget. Or would you?"

She traced a pattern with the tip of her finger over the palm of his outstretched hand. "What is it that prompted the question?"

"At the museum the other night, Paul Curtin came up to talk to me. Bright fellow." He took the pipe back and stuck it in the corner of his mouth. "He asked me about Uhuru Towers, Elly. He wanted to know what I thought. He's not the type that asks idle questions."

"Do you suppose he knows something? Or was he on a fishing expedition? You know the *Advocate* has your number from the point of view of subsidized housing. To them, you're Scrooge."

"It didn't seem worth the effort to get another quote from me on the subject. In New York City all public works are replete with a greater or lesser degree of sin. I felt that he might be intimating that there was something larger in back of it. The first thing that came to mind was the old budget switching game."

"I thought, with the Municipal Assistance Corporation monitoring everything, that was no longer possible."

"That's my understanding. I wonder if Uhuru is a sign of some new creative indiscretion. It would be odd, though, if Curtin were out to get something on Greene. He's the *Advocate*'s candidate. Melanie Parsons loves him."

"Well, I don't." She used his hand to pull herself to her feet. "My God, it's one o'clock. You want to take me to bed?"

He heaved himself from the couch and stuck his pipe in the ashtray. "I never turn down a pretty lady."

She slipped her arm around his waist and leaned her head on his shoulder. As he clicked off the lights on the way to the bedroom, she said, "George, are you going to take a look at Uhuru?"

"I might just do that."

As George and Eleanor Mason made love, Christopher Greene finally fell asleep, comforted by the thought that for every new stack of rules, there was a new stack of loopholes.

21

Paul Curtin thrashed inside the cocoon he had made of the covers on his bed. He reached out and pulled a pillow closer to his face, making a tunnel with his hand to let the air come in. Light came with it.

Someday, he thought, I will devise a system with enormous windows and lots of light for the daytime, and a foolproof drapery that guarantees absolute darkness so I can sleep in the morning. He kicked the covers onto the floor. As it was, he had neither.

He sat up and looked at the clock. It was half past eight. After he and Maryanne had come in from the country, they had gone to her apartment and cooked dinner for the kids. Because they would be going away with their father for the weekend, and wouldn't see Paul and Maryanne till Sunday night, they were allowed to stay up till ten, though it was a school day.

Paul showered and shaved quickly, dancing under cold water to get his circulation going. He felt logy and dyspeptic. And confused. He had grudgingly admitted to himself that he was grateful that Maryanne had accompanied him to see Jerry. Somehow, after that, the whole day she'd seemed like a different person. She'd made a commitment out loud, and for the first time, she was pressing him for a commitment—or that's how he saw it.

As he dressed he reflected that even sex had been different. It had always been good with her, but calmer. Sweet, with less hunger. He smiled. That scene in the car. Wonderful. And after the kids went to bed, she'd danced for him naked in the living room and they'd necked and made love on the floor for hours. He'd gone to bed at two.

Was his inability to sleep an indication of perceived pressure? Bullshit, he said to the mirror. Maybe you don't like the idea of her being right.

He walked into the kitchen, poured himself some orange juice, and paced, cradling the glass. Then he sat at his desk, pulled out his pocket note pad, and picked up the phone. Might as well make use of the goddamn day.

The number rang in his ear five or six times. At the point where he began to hang up, a husky female voice came onto the line. "Yes." It was hushed and throaty.

"Mrs. Gibbons?"

"Yes."

"I'm sorry to disturb you. My name is Paul Curtin. I'm a reporter for the *New York Advocate*. I was at your husband's funeral. I'm very sorry about your loss."

"Thank you."

"Mrs. Gibbons, do you think you could spare me a few minutes?"

"I don't know. Why? I really—"

"I'm trying to look into Uhuru Towers. I'd like to talk to you a bit about your husband."

"He was very proud to work on Uhuru Towers."

"I'm sure he was. I have been told that he was a very good foreman. A real professional."

The voice at the other end gained a little strength. "Oh, he was Mr. . . ."

"Curtin."

"Curtin. He was. He was dedicated. He was a young man. He wasn't but forty-seven. He knew all there was to know about bricks and masonry."

"Can I come out?"

After a brief pause she asked, "When would you like to come?"

"Now, if it suits you."

"All right." She gave him the address. He said he'd be there in three quarters of an hour.

Paul gathered his papers and stuffed them in his bag and went to get his car. Though it was a bit after nine, traffic was still heavy coming into the city as he drove in the opposite direction through Queens.

The Gibbons house was a two-family brick building in the middle of the block. Though it was winter, he could imagine the little plot of turf green with grass, and the window boxes full of flowers. A statue of the Virgin Mary stood in a little rock garden to one side.

He parked and crossed the sidewalk. The door opened before he could ring the bell. She must have been waiting at the window.

"It's very nice of you to see me, Mrs. Gibbons. It has to be difficult for you."

She lifted her chin. She was wearing a simple black dress. "I am sad. He was a good husband, and a good father. It's hard on the boy. We haven't got but the one. He'll be twenty-three. He's a graduate of Adelphi College." Her voice was full of pride. "He works for IBM." She led him into a small and neatly furnished living room. A polished upright piano bore an opened hymn book.

"Please sit down. Would you like some coffee?"

"No, thank you, Mrs. Gibbons." He watched her take her seat. She sat at the edge of a straight-backed chair, her hands in her lap, pulling at a white handkerchief. "You mentioned that your husband was proud of Uhuru Towers, Mrs. Gibbons."

"Oh, yes. He thought that it was important to black people in New York. He was a religious man, my Lloyd. He believed that the Lord wanted us to overcome our tribulations. And he said that the way to do that was hard work. He always said that there's no sense in complaining if you don't try to help yourself."

"I guess that's why he made sure your son got a good education."

"That's right." She swallowed, and hesitated a moment. "He said that if a man has the tools, there's no reason why he shouldn't succeed. He thought that Uhuru Towers was a tool for all the black people in the city."

"There are a lot of people who feel that way. I'd really like to tell how sorry I am. It seems such a waste, an accident like that." He waited, there was no reaction to the word. "Did he often stay late at night?"

She knitted her brows. "Not hardly ever." She twisted the square of cloth around her fingers. "I don't know what he could have been doing up there. He said he hated to stay around in the late afternoon in the winter when a building wasn't closed off. He was a careful man. He was always so careful." Her eyes brimmed and she brought the handkerchief to her face.

"Did he get along with all of the people on the job?"

She dabbed her eyes and answered, "Oh, he was very popular with the men." She paused again. "You haven't heard different, have you?"

"I have heard nothing but good, Mrs. Gibbons. I'm just doing a little research on the project. Sadly, your husband's death has become a part of it."

"He got on well with the men."

"How about his boss?"

"Gaines?" The tone of her voice changed. "Well, we never thought too much of him, to tell the truth. He leaned on Lloyd a lot. He only had a small crew before this job. They used to do little rehab jobs. There was times when it was only Lloyd and three or four others. I always felt that he wasn't our kind of people. He was . . . well, he didn't associate with nice people. Lloyd stuck with him because he had a hard time getting work. Being black in the construction trades in New York, I guess you know, isn't easy. Lloyd was with Gaines four years before Uhuru."

Paul looked down at his pad then up again, "And Marcus Hawkes? What did he think of him?"

"He didn't have much cause to deal with Hawkes. He told me that he was a blowhard. But, like I said, Lloyd was a very straight person. He tried once to go into business for himself, but he couldn't stand paying off to the building inspectors. Even the cops, if you wanted to work on a Sunday or a holiday to make a few extra dollars, the squad car'd pull right up to the job in plain sight and ask for money, or threaten to bust you, and drag you into court on a summons. Lloyd preferred to keep his own counsel. He worked a full day, but he left his work in the shop."

"Was there anyone he was close to at work?"

"Not really. There was just a bunch of laborers. Of course, there was Fred Giles and Al Jenks. They were with Gaines even before Lloyd got there."

"They don't live around here, do they?"

"Fred lives in Astoria, that's not far. Al lives over on Willis Avenue, in the Bronx."

"I guess they'd be at work anyway." Paul put the pad away. "There's nothing special that your husband has said about the job lately, Mrs. Gibbons? How did he say it was going?"

"Honestly, he didn't talk to me much about his work. He used to say there isn't much excitement in bricks and concrete. Last thing I remember his saying was that things were slow."

Paul rose and shook hands. "Thanks, Mrs. Gibbons. And again, I'm sorry."

She showed him to the door. "I hope that I gave you some help."

Paul turned on the radio and listened to music on the way back to his apartment. For all the good that had done, he might as well have stayed home. At least she said that she found Gaines unpleasant. Based on his one exposure, he couldn't see how she could come to another conclusion. Maybe he could get something out of his two coworkers.

As Paul drove down the Grand Central toward Manhattan, a bony black man in his early twenties slipped out of his ancient Chevrolet and walked across the street to a phone booth. Mrs. Gibbons's house was still in full sight. He cursed when he put the receiver against his head. He reached around and pushed the greasy sausages of hair away from his ear and dropped a coin in the slot.

"Mr. Gaines?"

"Yes."

"It's Tyrone Giggis, Mr. Gaines. Out by Mrs. Gibbons's house. She just had a visitor."

"You know who?"

"It was that tall blond honky that was at the cemetery. Should I stay here?"

"Yes. You just keep doing what you've been doing. You let me know who goes in and out of that house." Gaines hung up and sat back at his desk, a grim expression on his face. He was tempted to call Marcus, but he already knew what he'd say.

Leave it be. Then, he decided it would be better to tell Marcus anyway and picked up the receiver again. He knew that son of a bitch looked like trouble. He didn't like going away for ten days with all those loose ends hanging.

22

It was past eleven when Paul opened his front door and dropped his briefcase on the floor with a thud. He dropped his coat on a chair and headed toward the john in his bedroom.

"Jesus!" he yelled. "You scared me to death."

Maryanne was sitting on the bed with her feet propped on a pillow reading the *Times*. "You don't mind that I used my key? I spent my time in a worthwhile endeavor. Haven't you noticed? Your cage is clean."

"I've got to take a leak." He came out in a moment and sat next to her. "What brings me the pleasure of your company? I thought you were going to work today. I expected you to show up around dinnertime."

"I couldn't stand the idea of your taking a day off without me. Where were you? I expected to find you deep in the arms of Morpheus."

"I couldn't sleep. I got up and went to visit Mrs. Gibbons."

"Did she have anything to say?"

"Not a clue. What's in the paper?"

She made a bored face. "Nothing much. A bomb at a synagogue in Marseilles. A fire in the South Bronx. The Knicks lost, again."

He took the front section of the paper and scanned the front page. The *Times* doesn't front page calamity as a rule. This morning there was a picture of the ruins of the Bronx building, reduced to an irregular mound at the base of a partially standing wall. He read the story twice. They didn't know much. Paul read it again, then put the paper on the bed and stared out of the window.

"What's going on in your head? You've already done one interview today. You're supposed to be taking off the weekend to collect your thoughts."

Paul got to his feet. "I just want to make a phone call."

"Just you remember, this time is supposed to be spent reflecting. We're supposed to be together. I got rid of the children, remember?"

"O ye of little faith," he said sadly, picking up the receiver and dialing.

After a couple of rings, a gruff voice, muffled by a cigar rumbled, "Conforti."

"Morning, Matt. Paul Curtin. Who covered that big fire in the Bronx last night?"

"Phil Seelig. They dragged him out of his bed. You ought to see the pictures. Didn't you see it on TV?"

"I was just fooling around last night, and I got up late. I just saw the *Times* a minute ago. I'm supposed to be on R and R."

"It was spectacular."

"Phil's not around, is he?"

"Not here. He didn't file the story till after three. Joe Boyle's taking his place at Police Plaza."

"Then I know where to find him. Thanks." Paul held the button down till he got another dial tone while he looked over his telephone list.

"Hey, you said one call," Maryanne protested.

He held up his hand. "One minute." When a groggy voice answered the phone, he said, "Good morning Phil. Bright and shiny as a new penny, are we?"

"Aw, kiss my ass, Curtin."

"Where's the uncut copy you wrote on the fire?"

"I got it here. Maybe there's one downtown."

"I'll come get yours."

"Christ, give me a break. I'm dead. I didn't get to sleep until five."

"An hour. I'll bring you bagels and lox for breakfast." Paul hung up to forestall further protest.

"I thought that we were going to spend the weekend together."

"We are. I'm taking you. Have you ever met Phil Seelig?"

"No."

"Have you ever covered a story with me?"

"Just things like that party at the Met."

"That doesn't count. Today, you see me hot on the trail. Put on your shoes."

Forty-five minutes later, after a quick stop at Zabar's for bagels, Nova Scotia salmon, and cream cheese, they parked in the driveway of the high rise on the Henry Hudson Parkway in Riverdale where the Seeligs lived.

Phil greeted them at the door of his apartment in a worn terry cloth robe, scuffed slippers, and bloodshot eyes. "I'd invite you in, but I was planning to die. I am too old for this nonsense." Seeing Maryanne behind Paul, he asked. "Who's that? I may change my mind."

"Not only is she great-looking, but she has a Care package from Zabar's." Paul pushed past him, ushering Maryanne into the hall. "Maryanne Middleton, this is Phil Seelig, the last B-movie police beat reporter."

Seelig closed the door after them and led them to the living room. "He means he thinks that I'm over the hill." He grabbed a sandwich from the bag and took a bite. When it was chewed to manageable proportions he asked, "So what's the big interest in the fire?"

"Where was this fire exactly?"

"On Willis Avenue and 135th Street." He handed Paul a sheaf of yellow typescript. "Here. Do with it what you will, my good man. But if this is an article about housing, you're barking up the wrong tree. There ain't no housing left. Bricks, mortar, and tenants, all gone."

Paul riffled the papers, glancing over them, then shrugged his shoulders. "Just a . . . not even a hunch. I went out this morning to see Mrs. Gibbons."

"Yeah. She have anything to say?"

Paul shook his head. "Not so's I noticed. But maybe I didn't listen hard enough. One thing's for sure, her husband worked for that guy Gaines for four years, and she has the same impression of him that we got after four minutes. Who covered this fire for NYFD?"

"Chief Aiello. Nice guy. He was some harassed. He didn't have enough trouble. The mayor showed up, and then Senator Carney."

"What'd Carney want?"

"He came because he said the governor was otherwise

occupied on state business and wanted to send a representative to express his feelings, and his condolences."

"I'll bet Ken Miller wrote the damn statement."

"It's all there in your hand." Seelig yawned widely.

"Okay, okay, we know when we're not wanted."

"It's nice to meet you, lady. Even though you're with him."

Paul was quiet driving back toward the city. Maryanne looked out of the window at the Palisades, looming across the slate-gray river.

He turned at the Cross Bronx Expressway to the East Side. "Listen, how's your stomach? I want to go look at that fire."

She shuddered. "I guess I'll be okay."

"I'll take you home."

"No. No. I want to go."

Paul pulled the Corvette to the right and allowed it to coast down the ramp at 138th Street. It was still cold, but the clouds were scudding across the sky, leaving patches of blue. He drove down the block that parallels the highway, glancing across at the rickety buildings opposite. At the end of the street, just before the left turn onto the bridge to Manhattan, a row of police barricades reached out into the avenue, blocking access to the curb. An officer stood behind the barrier warily, swinging his stick.

Paul pulled up. "You're sure?" he asked, opening his door.

"I'm coming." She joined him.

The cop, sensing their presence as they approached him, turned to face them with the stick across his chest in a defensive gesture. He sized them up as they neared him, then let the stick fall to his side.

"This place is blocked off, mister. There was a fire here."

Paul pulled his press card out of his pocket and held it up. "I'm with the *Advocate*. I never attack on-duty policemen."

The cop glanced at the card and relaxed. "Sorry. They figured this post was only worth one man. In this neighborhood, when you don't work with a partner, you get nervous." He tapped his chest. "Even with a vest. What can I do for you?"

"I'd like to take a look around."

"I can't let you past the barrier. The fire marshals aren't through yet."

"Fire marshals?" Paul asked. "Is there something funny here?"

"Standard procedure. Who knows? They have to start sifting the trash." He motioned over his shoulder. "There's a lot of stiffs in there. At least what's left of 'em."

"How do you know? Is there a tenant list? What did you hear?"

"Nothing much. I'm just doing eight-to-fours. The guy I relieved told me that he heard that there could have been dozens of people in there. It was so quick that there wasn't really a fire. It just sort of blew out. The odds are it was a gas main. Con Ed's shut off the whole neighborhood. Poor bastards must be freezing their *cojones* off."

"Can we walk around the barrier?"

"Just so you don't go inside."

Paul walked slowly around the blackened rectangle with Maryanne at his side. Old law it was, ninety feet deep and less than twenty feet wide. An occasional wisp of smoke wafted upward despite the tons of water that had been heaped upon the debris by the pumpers during the night. A lone brick tottered on end, atop another, and slid into the ooze. It looks like the Blitz, Paul thought. This building wasn't burned, it was obliterated, destroyed without a trace, inhabitants and all. He grimaced as he caught the faint sweetness of fire perfumed by human flesh. Involuntarily, he reached up with his right hand and rubbed the scar on his shoulder. It throbbed in the damp cold.

There had been a village chieftain's house. His head was on a stake outside of the door. The building was smoldering. The rest of the chief's body and those of his wife and children, charred in the midst of the embers, had assaulted Paul's nostrils. It was a warning from the VC to collaborators.

He had been on patrol in Tay Ninh province. They'd followed a sloppy trail out of the village, two platoons—one ARVN, the other Cavalry, Paul's unit. They broke into a clearing three hundred yards out. There were ten poles dug into the ground. From each the corpse of an American soldier dangled by its hands. From the nylon topped boots, they could tell that they were Special Forces. Their genitals had been cut away. There had been a lot of vomiting and swearing. Then the firing had started. The ARVN had taken off.

Paul dropped on his belly next to a captain. He was in his mid-twenties, from the Bronx. His name was McFadden. "Jesus," McFadden said, "somebody ought to take pictures of this and send them to Jane Fonda." McFadden rolled onto his back and stuffed a magazine into his AR–15. "Then she can explain to these guys' mothers about the legitimate struggle for national identity. Of course," he said, rising to one knee and firing, "they'll be told that each of them died of one bullet in the heart. Almost no blood. Smiling."

After a few minutes the VC had pulled back, outgunned. Leaving a perimeter guard, McFadden had ordered everybody to take five.

A kid whose name no one had had time to learn stood trembling at the edge of the clearing, looking at the monstrous sight of his comrades sitting cross-legged on the ground, drinking water and eating C rations, talking in hushed tones almost inaudible above the buzzing of the flies around the bodies. Suddenly, he had pulled a jungle knife from its scabbard and run across to one of the dangling corpses and begun to cut the cords that bound it.

McFadden jumped from his seat screaming, "No, no, get off, you asshole!!! Claymore!"

Paul had dropped his canteen and fallen forward just as the body sagged. The cord to which it was attached pulled the trigger of the pie-shaped device concealed in the brush a few feet away. The plastic explosive it contained detonated, sending a thousand fragments from its cast-iron body flying in a deadly arc twenty yards wide. A jagged chunk had struck Paul's arm above the bicep, bounced off the bone, and spun upward, emerging from the top of his shoulder.

McFadden had been blinded in one eye. The nameless boy who had tripped the booby trap had been mutilated beyond recognition. They hadn't even been able to find his dog tags. It had taken almost eight hours to get the wounded out by chopper. Paul had been lucky. They'd sewn him up with only a nasty scar and an occasional ache as a souvenir. Except that sometimes in the night, he saw the dangling corpse, and just before it exploded, he saw that its face was his own.

"Ouch. Paul, you're breaking my hand."

"I'm sorry." He dropped Maryanne's hand as though it were

hot. "Jesus. I'm sorry. Let's get out of here. This place stinks of death."

He hardly waited till she had closed the door to pull the Corvette away from the curb. He took the bridge and drove a few blocks down Second Avenue, then pulled over to the curb. He leaned his head forward on his hands and closed his eyes for a moment.

"Paul." Maryanne touched his shoulder. "Paul, are you okay? Honey, you're white as a sheet."

He gripped the wheel with his hands till the tremors stopped, drew a deep breath, and sat back. "I saw a ghost. A lot of ghosts."

She sat still waiting for him to talk. Her mouth was like cotton.

"The wreckage. . . . It reminded me of a village in Nam." He shook his head to dispel the vision, which had popped back to haunt him. He didn't want to tell her about the ten penisless corpses staring at him from behind his eyelids, or the flies.

"It must have been a terrible fire. There was so little left. It's hard to imagine that there were people in there."

"They char, just like wood," he said brutally. He turned to see her recoil in horror. "Once more," he said, his voice soft, "I apologize. I'm sorry. I think I'd better take you home."

She reached out and took his hand. "I think maybe I should take you home. How about me driving, for a change?"

He shook his head. "I'm fine. Just a bad dream. It's hard to imagine that there was anything living there. You're right." He cocked his head, as though listening to a faraway sound. Then reached around behind him, and pulled his bag into his lap from the top well. He looked at the pad that he had used during his interview with Mrs. Gibbons. He flipped through the pages, then stopped.

"You game for one more stop?"

"Only if you're not going to have anymore bad dreams." Maryanne sat quietly thinking as Paul drove on. What the hell am I getting myself into? No sooner do I commit myself to this guy, than he starts to doubt himself, and has nightmare visions. What do I know about him? I know where he works. I know he was married. We've never discussed it. I know he has an autistic son. I saw him for the first time yesterday. I know he was in the army and that's where he got a scar on his arm. I know what he thinks about the *National Geographic,* pop art, symphony music, and politics. We have avoided the subject of marriage like the plague, though we spend virtually all of our free time together, and he treats my children better than any father I know. And they love him. But, he's touchy when I get close. I used to change my clothes in the bathroom when I was married to Forrest even after I'd borne him two children. I danced bare-assed to Ravel's *Bolero* for this guy in my living room last night. I didn't know what orgasm meant till I met him. He is inquisitive and bright and likes to write, but he seems to hate a job that gives him the opportunity to employ all those faculties. I am beginning to wonder whether or not I should be scared. But all I'm really scared about is that he'll leave.

"There it is," Paul pointed. "Uhuru Towers."

Suspicious eyes watched the car as it glided down the street. Men with empty pockets huddled in doorways and transfixed Paul and Maryanne as they parked and walked up to the chain link fence that separated Uhuru Towers from the street. Inside, a thirty-foot panel bore an artist's conception of the completed project, with imaginary green-leafed trees casting illusory shadows where only broken concrete and urban drabness now existed.

Maryanne looked up at the complex steel webbing and said, "I expect a giant to climb down any minute, chasing a small boy."

"And be he live, or be he dead, I'll grind his bones to make my bread," Paul quoted. He walked to the gate at the center of the fence and motioned to a guard. "I'd like to speak to the man in charge," he said, showing his press card.

"You wait here, mister," the man in the uniform said, heading toward the office trailer. In a moment, a light-complected Negro, short and stout, came down the steps. "Yes, sir. I'm Charles Hawkes. What can I do for you?"

"I'm Paul Curtin, Mr. Hawkes. I'm with the *Advocate.* I spoke to your brother briefly the other day, at Lloyd Gibbons's funeral."

"Yes. My brother Marcus is the president."

"Is he here?"

"No, I'm afraid not." Charles wanted desperately to run inside to call him.

"I just want to take a look around. Can you show me the plans, and a little of what you've built? I understand that it's going to be a real beauty."

Charles felt relieved. Why not? he thought. "Sure. Come on in."

"This is Mrs. Middleton. She's a friend of mine."

"Please, ma'am," he said, sweeping off his porkpie hat. "I hope you won't mind wearing a safety helmet. It's regulations once you've passed the building line." He pulled three of them off a rack next to the office trailer. "It's the insurance company and safety rules."

They spent a half hour going over the plans of the project, learning about the number and the kind of shops they hoped to have in the underground mall, and the offices, apartments, and elevators.

"Do you think that the citizens of Harlem will really be able to enjoy the building, Mr. Hawkes? It seems pretty sumptuous to me. Won't the rents be out of reach for most of them?"

"Oh, that'll work out fine. Naturally, the space available is limited. It's only one building, and a multipurpose one at that. But we'll be able to accommodate all kinds of people. All of the apartments will be essentially the same, but the rents are going to be staggered according to income. There will be people paying as much as two hundred dollars per room per month, and as little as thiry-five."

"How can you manage that?"

"We have a rent subsidy program."

Paul resisted the temptation to press further. Charles Hawkes was answering his questions by rote—like a litany. "When do you expect it to be finished?"

"We're aiming for occupancy in the early fall. The waiting list is a mile long already," he said with pride.

"I can imagine," Paul said, extending his hand. "Thanks for the tour." He took a last look at the skeletal structure, and tried to gauge its level of completion.

"It's going to be the center of a revival of Harlem," Charles Hawkes said, taking their yellow plastic hats. He watched them walk away. When their car pulled out into the street, he raced up the trailer's steps to call his brother.

Paul was quiet again and pensive as he drove home. They dropped the car in the garage and strolled back to his apartment. When they were inside, he looked at his pad again, and said, "I want you to do me a favor."

Maryanne picked up the phone and followed his instructions. She dialed the number of the office at the Uhuru construction site which was printed on Charles Hawkes's card. A male voice answered.

"Hello," Maryanne said, "this is the Chemical Bank loan department. Is there a Mr. Al Jenks there?"

There was a pause. "Al Jenks. He works on the masonry crew."

"May we speak to him, please? It's about his loan application."

"He shouldn't even have given you this number, lady. The men aren't allowed to receive phone calls on the job."

Paul motioned to her, and she continued, "Well, we've tried him at home and are unable to get him. Could you at least tell me if he's at work?"

The timekeeper grumbled, then said, "I'll take a look at his card." He dropped the phone on the desk with a clatter. A minute later, he returned. "Naw, lady. He hasn't punched in in three days. If he don't show up soon, they'll pull his card."

"Thank you, sir." She put the phone on the cradle and looked up at Paul. "He hasn't been there in days."

"I heard." He took the phone from her lap and dialed information. "Give me the phone number of Al Jenks. It's in the Bronx, operator. Yes, on Willis Avenue. Could I have that exact address? Thank you very much, operator."

Paul hung up, and looked in his lap at the front page of the *New York Times*. The address in the caption under the burned out building and the address of Al Jenks were the same.

"I think," he said to Maryanne, "that I would like a drink."

23

The long car had been parked throughout the day in the garage where the trucks that distribute the *New York Advocate* are loaded. Charles Brown, who had been Melanie Parsons's chauffeur for twenty years and her mother's twenty years before that, sat in his usual place in the backseat.

At six o'clock, he slipped on his shoes, pulled up his tie, and put on his jacket and cap. He swept the car with his whisk broom, then walked to the telephone on the wall next to the parking space. He rocked back and forth on his heels for a moment, waiting, then the phone rang. "Charles Brown."

"All right, Charles," Madeleine Shurtleff said. "Mrs. Parsons is on her way to the elevator."

"Yes, ma'am," he replied. Madeleine, a maiden lady, liked that. He looked in the wing mirror, adjusting his cap over his short white hair. He got into the car and with expert care turned it in the narrow space, and drove into the street in front of the Advocate Building. Leaving the motor running, he got out of the car and stood by the rear door, not opening it to keep out the frigid air.

When the saw the door of the private elevator open, he turned the handle. As she crossed the sidewalk, followed by Oscar Bornstein, he swept the door open before her. They climbed in and sat down. Charles closed the door and hustled to his seat where he waited with his ears cocked.

"Take me home, Charlie. I'm tired."

Charles Brown looked up into the rearview mirror. She seemed small huddled in the corner. "Yes, Miss Melanie."

She dozed against the gray plush throughout the trip north to the imposing house in Beekman Place. A wall extended from the edge of the house to the parapet that drops to the East River, shielding the garden from pedestrian view. A stone dog, seemingly alive in the glow of the streetlamps, sat perched atop the wall, looking across to Long Island.

When Charles emerged from the car and closed his door, Melanie's eyes snapped open. She wrestled herself forward on her elbow and sat at the edge of the seat. She brushed self-consciously at her hair, then took Oscar's hand and pulled herself erect onto the sidewalk.

The maid stood at the open door to take their coats to the closet on the opposite side of the spacious foyer, made larger by a black and white marble checkerboard floor.

Oscar followed Melanie through the double doors of the library and shut them. She sat heavily in a chair by the fire. He crossed the Aubusson carpet to the bar and turned on the light. Neat rows of cut crystal glasses were arrayed and rearrayed into infinity in the mirrored walls. He filled a glass with ice and then with Chivas Regal, then another with Madeira and brought the glasses to the table by the fireplace.

Oscar leaned against the mantelpiece and raised his glass in a toast. She nodded and took a swallow. Oscar looked up idly at the oil portrait of Melanie's mother hanging above his head. It had been painted by the same artist who had done the picture of her father in the office. Seeing both personalities through the same eyes gave a hint of the conflicts alive in their daughter.

Samuel Parsons, born Parchinsky in Nizhni Novgorod, escaped to the United States after great privation. It was 1881, and Alexander II had been blown apart by a nihilist's bomb on his way to the Winter Palace from an assignation. The government blamed the Jews and they were forfeit. Oscar remembered Mr. Parsons telling of how the Cossacks had taken his father's chin and most of his jaw when they had cut off his beard, and how he had sat next to him in the street listening to him gurgle and die for hours while the Russians rode about chanting "Hep! Hep!" mourning Christianity's loss of Jerusalem, and exacting vengeance in the name of the Lamb of God. Sam Parsons's face was warm and rounded by the kindness and understanding that suffering develops in the best of people.

Oscar turned back to Melanie. She had inherited the fair skin and blunt features of her father's face. The expression was her mother's. The matriarch in the portrait had blazing black eyes and the skin tones of her Mediterranean ancestors. Rachel Pinto came of Sephardic stock that had traveled the ocean and the continent to become shopkeepers, then merchants in Abilene, Texas. Her parents had scorned the ill-spoken Russian immigrant Samuel Parchinsky. But she had seen in him the determination of which success is wrought. In her life, she had deferred only to her husband, and considered her only failure that she had not produced a son. She had been rarely loved, often respected, and invariably feared. She glowered across the years from the painting in her black lace dress, a small dog clutched captive in her lap.

A long case clock struck a single tone as the hands came to 6:30. Oscar took a sip from his glass. It was time for the ritual to begin by which Melanie controlled her family in the same fashion that she controlled the affairs of the *Advocate*. The table next to her bore a number of objects: an address book, an ink stand, a block of note paper, and a white telephone.

As it rang, Oscar retraced his steps to the bar.

"Hello, Dora," Melanie said. "How are you, dear? Oh, good. Tell me all about it."

Melanie, who had been born in 1908, had three younger sisters, Dora, born in 1910, Elsie in 1914, and Sandra in 1918. Each of them called, according to the order of their birth, beginning at 6:30 sharp each evening. Between the three sisters and dinner, Melanie took calls from her daughter Andrea, married and divorced from Nelson Beldon, and her daughter-in-law Gena Koenigsberg, married to her son Buddy, like his sister the product of Melanie's first marriage, to Horace Koenigsberg. Each in her turn reported on the day's progress and was dispensed approval, disapproval, or advice.

The calls were not optional. Failure to report was a serious breach. It was still a source of curiosity to Oscar that Melanie enjoyed the power so much.

Oscar had become inured to the procedure. Dora was a good-natured matron lady, married with two normal children. Elsie had buried three husbands and divorced two others. She still dyed her hair the raven black of her youth.

For Oscar, Sandra was another matter. Of all of the services he had performed for the family, the only one he had begrudged was the rescue of her son, Phillip Kaster, from a Uruguayan firing squad for fomenting revolution when he was supposed to be a Peace Corps volunteer.

The source of his reluctance had not been his contempt for

Sandra's husband, who in a lifetime of foolishness had been too inept to conjure up a failure of sufficient magnitude to even dent her inheritance. Nor was it his dislike of Phillip himself, who was a self-important mannerless little boor, who now worked as a space salesman for the *Advocate* and lived in mortal terror of Melanie, though God knows, Oscar thought, it didn't help.

Just before the Second World War Oscar and Sandra had been playing tennis at the club. They'd walked over the shortcut through the woods behind the back nine. She'd stopped and confronted him.

"How come you never look at me?" She put her arms around his neck. "Everybody wants me but you." And everyone had had her, he knew. She kissed him on the mouth. He put his arms meekly about her waist and responded. She forced her tongue into his mouth, pushing and probing. He backed away.

"I don't get you." She shrugged her halter to her waist. Her small pointed breasts still gleamed with perspiration from the effort of their play. "Maybe you need some encouragement." She undid his fly and put her hand in his pants. She rubbed him and said dirty words. He felt nauseous. He pushed her away and ran. "Faggot," she'd yelled after him. Just a single word. They never discussed it again.

A week later, he and Danny Foster were in the shower. They had played a late round, and all of the lights in the clubhouse had been dimmed. Danny was a kid his own age working his way through school as an assistant pro in the summer. Three sons of members had burst in on them, hooting and shouting. "Faggots! Faggots!" They had been barely touching as the water had cascaded over their soapy bodies.

The gossip spread like plague. The Foster boy was fired. There was talk of bringing Oscar before the House Committee. Sam Parsons, outraged at the unfairness, had slammed his considerable weight down on the boy's side. The matter had been quietly dropped. As a favor to Oscar's humiliated father, Sam Parsons had taken him up to his plant in Rhode Island for the rest of the summer. As time had gone by, he came to regard him as the son he had never had.

It was a matter of pride with Oscar Bornstein that Sam Parsons had gone to his grave never knowing that Oscar had heard Sandra's laughing voice outside the locker room that night.

"Oscar, are you in a trance?" Melanie had hung up the phone. "Would you be an angel and get me another drink?"

As Oscar filled her glass, the phone rang again. It was Andrea. He shuddered. He had been invited to dinner because Melanie wanted to propose her addition to the board of directors of the *Advocate*. Or, worse yet, he feared, to suggest that she join the editorial board. She'd had one pass at working on the paper. It had been a catastrophe.

When Melanie was finally done, Oscar asked, "All the reports in, Mel?"

"I don't think that's funny, Oscar." She looked cross. "Did you see Buddy today? I haven't heard from Gena."

Oscar suppressed a smile. Buddy Koenigsberg, the elder of the two children of her first marraige, was a solid, cheerful individual whose salvation in Oscar's eyes was a lack of complexity. He was not terribly bright, but he was honest and direct. He was assistant publisher of the *Advocate,* and as such did much of the glad-handing with other publishers and represented the paper in the various industry associations. He worked long hours with Oscar, trying to master the business aspects of the paper's operations. He was squat and dark, as his father had been, and walked painfully, for after thirty-five years, bits of German shrapnel still floated about in his body.

Among his chief assets was his wife, Gena, whom Oscar viewed as a reward from heaven for Buddy's fundamental decency. She was an escapee of the Holocaust who had arrived in New York in 1946, bearing scars both mental and physical. The hard times had stood her in good stead. Their marriage, a year after they'd been introduced, had been opposed by almost the entire family. She had persevered. But at the same time, she had learned that if she wanted to keep her marriage intact, she would have to play by the house rules. She made her daily reports grudgingly. Since Melanie knew it galled her, she enjoyed Gena's calls most of all.

"I suppose I can't really complain," Melanie said to Oscar. "After all, she is a good mother to the boys. Of course, it would have been easier if she'd been a little more like the rest of us. . . . Well, I guess she's forsaken me," she said with a note of triumph. "It's time to go in to dinner." As the clock struck the hour, the phone rang. She turned to answer it.

"Yes, dear. I'm sure you tried. I suppose it is difficult getting through sometimes. Unfortunately, I can't talk now. I have guests, and it is dinner hour, you know. Good night, Gena."

24

On Saturday morning Maryanne Middleton opened her eyes and looked out at the unfamiliar shapes cast by the sunlight that poured around the edges of the shades in Paul Curtin's bedroom. He lay sprawled across the king-sized bed like a carcass. She stretched her arms above her head and her breasts slipped above the sheets. Her nipples hardened in the air. She raised herself on one elbow and looked down at Paul. She was still unused to feeling like this. She'd been a virgin when she married Forrest. Their sex life had been biweekly and boring even from the beginning. She slept with one other man between her divorce and Paul. They had done it twice. He was quick on the trigger and snored.

She smiled and ran the tip of her finger between Paul's buttocks gently. He moved groggily, then turned his head, and went back to sleep. She did it again, and a third and fourth time. He yawned, and turned over, erect. Maryanne lifted the covers away and eased herself down on top of him. His eyes were closed, but he was smiling. She rocked back and forth with an undulating motion of her hips till he held her still in his strong hands.

"Not yet," he said. "Wait."

She clenched her fists and sat still, kneeling over him, containing him, her heart pounding in her chest. He opened his fingers and she picked up the rhythm again. Perspiration trickled down her back. The pulse beat in her throat and her vision blurred. When she felt his back arch under her, she permitted herself to lock hard against his pelvis till she had come. She wanted to scream, but her breath had gone. Her legs trembled under her and she fell forward on his chest.

The bathtub was old, of cast iron with clawed feet, and high and wide. Paul played the part of the gentleman, his head resting between the nozzle and the faucet. His feet dangled over the sides. Maryanne occupied the other end, resting against an inflatable pillow held by suction cups to the tub wall. She wiggled her toes at him.

"What would you like to do today?" he asked.

She leaned back on the pillow and closed her eyes. "I can't imagine. What an incredible luxury. I can choose anything I want."

She pushed herself upright. "May I test your love?"

"I am ready to risk all."

"I desperately need a new dress."

"Then let's go shopping." He tweaked her toe. "I'll even buy."

"My God." She thought a moment. "Is Bloomie's all right?"

"How about Bergdorf's?"

"You'll be sorry."

They waited for the bus in front of the museum, then rode to the Plaza, and got off. Across the street, Bergdorf Goodman's gleamed.

The ten-story building, clad in white granite slabs, rises up to a green-copper-sheathed duplex in which the founder's grandson lives. The ground floor, reaching around from Fifty-eighth to Fifty-seventh streets, is encircled by display windows bearing some of New York's most expensive prêt-à-porter.

Maryanne, in her fur-lined leather coat over a white turtleneck and a Dress Gordon kilt, slipped through the revolving door, leaving Paul to trail behind her. She passed the Fendi bags with a glance and stopped at the elevators at the rear.

"Fourth floor, please," she said to the operator. "I'm going to take pity on you," she said to Paul in a low voice. "I was dreaming of an Oscar de la Renta that I saw, but I haven't the heart to even ask."

"How much?"

She shrugged as the door opened. "Let's say a month's salary. It's very pretty."

He followed her out of the door. "I should hope so."

They wove across the floor between arrays of picnic baskets and unusual table linens to a portal that gave on a room forty feet square. It was lined with racks of clothing in niches in the dove-gray velvet walls. Four cocktail tables were surrounded by overstuffed modern couches and chairs covered with the same material.

Maryanne looked about for a saleswoman then discreetly nudged Paul in the ribs.

Three matronly ladies stood huddled at the other end of the room waiting attentively upon two clients seated before them. The other chairs and the table they surrounded were spread like a banquet with a dozen dresses of various colors and fabrics.

Paul turned in response to the nudge and stopped in his tracks. Melanie Parsons frowned and pointed at one of the dresses and said, "I'm not sure, Andrea. I'm not sure at all that it will suit you."

Andrea Koenigsberg Beldon looked at the ceiling for help. "All right, Mother. I'll try the damn thing on again." She got up easily from the low couch, grabbed the garment from the chair, and stalked off to the dressing room.

"Do something," Maryanne said, between teeth clenched in a smile.

Paul put his arm through hers and walked across the floor to the nearest group of chairs and sat down. "No reason to intrude upon her private life," he said cheerfully, but quietly.

"We could go somewhere else," Maryanne said.

"Never retreat."

A woman in her middle fifties in a conservative chocolate-colored dress stepped from the draperies hiding the stockroom and strode determinedly across the floor. "May I help you, madam?" she asked Maryanne.

"I saw a Perry Ellis dress in the paper on Sunday. I believe it comes . . ."

"Yes," the woman said, toying with her single strand of pearls, "in mauve, and ecru, or navy, with a slit skirt."

"That's the one. I like ecru."

The woman appraised her. "Very nice with your blond hair. Seven?"

"Thank you," Maryanne said. "I'm a nine."

As she disappeared through the curtain to get the dress,

Andrea Beldon stepped out of the dressing room and whirled before the mirror, the hem of the red chiffon dress lifting above her knees. She stood still with her hands on her hips and looked over her shoulder to see the back. Then turned to her mother. "I still like it."

"If you say so," her mother said. "But you will try on the blue one?"

"If it will please you." She took the dress and retreated again.

"I don't see why she doesn't take them both," Melanie grumbled.

"And, if I may, Mrs. Parsons," one of the salesladies ventured, "I think she looked lovely in the green."

Melanie shook her head. "No flair, my dear. My daughter likes things with flair."

Paul and Maryanne turned their attention to the saleswoman, who had returned with the beige dress that Maryanne had requested. It was in rough silk, with a V-neck and a straight skirt with layered, padded shoulders.

"Would you like to try it on?"

Maryanne looked at Paul. "What do you think?"

"Looks lovely to me. Go."

As Maryanne left, Andrea returned. Paul looked at her across the width of the room. She was wearing a pale blue chiffon dress with a deep décolletage. In order to appreciate it fully, she had removed her bra, designed for a different neckline. The small breasts that she had resented at sixteen were a godsend at forty-five, still firm and erect. She was a small-boned woman, slender and athletic. Unlike her brother, she had inherited the Parsons attributes and was fair-skinned with blond hair. She wore it shoulder length and gently curled.

"You're right, Mother," she said looking in the mirror. "It's downright provocative. I like it." Her eyebrows arched above a sharp straight nose. Her cheekbones were high and prominent, her mouth a wide red bow, like her mother's. She looked in the mirror with frank appreciation, turning this way and that.

Paul could understand her feelings. She was leggy and glowed with the results of excessive pampering, exercise, and self-denial. I'll bet she's on the floor, panting like a St. Bernard, two hours a day, Paul thought. One hundred sit-ups. Two hundred leg lifts.

From what Paul had heard, it had not been ever thus. Melanie Parsons's youngest child had gone to Emma Willard and Vassar. She had been presented at the Christmas Cotillion, among the first and few of Jewish heritage who had been permitted. Upon graduation, she immediately embarked on the career for which she had been trained by marrying Nelson Beldon, a tall, upright, homely dullard who worked diligently in his family's large and successful textile business. In five years, Andrea and her husband established themselves in Scarsdale in a suitable house on five acres and produced two children, a boy and a girl. After five more years of garden parties and dull vacations, Andrea began to suffocate, as her mother had before her. She went to Melanie for advice. She had suggested that Andrea devote some of her time to outside activities.

Paul smiled as Andrea stood before the mirror and stretched her arms above her head, exposing her breasts above the neckline, then batting her eyes demurely, put her hands back on her hips.

She had taken her mother's advice in the wrong vein, as Paul had heard it, and began to sleep around enthusiastically.

It was from that newfound activity that the roots of her mother's antipathy for Frank O'Neil had sprung. Sex and politics, Paul sighed. The publisher of the only afternoon newspaper in the largest city in the United States held political views opposite to those of the governor. That was perfectly normal. The paper was New Deal Democratic. The governor was middle-right Republican. But the vendetta had started between the sheets, not at the polls.

It was not until Paul had been with the *Advocate* for several months that he had gotten the whole story. He had been wooed and won away from his job at the *Washington Post* by the temptation of exposure, and money in the biggest media market in the world. Mrs. Parsons had agreed to make him the highest-paid news gatherer on the staff, and had fought tooth and nail with the Newspaper Guild, even hiring an extra reporter who would be a guild member, to exempt him from membership to give added perks.

Her avowed purpose was truly comprehensive coverage of the state government and the governor. The *Advocate* was limited in size, compared to either the *Times* or *News*, but she was determined to make the paper both expert and readable in the narrow areas that it covered.

Therefore, it had come as something of a shock to Paul to find that her attitude toward the governor was vituperative and personal. Where he had expected a free rein, he found himself immediately thrust into a position which was not only partisan, but doctrinaire.

Nonetheless, he was delighted at the opportunity to work in New York, and admitted to himself, if to no one else, that he enjoyed his special status. While familiarizing himself with his new beat, he was stimulated by the idea of the dark secret between the publisher and the governor. His disappointment was proportionate to his interest. Where he had searched for some dark Byzantine plot worthy of New York's magnitude and sophistication, he found himself confronted with a scenario that would have been at home in Cedar Rapids.

His search had cost him the price of a beer. After a month on the job, he had taken Bernie Cohen, a forty-year veteran of cityside reporting, since retired, to the crummy bar on the corner, where they sat on rickety stools amid the smell of unwashed glasses and Lysol.

Paul heard the story from Bernie the first time, but he'd heard it many times in other places since. Its currency alone was enough to make Melanie mad.

It had been about halfway through Frank O'Neil's first term in office. By then, Andrea Koenigsberg Beldon had moved out of the house in Scarsdale, leaving the garden parties, and the husbands, including her own, and taken a lavish apartment in the city.

As an adjunct to her change in domestic life-style, Andrea had decided to make use of her birthright, and got herself appointed as personal assistant to her mother, the publisher of the *New York Advocate*. She arrived every morning in her own limousine, occupying one of the two spare offices in the publisher's suite.

As a reaction to her previous condition of servitude with boring and conventional Nelson Beldon, she used her position and money and the implied power of the paper to intrude into every social gathering she could manage. She particularly relished association with public figures, her pleasure increasing with their prominence. Without a hell of a lot to add to conversations, she quickly fell back on the reliable standard in the Big Apple, hard cash.

Lending her talents to the highly skeptical Pierre Du Fresne, the *Advocate*'s gossip columnist, she served as reporter, contributor, and participant in the maximum number of charitable functions. Buy a table for twenty, then have the organizers fill it with impoverished European nobility and slightly worn celebrities, and you're in line for an invitation to a pregala cocktail party on the next occasion.

On the principle that quick results require intensive effort, Andrea Beldon bought two tables at a bash for an orphanage in Puerto Rico.

The evening was not cheap at two hundred bucks a plate. But that was nothing compared to the cost of transportation. It had been decided by the organizers that the flavor of the occasion would be lost if it were held at the Plaza or the Waldorf, as such things often are. So instead, they made arrangements at Dorado Beach, the golf resort erected on a strand of beautiful beach by the Rockefeller brothers, thirty miles west of San Juan, Puerto Rico.

The considerable power of the organizing committee, which included a Rockefeller cousin, and of *tout San Juan,* was brought to bear on the reservations department. One hundred of the hotel's three hundred accommodations, including three quarters of their waterside bungalows, were set aside for the partygoers, despite the fact that it was Thanksgiving week. Everyone invited would stay the full six days normally required as the minimum at that time of year. It would cost eighteen hundred per room. Andrea Beldon laid out forty grand, air fare and all, for her twenty guests.

Frank O'Neil was approaching two anniversaries, one happy, the other sad. He had reached the end of his second year as governor of New York and of his fifth as a widower, having lost his wife Mary to a sudden stroke. As he became increasingly involved in the former, the pain of the latter began, however slowly, to subside.

The last of his eight children had left home for prep school. Ahead of him, only two remained in college. He had hosted the annual family Thanksgiving feast, and packed everyone back to school or home on Sunday afternoon.

O'Neil's social life had been limited to family engagements and close friends for several years. But since his election, he had been reported from time to time by the society and gossip columns as attending a charity function or a quiet dinner in a restaurant with one or two single women.

He had not taken a trip, or a vacation, except with his children. On this Thanksgiving, tired by a tough first session and the strain of legislative elections, he had decided to go away for three or four days in the sun. He wanted to take up golf again. He hadn't played since Mary's death.

He wanted to go to a place he had been before, with a first-rate course. He was very surprised to find that Dorado Beach, with its two beautiful Robert Trent Jones 18s, couldn't find a room for the governor of New York.

His ego prickling, he directed his secretary to find out why. In due course she came back with the address and phone number of the Santa Isabella Orphanage Benefit Committee.

"I'll take care of this myself," he had told her.

The volunteer at the end of the line had passed him along to the cochairman of the dinner committee, Mrs. Andrea Beldon.

As she talked to O'Neil on the phone, her mind conjured two images: his manly physique and handsome face and the bottom end of her invitation list. The conversation had lasted three minutes.

The governor had been satisfied. His reservation had been arranged. He would arrive Sunday night, after the ball, and stay till Wednesday, when the committee's reservations expired. Andrea was thoroughly excited and spent the rest of the day changing rooms and names on her list. Only the von Schumann und zu Heinkels, who were bumped from her personal list, were put out. They hadn't spoken a word to her since.

The ball had gone brilliantly. The house of Su Casa, a restaurant on the Dorado Beach property, had been dressed in chandeliers of beeswax candles, and the flickering lights on the stucco and the miles of silk and lace and tulle worn by the guests had stripped away the centuries. Music had drifted through the clear moonlit Caribbean night till dawn intruded at the edge of the sea.

Andrea Beldon allowed herself to be walked back to her bungalow by one of the heirs to the A&P. He was five years her junior and quite attractive. Normally, she would have invited him in. For once, she decided to husband her energies.

She had insisted on arranging the governor's short flight from San Juan Airport through the intraisland charter line. She knew that he was to arrive at four-thirty. She took off her makeup, drowned herself in cream, took a Seconal, and set the alarm for three.

She awoke to the insistent buzzing with eight hours sleep under her belt. She washed and checked to see that her legs and bikini line had been properly waxed at Gerard Bolet. Satisfied, she put up her hair, oiled herself till she had just the degree of glow, then slipped naked onto the patio, and lay face up in the sun.

It was an exercise in self-restraint for her to remain motionless, her pupils staring under the lavender plastic eyeshades, as she heard the doors of the semidetached suite which shared her bungalow open and shut as the new guest was installed by the staff.

There was a brief moment of concern when she heard two pairs of feet in heavy shoes grind sand into the concrete of the deck. The two security men grunted to each other in Spanish and went inside satisfied that she was not concealing a weapon.

She had lain stock still, pretending to herself to be blind, and trying to accustom herself to the world of darkness, when she heard a surprised voice say, "Damn. Excuse me."

She reached up casually, as she had practiced in her mind, and took off the blinkers. Leaning on one elbow, she looked across the patio into the shadow of the sliding door. "For what, governor? Welcome to Dorado."

Of course, Bernie Cohen hadn't been there, and Paul Curtin was one place removed from Bernie, but Frank O'Neil swore to everybody that that was what Andrea Beldon had said.

The rest of the story was prosaic enough. Frank O'Neil had been a vigorous and handsome fiftyish widower. She was a divorcee lying naked in the tropical sunshine. According to the apocrypha, O'Neil came back to New York white as a sheet, having gone swimming once and having played nine holes of golf.

From there, Paul thought to himself, it had been all downhill. She called persistently at his office, invited him to endless affairs, none of which he attended, and referred to his stay in her bed as "our tropic idyll" for weeks at lunches on the banquettes of Caravelle, La Grenouille, and Lutèce.

As time passed, and her fantasy diverged farther from the

reality, Andrea slipped a paragraph into one of Pierre Du Fresne's columns suggesting that the governor was about to make a very important announcement regarding Andrea Beldon.

When it was brought to the governor's attention, he called Du Fresne on the phone.

"Where did you get this tidbit?"

Du Fresne stuttered and blustered.

"You didn't place it, did you?" O'Neil said, suddenly getting the idea.

"No," he admitted.

"Can you say that it was a misprint?"

"Not if I wish to remain employed," Du Fresne said bleakly. "I'm terribly embarrassed."

"Don't you worry about it. I'll take care of it."

Three days later, Suzy Knickerbocker, venom all but obscuring the print, gleefully revealed that the daughter of the publisher of one of New York's newspapers (naturally one couldn't mention names) had made herself a colossal nuisance at the State House. Despite repeated rejections, she had thrown herself at the governor, who had expressed his frustration to close friends in an effort to find a gentlemanly way to explain that a one-week stand is not a proposal.

Paul had dug the story out of the file. It was the work of a professional. Lucretia Borgia would have been put to shame.

So was Andrea Beldon. And so was her mother.

Melanie herself avoided social gatherings for six months. Andrea Beldon, a recluse from unkind laughter, left the *Advocate* and her New York apartment. Her divorce from Nelson Beldon became final. She put her children in boarding school in Switzerland, then bought a house in Puerto Vallarta, another one in Portman Square in London, and spent the next six years globe-trotting and spending lavishly of the income of her trust funds.

Her hegira was laid bitterly at the feet of Frank O'Neil. Right or wrong, blood is blood. Melanie Parsons never forgave and never forgot. And as she got older, even her admirers wondered if her animus didn't distort her actions and her judgment.

Finally, terminally bored, Andrea Beldon had returned to New York six months ago, reputedly interested in making another go with the *Advocate*.

Maryanne Middleton returned from the dressing room with a smile and the Perry Ellis dress.

"It fits you very well, indeed," Paul said appreciatively. "Do you like it?"

"I love it. May I have it?"

Paul smiled at the saleswoman. "Give me the bad news."

She looked at him with satisfaction. "I was sure you would be pleased. The dress is really her." She sat down at the table and began to write on her billing pad. "Will this be a send?"

"Oh no," Maryanne said. "I think I'll wear it out. You can pack my skirt and sweater."

Paul scanned the bill, wrote a check, and handed it over with his driver's license. The saleslady was back in a minute with a shopping bag.

"Thank you, sir." She handed back his identification. "And thank you, madam."

With the transaction complete, Paul rose to leave. A little unsure, he bowed his head politely in the direction of Mrs. Parsons. She raised her hand and beckoned to him.

Taking Maryanne firmly by the hand, he crossed the floor to her. "Good morning, Mrs. Parsons. Do you know Mrs. Middleton?"

"I don't believe we've been introduced." She extended a gloved hand. "I was afraid that you were going to leave without saying hello. You do know Mrs. Beldon?"

"Of course. Good morning, Mrs. Beldon."

Andrea Beldon brushed the hair away from her face and looked squarely at Paul. After an uncomfortable moment she said, "I've seen Paul around the office. It's good to have a man around at a time like this." She spun in the blue dress, coming to a stop a foot from him. "Do you think I should take this one?"

"You look lovely in all of them."

"Oh? Have you been watching?"

"I was sitting across the floor."

Andrea Beldon turned and snapped her fingers at a saleswoman, who moved quickly to her side. "The gentleman likes them." She looked around at the dresses draped over the couch and chairs. "I'll take them. Have them sent." She turned in front of Paul, giving him her backlit profile.

"I'm looking forward to seeing you in the office Monday,

Paul," Melanie said. "I trust that you've been using your time to good advantage."

He smiled easily. "I can't imagine a better way. I believe we have something to discuss."

"How nice. I'll see you then. Good-bye, Mrs. Middleton," Melanie said formally. "It was nice to meet you."

"Bye, Paul," Andrea Beldon said. "Thanks for the help. I'll see you at the office."

Paul and Maryanne didn't talk again until they were on the street. Paul cleared his throat. "A little awkward."

"You could say that," Maryanne replied acidly. "Just don't ever tell me that you are staying late at the office if Andrea Beldon is in town."

25

"Shit," Frank O'Neil said distinctly. He looked up in despair at Florence Gable, his secretary of twenty-five years.

"I'll deal with her. You take the phone," Florence said, sensing that he wanted a suggestion. He nodded agreement, and she walked out to her office. They'd come in Saturday morning to try to reduce the staggering pile of mail that had accumulated over a week split between Albany and New York. It was always hell during legislative sessions. And now, Allison had appeared unannounced, and the governor's twenty-six-year-old second son, Jack, was on the phone from Boise.

"Can you take a seat for a moment, Mrs. Forrestiere? Let me take your coat. I'll get you a cup of coffee." Florence took the coat and looked pointedly at the light on the call director. Then she winked. "A caller from the West." She left Allison in her wake, half-convinced that it was the Western White House.

"How are you, Jack?" the governor asked. "And Ellen and the children? Can Timmy talk yet?"

"C'mon, Pop. One question at a time. Everybody's fine. How the hell are you?"

"Never better."

"Dad." There was a pause. Frank O'Neil smiled. How much? he wondered. "I've got some terrific news. I've got a new job. In New York."

Frank beamed. Jack favored Mary the most, with his turned-up nose and blue eyes. He was an architect, two years out of Yale Graduate School. He had started his apprenticeship with a builder of ski resort condos and hotels in Idaho. "That's wonderful. Let's have some details. Where? When? With whom?"

"Would you believe I. M. Pei?"

"No. Fantastic."

"I need a little advice . . . and maybe more."

"Talk."

"It's like his, Governor." That sounds serious, Frank thought. "He's offered me $35,000. That's pretty good for a third-year apprentice. Assuming I don't muff the chance, it will end up at $50,000 by the third or fourth year. The problem is that I am going to have to work my ass off, Pop. If I want to make it, I'm going to have to put in a lot of twelve-hour days and plenty of weekend work. That's what it takes to make it in New York. If I don't like it, there's a list a mile long of guys who would be glad to have the chance."

"So? You're not afraid of a little work, are you, Irish?"

"Not at all. But I am afraid that if I get a nice little house in the suburbs and leave at five-thirty every morning and come home at ten o'clock every night that I am going to end up with no marriage. And I don't know if I can afford the city with a wife and two kids on my starting salary. What do you think?"

"Not easily. Not Manhattan for sure." Frank O'Neil already had jumped his son three moves. Perspiration began to appear at his hairline.

"That's what I thought. I hate like hell to ask, Pop, but do you think . . ."

"That I could help you out for a while till you get over the hump."

There was an embarrassed silence. "In so many words."

O'Neil licked his lips, trying to calculate in his head.

"Look, Pop," Jack's voice was earnest at the other end, "if you can't, you can't. We'll figure out something."

"No, Jack. Don't you worry about it. You take the job, son. Dad will work it out."

"I love you, Pop."

"Yeah. Yeah. I'll bet you tell that to all the governors. I love you, too, Irish. Call me when you get the details straight and we'll find a place for you to hang your pajamas. When do you think you'll be in?"

"I'm supposed to tell them yes or no on Monday. Maybe I'll be in the week after." There was happy laughter in his voice. "Thanks, Pop. You never let me down."

"Love to you all, son."

The phone went dead in Governor O'Neil's hand. Jesus Christ Almighty, what have I gone and done now? he thought. That's another thousand a month, or maybe fifteen hundred to make up what the kid can pay for rent and what it'll cost for two bedrooms in Manhattan. The shoe box he received from Hawkes contained twenty-five thousand dollars. That was enough to pay off some of his overdue bills and to cover out of pocket expenses that couldn't be traced by the IRS when paid in cash: restaurants, theater tickets, department store purchases, even some of the food for the house. The allowances that he gave to four of his eight children were in cash. The presents that he bought for Allison. He got a shoe box like that every sixty days. Over the two years of Uhuru Towers construction he would get about $300,000 in unmarked bills. By then, please God, he would have married Allie, and the problem would have been laid to rest. In the meantime, Hawkes had been his salvation. He had been flat broke when he met him and had borrowed to the hilt on every asset. The rising curve of interest rates had done him a greater disservice than his constituents. You can't act the part of the governor of the state of New York on eighty-five thousand a year, perks or no perks. And it wasn't as though he'd dipped into the public till to feather his nest. There'd be a little spillage, that's all. And adding Jack's problem to his own list of woes, Frank thought, even with the graft from Hawkes, he'd be lucky to break even.

Governor O'Neil listened to the click on the other end of the line and reached forward to hang up his receiver. Instead he jiggled the hook till he had a dial tone and composed his brother's private number at O'Neil Maritime and Fuel.

The phone rang a half dozen times, then was picked up, and after a pause, a high nervous voice answered, "O'Neil."

"Dennis, it's Frank. You took awhile. I thought you were in the country."

"No. No, Frank. I was here. I was on the couch, reading. I sent Corinne out with Billy. I just have too much to do to get away this weekend." He stopped talking and waited. The governor could hear his shallow breathing on the other end of the line.

"How's business, Dennis?"

"Not very good, Frank."

"I'm sorry to hear that." Talking business to his elder brother had become awkward over the past several years. "Dennis, what about the year-end dividend? We're in mid-February."

"I'm not a hundred percent sure, Frank."

"Sure of what?" The governor's voice took on a slight edge. "I need some money, Dennis. Jack is coming back from Boise. He's got a job here with I. M. Pei."

"That's great, Frank."

"Yes. But he needs a little help. He's probably going to need it for a couple of years. I want to know how much I can expect from the Christmas dividends, Dennis. I want to take that money and put Jack on the payroll as a consultant."

"I . . . I can't do that."

"Why not? Just don't pay dividends on the C stock. I'm the only one who owns it."

"I just can't." Dennis O'Neil's voice rose a half octave. "There aren't going to be any year-end dividends this year."

"And how is that?" the governor asked coldly.

"We're in to the Chase for a ton. Until the refinery starts to make money again, they won't let us take out a cent."

"Does that include your salary, and Billy's?"

"Goddamn it, Frank. We work here. If there's a budget deficit next year, is the State Senate going to vote that you shouldn't get your salary?"

"The state of New York is operated for the common good of its citizens. It is my understand that O'Neil Maritime and Fuel is supposed to be run for the benefit of its stockholders. All of them." Frank O'Neil literally bit his tongue as he finished the last sentence. His lips twitched in reaction to the pain and the slightly salty taste of his own blood. What the hell could Dennis do? He wasn't terribly good at being the president of the company. From the time of the first Arab oil embargo the company's refining business had been adversely affected by declining profit margins as feedstock costs skyrocketed and customers cut back. More and more residential consumers switched to natural gas. The delivery business slowed down. As the unions strangled New York Harbor, the tug business became less and less profitable. The dividends on which Clan O'Neil depended so heavily began to diminish. Jesus Christ, the governor wanted to scream into the phone, what are you doing with my birthright, you fool? I need the money! Instead, hearing the soft sobbing at the other end of the phone, the governor swallowed. "All right, Denny lad. I know you can't help it."

"I've done what I can, Frank. I haven't your gifts." He coughed, muffling the sound with his hand over the receiver. "I'm really sorry, Frank. God, I wish you could get in here and help me."

"But I can't, Denny. We both know that. My position won't permit it. I've pulled what strings I can. I thought the new fellow you hired last year would help a lot."

"He does, Frank. But, God, it's hard. It's just that the business isn't the same. I . . ." There was more coughing.

"Take a nitroglycerine, Denny," Frank said, his voice laden with concern. What the hell had he called for in the first place? In time, the new executive that had been hired from a major oil company might be able to stem the effects of mismanagement and plain bad luck. For the moment it seemed that the O'Neil family would be lucky if their assets weren't eaten up by losses. Calling his weak older brother and aggravating his angina were not practical answers to Frank O'Neil's personal problems. He'd have to work them out some other way.

"I took the pill, Frank. I feel much better."

"Good, Denny. Listen, you take care of yourself. When you get the year-end figures together, let me see them. I might have an idea or two. Best to the family."

"You too, Frank. I'd love to get together real soon. And, Frank, I'm sorry I can't be more help."

"Real soon, Denny. It's all right." The governor lowered the phone to its cradle. Real soon. They had seen each other at the ritual Christmas party. It must have been six months before that.

O'Neil rose and walked to the door in the corner of his office that led to his private bathroom, complete with stall shower. A massage table rested folded against one marble wall. It hadn't been used in months. O'Neil missed the regular sessions.

He took off his coat and hung it on a hanger, then brushed it off. He ran a comb through his thick hair, straightened his tie, and splashed his face with eau de cologne. He replaced the jacket and checked himself over in the full-length mirror.

He sat at his desk, pushing the papers before him into a neat pile, and reached out to press the intercom button.

"Yes, Governor."

"Flo, would you show Mrs. Forrestiere in, please."

When she had closed the door behind her, Frank O'Neil got up from behind his desk and opened his arms. Allison walked to him and turned her face to avoid smudging her makeup. He took her chin in his hand and straightened it, looking directly into her eyes. "None of that, now." He felt the shiver run through her body. She opened her mouth as he leaned to press his lips against hers. He felt her breasts beneath the silk of her dress.

She leaned against him with her head against his chest. He felt very tired.

"I dropped in, in the hope that you wouldn't be too busy. Would you like to take me out to lunch?" She stepped back from him and wiped his lips. "You're going to have to go to the john and wash your face. I must look a mess."

"Not to me, you don't."

"You'll never guess who I saw this morning as I was coming out of Bendel's; Melanie Parsons and her horrid daughter, Andrea. They looked a fright. The old bag must be a hundred." She walked past him into the bathroom, prattling as she redid her face. He looked down at the stack of papers and weighed their relative importance.

He pushed the intercom button and said, "Flo, can you clean up when I leave? I'll be taking Mrs. Forrestiere out to lunch."

26

George Gaines was driven to the airport by two young men. Despite the cold, they both wore brightly colored African shirts made of cotton over blue jeans. Their hair was wound into serpentine coils. Though neither of them was smoking, the pervasive odor of marijuana hung in the car.

One of them pulled the car to the door of the Eastern terminal. The other got off with Gaines and carried his two bags directly to the check-in counter, circumventing the skycap on the sidewalk.

"First class to St. Petersburg, please. The name is Gaines."

He licked his lips and watched nervously as ten days' summer wardrobe and two million dollars in small unmarked bills slipped away on the rubber conveyor belt.

Gaines went up to the plane, stretched out in his seat, and drank his champagne, wondering for the tenth time whether the risk was greater that the suitcase full of money would be lost in transit or opened at the security check before boarding. In any case, since Marcus had said check it, that was what he had done.

The Hawkes family had provided a more secure atmosphere for its growing sons than George Gaines had enjoyed. It had permitted Marcus to get the elements of an education, of which George was deprived.

After Jeremy Gaines fled from New York to the land of his birth, his son George had been without a father. His brothers had died of disease and poverty. His mother was turned into a stooped crone, eking out a living on worn knees.

Gaines had been born five years after Marcus Hawkes, and was only ten when the change in circumstances cast him into the streets of New York, virtually on his own, often with an empty stomach. In school he became a discipline problem as he used his comparative size and strength to steal food and money from his better-heeled classmates. By the time he was fifteen, he was the size of a man. Each week, a new gas station attendant or storekeeper somewhere in the city learned to fear him. His first big score was made with the cooperation of a pretty blonde whore in her mid-twenties, whose scrawny middle-aged mulatto pimp had taken to beating her beyond the limit common to such arrangements.

George Gaines shifted lithely in his seat on the plane to St. Petersburg and motioned to the stewardess for another glass of champagne. He smiled as he watched the sparkling liquid trickle into his glass.

The blonde whore had initiated George Gaines into the joys and mysteries of sex with pleasure, combining as he did the endowment of Atlas, the exuberance of youth, and the patience of Job. He broke the pimp's back, leaving him a quadraplegic in a garbage-filled alley. They split his two-thousand-dollar bankroll and the two hundred they got from a fence for his watch, cuff links, and belt buckle.

When she left him after six months for a more stable life, he approached his father's old friends among the Rastafarian community.

In 1946 a teacher caught him dispensing ceremonial herb in the lavatory during lunch break. After the beating George gave him, the teacher required a week's hospitalization. To avoid the certainty of reform school, he slipped onto a cargo ship with the aid of the Rastas, and bribed a crewman to feed and hide him during the six-day crossing to Jamaica. He slipped over the side and swam ashore outside Kingston harbor with nothing but the sopping clothes on his back and a hundred dollars.

He found that his father's arrival from New York six years earlier had coincided with the release of a Rastafarian preacher named L. P. Howell from the insane asylum where the colonial police had placed him. Using donations gathered from the faithful, Howell bought the Pinnacle, an ancient ramshackle plantation high in the Jamaican mountains, and designated himself the Viceroy of Haile Selassie on the island. With a thousand followers, among whom Jeremy Gaines had hidden, he withdrew from civilization, and there George found his father.

Howell's orthodoxy had slid toward violence, teaching that

purification would only come after the white man had been driven from the earth, and all blacks accepted Jah, the Rastafarian name for their God, even if they needed to be proselytized by force. The faithful began to raid their neighbors, burning out the whites, converting the blacks, and stealing indiscriminately from both.

Jeremy Gaines nonetheless prodded Howell, whom he saw as complaisant and forbearing. Wreathed in a cloud of marijuana smoke for all of his waking hours, he was given to visions and violent temper tantrums. He walked about in a loincloth with a graying beard that flowed almost to his waist and long plaited hair, swaying and chanting, frightening even to his own kind.

George Gaines had grown tall and powerful, but he reasoned that if the brethren of the Pinnacle continued to raid their neighbors, they were sure to call down the wrath of the British government upon themselves. His father was the first to denounce him.

He was thrown bodily through the gate with his few belongings. He gathered them together and walked down the road toward Kingston. Once there, in his tatters and dreadlocks he bumped white people from the sidewalks, calling them buckra and pussy clots as he shouldered them aside. They called him rude boy.

Late in the afternoon of his first day, three policemen apprehended him and pulled him into an alley off Bay Street. Two of them forced him to his knees and held him while the third beat his back with a rubber truncheon until he fainted. They they turned him over and beat his chest and arms. Then they kicked him awake and warned him against further rudeness. He lay against the wall of a tin shack in a Rasta slum for three days, barely able to move.

The following day, he went to a barbershop and had his locks shorn to a tight cap of curls. He spent three hours in a steambath cleansing his very pores. He bought some colorful sports clothes and began to hang around the dock where the rich white tourists came to charter day fishermen or sailboats to the outlying cays. In a month, he was taken out by half a dozen lone woman who would never tell their husbands what they had done during their outing.

With some cash in his pockets, he soon attracted two teenage whores, and in two more months, he had enough to fly back to New York. As a juvenile offender, he had no police record. He showed his birth certificate to the customs agent, and took a cab to his mother's tenement apartment.

Decent work was still scarce if you were black. He nosed around in the Jamaican community of Brooklyn and got a job as a day laborer. He showed himself to be handy with his fists. He was put on as a supervisor by a small black construction company, as a motivator for the crew.

One day he quit and went to the competition. "I want to buy in," he said.

"What can you do, boy? I don't need no partner." His accent was thick as molasses. White bristles quivered on chocolate jowls. He held his hands folded over the checkerboard shirt that covered his paunch.

"You got a lot of business?" Gaines asked.

"As much as you can get fixin' up people's old houses in Harlem. Every now and then some old Jew boy wants to get his tenement fixed cheap, he'll look me up. I ain't union. I'm a old colored man. That's the kind of work I'm going to get."

"Have you got all of the business from the colored?"

"Naw. There's plenty of others scratching around just like me. No unions. No big jobs. Good thing that there's barely enough little shit to go around."

Gaines gave the man an envelope. He looked through it.

"Shit," he said. "Shit. Three thousand cash. What do you want me to do with that? Buy the Chrysler Building?"

"I'll make you a deal. You teach me the business, and I'll show you how to turn that three thousand bucks into big money. And you've got no risk, cause it's my three thousand."

"How do you expect to get paid?" the old mason asked, scratching his stubble and eyeing Gaines suspiciously.

"A dollar an hour. But if it works, in six months I get half of the business. Is it a deal?" Gaines stuck out his hand.

The man hesitated. "What do you mean if it works?"

"If the business hasn't doubled in six months, I quit, and you get to keep the three grand."

The man took Gaines's hand.

George Gaines used the cash to bride building inspectors and cops, buying closed eyes to work illegally on holidays and Sundays. He paid bonuses to the skilled workmen of other small contractors, either to join him or to sabotage their work. The edge made a difference. In six months the business had not doubled, but quadrupled.

It took two years for Gaines to learn the masonry trade to the level of his partner's skills. Three months later, the old man slipped on a scaffold and plunged to his death on a Harlem sidewalk. His widow sold his share of the business to Gaines for a pittance.

Gaines moved uncomfortably in his plush seat and glanced down at the colorless winter landscape beneath the plane. That year had been both a beginning and an end. Shortly after his partner's death, the Jamaican police, pushed beyond their endurance, raided the Pinnacle. Only one Rastafarian was killed. A crazy old man in a lioncloth and beard had charged the assistant commissioner's car, carrying a banner with a portrait of Haile Selassie in one hand and brandishing a spear in the other. He had badly wounded an officer before they shot him dead.

George Gaines never slept a night that he did not dream of his father falling in a hail of bullets, waving a banner of Jah.

The memorial service had been held at the Rastafarian Temple in Brooklyn. Among the few mourners were a slender graying old man and his two incongruously fat sons. It had been years since George Gaines and Marcus Hawkes had met. After the service had ended, Phineas Hawkes took Jeremy Gaines's widow home, leaving their sons to become reacquainted.

Gaines tightened the seat belt and pulled himself into an upright position as the plane took a pass over Tampa Bay and turned to land at St. Petersburg Airport. Marcus was a great maker of speeches and promises and a great theorizer. He had always told George that it was his aim that the earnings and assets of black Americans be in proportion to their percentage of the population.

Gaines smiled. It was possible that once Marcus Garvey Hawkes had believed in the causes that he championed or invented, just as Gaines had believed back in the mists of time in the holiness of Jah. For George Gaines the Rastafarian movement had become nothing more than a source of muscle and a pipeline for his sidelines in the marijuana traffic and prostitution. He had long shed the glassy stare and the dreadlocks, convincing his brothers that his conventional appearance provided them with a necessary channel to the nonbelieving world. Because he made sure that everyone profited with him, his explanations were accepted, along with his life-style. He had come to occupy the position of elder statesman and mediator, as the influx of Jamaicans after the war enlarged the community greatly. With the expanded market for their products and services, the various Rastafarian bands began to vie for power and territory. Not infrequently, the struggles ended in death. But because their violence was largely restricted to their own kind, the New York police tended to let them sort out their problems among themselves. That attitude provided immunity for much of George Gaines's illicit activity.

Marcus Hawkes had chosen another path. He had become estranged from his roots. Though he wore a Jamaican flag in his buttonhole, he had made his place in the Harlem of the southern Negro migrant, stumping the black community like an itinerant preacher. He had been gifted with a glib tongue and a resonant voice. He used his wiles and his popular political sentiments to gain entry to legitimate black enterprises, and without investing anything but hot air, often was able to make off with a profit.

Gaines smiled in appreciation of his skills. He had no complaints with his partnership with Marcus. They'd augmented their small contracting business with theft and fraudulent bankruptcy and acquired decent homes far from the communities that they had fleeced. But there had been no cushion, no security. Till now. Till Uhuru.

Gaines thanked the stewardess as he walked to the gangway. He blinked in the unaccustomed Florida sunshine and opened his jacket in its heat as he hurried across the runway to the baggage claim area. He paced back and forth in front of the conveyor belt for ten minutes as the plane was unloaded. He put his hand in his pocket and fingered the two tightly rolled marijuana cigarettes which had been pressed upon him as a gift by his chauffeur. He was almost tempted.

With great relief, he reached out and pulled the two bags from the line, hefting them to reassure himself, then checking the locks.

"Boy," he called out to an elderly Negro with a handtruck, "take my bags to Red Carpet Flying Services."

* * *

At the same time, Marcus Hawkes stood on the porch of his house and waved with his right hand at the car pulling out of the driveway. His wife and two children waved back. He thought enviously of George Gaines comfortabaly ensconced in the warmth of the Caribbean. His left hand was stuffed into his pants pocket against the winter cold. He shuddered and turned hurriedly through the door.

When he was sure that his family was well gone on their expedition to the steep hill in the town park with their sleds, he double-locked the front door from the inside, then crossed the house, locked the back, and descended to the basement.

A single bulb flickered on in a ceiling fixture, throwing shadowy light on the roaring gas-fired boiler and the gleaming cylinder of the hot water heater. He edged between them, holding his stomach. Once through the crevasse, a space of three feet existed between the machinery and the wall. A camp stool leaned precariously in a corner.

Hawkes took a penknife from his pocket and sat on the stool facing the wall. He pivoted a cement block silently out of the way. A steel box rested in a metal sheathed compartment. He worked the combination then pulled up the hinged lid. A 9 mm pistol glinted dully in the half light. He undid the buckle of his wide belt. The zippered compartment inside of the belt contained ten thousand dollars in hundred-dollar bills. In addition, there was a small package of tissues. He opened it and looked with wonder at the brilliant stones. Carefully, he extracted a leather pouch from the box and loosened its top. He rolled the gems, all between one and two carats and of finest quality and color, into the pouch with the rest of his collection. He added the hundreds to one of the thick stacks in rubber bands at the back of the box. He hefted the pouch again. It never failed to amuse him that something so compact could be so valuable. Carefully chosen for consistency of quality and relatively small size for easy convertibility, the pouch contained about four-million-dollars' worth of gemstones.

He put the pouch back and pulled out a white plastic travel envelope. It contained a passport, a one-way ticket for one to São Paulo, Brazil, and some accounting records.

In addition, there were a dozen cash requisition forms to draw on funds of the state of New York for building materials.

They were made out in blank to the Gaines Masonry Corporation, and countersigned by the governor; some by hand, and some by the carefully guarded machine which reproduces the signature and simultaneously embosses it with the Great Seal of the state.

Hawkes looked critically at the stacks of bills. He always kept a reserve for his own needs, but beyond that, by the beginning of the next month he had to have enough to fill a shoe box for Frank O'Neil.

He felt better about his relationship with Chris Greene. He sensed something akin to a tingle in his fingers as he scanned the accounting sheets and memoranda that bore undeniable witness to the mayor's knowledge and complicity in the systematic misappropriation of funds from the Uhuru Towers project. It was just as binding as his relationship with O'Neil, Hawkes thought, and a damn sight cheaper.

Hawkes replaced the papers in the envelope and put it in the box. He occasionally felt a twinge of regret about leaving his wife and children, but the house was in her name and he'd seen to it that there would be some money in the bank. He shrugged. They'd make out. With the cost of living being what it was in Brazil, he'd be set to live like a king for the rest of his life.

After replacing the cinder block, Hawkes pushed himself upright again, kicked the stool into its corner, and squeezed himself through the gap. He retraced his steps to the ground floor, put on his coat, and went for a walk, whistling and waving to his neighbors.

Of the numerous ways to get from the United States to the Cayman Islands, Gaines had chosen Red Carpet Flying Services, unencumbered as it was by computerized passenger lists and the keeping of records.

The small turbo-powered plane took twice as long to cover the five hundred miles as a scheduled jet would have, and its more pronounced reactions to gusts of air gave Gaines moments of concern. He considered his discomfort a reasonable price for relative anonymity and his proximity to his baggage, which he had placed aboard with his own hands and which he would unload the same way.

The entry formalities were minimal. No visa is required of

holders of American passports. Customs examination was a smile and a wave of the hand.

Carrying his two bags, George Gaines looked about the neat small lobby. A cadaverously thin man in a tropical suit with Bermuda shorts stood at parade rest near a small lectern marked Special Customs.

"Mr. Gaines," he said, extending his hand to help with the luggage as he strode forward. "I'm Arthur Watley, with the Bank of Cayman."

Gaines hesitated a moment, pulling the money-filled suitcase protectively against his leg. He looked into the watery blue eyes above the long nose and drooping blond moustache and relaxed.

"Warm, isn't it?" Watley said, as they walked under the slowly turning ceiling fan and out into the Caribbean sunset. "It isn't usually this warm this late in the day."

Gaines resisted the temptation to hurdle the small talk and nodded as the man prattled on in an English accent. He dropped Gaines's bags into the trunk of his old Morris and held the door for him.

When they pulled out into the road, Gaines said, "Where are we going? I hate to keep this bag with me."

"Oh, we're going straight to the bank, Mr. Gaines."

"On a Sunday night?"

Watley smiled. "In the Caymans, Mr. Gaines, our banking community is in the habit of making unusual arrangements for its clients. We provide whatever service may be necessary. There is no reason for you to be inconvenienced in a transaction of this size."

Gaines sat back and watched the palm trees go by till they entered the outskirts of George Town, where twelve thousand of the Cayman Islands' fourteen thousand inhabitants live. He put his hand to his mouth to stifle a yawn. Whatever quaintness the town may have had once was submerged in the airy neatness of the five-story bank building erected along Edward Street since the passage of the Trust Company Act of 1966.

Watley pulled his car around to the rear of the Bank of Cayman Building and led Gaines, who insisted on carrying his case himself, to the back door, where two uniformed guards waited. Another Englishman in a white suit sat at a desk in front of an enormous safe reading a newspaper.

"Mr. Gaines," Watley said, "this is Alfred Jocelyn, one of my coworkers."

Jocelyn extended his hand and indicated the two chairs in front of the desk. "Please, gentlemen, sit down. Mr. Gaines," he said, pushing a printed form toward him, "the formalities will only take a moment."

Gaines scanned the form quickly. It provided for the deposit of the money in the unnamed, numbered account which he and Marcus Hawkes had opened for the purpose. He filled it in and signed the bottom line. He was given a conformed copy signed by the two bank officers. He watched as first Jocelyn, then Watley counted the money twice each. When they were done, Jocelyn impressed the paper with a seal.

On the return trip to the car, Gaines permitted Watley to carry the empty suitcase.

"I'm sure that you'll enjoy the West Indian Club, Mr. Gaines," Watley said. "It combines quality with discretion. There are only nine apartments. No lobby. No bar. The maid will cook for you if you wish."

When Gaines had seen Watley safely out of the door, he unpacked his bags and placed the receipt for the deposit in a stamped envelope addressed to a post office box in Ocho Rios, Jamaica. Leaving the door on the latch, he stepped out into the gathering dusk and dropped the envelope into a mailbox in front of the club's main door.

When he returned to the apartment, a West Indian maid wearing a colorful kerchief and a white uniform was turning down his bed. She started when he appeared at the door, then smiled and said, "Can I do something for you, sir?"

Half an hour later, she lay on her back holding her thighs in her hands to keep her legs in the air as George Gaines made deep thrusting motions above her. Her white uniform was strewn across the couch. Perspiration ran from under her kerchief as she pushed against him, grunting with pleasure, eyes closed, mouth open.

Arthur George Watley was sitting on the veranda of his neat white cottage at the other end of Seven Mile Beach. He took a long satisfied sip from his frosted gin and tonic. He put his hand in his jacket pocket and rolled the three small stones he had received in the parcel between his thumb and forefinger. They had been posted to him as a gift by Marcus Hawkes. It

was odd, Watley thought, that gems don't seem to acquire the
repugnant cold of other stones. When touched, they seem to
absorb and reflect human warmth.

He tried to consider what he had done in an objective light.
An account had been opened at the bank by two gentlemen
with a considerable cash deposit in American dollars. At their
request, no statement of the account was rendered, other than
the deposit receipts which were provided as a matter of course.
Since it was a safekeeping account, no interest was paid,
therefore minimizing the records.

Each of the signatories to the account had joint and several
control over the funds. He had simply followed instructions.
As after the first deposit, Arthur Watley had transferred 90
percent of the money out of the joint account immediately after
the two millions dollars had been put in, and depsoited it in the
National Cayman Bank, across the street, in another anonymous numbered account under the sole control of Marcus
Garvey Hawkes.

He took another swig. And he, Arthur Watley, was completely covered. In the same package as the diamonds, he had
received a letter of instructions with a signature guaranteed by
a large New York bank. He rattled the diamonds together
again. All he had done, in accord with his side agreement with
Marcus Hawkes, was to keep this perfectly legal transaction to
himself. He leaned back in the rattan chair, put his feet up on
the balustrade, and watched the yellow moon rise above the
Caribbean.

27

Paul hunched his shoulders against the wind and pulled up
the zipper of his leather jacket, then tugged the cuffs of his
gloves so that they covered the ends of his sleeves. He trotted a
couple of steps to catch up with Maryanne as she walked across

the playground at the end of Long Beach. He gave her his arm as she climbed over the low fence, hopped it, and walked beside her on the sand toward the rolling breakers of the Atlantic Ocean.

"It's so different from the Sound," she said, looking across the gray water. "In the summer, when you look across from Connecticut, or back from Long Island, even if there's a storm, you get a sense of shelter—protection. But here on the other side of the island, even on the nicest day, you feel pretty feeble."

"Cheerful thought to top off a nice weekend."

She stopped and turned to face him. There was a wool cap pulled down over her forehead and a scarf wrapped around the lower part of her face so that her mouth was hidden. She stuck her gloved hands under the arms of her quilted down coat. "I have had the best weekend of my entire life."

He kissed the end of her nose. "So forget the angst and the smelly old ocean. We came out here for a walk and to go to Brown's." He turned back his glove and looked at his watch. "Which reminds me, didn't you tell Forrest to have the kids back anytime after six? It's four o'clock, and it's an hour back to town."

She turned toward the sea again. "Can we walk a little farther?"

"Sure. I'll tell you what. Let's walk to Brown's and buy the lobsters, and then we can come back while they steam them."

She nodded and followed him back to the road. In a couple of silent minutes they stood in front of the lobster dock. A tall teenager with an Irish face led them into the storehouse of metal tubs with the sound of aerated seawater bubbling through them. They looked down to choose among the huddled crustaceans, moving like prehistoric monsters in slow motion across their crowded neighbors.

"A one and a half, a two and a half, and two fives," Paul said.

"Five? You're nuts," Maryanne said.

When the kid dug after the lobsters Paul said, "Cool it. You'll need the strength." He walked after the young man who had dumped the lobsters into a pan and was putting it on a scale. He gave Paul a price. "Okay, mister?"

"Steam 'em. And pack up five pounds of steamers to go with."

"Okay. Figure forty minutes."

"Perfect. Let's go, toots." When they hit the beach again he said, "Are you crying?"

"Uh-huh."

"Why?"

"I've had a very nice weekend."

"I'm glad it wasn't any better. I might have to pull your head out of the oven and turn off the gas. There will be lots of other weekends."

"Will there really?" She wiped at her nose with the back of her glove. She dug into the damp sand with the toe of her boot. "What are you going to do, Paul?"

"I don't know, babe. I don't want to lie."

"You had a good weekend, didn't you?"

"Why ask?" he put his hand on her shoulder. "It was better than a three-month vacation in Tahiti."

"Has it changed anything?"

He kissed her forehead. "Are you asking me if I know what I want to be when I grow up?" When she didn't answer, he put his arm around her waist and walked her up the beach. "How much choice do I really have? I need money from somewhere to take care of my boy. I suppose I have a better deal than anybody has a right to expect. But I don't like what I do. And I'm afraid I'm going to find myself sitting under a lap robe in a wheelchair at the age of eighty-six and wondering why I feel like I'm checking out without ever having checked in."

"And me and the kids? Where do we fit in this somber picture. I told you, I'm ready for anything from Scarsdale to Centralia, Illinois. But I want the feeling that you're not just bitching or running. I want to know that you're taking hold."

Guilt prompted a burst of bad temper. "So tell me what you want me to do. Tell me what's going to make this fucking city any more palatable. Or better yet, Melanie Parsons?"

"What does this have to do with them? They're circumstances in your life. This weekend was a circumstance in your life. But just because flowers smelled better for forty-eight hours, and you got laid three times a day doesn't change the fact that tomorrow is going to be Monday, and one set of circumstances will have changed back into another. And you still won't have decided—not what to do when you grow up—but if you're going to bother to grow up at all."

Paul shook his head and watched Maryanne run away across the sand and onto the road, then disappear around the corner toward Brown's Lobster Dock. He looked at his watch. It would be twenty minutes before the damn lobsters were cooked. He didn't know whether to run after her or not. He hesitated, then walked away down the beach. It had been the same with Faith, his first wife, after Jerry was born. He couldn't give her fixed answers, reasons why. She couldn't sustain life on her own strength, and he hadn't been able to share his effectively with her, and she'd gone off the deep end and died in a car wreck with another man under the influence of alcohol. Jerry was eighteen months old. Faith would have been twenty-six.

He still didn't have any answers.

As he turned back up the beach to get Maryanne, the sweetness of the weekend gone sour, he spotted her trotting across the road toward him. When she saw him, she took her hands from under her arms and began to run in earnest. When she got to him, her nose running and tears streaming down her cheeks, he wrapped his arms around her and hugged her to him. She tried to talk but the words strangled in her throat. He pushed her away and put his hand over her mouth.

"Listen. Quiet. Stop. Listen to me. When Jerry was born and we knew he was a Mongoloid," the word sounded like breaking glass in his ears, "Faith needed help. I just couldn't seem to give her enough. I was too aloof. Too cold. I don't know. It didn't seem to me I was those things. But that doesn't matter. She started to fuck around. In front of me, even. Anything to catch my attention. It was awful. I couldn't even get mad. She drank. She took a kid who worked in the gas station a few blocks away for a spin in her car. They were coming back from Lake Ponchartrain. They must have been fucking in the bushes. They were sloshed. Blind drunk. They missed a curve. She was decapitated." His throat hurt becaues he was screaming the words into the biting winter wind against the roar of the ocean and the pounding of his heart in his ears. "And I won a prize and a job groveling in the stench of New

Orleans corruption. And I came to Washington with my idiot son, and the vision of the headless body, and the distorted head rolled under a bush. And I love you to death and I don't know what the fuck to do." He shook her by the shoulders. Then screamed again at the top of his voice, "But I think I have a motherfucking idea. Now stop crying and let's get the lobsters."

They cried together silently all the way back to Brown's, then wiped their noses and took their lobsters home. On the way in to New York, they talked, and decided where, at least, they would begin.

The plates were cleaned and put away, and the children had subsided from the excitement of their weekend, their homecoming, and the lobster and gone to bed. Paul sat on the sofa with his feet up, a pad propped on his stomach. Maryanne sat cross-legged on the floor next to him, toying with a glass of beer.

He tried to solve the question of Uhuru Towers as a puzzle diagram, with the project as the central figure, radiating lines to various corollary squares and circles on the yellow paper. The information provided by Jeff Jackson's informant indicated that there was a fraud of magnitude at Uhuru Towers. Lloyd Gibbons may have been in a position to uncover or blow the whistle on the fraud. Ergo, he was murdered. Al Jenks worked on the same crew as Lloyd Gibbons, according to Gibbons's widow. It would make good sense to get in touch with Al Jenks. Only Al Jenks hasn't reported in to work in several days. A good reporter would take the next step—chase him down at home. Only, it seems that by coincidence, his house burned down, killing everybody in it. Logical conclusion: the informer is right. There is a scam big enough to have prompted the murder of two men on purpose, and maybe a couple of dozen more thrown in to the bargain at no extra charge.

Paul drew a line through the asymmetrical design. So much for logic. Now, on to proof. None. A rumor, given without evidence by an unnamed stranger leads me to believe . . . The pencil point broke. He dropped the pencil on the floor and took another one from the table.

What to do? If he went to the police with the evidence at hand, they might set someone to look at it. They might not. Without an investigation of Uhuru Towers, and some proof of fraud, the deaths could only be looked upon as coincidental in the absence of evidence of intent. If he went to the police with Jeff's informant, he was taking a chance on making himself an unintending accessory to his murder.

Assuming that the authorities were out of the picture, at least for the moment, how could he pursue the case if Melanie Powers kicked him out on his ass? Or gave him a new assignment? Either one of which was likely to happen unless he could buy time or attract her interest.

He looked down at Maryanne and suffered a chill. The stench of death, and the freshly turned memories of Vietnam made him suddenly conscious of his own mortality. To what degree did his involvement represent physical danger to Maryanne and the kids? He would not be the first reporter who had died with his nose in somebody else's business. He shuddered as he thought about poor Don Bolles, legless and bleeding to death in his bombed car in Phoenix, mumbling the name of a big businessman whose trail had grown too warm.

He put down the pad and the paper. "I'll try it the hard way. I'm just going to tell Melanie what I know—or almost all. I think that there's a fraud at Uhuru. I want to pursue it to the end. She gets O'Neil with his pants down. I get the time to get the whole story. And, I keep faith with Matt and Jeff by running down the informant's story, without risking his neck."

"And what about the Willie Avenue fire?"

Paul crumpled up the yellow sheet and threw it into the wastebasket. What he hadn't told Maryanne, she couldn't guess. And if she didn't know, it couldn't hurt her.

"That's another kettle of fish. One story at a time. I'll fit it in."

Maryanne wrinkled her nose. "I don't get it. I thought you saw some connection."

Paul patted her head. "It's a matter of priorities. It's my problem, anyway."

She looked at him, annoyed, and ducked the patronizing hand.

"Too complicated for a girl, huh? Well how about a problem that concerns us all? Now that we've decided to spend our lives together, where and how are we going to do it? Do you suppose you could put your great, big male brain to work on that?"

"It depends. If I can get some breathing room from the old bat . . ."

"Then maybe we'll stay in New York."

"Right. If she cans me, or busts my balls, we go."

"Together?" she insisted.

"The four of us. Together."

28

The relaxed mood that Oscar Bornstein had developed over the weekend by reading in front of the wood fire at his country house and playing tennis at the nearby covered courts was rapidly being dissipated in the course of his Monday morning discussion with Melanie. She had been none too satisfied with his reaction to her proposal on Friday night that Andrea join the board. While there had been a temporary change of subject, Oscar knew that it was merely a continuation of the same argument from a different tack.

She glared at him and said, "You still haven't come to grips with the question. How do we get Bergdorf and Saks to advertise in our paper?"

"We have talked this to death a thousand times. It isn't from want of trying, Mel. Face up to it. Change the readership to conform to their clientele and start publishing in the morning. Our paper comes out when the reading public is at work in their offices. Some of them pick the *Advocate* up and read it at lunchtime. But a lot of them carry it home on the train or the bus, not only out to the suburbs, but to Queens and Brooklyn, or wherever. Then it hits the trash bin, or sits with them in front of the television set. People don't buy our paper on the way to go shopping. And our profile reader doesn't shop the deluxe stores. Just be grateful we get the supermarkets and the discount stores."

"We're still the only real afternoon newspaper in the biggest market in America." She pouted, depressed.

"That doesn't change the purchasing patterns of our readership. We've tried to convince the big stores for years. They just point to the average income and education levels, and the discussion comes to a halt. And don't think that steady increases in line rates help, either."

"The *Times* raises theirs all the time."

"Are we the *Times*?"

Without looking up, she said, "I want to appoint Andrea to the board of directors."

Oscar shrugged, concealing his self-satisfaction. "It's a private corporation. You control the stock. The board, as it is now constituted, is just you, me, and Buddy. If you want Andrea on . . ."

She looked up sharply, irritated. "You know that's not what I mean. I want to put Andrea on the editorial board. And on the board of the *Advocate* itself, not of the holding company. I want her to be associate publisher. I'm thinking in terms of succession."

Oscar made no effort to hide his smile. "Thinking of stepping down, Mel?"

She tilted her chin in the air. "Certainly not. I'm going to be carried out of here. I just want to feel a sense of continuity."

"Buddy sits on the board. In time . . ."

Melanie folded her hands on the desk. "I think I'm hurt. I'm not used to your diddling the truth with me, Oscar." She leaned forward. "Oh, Buddy is a nice boy . . ." she laughed hoarsely. "There's your trouble, right there. Buddy is fifty-two years old and we think of him as a boy. He lacks the gusto, the—" she searched for the word, ". . . the balls for the job. I don't think that he has either the intestinal fortitude or the intellectual capacity to be the driving force behind a newspaper."

"And you think that Andrea has?"

She hesitated for an instant, then went on. "She has the drive. She can buy the rest. Just as I have."

"Do you want to cut Buddy out?"

"Certainly not. I've left his training to you. Perhaps he can run the business end of the paper. At least he might keep it afloat, if you don't die too soon. But he lacks passion, Oscar. He hasn't the fire or the political point of view."

"How do you know that Andrea will share your views? How

do you know that she won't turn the paper completely around?"

"You won't understand this, Oscar," she said leaning toward him, "not having children of your own, but we talk, Andrea and I, profoundly. And what I say sinks in. I know," she said with pride.

Oscar closed his mouth and averted his eyes. She had taken what he had said into consideration, thought about it over the weekend, and decided to do as she pleased. Well, it was her newspaper. He looked at his watch. It was nearly eleven. He would be relieved when Paul Curtin showed up, whatever the outcome.

When Madeleine buzzed to announce Curtin, Melanie perked up, patted her hair, and sat straight in her chair.

"Take a seat," she said, as he entered.

He was dressed in a sports coat and slacks with a white shirt and tie. He was carrying a manila envelope and a yellow pad. He crossed his legs and sat back against the chair.

"You look refreshed," she commented. "She seems very attractive, Mrs. Middleton."

"Oh, she is," he said, unperturbed. "We had a lovely weekend after we met you shopping."

"I would be pleased with anything that would provide you with a little inspiration. What have you got for me?"

Paul had made up his mind the previous evening to minimize Maryanne's exposure to whatever personal risks might arise from the case. At the same time, he had determined that to fend Melanie off, he would have to meet her head-on.

"I'd like to talk to you alone."

She pushed back in her chair. "There's something that you can't say in front of Mr. Bornstein?"

"Yes. It's confidential."

Melanie glanced at Oscar, her eyes asking his opinion.

Oscar Bornstein rose from his chair. "Of course. If you'll excuse me, Mel, I'll be in my office."

She watched him leave, then turned back to Paul.

"To tell the truth," he said, "I may well be jeopardizing an informant's life by discussing the matter with you."

She nodded curtly. "You may rest assured that what you say will stay with me."

"I hope so," he said pointedly. "I have been informed by a

source I consider to be sound that there is a massive fraud being perpetrated at Uhuru Towers."

"Do you have anything concrete?"

"The man is in mortal terror of his life. He came to this newspaper because he's afraid to go to the authorities."

"That isn't printable."

"I believe the man, Mrs. Parsons. There was an accident at the building site. He tells me it was a murder, and that it was committed to prevent the dead man from shooting off his mouth. Another man who worked with him is missing. I think that he's dead, too."

"And you can't put a name to them? Nothing will be served by going into print?"

"If you and I don't keep faith with this man, and keep this story out of the papers until we have some proof that will demand legal action, we might be responsible for his death."

"Don't get preachy. I told you I'd keep it to myself. I want more facts."

Paul looked up at her. He was committed anyway. "The man Gibbons, who was killed, had an assistant. His name was Jenks. I heard about him from Gibbons's widow. He's missing. The building he lived in burned down. Is that coincidental enough to suit you?"

She scratched her chin. "It hardly seems plausible. How can a project that gets so much scrutiny get out of hand? You know what the breadth of its support is."

"This is the story you've been looking for, Mrs. Parsons. This is how you get the drop on Frank O'Neil."

She waved her hand in dismissal. "Of course, he's in it. But, how about Chris Greene? How about all of that community support?"

"Community support is attracted by shiny objects. That's how we got Manhattan Island for twenty-four dollars worth of beads. And don't worry about Chris Greene. The bulk of any blame will fall on O'Neil. This is his baby. If Greene sees that O'Neil is hooked, he'll switch sides so fast your head will spin. Unless he's been bought, he'll be quick enough to disavow Uhuru Towers."

"I think that's repulsive."

"I agree. But that's Chris Greene."

"And you think that the black community will forgive Greene for changing sides on the issue?"

"Short of dyeing himself black, he's doing all he can to curry their vote. He knows that he's got to leave New York with them in his pocket on Election Day. Besides, we can't ignore the story in any case. Unless, of course, you are prepared to turn your back on a swindle complicated by multiple murders."

"Without a shred of printable material or submissible evidence." She glared at him. Of course, she couldn't turn it down. "What do you want from me?"

"I need time. I need to be left to my own devices without interference."

"You have to have a story for the rest of the editorial board. The whole paper will be buzzing if you don't have a plausible cover. You might as well tell them everything."

"I'll tell them that I'm doing a follow-up story on housing. Let's drop Uhuru altogether. I'll tell them that I'm working that fire on Willis Avenue."

"That's not your beat."

"I'll tell them that it's part of a bigger story on the decline of the housing stock and the ineptitude of the O'Neil housing program."

"It sounds weak to me. Oscar will want to know why you asked for the private audience."

He looked at her frankly. "He does exactly what you tell him to do, including keeping his mouth shut. As for the others, stuff it down their throats. You do it all the time."

Her eyes were slits, and her mouth drooped. "I see O'Neil's head in the noose. So I think I'll let you do this, and then fire you. You are a rude little bastard." She picked up the phone. "Madeleine, ask Mr. Fabrikant and Mr. Bornstein to come up here. Now, Madeleine." She leaned back and looked at Paul malevolently. "It's a good thing for you that it's a giant fraud and multiple murders you have to hang on O'Neil. I don't think I could stand you for anything less."

The first knock on the door came in a minute. Bornstein walked in saying, "I was on my way back up, anyway. You have to look at some equipment orders." He held up a folder. "I have to get them off my desk in an hour, or we'll be pushed back a whole delivery cycle." He slipped the folder under her nose.

As she was looking through it, Fabrikant knocked and entered.

Melanie signed the forms that Bornstein had put in front of her and waved at a chair with her pen. "Sit down, Max. Curtin wants to make us a proposition."

After ten minutes, Fabrikant shrugged. "So where's the startling revelation going to come from? What shall we do? Hang O'Neil for all of the deaths in all of the tenement fires?"

"No," Paul said, annoyed. "But it might be interesting to our readers to see the connection with the administration's failure to provide more public housing and a lot of senseless deaths in a firetrap."

Fabrikant raised his voice a notch. "Well, I don't think a whole lot of rhetoric is going to serve either the readers or the paper."

"I think it's the kind of tone we ought to take," Melanie interjected. "Maybe we need something to get people stirred up. We're not addressing the occupants of the reading room at the University Club. Oscar was just instructing me in the tastes of our readership, weren't you, Oscar?"

"In another context. But I agree with Max that equating the governor's housing program and the reason for those tenement deaths shows a certain lack of class. Frank O'Neil doesn't set fires and kill babies. It's not likely that the most enthusiastic building program would have prevented that fire."

"No. But if you think about what he does build," Paul said, "white elephants like the Albany Mall, the silly-ass federal office building on 125th Street, and Uhuru Towers, it is possible that those people would have moved to better housing. Appearances and monuments come ahead of necessities at all levels of government." With silent thanks to George Mason, he said, "It's circuses without bread."

"I like it," Melanie said with finality. "After all, gentlemen, we don't have to print it if we don't like what we see." She brightened visibly. "And then we can fire Mr. Curtin."

"How nice for you," Paul said.

"Are we agreed?" she asked softly.

Max Fabrikant drew a breath. "We might put it to the editorial board. There are four other senior editors." Melanie smiled implacably. Max continued, "But since there will probably be a consensus anyway . . ." His voice trailed off.

"Well, it's settled, then. I'll expect to hear from you regularly, Paul. You're going to have my personal interest."

Paul, Oscar, and Max stood silently in the foyer outside of

Melanie's office, waiting for the elevator. Without exchanging a word, Oscar exited on the fifth floor. Max and Paul continued to the fourth.

"You certainly know how to bullshit," Max said. "You don't think that smokescreen is really going to provide any new insights, do you?"

"No, Max, I don't," Paul said with a smile. "But it'll move the proles. And that's what the Boss Lady wants. She wants them all out there on Election Day, voting against Frank O'Neil. So that's what you want, too. Isn't it, Max?"

Max gave Paul a stare and headed back toward his office, looking at the floor. Shit, Max said to himself. There are three newspapers left in New York. Where would I get another job? I remember when there was no bullshit on the front page, only news. I remember when there was no television. He slammed the door of his office and slumped behind his desk. Ah, fuck it! He smiled. It's payday.

Paul stopped at his desk to see if he had any messages. He stuffed his file back into the drawer and locked it again. She was right. My cover story was thin. Max and Oscar didn't buy it for a minute. But I was right, too. She said shit, and they squatted. I bought my time. He had a sour taste in his mouth. He'd feel better when he got to work.

29

By the end of the first week following his meeting with Melanie Parsons, Paul Curtin had augmented his background in the lore and regulations of the Housing Department of the state sufficiently to begin looking for a source on its staff that might give him insight into how the Uhuru scam worked.

He drove down to the World Trade Center and wandered around from desk to desk amid the appalling impersonality of the Division of Housing and Community Renewal like Diogenes, looking for a man to buy a drink.

After a day of rebuffs and another morning of being passed along through a chain of bored or intractable civil servants, he fell upon a fortyish bald black man named Eustace McGee.

"Hey, listen," Eustace said, regarding him with suspicion. "I don't know why I'm talking to you at all. I could lose my job. I've already got twelve years in. You never know who you're going to piss off if you talk too much. I'm thinking about my pension."

"Listen, Eustace, there's nobody standing in this room but you and me. I need some information. I'm not asking you to testify, or stand in front of a camera. I am going to forget your name, address, and telephone number as soon as I walk out of here. I'm not asking you to name names. I want to do some digging, and I don't have the tools."

"I don't mind helping you out. I just don't want them tools to dig my grave." He scratched his chin, thinking it over. "Okay. You can buy me some lunch."

Paul walked out first, waiting for the elevator amid the rattle of heels on the cold linoleum floor and suffering the stomach-churning drop to the bottom of the tower. He walked through the vaulted canyon, built to maddeningly inhuman proportions, and onto the street.

Ten minutes later, Eustace joined him at an inviting Italian restaurant a couple of blocks to the south. They chose a table in the rear.

"I want to ask the first question," Eustace said. "Why me? Did somebody send you to me?"

"God's honest truth? Pure chance. I spent half of yesterday trying to get an appointment with the director of the division. When I finally saw him, he was superhostile. Polite, mind you, but just uncooperative. The best I could get from him was an introduction to the public information section. I've been walking around the halls of the state bureaucracy for four years. By now, I know when I'm being stiffed. When I realized that the flack they passed me to wasn't going to tell me anything except what you can find out in the library, I listened politely, thanked him, and decided to strike out on my own. There's an information board downstairs in the lobby. It has everybody's title and section on it." He pulled out a steno pad and showed it to Eustace. "You're the fifth name from the top."

Eustace smiled at Paul. He had a big head with a close-out black fringe around a shining dark dome. There was a pencil-thin moustache on his upper lip, and his eyes danced with good humor. "You're learning. In housing, people learn to mind their own business. There's too much money on the table. You don't want to say anything. First thing you know, you mess up a deal for some big contractor, he bitches to his congressman, or the governor, and you find yourself transferred to some hole. You get in the way of some union deal, you end up with no kneecaps. What do you want?"

"Let me ask you a question first. Why did you come to lunch?"

Eustace cocked his head and gave a little chuckle. "You came in to my office and said you needed some educating. You said you wanted to understand how payments in the state housing program are made. I'm a reasonable person to ask. It's my end of the business." He hunched his shoulders and leaned forward. "You're on to something. You don't care about procedures in the department. You smell a rat, but you don't know how the scam works. Why else would you want to hear about a lot of paperwork bullshit."

"So what are you? A public-spirited citizen?"

"Not likely. There's two sides to it. I care about my pension, but I'm wasting my time. The problems in my job don't interest anybody but me. It would be nice to see that change."

"That sounds public-spirited to me," Paul said.

"Maybe. All anybody cares about on the outside is results. Is there enough good housing? Are the buildings safe? Are they going up fast enough? Cheap enough? I see what goes on every day. Every once in a while some asshole gets caught with his hand in the cookie jar. There's a big cleanup campaign and some people get their asses fired. Then it goes on, just like before." Eustace leaned forward again. "One of these days, I'm going to get left holding the bag. Nobody talks because everybody's indifferent or afraid. I'm not a hero, Mr. Curtin."

"Paul, please."

"Not a hero, Paul, then. I'm no different than anybody else. I'd like to think I amount to something. I've been sitting around for twelve years taking the slow train to my pension watching all kinds of bad shit go down. Stealing. Bribing. You name it. Just the same, a lot of good gets done here. Most of the people are decent and honest. If you are going to do another one of those big scandal stories, I'd like to see that the guys who are clean and who do put in their time without being on the take get a square shake."

"What if I told you I wasn't doing a scandal story?"

"I'd eat my lunch and fill you with a lot of bullshit, because I'd know you were a liar."

"Fair enough. I won't lie."

"Okay. You ask the questions. Don't tell me too much. I don't want to know. It might not be healthy."

"I found you at random. Nobody knows we're here. I'm never going to call you again."

"Okay. Shoot."

Over the course of the next hour, Paul and Eustace touched on the procedures of establishing, bonding, and paying for a government-backed project. They proceeded from small infractions and frauds like substituting inferior grade materials for those specified in the building contract, up the ladder of dishonesty to the upper strata, such as bid fixing, and the possibilities offered when the local group sponsoring a project chooses a builder.

"Then the only absolute requirement," Paul said, "is bonding."

"That's right," Eustace said, nodding agreement. "If you can get the Prudential Life Insurance Company to bond you for the fifty million, or whatever, the job is worth, everybody else—the sponsor, the government—will accept your skills as a fact."

Paul continued to edge carefully closer to his central purpose. "This sponsorship business, Eustace, it's community level group action, right? Recognized groups acting as a catalyst for new building in their neighborhoods."

"Sure. But it can't be just anybody. To begin with, they need seed money to get the project off of the ground. Some of the time the big foundations, like Ford, will supply the money. They do a lot of looking before they leap. That doesn't mean that mistakes can't be made. Bad sponsors or bad contractors. There's no shortage of crooks."

Paul finished his drink and asked casually, "How about Uhuru Towers?"

"Never happen, man." Eustace held up his glass and the

waiter came by. Paul ordered another round. "There are three sponsors, not one. And the governor and the mayor are fighting over credit for Uhuru like kids with a new toy." He shook his head from side to side.

"You seem awfully sure. If I wanted to look into it further where would I go?"

"If it was me looking, I'd go up to the Urban Development League on 117th Street. See Reverend McCaig. He's the spokesman for the sponsoring groups."

"And he wouldn't be involved in a rip-off?"

Eustace sat back in his chair and took a swig. "Old Don McCaig? No. He wouldn't steal nothing. He just a frizzy-haired, bearded old nigger who thinks he talks to God. You wouldn't want to invite him to the Plaza for a drink, but he's a pretty decent old cuss."

"Is he the one who pays the bills?"

Eustace shifted in his chair again. "I'm beginning to think that you know something I don't know."

"What makes you say that?" Paul tried to sound casual.

"I told you, my friend. I've been around twelve years. I said to you not to tell me too much. Anything about Uhuru Towers is too much. You don't need inside information to know that there are a lot of people who would be very upset if something got in the way of Uhuru Towers."

Paul was tempted to ask him if he knew something specific, but he watched Eustace's face close like a door, and thought better of it. "Well, let's change the subject, then. I was only using an example, anyway. How do bills get paid in general? Does the state send the contractor a check? Does the sponsor?"

It took Eustace a moment to get back into the easy give-and-take they'd had before Paul had pressed him on Uhuru. He talked his way through a couple of minutes of murky generalities, then said, "It's all based on requisitions against percentage completion of the work. As you go along, you put in periodic requests for payment for materials and manpower expended against certificates of completion. You need approval from the planning department of the Housing Division, then the numbers go up to the comptroller in Albany for audit, then to the paying bank."

"Could there be a leak at the comptroller's office?"

"No," Eustace said firmly, shaking his head. "How would

you do that? What are you going to do? Fix the comptroller?" he said laughing. "Or maybe Frank O'Neil?"

Eustace looked at his watch. "I'd better be getting back to my pile of paper. I hope I've been some help."

"I've learned more in an hour and a half from you than I did in a week reading all those regulations."

"They're meant to confuse you, not help you. Don't feel bad." Eustace shook Paul's hand. "I think it would be better if we leave separately. The more I think about it, the less I like the idea of being seen with you."

"Thanks, Eustace. See you. And I won't forget. Never saw you in my life." Paul watched him go through the door, then ordered another drink, and began to read his notes.

<h1 style="text-align:center">30</h1>

Paul looked up from the yellow pad on his desk with annoyance. His elbow struck a pile of cardboard-bound housing authority regulations and spilled them to the floor. The doorbell rang again. "Ratshit! I'm coming."

He pushed back the chair and walked across the living room, a frown on his face at the interruption in his train of thought. He turned the handle and looked out into the hall.

"I understand that the prisoners are being permitted conjugal visits today," Maryanne said. "I thought I'd drop over and see if I could get a little piece for myself."

Paul took her face in his hands and kissed her softly and longingly on the lips. "Would you be offended if I invited you into my bachelor apartment?"

She stepped inside and closed the door behind her.

"What brings me this fortuitous surprise?"

"Today is Wednesday."

Paul looked at his watch. "It is. At ten-thirty in the morning." He looked up at her sheepishly. "Did we have a date? Have I forgotten something?"

"No." She handed him her coat and dropped onto the couch. "I don't want to seem possessive, mind you, but I wondered how come I had not received so much as a telephone call since you left my steaming sheets on Sunday night."

"Huh?"

"Paul, you saw me twice last week. You haven't called me in three days. I was starting to break out in acne. I felt like the cheerleader who screwed the captain of the football team, then sat by the phone waiting to be invited to the prom. And the phone didn't ring."

He flopped down next to her. "I'm sorry. Look at that pile of papers over there. I got them on Monday, and I've been buried in them ever since." Paul had hoped that the press of her own business would have taken the edge off of the reduction in his attentions. He didn't want to explain.

She cast a disapproving glance around the room. "This isn't the compulsive man I have grown to love and admire. Are those socks that I see straggling under that chair?" She reached out to touch his face. "And you haven't shaved. Have you taken drugs and strong drink?"

"No."

"Then would you mind telling me just what the hell it is that you are doing?"

He smiled. "I'm working. You're going to have to make up your mind, my dear. When I mope and hate what I do, and feel frustrated and shitty, you are unhappy. When I become immersed in what I am doing, the same."

"How feminine of me. I want some attention."

Paul leaned over and kissed her cheek. "There."

"Sport." She kissed him back. "I was really starting to worry. I wondered what had become of you. I was on my way to see Harry Lesser again about that damn co-op venture. He lives two blocks from here. I decided to stick my nose in the door."

"I've been sitting here busting my ass. I probably would have surfaced this afternoon anyway. I don't think there's anything left in the icebox."

She looked at her watch. "Just so you're okay. I've got to go. The kids miss you." She got up from the couch and took her coat.

He grabbed her hand and pulled himself up after her. "I've really been buried. But, I feel like I'm making some progress."

"How long do you expect to be so occupied?" she asked evenly.

"I don't know. A couple of weeks. Maybe three. I need concrete results before I can go back to Melanie."

"I've got to go." She turned back at the door. "I love you, Paul."

Her face was sad. I'm probably fantasizing about the risk anyway, he thought. A lousy dinner can't hurt. "How about I get some Chinese food?"

She smiled and stepped into the hall. "I love you," she said, walking to the elevator.

"I'm forgiven?" He asked.

"I love you," she said again, as the elevator door closed, and she dropped from sight.

Paul closed the door and looked around the apartment. Maryanne was right. Christ, what a sight. He put his hand on his forehead. Oh shit, he thought. I've got to go up to the Urban Development League. He ran to the bathroom, stumbling over the shoes he'd left on the doorsill. It was a good thing that Maryanne had showed up, or I'd have missed the frigging appointment.

Bathed and neatly dressed, Paul drove to his scheduled meeting at 117th Street and Seventh Avenue. His week's work had brought him to the conclusion that housing fraud, like welfare cheating and stealing Social Security checks, is based on a thorough understanding of the system and the weaknesses built into it by its designers to serve their political aims, rather than its supposed social purposes.

In Paul's experience, all public assistance programs had the same flaws. Too much of the money, sometimes more than half, went for administrative costs and salaries, diluting the impact on their beneficiaries. Examination and auditing procedures were slipshod and slow. There was too much use of the average and the median. When you deal in billions, Paul thought, a little rounding off here and there amounts to waste in millions, squandered or stolen.

In order to avoid affronts to personal dignity, the legislators dictated client interviewing procedures that were too convoluted for either those who administered them, or those whom they were intended to screen: the elderly, the indigent, the linguistically or culturally estranged. But at the same time, they left the door open for the barracks lawyers and the cheats, who played the system like a violin.

Seventh Avenue is a broad, tree-lined boulevard. As 125th Street has been the heart of Harlem, radiating the culture, entertainment, and business of the community, so Seventh Avenue, its base firmly rooted in Central Park, wide and straight, provides a backbone.

In its beginnings, after the turn of the twentieth century and through the First World War, the avenue had served as a home for Jews who had gained sufficient affluence to escape their Lower East Side ghetto.

At the end of the Great War a resurgence of the Klan, a decline in agriculture, and talk of a new industrial revolution in the North brought droves of Negroes to New York. Even before the Depression, the Jews had given way to the next wave of immigration, and by Roosevelt's first inauguration, Seventh Avenue north of the Park was all black.

Paul pulled up in front of a row of old-law tenements that lined the street. A large painted panel indicated the location of the Urban Development League.

He knocked at the door and was greeted by an attractive black girl in her twenties dressed in a gray sweater and skirt and penny loafers. She had a round face and inquiring eyes topped by a medium Afro. "Hi, I'm Paula Dennis. How may I help you?"

"I'm Paul Curtin of the *New York Advocate*. I have an appointment with Reverend McCaig."

The girl led him to a narrow space where two wooden armchairs bracketed a dirty standing ashtray. "Please have a seat, Mr. Curtin. I know that he's expecting you. I'll be a minute."

Paul waited, balancing his attaché case on his knees. The door through which the girl had disappeared opened again. A tall black man in a rumpled suit with a clerical collar strode briskly into the room and stuck out his hand. "Paul, I'm Don McCaig. Let me lead you through the lion's den."

Paul followed after him into a large room humming with voices. Fifty people sat at desks, hands cupped over their free ears, talking into telephones. Paul found that he had to lengthen his stride to keep up with McCaig, who despite his wild graying hair and wizened features, moved with the energy of a young man. At the back of the room there was a single, glassed-in office; Paul closed the door after him.

"This is one of our busiest times, Paul," McCaig said, slumping down into the chair behind the beat-up desk. "This is the landlord season. Every year people who are old and afraid or don't speak very good English have their heat turned down or off by neglectful or greedy building owners." He smiled a gold-toothed smile. "We call them up to remind them of their legal obligations."

"You should have been a track star," Paul said, mopping his brow.

"I was. I chased sheep over some of the most miserable sharecropped land in Virginia. I still keep in shape running a step ahead of the young hoodlums." He cackled and slapped his thigh. "You look to be in pretty good shape yourself. What can I do for you?"

"Not much more than I told you on the phone. I'm just taking a hard look at New York housing with an eye on the election."

McCaig made a tent with his hands and said in a cracked voice that was half drawl and half New York nasal, "If I were Frank O'Neil, based on the condition of housing in this state, I'd be mighty nervous."

Paul returned his smile. "I surely hope so." He leaned forward in his seat. "I'd like to know something about Uhuru Towers."

"That's not a short story." McCaig rocked the chair onto its back legs and stuck his feet in an open drawer. "Where to start? With why? How? It's occupied so much of my time over the past years. I was watching the city I live in fall apart. People who pay the taxes were leaving by the carload. The ones who were left didn't know how to take care of what they had. Pride dies. People get angry and stay that way. The combination gives you more dirt and crime, and less hope. And round and round. I wanted to bust up the cycle. I guess people thought I was a nut case when I started."

Paul sat back in the chair. "You don't seem like a nut case to me, Reverend McCaig. But I wonder if you still think that Uhuru's practical."

"Uhuru means freedom in Swahili. That's symbolic. But the building—that's a concrete and steel revelation to the brothers out there that the white population is interested enough in the renovation of the center of this city—the part of the city where the black folks live—to build something that can be looked at with pride."

Paul moved slightly in his chair. McCaig's eyes were hooded by heavy brows, and bored into Paul. His voice rumbled in his chest. "How many times have you seen a black man in a Cadillac and said nigger rich? Maybe not out loud, but felt it? What right does a man who doesn't even live in a decent neighborhood have to ride in a car like that?" He straightened up in his chair. "Do you know that blacks drink half the Chivas Regal consumed in America? Every little sliver of status is an escape from self-contempt, and an inch closer to hope.

"Uhuru is a powerful symbol. It's going to provide first-class housing for six hundred families. It's going to provide the first new attractive stores in Harlem in two generations." He leaned back in the chair again and scratched at his scraggly beard. "Oh, I know what people think," he said softly. "The niggers'll break the windows and steal all of the merchandise in a week. And if they don't, the spics will. I think my people, like all people, will rise to a landmark of their pride. And I think that instead of chasing black people out of the center of the city because we want to gentrify the area, to take over their substandard housing, and turn it into something profitable and livable for white folks, we ought to give them a chance to find a permanent place in the sun, too. This is their city as much as anybody else's. If you want us to act middle class and stop acting like a bunch of hoodlums, then you better give us a chance and some of the goods to do it. Middle-class blacks run from Harlem. I want them to come home. Uhuru might attract them, and some investment dollars with them. I think it'll make the system work right here on 125th Street."

"Is that symbolism—the identification angle—that settled you on a black contractor?"

McCaig frowned for the first time since Paul had entered his office. "No sense telling you what you already know about the difference between black unemployment and white unemployment. I am getting to be an old man. I have waited my whole life to see my people get a bigger slice of the pie." He put his hand to his neck. "Three years at Alabama Bible College while I washed dishes and cleaned white folks' outhouses doesn't give me a direct line to the Almighty. But I try to talk to and to see a lot of people and to know them.

"I've seen Marcus Garvey Hawkes hanging around here for twenty-five years. He preaches worse than I do. Always the same theme. We are fifteen percent of the population, we ought to get fifteen percent of the work. He's been mooching from one sponsor group to another for years. He went bust a couple of times trying to do rehab work with no cash. But that doesn't make him different from any other black contractor. He can't get a bond from the insurance company. Therefore, he can't get decent jobs or bank financing. Therefore, he can't work and has no experience or track record, which means no bonding. And so on." McCaig slumped in his chair, his shoulders rounded as though he bore a heavy weight.

"I don't know if he's the right man, Paul. I can't know for sure. But he is a black contractor who has managed to get the backing of a major American company. And from what we can see—and you'd better believe that the more militant members of this community have looked very hard—Hawkes is actually doing the job himself with black supervision, black labor, and black subcontractors. That shows that Uhuru means more than neighborhood pride. It means skill development, too. It means more jobs for blacks in the—" He stopped short and laughed. He'd been ticking off the points on his fingers.

"I get the point," Paul siad, jotting a note on his pad. He looked up again. "Are you saying he was the only game in town?"

McCaig rocked the chair forward and hesitated before he answered. "You can make a case for that. He was the only black contractor who had found a solution to the absence of minority bonding capability without selling control of the job, or his soul, for the opportunity. The company behind him—Burton Industries—these are real solid people. If they're willing to take a chance on Hawkes and to give him control of a fifty-million-dollar job, who am I to ask a lot of uninformed questions? Whatever doubts I had, or the other sponsors, they were set aside on that alone."

Paul saw that McCaig was looking over his shoulder through the glass at the crowded floor behind him. He rose and extended his hand. "Don, I don't want to keep you any longer. Thanks a lot for the time."

McCaig got to his feet and opened the office door. He clapped Paul on the shoulder. "Thanks for your interest. Treat us kindly, brother. This community needs Uhuru. These people out here need it." He saw Paul to the sidewalk. "I've got to get back to my slumlords now. You know, I think that some of them even look forward to my calls."

Paul walked to his car. Two young men in their early twenties were leaning against the front fender. They were wearing black leather jackets studded with chromed nail heads. Their hair was covered by caps from which tight curls writhed at random like snakes in the March wind. Paul's mouth went dry. He opened the door of the car and sat down without a word. When he started the engine, they lifted themselves in a leisurely fashion, sneered at him, and sauntered down the street.

31

Paul had parked on Fortieth Street, next to Bryant Park, ignoring the gaggle of drug dealers plying their trade on his way across to the public library. He trotted up the marble steps to the third-floor reference room and requested all available materials on Burton Industries. He read for an hour, then went to the Xerox machine, and spent nine dollars of the *Advocate*'s expense money getting everything copied.

It was six o'clock by the time he had been to Chinatown, waited for dinner to be cooked and wrapped, and fought the traffic back uptown to Maryanne's apartment. He listened with feigned interest to school stories till the children went to bed.

Paul helped to clear the table, then excused himself to use the telephone. He thumbed through his address book looking for the home number of Abe Schneider, the real estate man in the *Advocate*'s financial department whom he had consulted before.

"Abe, this is Paul Curtin. How about some help?"

"What have you got in mind?"

"I need some information and an introduction."

"If I've got it, you can have it."

"I need to know who owned a building that burned down in the Bronx. Also, do you know anyone at Burton Industries who might talk to me about their Hawkes Building venture, and the building they're putting up on 125th Street."

"I can't promise any miracles," Schneider said. "You call me at ten-thirty tomorrow and I'll do a little spade work for you. As it happens, I have a friend or two at the Bureau of Buildings and Real Estate. What's the address?"

"What was the address," Paul corrected, "523 East 135th Street. How about Burton?"

"It's your lucky day. I go fishing with a guy named Len Jarvis. He's their PR director. I can give him a call."

"Is coming through the PR department going to hurt me?"

"On the contrary. If you come through Jarvis, they'll be less concerned that you're going after their scalps. You just need some facts, right? I'd hate to have you fuck a friend."

"That's all, Abe. Just some information." Paul's conscience twinged. "Where are they?"

"They used to be on Park Avenue. Then they got smart," he chuckled. "They're in almost tax-free Hampton, New Hampshire, forty minutes north of Boston."

Maryanne walked in as Paul picked up the phone. "Did something happen to you today? You were pretty distant at dinner. Petey asked me if you were mad at him when I put him to bed."

"I'll deal with that right now." Paul walked down the hall to Petey's room and sat on the floor next to the bed. "Petey, old man, I have a problem."

"You do?" he asked in wonderment.

"It even happens to me. I was working on a story today. I thought about it a lot, and it frightened me."

Petey pulled himself up and leaned on his elbow. "I didn't think you ever got scared."

"Oh, but I do. And I get preoccupied with my work. But

that doesn't mean that I love you or Mom or Alex any less. Do you think that you could keep that in mind?"

"I'll tell Alex in the morning. She was worried."

"Thanks, Pete," Paul said gravely. "I could use the help."

Maryanne sat cross-legged on the floor in the living room reading the *Advocate*. "What was that about?"

"Man talk. The matter is settled." He took a drink and sat on the couch. "I got a chill today. I went to do an interview in Harlem. When I came out there were a couple of tough kids sitting on my car. They scared me."

She frowned. "Is that what you told Petey?"

"Minus the details. I just didn't want him to go to sleep feeling unloved."

She put the paper down deliberately. "Listen, are you sticking your neck out?"

"How do you mean?"

"Stop fencing. Are you doing something dangerous? Does that have something to do with your sudden scarceness?" There was a tremor in her voice.

"Don't get carried away. I went in to talk to this crazy old Reverend McCaig. When I left, there were a couple of tough-looking Rastas sitting on my fender."

"Bullshit," she said evenly.

"All right. Enough." He finished his drink in a swallow. "I don't like the smell of this story. I didn't like the Rastas on my fender. They weren't a reincarnation of Bob Marley. I will call you regularly. We will have dinner once a week. But that's it for the duration."

"Jesus," she said, half angry, half scared. "You are doing this to prove something to that old bitch?"

"I am doing something because it may be worthwhile."

"Well, I don't want you to do it if you're going to get hurt in the process."

"And I don't want to hear from you on the subject or see your nose in my business, Maryanne." He lowered his voice. "You got that?"

"I'm afraid."

"That's my line. Just don't make it harder for me."

"I thought we were going to share."

"Not this."

"Okay," she conceded, her voice barely audible. "You going to go now?"

He nodded.

"In a while," she said, extending her hand to him and getting to her feet. "When you feel the cold wind on the back of your neck, you need to reestablish your contact with life." She pulled him upright. "I want you to help me move some furniture."

In the bedroom Maryanne pulled off her sweater and kicked off her shoes. She stood at the end of the bed and undid the snaps on her skirt, dropped it to the floor and pulled off her pantyhose. Paul stood in the doorway and watched her hang and fold her clothing. When she was done she turned to him and beckoned, like Peter Pan in her blue bikini briefs. "To work."

"What are we moving?"

"The mirror."

"God." He looked at the rococo gold frame on the wall above her long dressing table. It was five feet high and three across. "It must weigh a hundred fifty pounds."

"That's why I need help."

Paul stripped off his jacket and shirt and pushed the dresser forward till there was sufficient space for them to stand between it and the wall. They held the mirror by the corners and lifted it from the hooks on the wall.

"It's not as heavy as it looks," Paul said with gratitude. "Where do you want it?"

"There on the floor at the foot of the bed."

They walked across the floor, then rested the frame on the carpet and leaned it against the wall. Paul brushed the hair out of his eyes and straightened up, looking at her body.

"What is this in aid of?"

"Look in the mirror. What do you see?"

"The bed."

She slipped her briefs off and threw them across the room, then sat at the foot of the bed. "Come here, Paul."

He turned toward her. She undid his belt buckle and the buttons and the zipper on his slacks, then slipped them down around his hips. He bent to help her, but she pushed his hands away.

"I want to do this all by myself. You've had a hard day." She shimmied the pants to the floor, pushed Paul back, and knelt at his feet, undoing the laces on his shoes. He shifted his

weight and she slipped off one shoe and sock, then the other.
The room seemed terribly warm to him, and a film of
perspiration formed on his upper lip. Her back was a porcelain
arch.

Without looking at his face, her hands moved upward,
grazing his calves and thighs, hooked the waistband of his
shorts and pulled them to the floor. When he was naked, she
rocked back on her heels and looked at him.

His pulse pounded in the side of his neck. He quivered as her
fingertips played over him.

He was shaking when she pulled back from him and rose to
her feet. She knelt on the foot of the bed and, resting forward
on her hands, looked at herself in the mirror. "Take me," she
said. "I want to watch." She looked at him as he moved to
stand behind her and watched him thrust till the image blurred,
his fingers digging into the softness of her hips.

When the alarm rang at 6:30 in the morning, she looked at
him sheepishly. "I'm sorry. I couldn't think of another way to
keep the kids from finding you here in my bed."

"It's in a good cause," he yawned. "When this business is
over, we'll do this more often. You want me to put the mirror
back?"

"No. I like it just where it is. And whenever you want, you
can stay permanently."

"Soon." He kissed her. He showered, dressed, and slipped
quietly out of the door, and went to his apartment.

He stayed in bed for a couple of hours, then got up and
sorted his papers, yesterday's chill of fear dissipated in last
night's warmth. He made a quick pass at straightening and
dusting and ran the ancient Hoover for a few minutes,
whistling as he worked.

At half past ten he called Abe Schneider. "Morning, Abe."

"I was just going to call you. How fast can you get on the
shuttle?"

"Instantly. Where am I going?"

"Hampton, New Hampshire. Luck is smiling on you. You
have an appointment with Burton."

"You are a peach."

"I don't suppose that you have anything worth sharing with
a colleague."

"Not up your alley, Abe. But if there is something, I'll holler. I promise."

"I'll hold you to that."

Paul took down the appropriate names and addresses, grabbed his briefcase and his coat, and headed out of the door. The FDR Drive and the Grand Central were providentially empty at mid-morning, and he found a parking space in front of the Eastern shuttle terminal. Panting, he made the second section of the eleven o'clock to Boston.

After the stewardess took his credit card, Paul undid his tie and opened the briefcase for a last look at the essentials. Burton Industries: sales $2.5 billion. Substantial, if erratic, earnings growth over fifteen years. Basic product lines: roofing, floor tiles, lumber insulating materials, wallboard, and assorted construction materials. Plants throughout the United States. Forest reserves on every continent except Antarctica. The board of directors, a Who's Who of American Industry.

Before one o'clock Paul was driving his rented car out of Logan Airport and north on I–95. In less than an hour he had crossed the Massachusetts-New Hampshire line. It was a hundred yards to the Hampton turnoff.

Just beyond the toll booth a large white sign was lettered Burton Industries. Paul swung the car into the driveway, which coursed through a half mile of woods still covered with snow and thick with blue spruce.

He parked in a large circle fronting a red brick and white clapboard building in the style of an Ivy League university library, with balance born of the Age of Reason and topped by a carillon spire.

He brushed his feet on a large cocoa fiber mat and entered the building. Its vastness was muted by adherence to the colonial theme. The central hall stretched into the distance, polished oak floors glinting like rails on either side of a patterned runner. The entrance maintained human proportions by the use of a room-size Oriental rug and groupings of period furniture. An attractive woman sat at a mahogany desk with brass fixtures. Paul stepped forward to introduce himself. "I have an appointment with Len Jarvis."

"I'll let him know you're here, Mr. Curtin," she smiled brightly. "In the meanwhile, if you'll just put your coat in there," she indicated a cloakroom near the front door. By the time he had returned a cheerful middle-aged woman stood at the desk awaiting him.

"Mr. Curtin, I'm Mr. Jarvis's secretary, Ginny. Please come with me."

Leonard Jarvis was standing at his desk talking on the telephone. He was thin and fiftyish with close-cropped gray hair, and a tan over red cheeks. After a few further words, he hung up and crossed the room to meet him.

"You're Paul," he said, extending his hand.

"I am. You're very nice to meet me on such short notice."

"That's what I'm here for. We are always receptive to the press and security analysts. If the newspapers and Wall Street don't understand us, how will they get to love us?" Jarvis ushered Paul to a chair.

"I'd like to talk to someone who can give me the background on Hawkes Building. Why it was started. What the relationship is. How things are going. A little of the practical and the philosophical together." Paul leaned back in the chair again. "I'm asking too much, yes?"

"Yes. But, I will go down the hall and see if we can help. There are two people that you want to see: John Holderness, who is our vice-president of the Building Products Division and is directly responsible for Hawkes, and of course, Kurt."

"Kurt?"

Jarvis smiled. "Kurt Englander. He's our president." He started out of the room, then turned back at the door. "By the way, while I do all of this road paving, I appreciate Abe Schneider's interest, and your own, but would you say that your intentions were honorable?"

Paul cupped his hand in his chin. "Let's say that I came up meaning no harm. I want to learn, not to collect scalps."

"I'll take you at your word," Jarvis said and disappeared. His secretary came in and asked Paul if he wanted coffee. By the time he was through with the cup, Jarvis had returned.

"If you can wait ten minutes, Paul, I have you all set to meet both John and Kurt in Kurt's office." He sounded a little tense. "You're really lucky. They've both been on the road."

Jarvis led Paul back to a large room with a many-paned bay window dominating the far wall. The window opened on a valley that stretched east to blue hills, and to the sea beyond. The room was decorated as a sea captain's cabin, with a massive sea chest desk and a large leather-covered chair. Couches and a table occupied a niche between matching book-filled breakfronts at the end of the office opposite the door. An antique globe stood to one side of the desk. The remaining wall space was covered with prints of sailing ships.

The first of the two men to whom Jarvis introduced Paul was John Holderness. He was a couple of inches taller than Paul, at six four, but outweighed him by fifty pounds. His hair was dark and thinning and brushed back over his scalp. Like Jarvis, he had a florid face tanned by skiing in the New England winter.

Kurt Englander struck Paul as an unlikely combination of northwoodsman and Prussian officer. In his early fifties, he was of middle height and trim, though solidly built, looking ten years younger than his age. His head was shaved completely. His face was round and blunt featured. His eyes were a pale, cold blue. Baleful was the proper word, Paul thought.

"Nice to see you, Mr. Curtin," Holderness said.

"Yes. We're pleased that you took the time to come up from New York to see us," Englander said in a flinty baritone voice. He turned to Jarvis and said, "Thank you, Len," dismissing him.

Jarvis waved at Paul heartily and backed out of the room, saying, "Please drop in and see me on your way out. And if there's anything that I can do. . . ." His voice trailed off, and he closed the door behind him.

Englander sat down in a chair next to the coffee table facing the interior of the room. When Holderness sat on the couch, Paul naturally selected the remaining chair which faced the window. He blinked in the reflected glare from the snow.

"Would you like some coffee, Mr. Curtin?" Englander asked. Paul found his voice curiously monotonous.

"No, thank you. I had some with Mr. Jarvis."

"Len tells me that you've come up on very short notice to talk about our urban renewal venture. Both John and I are just back from long trips. We may have to delay some of our answers until we get current. But we'll do our best."

Paul took out a pen and flipped his pad open. "I'll try to be brief. I'd like to repeat what I told Len. This is background for a story on housing conditions for the poor in New York. I'm not poking around for dirty laundry."

"We appreciate that, Mr. Curtin," Englander said dryly. "We'll try to be equally frank with you. Now, shoot."

"Why did you go into this venture in the first place?"

Englander frowned and thought a moment, "Two reasons. Large companies have been slow to involve themselves in urban renewal on the national scale. With the rising cost of single-family homes it seems clear that in small towns or large, a lot of multiple-dwelling units are going to be built in the future. Decaying conditions in most city centers—New York isn't alone—are going to require a lot of rehabilitation of existing properties. The scale will be huge. Therein," Englander smiled, "lies the first reason. Money. Somebody is going to make a lot of money rebuilding the cities. Why not Burton Industries?"

"And the second reason?" Paul prompted.

Englander focused his smile on Paul, who felt a chill. "That's a little more complicated. Call it capitalism with a human face. Let's say that I believe that the corporation has social responsibilities as does the individual. If we don't exercise them on our own, we will be," he searched for the right word, "urged by less pleasant means to do so."

Englander paused, unblinking, giving Paul a chance to catch up with his notes. When Paul looked up, he went on. "In trying to combine the two imperatives—making money and acting responsibly—we found that we needed a partner. It's no use moving into a city center, tearing down the old ghetto and building a new one, leaving the inhabitants to move back in as jobless and uninvolved as they were before, and with the profits from the renewal moved far from the area. Our partnership with Hawkes is an attempt to break the cycle, build some goodwill, and make some money doing it."

"Urban renewal has been with us a long time."

"Not as an organized, large-scale money-maker. We're not doing social justice or proposing philosophy here, Mr. Curtin. We're in it to make money. We've believed that we would do some good as we went along."

"Is it profitable just for you? Or is there incentive enough for everybody?"

"I sure hope so."

"Enough for Marcus Hawkes, Mr. Englander? Enough to keep him straight?"

"I'd hope so, my friend. Hell, he and his management own fifty point one percent—that's control. It wouldn't do to have control in our hands. Let's say they do a hundred million dollars a year in construction. Two, maybe three million in profit. At five times earnings, that's worth ten to fifteen million dollars in stock market terms. And that's year one. You can triple it, or quadruple it, if they're any good. Hawkes owns a third himself. I'd think somewhere between two and ten million would keep him interested."

"I'd think so. I would be," Paul replied.

"I've done a lot of checking on you in the past twenty-four hours, Mr. Curtin. I'm satisfied with what I hear. Ask your questions, Mr. Curtin."

"How is your partnership with Hawkes working out?"

"Fair. From what we can tell, they're a bit behind in their projects, but that happens to builders with a lot more experience in New York."

"If he was inexperienced, why did you choose him for a partner?"

"A reasonable question. He's been in the industry for years. He got good marks from the employers we contacted. And believe me, we checked to the limit of our capabilities. And he came with enthusiasm and ideas. As for his experience as a general contractor on his own," Englander raised an eyebrow, "what can you expect? There isn't a host of black contractors to choose among. No jobs. No experience. If we'd had a big choice, we wouldn't be having this little chat, would we?"

"Then you must keep a pretty tight rein on them—controls and so on."

Englander got up and walked to the window, standing with his hands in his pockets, looking out over the dark wavering forest. "I'm afraid we don't have that luxury. Do you want to speak to that, Jack?"

Holderness's voice was an airy tenor inconsistent with his physique. "It's not like dealing with a subsidiary, Mr. Curtin. We don't have political problems with our subsidiaries. If somebody screws up—bang, he's dead. If we do a joint venture and we don't have the numbers on time two months in a row, we have a team of B-school types on their ass. We've got the systems, Mr. Curtin, but we don't have the clout, where Hawkes is concerned. We can't lean on them. We bought the whole concept to get a shot at those big urban renewal bucks. If we crowd these guys, the whole ghetto is going to start screaming Oreo—black on the outside and white on the inside. Ergo, no control. Reports we do get, incomplete and a little confused and always late. But that's not control, especially when you can't check their accuracy."

"That doesn't sound like a basis for real confidence. Do you have doubts about the accuracy of their numbers?"

Holderness turned back to him, smiling. "Even if we don't, you can't steal much, or for long. Our auditors would catch it at the end of the year. Even stealing cash, in a few months your trial balance won't reconcile. But, besides worrying about getting caught, who would blow a chance to be the richest black businessman in America to steal a few bucks, or even a million?"

Englander, who had continued to look out of the window, cleared his throat. "It seems unlikely to me, too. Especially in consideration of his bipartisan political support."

Paul cocked his head, but said nothing. Nobody had answered his question.

"We've been interested by the high praise he's gotten from everybody in the Big Apple." He turned to Paul and weighed his words. "We were hoping that we'd chosen the right partner. Of course, we never expected to get strong recommendations from the governor and the mayor. It makes you wonder what they know that we don't."

"I don't get it."

"I'll simplify it for you, assuming this is off the record," Englander said.

Paul bristled. "I don't see the point of having an interview if you can't use it, or in giving one if you don't want your views known."

"For the moment, I don't think what I have to say will serve as anything but an interesting curiosity. But that may not always be true. You may want very badly to know what I have to say. It may be in my interest for you to have the information early on."

"Then let's say," Paul answered in a more accommodating tone, "that I am gathering material for my files, and that before I use it, I'll call for your okay."

Englander looked out of the window again. "I have gone to considerable trouble to check your pedigree, Mr. Curtin. I hope that I am not making a mistake in judgment. No man likes to be sandbagged twice the same year."

Paul made a show of putting his pencil and pad away in his briefcase.

"Construction is a tough business, Mr. Curtin. It's like quicksand. You want to stick in a toe. Then the first thing you know, you're up to your armpits. The theory behind Uhuru is fine. Do well by doing good. But we've been concerned as hell about the viability of this operation from the beginning. A few bucks for a look-see is one thing, but once you're past the seed money stage, and you're committed to build, you're talking telephone numbers."

Englander walked across the room and sat down behind the desk again. "We wanted to start slowly. A little job here. A little job there. That didn't suit Hawkes at all. It would prove to the black community that we didn't trust him. Tokenism, he called it. I stood my ground on one big gamble after another until Uhuru Towers came along. I took one look at it and told him he was nuts to even comtemplate anything that size, sixty to seventy million dollars with an infant company. He told me I ought to have more confidence. But he seemed to accept my decision."

Englander pushed the chair back from the desk. Paul could see the muscles in his jaw working. "Not long after that, I got a call from a friend telling me that Frank O'Neil was interested in making my acquaintance. We met by accident, as the saying goes, at an intimate cocktail party given by a mutual friend. He explained that Uhuru Towers was his personal marker to the black community. He wanted it built, and by a black builder. He had nothing but good things to say about Marcus Garvey Hawkes. You might even call it a character reference. I got the idea. We would be protected. The governor would see to it. I bought it."

For the first time since Paul had entered the office, he saw Englander's ice-blue eyes flicker with emotion. "It wasn't easy selling the board of directors of Burton Industries on guaranteeing a seventy-five-million-dollar bond for Hawkes Building. Needless to say, I was unable to give the directors all of the reasons for my confidence in the project, so I just muscled them with my own track record and credibility." He looked at Paul again. "I'm not given to that kind of risk taking."

"But this time, you stuck out your neck," Paul said.

"I did. The other side of the coin is pretty, Mr. Curtin. If we can get Uhuru Towers built decently and near budget, it'll open the doors to the municipal vault in every big city in America. And we'll have changed the way the country lives, and have taken a real shot at urban decay."

"And, since it was your risk, you get the credit, leading who knows where. But—"

"Ah. But. We've been getting a lot of hand holding from the governor's office, Mr. Curtin, lots of moral support. The building is falling behind. Our information is soft. Before I went on a trip to the Philippines, I put some wood to Mr. Hawkes. I said I expected to be informed when I got back. He didn't blink an eye.

"When I got back somebody else wanted to see me. This time it was Christopher Greene. I couldn't imagine why, since we have diametrically opposed political views. But, I'll bet by now you can guess what he wanted." Englander got to his feet again. "Right the first time. He wanted to sing the praises of Marcus Garvey Hawkes. He also told me that my association with Hawkes was the source of the high esteem im which both I and Burton Industries were held by him. I guess whoever wins in November, Marcus and I are going to have a friend in Albany."

"Beware of Greeks bearing gifts," Paul said.

"Beware of politicans bearing sandbags and handcuffs. I have no reason to be anything but grateful to the governor and the mayor for their support. While I'm sure that it really isn't newsworthy now, it might just be someday." Englander crossed the room and shook his hand. "Thanks for coming up. It's always a pleasure to meet the press. I'm not sure that you got what you expected, but I think you've got a clearer picture of urban renewal. If you print something, I'd like very much to see it."

"Thanks for your time. It will be interesting to see if these anecdotes do become news."

Despite a traffic jam at the Callaghan Tunnel under Boston Harbor, Paul made the six o'clock shuttle. He drove the car into the city by instinct, preoccupied by his interview at Burton Industries. Englander had accepted his request for an interview as opportune. He'd done some homework, looked him over, taken a few references, and decided that he'd make a good neutral witness if his nightmares came true. If he's backing and filling, he must really be feeling the heat. And those phone calls from Greene and O'Neil . . . I guess I'd be feeling the heat, too.

32

The day after Paul Curtin visited the Reverend McCaig, Paula Dennis, the young woman who had greeted him at the door of the Urban Development League, was taken to lunch at Jim McMullen's, a fashionable watering hole on upper Third Avenue.

Her invitation had been extended by a tall and well-groomed former Ivy League basketball player, who after law school and a year's clerkship with the chief judge of the Second Circuit, had become an administrative assistant to the mayor. As a black member of Greene's team, he'd been assigned to keep tabs on Uhuru's sponsor groups. On his first visit, he'd found an instant solution to his contact problem. From time to time, he was able to garner information, eat in a nice restaurant at the city's expense, and then get laid.

After Paula Dennis and he had showered and dressed, and she had left his bachelor studio to return to her work, he looked at his watch and decided that it was too late to go back to City Hall. He called the mayor on his private phone.

Chris Greene was tempted to rush over to see Melanie Parsons when he heard that Paul Curtin had been sticking his nose into Uhuru Towers again. Then, he thought better of it. Unseemly. Precipitous. Those were the first two words that popped into his head. He decided to sleep on it. He didn't sleep very well.

At ten-thirty the following morning, Chris Greene used his

private phone to call Melanie Parsons on the unlisted wire she had given him.

"Mrs. Parsons, this is Chris Greene. Good morning."

"Good morning, Mr. Mayor."

"I want you to know how much I appreciate your editorial support," he pushed the early edition of the *Advocate* around on his desk, then finding the page, continued, "for higher parking lot taxes."

Melanie raised an eyebrow. What does he really have to say? she wondered. "Our feelings are the same as yours, Mr. Mayor. If they want to come in to the city and pollute our air, we might as well derive some fiscal benefit from it."

"And there was another thing."

"Yes."

"You've been very supportive of my efforts to convince the black community to get out and vote. I think we both know that that's the key to getting Frank O'Neil out of the Governor's Mansion." She'll like that better than talking about getting me elected, he thought.

He knows how to reach for the right strings, she admitted, replying, "That majority in urban areas will certainly make the difference." What's the damn sparring about?

"I am convinced that the success of the Uhuru Towers project and my identification with it are keys to a wide margin in that vote."

Melanie frowned. Why is he pushing? "We've always shown support for Uhuru, Your Honor." Paul Curtin's words intruded into her consciousness. Greene won't mind changing sides on Uhuru, Paul had said, unless of course, he's been bought.

"I've talked to all of the people on the Greene team, Mrs. Parsons. I don't meant to preach to the already converted, but I wanted to express to you personally that Uhuru is a keystone issue for me, and that your support on the issue is vital for me in stopping the O'Neil avalanche. I hope that you're not offended by my unabashed lobbying. I wasn't sure if I should impose on our personal relationship this way. But I thought it was that important."

"I'm glad that you feel that you can confide in me, and call on me, Mr. Mayor. I am sure you know we're behind you."

"I'm proud of it. Thank you very much. I hope we'll be seeing each other soon."

"Of course."

Greene was still uneasy when he hung up the phone. He wasn't sure whether she'd made a commitment on Uhuru or not. He blew out a deep breath. He'd done what he could.

Melanie Parsons stared at the telephone. After three and a half decades of public life, she'd become attuned to the subtle nuances of human behavior. The phone call from Christopher Greene had been a crash of cymbals.

As anxious as she was to bring O'Neil to his knees, and therefore committed to his opponent, she did not want to be manipulated by Greene.

Her whole life had been dedicated to shrugging off the mantle of male-imposed helplessness which her sex in her generation had inherited. Melanie sat in the straight-backed chair and looked across the table at her father's portrait. He was the first man who had looked past her gender and into her heart and intellect. He had permitted her to postpone her interment in the social whirl of post-World War I America by attending law school.

By the end of her first term, the pressure for her to make a suitable match had become intolerable, even for Samuel Parsons. His wife and his younger daughters tugged at his sleeves and nattered endlessly that Melanie's spinsterhood was a roadblock to her sisters' social advancement and marital opportunities. Despite his own disinclination, and Melanie's reluctance, at the end of the year she withdrew from school.

Despite her unfeminine interests, she was clever and amusing. She was a pretty girl, with a mass of shimmering brown hair. Though she was not tall, her character showed in an upright posture which gave her a presence. She had a round face and pudgy little nose, with eyes that were dark and flashed with rage and humor, and big breasts and pretty legs.

It was a time of paradoxes—the summer of 1926. Blond investment bankers bustled against European nobility in boaters and white flannel trousers at the gangway of a yacht owned by a formerly impoverished Russian Jew. But, then, RCA was selling at 600 on the New York Stock Exchange, and David Sarnoff's modest pedigree didn't seem so important.

The party was given in honor of the daughter of still another such parvenu. Samuel and Rachel Parsons stood with their oldest children, Melanie and Dora, in the receiving line with their friends.

The guest list was a Byzantine amalgam of the business, professional, and social worlds. After a quick review by the host to make sure that no one important to him had been omitted, the matter was turned over to Mrs. Sarnoff, to decide what emphasis should be placed on noble birth, Mayflower heritage, and cold, hard cash, and eligibility.

Melanie danced with each of the eligibles twice. Fifty whirls past the teak and the polished brass listening to the gamut of postadolescence from bravado to agonized silence. Willing the pain in her feet and legs to subside, she passed a few moments in conversation with ten survivors. Half a dozen asked if they might call upon her. She accepted four. From the middle of the list Horace Koenigsberg emerged. Like so many compromise candidates, in the absence of serious faults, there was a lack of virtues.

He was quite tall. Melanie liked that. He was rather handsome. She liked that, too. He was shallower than she had imagined at first. Horace was the type who is often mistaken for cool and clever by dint of a silent smile, when in fact, he has nothing to say.

He was the scion of one of New Orleans's oldest and most respectable Jewish families, though only vestigial wealth remained. He was looked upon as something of a catch, and Rachel Parsons wanted him for a son-in-law.

God, Melanie thought, sitting in front of her father's portrait, peering into that time-tinged mist, if any ship of matrimony had been launched in high style, it was that ill-balanced, badly designed, and unwieldy craft.

Nothing was spared in the undertaking except good judgment. There had been seven hundred and fifty people in attendance at the Plaza Hotel. The breadth of the social canvas was a masterwork. There were Loebs, Lehmans, and Schiffs. There were Whitneys, Vanderbilts, and Goulds. There were Rhinelanders and Van Rensselaers. They were uniformly congratulatory and resplendent, as though their good wishes, like their finery, could be acquired by the yard.

Melanie accepted the moment stoically. She stood expressionless outside the double doors at the rear of the Grand

Ballroom, an ornament in white satin and lace. In her hands, she gripped a large bouquet of white orchids and lilies of the valley.

At her side, Samuel Parsons shifted from foot to foot, adjusting the carnation on the lapel of his cutaway coat. Melanie noticed the frown on his face. The diabetes which was to take his life had already affected the circulation in his legs.

"Your legs hurt, don't they, Papa?" Melanie asked. Her voice sounded hushed to her, the way it does when you whisper after bedtime when you are a child.

He shook his head sadly. "No. Not much. I have other concerns."

She turned toward him, sweeping her veil away from her face. "What is it, Papa?"

Avoiding her ten-foot train, he stepped around her and gripped her arms in his hands. "In business, if I make a bad decision, I change my mind. I look in the mirror and say, Sam, you are old, diabetic, and foolish. Take the first markdown."

Melanie swallowed and forced a smile. "Where is this taking us, Papa? This lesson in high finance?"

"Melanie, marriage isn't a line of goods you can drop at a moment's notice. Taking a loss after you have made the major commitment of your emotional life is more costly, with lingering effects."

Dear Papa. She touched his cheek. "Shall we beat one more time around the bush? Please, Papa. Say it."

"Melanie," she could feel his grip tighten on her arms almost to the point of pain, "if this marriage is not what you want for the rest of your life, in a matter of five minutes, this gathering can be turned into one of the nicest dinner-dances of the New York season. Once that glass is shattered beneath Horace's heel, it will be too late. It is a thousand times better to express regrets one minute before than one minute after."

She swallowed hard and looked him in the eye. "I've made my choice, Papa."

Her life with Horace Koenigsberg was numbing. As in everything, Horace clung dully to the white line in the middle of the road. He appeared at his office regularly, accomplishing nothing. Their sex life was perfunctory, but she dutifully bore two grandchildren for her parents to adore. In the absence of a focus for her interests, she dissipated into Mah-Jongg, bridge, and golf and entertained.

The only relief from the tedium was her weekly visit to her father. The Depression had settled in, and the world had turned upside down. Friends she had known disappeared from her life. Rich men became poor. The poor became paupers.

"How are you, my dear? How are things at home?"

"They are fine, Papa. The children are well. The servants are well. The dog is well. Even Horace is well."

"How nice. Has anything interesting happened since last Wednesday?"

"Not in my house, Papa."

Samuel Parsons moved restlessly in his bed. A blanket covered the stump of his amputated right leg, lost to gangrene six months earlier. His agile mind had permitted him to preserve the bulk of his fortune, but no skill existed to maintain his eroding health. He looked at his daughter across the mass of business papers strewn about him. "Well, I expect that one day I shall be inundated by this mess. I am getting too old and incompetent. You don't suppose they took a part of my mind with my leg?"

She looked at him with affection. *Which of us invalids is here to cheer the other, Papa?* "Oh, I don't know, Papa. It seems that we have more servants than ever. Mama has always said that the measure of wealth is comfort, and that comfort can only be provided by servants."

He waved his hand in dismissal. "Nonsense. Not having to make your own bed only frees you from a small task. If you are freed of all the small tasks, then what will free you from tedium? Not servants."

"Papa, do you feel trapped in that bed?"

Not so trapped as you are, my daughter, he thought. "No. My mind has wings. My ears and eyes bring me what others see and hear beyond the bed and the room. My imagination does the rest."

"My imagination has withered. I get around, and I see, and I hear for myself. But the impressions are flat and gray."

Samuel Parsons pushed himself higher onto his pillows. "You should have finished law school. That's my fault."

"I don't mean to imply that, Papa. It's no one's fault. It's the way of the world. I have nothing meaningful to do, nothing that matters."

"Does your home matter?"

She hesitated. "All right, Papa. I admit it. I have learned to tell servants what I want done. My children seem normal and happy. Is that the sum total of my life? I suppose so. It's the world we live in. I should be grateful. There are few women as fortunate as I am."

Samuel Parsons looked at his daughter ruefully. "That's not enough for you, is it? It's enough for Dora, it's enough for the other girls. But it's not enough for you."

"Papa, am I such an ingrate?"

He looked across the room through the window. "I am not even physically trapped, so long as I can look out into the garden at the river and Long Island."

Melanie looked at him quizzically.

"Our world is changing. Perhaps our money will insulate us from some elements—perhaps not. If I were young I would want to be at the forefront. A new social order is going to come out of this Depression. If we want to persist, we should take a part in the transition. What do you know about Governor Roosevelt?"

Which bush are we beating around this time, Papa? "A bit. I read the papers."

"A successful revolution can only be carried out by a member of the old order. Otherwise, there is only time for vengeance and reprisal. Roosevelt is the man."

"Yes, Papa. And so?"

"I was just thinking."

"I can see that, Papa." Please, Papa.

"Why don't you see if you can get involved with Roosevelt's campaign."

"What about my family responsibilities, Papa?"

He cleared his throat. "I think it is very important that people make sacrifices for family. I remember telling you that, once." And you have paid for my clinging to convention, he thought. "I am beginning to wonder what the extent of such sacrifice should be. Surely, not the immobilization of an active mind. Perhaps your children will be better served in this new world-to-be by a mother who was active in the transition." He lay back against the pillow, suddenly tired. "Why don't you give it some thought?"

Melanie left the room with her temples pounding. She drove about aimlessly. Though it was a chilly March day, she rolled down the windows of the black Packard and let the wind whip around her.

Can he mean that I am free to leave? she asked herself. Can he be giving me that license? She remembered him standing with his hands around her arms at the Plaza. Better a minute before, than a minute after. She told him she had made her choice. While he lived, she would not renege. But, there had to be a middle ground.

By the time that she arrived at home, she had made peace with herself. She ordered the servants about with her customary competence and dropped into the children's wing to say hello and check with Nanny.

Horace came home from another empty day at the job which his father-in-law had created for him. He drew himself a scotch and soda and sat in his overstuffed chair. "How was Dad today, Melanie?"

"All right," she said, strain showing in her voice. "He wants me to look into something for him."

"Oh?" Horace said, with mild interest.

"He thinks I ought to take a greater part in the world around me. He suggested Mr. Roosevelt's campaign."

"I can't imagine what's on his mind. It's hardly your cup of tea, my dear," he said with the annoying trace of a drawl.

Her look chilled him to the bone. "Nonetheless, I will be getting involved."

Though she hadn't raised her voice, he had the impression that she had shouted at him. "Why, of course, my dear." He sipped at his drink and picked up the evening paper.

Such had been her Declaration of Independence, ignored even by the man to whom it had been made.

She began to read omnivorously—papers, magazines, books. She attempted Keynes, battled to the last page and returned him to the library, read but undigested.

After a month, she began to discuss her findings with her father. He was patient and receptive. "You sound very knowledgeable, Melanie. If you keep this up, I may hire you myself."

' At home, Melanie fell victim to headaches. Horace became sufficiently alarmed to suggest that she see a doctor. She sniffed a lavender hanky and said that they would pass.

Three months after their first discussion on politics, Melanie presented herself at the Beekman Place house dressed in blue silk. She wore a smallish hat with an elegant peacock feather and carried a clutch bag.

Samuel Parsons pushed his spectacles back on his nose. "My goodness. Is this a fashion show? I was just expecting another visit to the invalid ward."

"No. I just felt like dressing up." She broke into a smile. "I have never been able to lie to you successfully."

"Too true."

"There's a benefit for Roosevelt at the Morgenthaus' this afternoon. They're trying to raise money, but I heard that they need volunteers as well."

His eyes twinked. "Are you prepared to lick stamps and march in torchlight parades?"

"Is that how one starts at the bottom?"

"So I am told. Are you ready to face all of these political types?"

"I'm better read than I was when I started. I've got to make a beginning."

"Let's make it a good one, then. I don't think you are the stamplicking type. We want a better showcase for your talents. If you want to step forward, it's going to cost money. That's what they all want. But you know that already." He opened the drawer of his night table and pulled out a book. He wrote a check and handed it to her.

"That should be enough to impress them. Give them twenty percent of it today. Be the second- or third-largest donor. Enough to be noticed, but not enough to seem the parvenu or the fool."

She looked at the check. It was for $100,000. "Thank you, Papa."

The gathering at the Morgenthaus' was more eclectic than she had imagined. There were Tammany Irish, upper-class Jewry, and odd foreign characters who looked like Wobblies and anarchists.

It cost Melanie only $10,000 to play her opening card. She listened to radical speeches by members of the IWW and the

International Labor Farband. If half of what they suggested came to pass, she could not imagine that America would emerge from the economic storm through which it was sailing.

She saw that Mrs. Roosevelt and Mrs. Morgenthau clapped politely and nodded in appreciation and interest for each speaker. She did likewise.

At the end of the affair, Melanie was introduced to Mrs. Roosevelt. She was polite without being diffident. Mrs. Roosevelt recognized her as a new source of funds immediately and invited her to tea two weeks hence.

"I know," Mrs. Roosevelt said, "that Franklin will be pleased to meet you. Will you be bringing your husband?"

"No, Mrs. Roosevelt. This is very much my own undertaking."

As Melanie took her coat from the maid, Chapin Morgan, a banker who had climbed early onto the Roosevelt bandwagon, stepped forward to introduce himself. He was about thirty, Melanie judged, several years younger than herself. He was tall and suave, dressed in Brooks Brothers' unchanging style. "May I take you somewhere, Mrs. Koenigsberg? My car is downstairs."

"My car is in front of my father's house on Beekman Place. It would be lovely if you could drop me there."

Morgan's car was a royal-blue Chrysler saloon with dove-gray upholstery. The seat had the feel of cashmere to it as she slid in. The doorman closed the door behind her.

"Beekman Place, wasn't it?" She nodded, and he stepped on the gas. He glanced at her sidelong in the mirror. On a whim he said, "Say, you wouldn't join me for dinner, would you?"

"Thanks. I've got to go home. Scarsdale," she said with a nervous laugh.

At the first light, he said, "How about a cocktail, then?"

"I'd rather not."

As he pulled away, he said, "I hope you're not offended. I don't ask pretty strangers out all of the time."

"Oh, no. It's very nice of you. I don't like speakeasies. I'm not comfortable in them."

"We could have a drink at my place," he blurted.

She looked at him and began to laugh. His face was red as a beet. "Do you ask strange women to your apartment all the time?"

He grinned. "Not really."

"Okay, I'll stretch my luck."

They sat together on the couch of his four-room apartment, appreciating the view of the park. He had mixed them five to one martinis made with gin smuggled in from the Caribbean on his Christmas holidays. She felt giddy and warm.

Chapin was quite as stiff as she, sitting at the edge of the sofa, his knees together, balancing the glass. Finally, as they talked about Roosevelt, and his promise to repeal the Volstead Act, he put the glass down and reached awkwardly for her hand.

She withdrew it. Inadvertently, he brushed against her breasts. The touch of his fingers augmented the tingling sensation that two drinks and the heat of the radiator had produced. She rested, passive for a moment, not considering the consequences.

Chapin, stunned by his own audacity and her failure to evade his grasp, turned his hand and touched her nipples, as they hardened and protruded through the silk.

Her pulse roared in her ears. In a moment, she was committed.

He stood, and helping her gently to her feet, guided her, cupping her breast in his hand, into the bedroom.

She stood docilely in the middle of the room, wordless, as he murmured to her, nibbling at her with his lips, removing her clothing one article at a time. When he had done, and she stood before him in the soft glow of the bedside lamps, she realized that no man had ever seen her unclothed in the light.

He brushed against her and nuzzled her as he removed his own clothing. When he had put the last of it on the back of a chair, she forced her eyes down to his groin.

She reached curiously to touch his erect organ, stripping the unfamiliar foreskin back and forth several times. His breath caught in his throat.

He picked her up in his arms and lay her on the bed. After twenty minutes of gentle, persistent attention, he gave her the first orgasm of her life. She was still for a few moments afterward.

"Can that happen again, Chapin?"

"Of course."

"Show me how to make love, Chapin."

Two hours later, after they had dressed, he went to the door to take her to her car.

"You're very sweet." She kissed his lips. "I'm going to take a cab. Listen to me, Chapin. We're never going to do this again."

"But why?"

She smiled and touched his cheek. "It simply won't do. I thank you. Now I have been to bed with two men in my life. For your information, you are far the better. Just the same, I don't need an awkward liaison. A Jewish matron with two children in Scarsdale will provide you with more problems than pleasures in the end. But I will tell you this, if ever I need you for something, I will not hesitate to call on you. If ever you should need me, remember that I am in your debt. Good-bye, Chapin."

She returned to the house in Scarsdale in cold fury at Horace, mourning the hollow nights she had wasted in his bed, glorying in her newfound joy. She announced that, henceforth, she would be sleeping in a separate room. It was the evening of the last day that any man imposed himself upon her without her prior consent. She had made herself free.

Melanie Parsons put her hands on her knees and pushed herself to her feet from the stiff chair in front of her father's portrait in her office at the *Advocate*. Twenty-five years after that afternoon in his apartment, Chapin Morgan tottered at the edge of failure in his effort to take control of a small electronics company. To Oscar Bornstein's horror, she lent him ten million dollars on his signature. In a few weeks, the money was returned with interest, together with a few shares in what became a billion-dollar conglomerate. She received two dozen roses on every birthday and another two dozen on the anniversary of the fund-raising party at the Morgenthaus.

She sat behind her desk and mulled over her conversation with Christopher Greene. It always becomes necessary, sooner or later, to judge the sincerity of the people with whom one comes in contact. With her sweet reminiscence of Chapin Morgan close at hand, she made her decision about Christopher Greene. She had considered calling Paul Curtin to tell him about Greene's phone call. She put the idea out of her mind and called Madeleine to bring her another cup of tea.

33

Paul Curtin was typing up his notes on his visit to Burton Industries when Abe Schneider called.

"How'd it go, Paul? You get anything?"

"That's a hard question to answer," Paul said candidly. "I saw your friend Jarvis. He got me in to see both Englander and Holderness, the top dogs. They were very cordial. It was damn nice of you. I don't know what I expected to find out." Less frankly, he added, "It was interesting, but it didn't change my world."

"What did you think of Englander?" Abe asked.

"Bone chilling. A very smart man. Very strong. He scared me to death. Is he straight?"

"So I am told," Abe replied. "But, not to step on his toes, please. He neither forgives nor forgets. But if he tells you something, you can bank it."

"At least I have a better idea of why Burton got into the Hawkes deal. I owe you that."

"Think nothing of it. Any signs that it's not working out?"

Paul could sense the old newspaperman's instincts hard at work. "It's hard to tell," he said, noncommittally.

Abe knew when he was being brushed off. "Okay, Junior. I'll leave it be. Now, about your building. Not much, Paul. It was registered to 523 East Corporation. The only address given is P.O. Box 122, Morrisania Station, Bronx, New York 10451."

Paul scribbled the information on a pad, looked at it, and said, "But what do you do if the water isn't running or something? How do you complain?"

"I guess it's just tough titty. Maybe there was a super-intendent."

"In a hole like that?"

"They probably have a guy that covers a whole bunch of them in the same neighborhood. That's all I've got, old buddy. I've got to run."

"Thanks again, Abe."

"You owe me a cigar."

Paul looked up the address of the Morrisania Post Office, took a note pad, and went to his car. He took the drive up to the Willis Avenue Bridge, looking over at the charred rubble of 523 East, and continued up to the Grand Concourse into the Bronx.

At a distance, the avenue seems aptly named. Two generations ago, it was the borough's main artery, and its Park and Fifth avenues combined. An eight-lane roadway separated by two islands marks its northward path from the Harlem River to the city limits. The concourse is lined on both sides by buildings that convey the sense of the twenties. Though most of them are less than ten stories tall, many have carved stone facings, and large windows give evidence of high ceilings and spacious rooms.

As Paul left the central roadway, he opened his window to ask directions from a pedestrian. The cancer which had consumed the south Bronx had begun to encroach on the concourse, the smaller buildings first, and the stench of garbage that is a concomitant to poverty in New York was tangible even in the crisp March air.

With help from two passersby, Paul was able to locate the post office off 190th Street. He parked the car and entered the dingy building, which crackled with steam heat and was redolent of unwashed humanity.

The first clerk he saw told him it was impossible to have the name and address of the lessee of the post office box. A second was even more positive. Persistence and loud protestations brought him to the desk of a fat man reading the *Daily News* and eating a monstrous meatball sandwich. It had dripped on the front of his shirt. Paul showed his credentials, then explained that he was looking for a slumlord.

"This ain't nothin'. They're all like this, the landlords around here." He whispered confidentially. "They don't want none of these spics and niggers knowing where to find them. Afraid they'd come and kick their fuckin' asses off. You know," he said in a low voice, "like when they cut off the heat and shit like that." The man snorted and took another bite. "Serves 'em right. Ought to pay their fuckin' rent just like the rest of us."

After a bit of cajoling and sympathizing with the man over the evolution of his neighborhood, Paul secured the street address of the company that proved to be the owner of more than twenty buildings, each with its own anonymous post office box.

The J and G Realty Corporation was located on Fordham Road, not far from where it bisects the concourse. The offices occupied the second floor of a two-story brick building that had been built shortly after the Second World War. At first, he had been tempted to make an appointment by phone, but decided that since they had gone to considerable trouble to maintain a low profile, they might not welcome the press with open arms.

The doorway to the upper floor was lodged between the two storefronts that occupied the lower level of the building. The stairs were narrow and steeply pitched. The glass door showed the marks of many hands and the gold lettering was chipped and faded. Behind it there was a large room with dirty beige walls bisected by a chest-high unpainted plywood counter. The scuffed black vinyl floor was dotted by a dozen desks occupied by women typing or shuffling papers.

A plump woman in her fifties, with a pencil stuck in her curly gray hair and spectacles dangling by their earpieces from a chain around her neck, walked aggressively to the counter opposite Paul and asked him in a loud, nasty voice, "What can I do for you, mister?"

"I'd like to see the proprietor, please."

"The who?"

"The owner. The boss."

"For what? In reference to what?" the woman said, clearly obstructionist.

"Are you the boss?"

"No, I'm not. Listen, I'm busy. You want to tell me what's on your mind, or can I go back to work?"

Paul pulled out his press card and leaned across the counter. "If you don't tell the boss that I'm here, you may just find yourself all over the front page of the *New York Advocate* and out of a job," Paul said cheerily. Then he snapped, "Now move it, or I'll start making some real noise."

The woman turned slowly and walked with insolent deliberation to a door at the back of the room and knocked. She stuck her head inside and said something. There was a small commotion. She closed the door again, beckoned to Paul, then walked back to her desk, ignoring him.

Paul assumed that he'd been summoned to the office and made his way around the counter. He knocked and a brassy female voice told him to come in.

The woman was like the first, but better dressed. "I'm Mrs. Greenstein," she said importantly. "What do you want?"

Paul passed her his press card. "I'm Paul Curtin. I'm with the *New York Advocate*. I'd like to ask you a few questions. I won't be long."

She handed back the plastic laminated ID and stepped away from the doorway, where she had effectively blocked his view into the office. Behind her, a middle-aged man sat at a desk in a corner. He was fat and his collar was open, revealing a ruff of black hair at the base of his throat. His face was porcine with tiny eyes, divided from a double chin by a slash of a mouth with a long black cigar in the corner.

He mopped his bald head with a handkerchief, removed the cigar from his mouth, and indicated a chair at the side of the desk. "I'm Max Jacobs. Sadie, maybe he'd like a cup of coffee? You'd like a cup of coffee, Mr. Curtin?"

"No, thank you. I want to get some information on the building that burned down."

Sadie sat down next to Max. There was a pause, then Max said, "Which one, Mr. Curtin? We had three in the last six months."

Casual, Paul thought. "I wasn't aware of more than one."

Jacobs shook his head knowingly and puffed at his cigar. "Mr. Curtin, are you looking for something special, or just a standard slumlord story?" He laughed humorlessly. "Oh, even us slumlords read the *New York Advocate*. They teach us in Scrooge School, where we learn to be mean to orphans."

Paul moved uncomfortably in his chair, looking for something to say.

Jacobs waved his cigar. "Go ahead, Mrs. Greenstein. Tell how you were a guard at a concentration camp until they found out that you were Jewish and fired you. Mrs. Greenstein hates children, too. Don't you, Sadie?"

Paul raised his hands above his head. "I surrender. I give up. I won't prejudge you if you don't prejudge me."

"Good," Jacobs said, stuffing the cigar back into his mouth. "That's a beginning. I'll try to forget that you are a mudslinger trying to hang me from my own tsitsis. You'll forget that I'm a monster who likes to watch black children turn blue with cold."

"I'm investigating the fire at 523 East 135th Street. It's a background for a story on housing under the O'Neil administration."

"You be a good fellow," Jacobs said. "If you find anything worthwhile that happened to housing since O'Neil is governor, you'll let me know."

"What happened to that building, Mr. Jacobs? Do you know?"

"I'll tell you what I told the fire marshals. I'll tell you what they told me. It was an old building, 1903. There was probably a gas leak somewhere in the basement. It accumulated under the floorboards. Then, there was a spark. Or, it could have been the flame from the boiler. Then, it blew up. And in that wind, that rotten old building burned to a crisp." He looked up sharply at Paul. "I know what you think. You think I'm indifferent. That I forgot that there were people in there. No, I didn't forget. The other two buildings that Mrs. Greenstein and I owned that burned, they were empty. Them maybe, we could forget. We won't forget 523. I asked about arson. I couldn't believe that it burned by itself. It was such a mess that they couldn't tell. The marshals said that the usual things, the ones that show up right away, weren't there. There was no sign of flammable fluid on the beams that they could see. There was no hesitation between the fire and the explosion, which happens when some crazy sets a bomb. Whoosh! It was there one minute, and gone the next. They are calling it fire from accidental causes."

"But how could you let it get into such a condition where it could blow up like that? Why didn't you rehabilitate it?"

"I want to show you something, Mr. Curtin. You want to report on something? Report on this." Jacobs drew a statement out of the desk drawer and passed it across to Paul with two other pieces of paper.

"This is why I asked about arson, Mr. Curtin. The fire

marshals said there was no evidence of arson. But there's no evidence of negligence, either."

The bill Jacobs had passed was for $200 for repair of gas lines dated the week before the fire. The others were fire inspectors' reports, the first dated three weeks earlier, indicating an unsatisfactory condition, the second the day after the repair bill showing that the fault had been corrected.

"Nobody wants to hear about that, Mr. Curtin. They'll say that I got the repair company to send me a bill for doing nothing, and that I bribed the fire inspector to give me a clean bill of health on his second visit."

"Did you, Mr. Jacobs?" Paul asked. "Were the repairs legitimately performed and inspected? Or was there a little hand-holding?"

Jacobs spit the end of his cigar into the wastebasket. "Both the repairs and the report were legit. Let me tell you something, Mr. Curtin." He poked a stubby finger angrily in Paul's direction. "You think it's easy to be a landlord in this city? I own these buildings with Sadie Greenstein, like I owned them with her husband Jack, rest in peace. Some of them have been in the family fifty years, since they was built.

"The taxes on 523 East went from $5,800 in 1969 to $21,000 in 1980. If I raise the rents the same proportion, I go to jail. The cost of gas went up four hundred percent. It's only two years that I could get some of the money back. In the whole building, there was only one family that wasn't on some kind of welfare. The welfare, they make out the rent checks in the name of the tenant and the landlord jointly. For ten percent the check cashing service forgets there's only one signature. Go collect. Go evict."

Jacobs got up and looked out of the window. "I remember when this was a nice shopping street. Now you can't even walk on it in the daytime, that you wouldn't be afraid. I would like to have some pride in my properties. I would also, God forbid, like to make a decent return." He spun around to face Paul. "There are times when there isn't enough heat in my buildings, and it's my fault. And there are times when I put in new copper tubing, and in three days the scum next door rip it out and sell it by the pound for bubkis. Then they call 'Eyewitness News' to complain about no heat." He slumped in the chair. "All right. I had my two cents' worth. What else do you want?"

"I want the tenant list for the building. I'd like to know anything you know about the tenants. Anything at all."

"The only people I knew were the Jenkses. They were the family that wasn't on welfare. The husband, Al was his name, used to do an odd job or two around the house for me. I'd throw him a few bucks. The others, they were just families, black and Puerto Rican. Lots of kids. The place was always full of kids.

"Did you have a super who covered that building, Mr. Jacobs?"

"Yeah, Manny Hernandez. He's been with me ten years. I own a few other tax-payers in the same area. He keeps an eye on them. I can't do it. I'd get lynched."

"Because you're the landlord?"

"There's that. Plus, I'm white. I'm a Jew. And I'm there. Someday the city is going to end up owning all of these buildings. Then what will they do? There won't be nobody to pay taxes, and fixed rents won't cover rising costs." He shook his head glumly. "Sadie, give him the tenant list and Hernandez's phone number."

Paul checked out Jacobs's story with Archie Fallon at the Inspector General's Office of the fire department.

"I'm from a big family. Seeing kids in a fire tears me up. Sometimes, I get so sick I walk over to church. I went to mass in St. Paul's when I came back from that Willis Avenue site. I've been in the job my whole life, like my father. I ought to be used to it by now."

"How can anyone get used to death?" Paul asked. "There were lots of kids, huh?"

"You can tell by the size of the bones, when you're sorting the debris." Fallon's voice was flat and emotionless.

Paul nodded. "Has anyone got a final count?"

"You could try the Bureau of Records and the Coroner's office."

"The owner told me that you gave it a clean bill—no arson, no criminal negligence."

"We gave it a good toss. No sign of flammables. No sign of explosive devices. You can tell. Discoloration of the beams and floors. The way materials are fractured."

"Then it was a gas leak, as he said. Isn't that negligence?"

"The place was just inspected. The certificate was clean. We checked the inspector out. Not a mark against him. Never taken a dime. We grilled him. So did the cops. Maybe another part of the gas line gave after the first repair."

Paul took the copy of the NYFD report Fallon gave him to the bar at the Lion's Head and read it over a double scotch. It told him nothing he hadn't heard. He decided to give the super a call.

The number rang five or six times. As he started to hang up, there was a click at the other end of the line. "*Diga me.*"

"Mr. Hernandez?" Paul asked.

"Yeah. Who's this?"

"My name is Curtin. Mr. Jacobs gave me your number. I'm a reporter. I want to talk to you about the fire on Willis Avenue."

Hernandez hesitated, intrigued. "Jacobs give you my number? I work my ass off, man. When you want to see me?"

"Whenever you want. Where do you live?"

"In one of Mr. Jacobs's other buildings. Just on the Manhattan side of the Willis Avenue Bridge."

"You had dinner yet?"

"Nah."

Paul scoured his mind for a suitable meeting place. "You know the Madison Avenue Deli?"

"On Eighty-sixth Street, the big fancy place?"

"Is that okay? In a half hour?"

Paul beat Hernandez to the restaurant by a couple of minutes. He was middle-aged and swarthy with rough hands. He'd put on a suit. Church clothes, Paul thought.

After they were seated, Paul said, "I appreciate your taking the time. You put in long hours, huh?"

"I work like a dog. I cover all their buildings in the south Bronx, nineteen of them."

As they talked, the waitress brought them their dinner and some beer.

"Is Jacobs a good boss?"

"Yeah. I work for him ten years. He treat me good. Mrs. Greenstein, she yell a lot."

"Is he a good landlord?"

"There ain't no such thing," he said around a mouthful, "as

a good landlord. But we don't run no dives. The heat comes up. The toilets flush. But them buildings is old, man."

"Was 523 worse than the others?"

"Hell, no," Hernandez said, finishing his second beer. "Some asshole try to steal some pipe. He make a leak. That's the day the building inspector show up. It's always like that. We get it fixed right away. Even had a plumber do it. I don't like to fool around with gas."

"So you think it was an accident, too," Paul said.

"It wasn't no torch job. Who would bother?"

"You never know. Maybe they were trying to get rid of somebody in the building." Paul let the bait dangle.

"Them stiffs?" Hernandez laughed. "Them poor bastards didn't have a nickel between them."

"Jacobs told me one of the tenants used to help you out a little."

"Who? Al Jenks?"

"That was the name," Paul said casually.

"He was a mason. He used to give me a hand weekends for a few extra bucks."

"A straight guy? Never mixed up in anything funny, was he?"

Hernandez stopped eating, and looked up. "We used to have a beer together. He had a wife and a bunch of kids. It was a shame. He wasn't never mixed up in nothing."

Paul shifted uncomfortably. "Did you see him the day of the fire?"

"Nah. I was there the day before. His old lady asked me if I seen him that day."

"Why?" Paul asked.

Hernandez shrugged. "I don't know, man. Maybe he tied on a load and forgot to sleep in his own bed. Al liked pussy."

"Did you see him after that?" Was he already dead by then? Paul asked himself.

"How come you so interested in him, man?"

"I thought he might know something about the fire, when Jacobs told me he worked on the building, too. Have you seen him since?" he insisted.

"Since the fire? Shit, man, he's in there with the rest of them, all fried up."

Paul spent too long falling asleep, thinking about Fallon's

comment that in the absence of concrete evidence, suspicions get you nowhere. The facts of Al Jenks's disappearance, the where, why, and when, were conveniently buried in the debris of the building in which he had lived, and Paul was running out of strategies to disinter them.

34

Paul awoke with a dull headache and called Jeff Jackson.

"Listen, I'm about out of inspiration. Can you take me uptown tonight, and see if we can find somebody to talk to about Gaines and Hawkes? Somebody from the neighborhood."

"I'll see what I can find."

"My place at six?"

Paul dressed and went downtown to the Department of Birth and Death Records. As he walked in, he made note of the department head's name on a wall sign.

"I'd like to speak to Mr. Carluccio, please," he asked politely.

Carluccio was a hard-faced man of middle years with dark hair. "What can I do for you?"

"I need a list of the people who died in a fire about a month ago."

"They'd be listed by date."

"They all died the same day."

"You could still have hundreds of names of deal with."

Paul took out the tenant list. "I have this to compare it with. I'd like to see the death certificates."

In an hour, using the list as a base, Paul had picked out twenty-two certificates with matching names.

Paul's next stop was the morgue on East 29th Street. As he walked through the doors, a voice reverberated matter-of-factly from the cold walls, "Meat wagon's comin' in. Open the garage."

After some negotiating, Paul found himself in the office of Dr. Ernest Hollings. He was in his mid-forties, cadaverous, with shining black skin and a pencil moustache tucked under a broad nose. His eyes were red and veiny from lack of sleep.

Paul put the death certificates on the desk. "How do you know that the people on these pieces of paper are the ones who really got buried?"

The doctor took the certificates and shuffed them. "We collect the bones, and whatever else might remain, dental work and so forth, and we sort them."

Paul's face reflected his distaste.

Hollings continued. "It was a nasty fire. An explosion. Great heat. Under normal circumstances, even in a fire, visual identification is usually possible. Disgusting, revolting, or heart-rending for a relative or friend—but possible." The doctor stopped talking, lit a cigarette, and offered the pack to Paul.

"No, thanks. Then, I guess you've made a positive identification of all the people in this building."

"I said under normal circumstances," Dr. Hollings said, blowing out a cloud of blue smoke. "If the fire hadn't burned so hot, or so fast, the fire hoses might have saved something. If there hadn't been a blast to scatter things around, or a collapse to bury them. We dug out what we could, and tried to match it on the floor of forensic lab number two, upstairs. It took two days to get the remains here. It took two more to finish sorting."

"Did you have a tenant list to work against?"

"That, and the 1980 Census form for the building, though who knows how accurate it was. If we hadn't had them, we wouldn't have known where to begin. We took the list and counted out complete sets of major bones, male first, then female, adults then children."

"Were there any discrepancies from the lists?"

"When we were finished, we checked against dental charts, and people came to make identifications."

Paul drummed his fingers on the desk, then decided to say what was on his mind. "Was there anybody in that fire who didn't get a death certificate? Was there anybody who got a death certificate who might not have been there? Is there any doubt? Any possibility?"

Dr. Hollings crushed his cigarette in the ashtray and leaned across the desk pugnaciously. "None of the dead has complained. Are you suggesting that we mix and match so the count will come out even? Death and papers? No one has come forward."

"I didn't say that," Paul replied angrily. "Sometimes, I have to ask hard questions, too, Doctor. I want to know if there was a man named Al Jenks in that fire—for sure. Surer than this piece of paper that says he was there." He pointed at the death certificates.

"No, goddamn it!" Hollings slammed his fist on the desk. "I can't tell for sure. When you're looking at three-quarters of the skeleton of a child, so burned that you can't tell if it ever had skin, much less what color the skin might have been, but the lower half still has enough flesh to make out prepubescent genitalia, you know it must have been one of the six girls between the ages of five and twelve who died in that fire, and who were supposed to have lived in that house, so you tie a name to it. There were also four boys, five adult females, and seven adult males. We did pretty good with the children and the women. We got stuck on three of the men. We guessed."

Paul sat back in his chair and shuddered. "I'm sorry, Doctor."

"So am I. So am I."

Paul sat at the curb in his car for twenty minutes. He knew nothing more concrete that he had before. Officially, Jenks was dead. Dead, in the officially accidental fire. Maybe he was in there. Maybe he wasn't.

But who could have taken his place? It could have been any one of a million males of similar age and size. He might not be reported missing for weeks, or ever.

In New York City, filled as it is with common-law households and double entry welfare fraud, men come and go like the spring wind, dropping their seed, fertilizing the land, and then moving on. Only the women endured.

35

Paul sat in a booth with Jeff Jackson in the Red Rooster on 138th Street and Seventh Avenue looking out at the crowded dining room and bustling bar.

Jeff looked at his watch and said, "He ought to be here in a few minutes. He's never late. Take a look at the menu. Best soul food in Harlem. Sooner or later, you see everybody you ever knew or heard about."

In ten minutes, a portly man in a three-piece gray suit appeared at the archway to the dining room. Paul judged him to be Jeff's age, or older. His face was illuminated by good humor. Bushy gray eyebrows flared wildly above eyes creased by time and a thousand smiles.

Jeff slipped out of the booth and headed toward the man, who was already waving in their direction.

"Mason, this is my colleague, Paul Curtin. Paul, this is Mason Rhodes."

"Colleague?" Rhodes said questioningly, as he slid into his chair. "My God, Jeff, have you found work?"

"You'll have to put up with Mason's brand of humor, Paul. It's part of the package. Mason is an insurance broker. You might say, he's Harlem's insurance broker. He knows everybody and everything. We were in the war together. While I was risking my life running coffee for the white folks in Paris, Old Mason was with Percy Sutton and the rest of the 99th Fighter Squadron—the Black Eagles—getting his segregated black ass shot off fighting Krauts in North Africa and Italy."

"That's where," Rhodes interrupted, "I began my lifelong interest in other people's security and well-being."

"You see, Paul," Jeff said. "He sells everybody. Even I have insurance, though I don't remember what for."

"You need a refresher, boy?" Mason Rhodes asked.

"Please, no. If you want to talk, make it something besides insurance, Mason."

When he was no longer able to lift his fork, Paul leaned back in his chair and opened his belt and the top button of his trousers. He wiped the grease from his lips with an oversized gingham checkerboard napkin. His plate was a pile of cadaverous leavings; chicken bones, ribs picked to gleaming, and traces of beans and black-eyed peas. "God," he said.

Mason, who seemed to be able to talk and eat simultaneously, went on, "Both Gaines and Hawkes are the get of that first wave of Jamaicans who came over here with Marcus Garvey during the First War. Even my old man, and he was as conservative as hell, belonged to the Universal Negro Improvement Association. When you look back, old Garvey had a lot of good ideas. He was just born too soon. Most of the folks that were involved just chalked it up to experience. Some of them all but curled up and died. They were that disappointed."

"That's ancient history, Mason," Paul said.

"Apples don't fall far from trees. George Gaines's father was a crazy. He ran back to Jamaica because he was wanted. He ended up dead in a police raid, I think. He was a Rasta, you know. Some of them get involved in rough trade. I hear that the younger Gaines has kept his old ties, even though he's wearing business suits, and has given up those greasy dreadlocks."

Paul felt a shiver run the length of his spine. He could still see the smirks on the faces of the boys that had been sitting on his car in front of the Urban Development League, coils of hair straying from their caps. Could Gaines be having him followed? He shrugged off the chill. "And Hawkes?"

"I know he served in the war. Won it all alone to hear him tell it. He was a demo expert. He got his training on the beaches in France. That's how he got his start in business here, knocking things down, not building them."

"I wonder if he keeps in practice?" Paul mused.

"Sure he does," Mason Rhodes said. "Hell, the biggest problem in Bed-Stuy and the South Bronx is clearing the land. There isn't much money in it, but Hawkes used to make ends meet doing demolition, twenty, twenty-five years ago."

When Paul dropped Jeff off at his door a couple of hours later, he said, "Another nail in the invisible coffin. On top of everything else, Gaines has a hoodlum background, and Hawkes has expertise with explosives. Shit."

"Exactly. Shit. All it does is to shore up your suspicions, but not a drop of proof."

"Sooner or later, there's got to be a break," Paul said stubbornly. "What the hell could have motivated them to kill all those people? It must be the rip-off of the century."

"Don't count on it. Trying to tie the magnitude of the crime to the magnitude of the purse doesn't work in New York. I've seen three kids kill a blind newsy after they robbed him of $3.25. For all we know, this whole thing may have been triggered when Gibbons caught Hawkes and Gaines stealing bricks to build a patio and a barbecue."

"It's time to stop farting around and start pushing. I'm going to go see Hawkes and ask a few pointed questions."

"Watch it, Paul."

"Don't worry. I won't tip off your contact."

"I mean watch out for yourself."

When Paul parked his car and walked home, Tyrone Giggis climbed off his motorcycle and called George Gaines from a telephone booth on the corner of Madison Avenue. "I done like you said, Mr. Gaines. He spent most of the night at the Red Rooster. He was talking to some old dude in a gray suit. A brother. Then he drop off the little black guy who works on the paper with him. Now he's home."

"You go home, Tyrone. But you come back to his place tomorrow morning around eight. You just sit there and wait for him."

"Yes, Mr. Gaines. Good night."

Gaines put the phone on the hook slowly. Marcus was taking all of this too lightly. Curtin was sticking his nose in everywhere. Now, he was asking questions about the fire on 135th Street. Let Giggis tail him for the time being, he thought, his eyes closed, his fist clenched, but Marcus or no Marcus, sooner or later, we're going to have to do something about Paul Curtin.

PART TWO

36

When Paul called Marcus Hawkes the next morning he had not
yet arrived at his office, but his secretary promised that she
would have him return the call when he got in.

He had showered and dressed and was fussing over a second
cup of coffee when the phone finally rang. It was nearly ten.

"Mr. Curtin."

"Yes."

"Marcus Hawkes for you, sir. Just a moment, please."
There was a thirty-second pause. Paul imagined Hawkes
watching the sweep second hand of his watch out of one eye
and the phone with the other.

"Mr. Curtin, what can I do for you?"

"Can you spare a few minutes? I'd like to ask you some
questions."

"Gladly. When?"

"Whenever you're ready, Mr. Hawkes. I'm ready right
now."

There was no trace of hesitation. "Come right on down."

Paul entered the lobby of the shining glass and steel tower on
the Avenue of the Americas twenty minutes later, armed with a
small note pad, two pens, and a surfeit of pent-up hostility.

The offices of Hawkes Building Company were immediately
impressive. An attractive black woman in a chic suit stepped
from behind the reception desk to take his overcoat.

"Who may I say is calling on Mr. Hawkes?"

There was a hiatus of two minutes, then a door at the rear of the foyer opened. A middle-aged woman, black and thin, with sharp eyes, greeted him. "I'm Eleanor McGuffy, Mr. Curtin. Please come with me."

When she ushered him into the office, Hawkes was sitting at his desk writing furiously on a yellow pad. She knocked diffidently, and he looked up.

Backlit as he was by the window wall, the sun risen to the east behind him, Hawkes loomed like a Buddha, overlapping his chair. It took Paul a moment to become accustomed to the light.

Hawkes walked around from behind the desk, all three buttons of his suit jacket closed. He smiled a cannibal's smile. "I'm glad you could come. Sit down. Let's have some coffee."

Eleanor McGuffy appeared again with a tray bearing a service of Coalport china and sterling silverware. She poured for them.

As she retreated, Hawkes said, "Please hold all of my calls."

"Nice office," Paul commented.

"I hope I can show you that it's more than a showplace, Mr. Curtin. It's an efficient operating format for a busy company. How would you like to start? We can do the grand tour, if you like. If it would please you to just sit here and chat, that would be fine as well. I am entirely at your disposal. How much time can you give us?"

"I'm flattered. Whatever it takes."

"We want to make sure the impression the public gets represents what is happening here. We are willing to go to whatever lengths necessary to accomplish that end," Hawkes said pleasantly, but deliberately. "It would be a shame to see this unique experiment misunderstood."

Is it his overripe vocabulary or his exaggerated good manners that piss me off the most? Paul asked himself. Aloud, he replied blandly, "Oh, I agree. I think it's very important for the public to find out what's going on here."

"Well, then," Hawkes said, rubbing his hands together, "our aims coincide. Why don't we start with the Cook's tour."

Paul followed Hawkes down a long corridor whose walls were studded with office doors, some open with occupants busy at their desks. At its end, it branched in two directions.

"We've come to the crossroads, Mr. Curtin. To the left is our data processing center and our computers. To the right is the planning department, with some of the best young architects in America. It's the symbolic boundary between the technical and the creative."

Hawkes turned to the right. "I prefer the creative, of course. Black people haven't had much opportunity to express themselves in architecture during the past three hundred years." As he walked quietly past the men at their drawing boards, he commented, "Most of these men were consigned to commercial art or sign painting when we opened up. One is a graduate of the Yale School of Architecture. He spent six years in the City Department of Buildings." He let the sentence hang.

"Is there anything about Uhuru Towers on those boards?" Paul asked.

"Oh, no," Hawkes replied. "It's much too late to find Uhuru in here. That's an almost finished work, Mr. Curtin. In your terms, it's like trying to scoop the competition. Our eyes are fixed on tomorrow, on our new projects."

"Newspaper people have their practical moments, too. I've spent most of my career harvesting very small pieces of information in the present. People are involved in what's going on now, especially with public funds." Paul smiled. "You know how things are."

"Naturally. Naturally," Hawkes said, rubbing his palms again, the picture of good humor. "Let's go look at the practical side. Let me show you our DP center."

They crossed the corridor into the opposite transept, through curtained glass doors with a painted sign warning all comers to close the doors behind them. The room was sterile and sparsely arranged with the appurtenances of technology.

Paul felt himself drifting. He was being jollied along, questions blunted, thrusts turned aside. He decided to press on before he found himself standing outside in the street, defeated.

"Mr. Hawkes, I appreciate your time, but I'm sure you have more important things to do. I'd like to meet some of the line people and talk to them about Uhuru Towers. I think that project would make a good base for an article. After all, it's the biggest thing you have going, a flagship undertaking."

Hawkes chuckled. "Looking for a burr under my saddle, Mr. Curtin? No need to press. Follow me."

Hawkes picked up his pace and led Curtin on what he said was a short cut. In fact, he swept him through the billing department, purchasing, and government liaison, reinforcing the impression of busy hands and substance.

They emerged from the back office at the midpoint of the main corridor, and entered an office whose corkboard walls were cluttered with blueprints transfixed by pushpins. A desk was awash in papers.

In a corner, Paul saw a man of immense size coiled like a spring in a leather and chrome chair. He held the receiver of his phone between two fingers, like a toothpick.

He said in a measured voice, all the more frightening because it was soft, "Well, you tell that motherfucker that if he don't get that concrete poured between now and tonight, he's going to sleep in what's left of it. Do you understand me? I mean, do I make myself perfectly clear?" He hung up the phone while the man at the other end was still talking.

Hawkes cleared his throat. "Mr. Curtin, this is Mack Bell, our vice-president of construction. Mack, this is Paul Curtin of the *New York Advocate*. Go ahead, Mack. Tell him the truth. That was really your old grandmother you were talking to on the phone."

Paul watched in awe as Bell unwound himself from the chair. The six-foot-four-inch frame was broad and spare. He wore a button-down shirt with the tie pulled away from the open collar. The sleeves were rolled to the base of biceps they could not contain. Great ropes of black sheathed muscle ended in hands like hams.

"You're just going to have to excuse me, Mr. Curtin. I don't have much time for amenities." He smiled infectiously. "I suppose civilians aren't used to construction talk. Hell, I was being polite. If I'd been face to face with him, I might have bitten his ear."

Paul laughed good-humoredly. He liked Bell immediately. No nonsense here. "Mr. Bell, Mr. Hawkes tells me that everything that's wrong with Uhuru Towers is your fault."

Bell smiled back. "Now, I think that's a crock of shit, Mr. Curtin. Because Marcus knows that if he told something like that on me, I'd get pissed off, and walk out, and leave him to finish the goddamn thing himself. There is no way in the world, Mr. Curtin, that Marcus would risk that. Ain't that a fact, Marcus?"

Hawkes raised his hand piously. "I never would."

Paul smiled, thinking to himself that those were the truest words he'd heard from Hawkes's mouth since he'd arrived.

Hawkes went on, "For some reason he hasn't shared with me, Mack, Mr. Curtin has decided to narrow his focus onto one small aspect of our operations—Uhuru Towers. If that's what he wants, help him out." Hawkes turned to Curtin. "I'm going to my office. If you want me, I'll be there. I don't have any secrets from the press about Uhuru Towers, or anything else. Maybe you think that our cooperating with Governor O'Neil puts some kind of onus on this project. Your feelings about him politically are pretty clear." Hawkes puffed himself up like an adder. "Well, we wouldn't have any part in a politically inspired charade on the black community. No one here would. We have bipartisan support. Mayor Greene is with us to the hilt. You want to talk Uhuru, you talk to Mack. I'll be waiting." He turned on his heel and made his exit stage left, exuding dignity from every pore.

Both Mack Bell and Paul stared after him for a moment. Curtin spoke first.

"You're busy, aren't you? It's a lousy time."

Bell waved him to a chair. "It's always a lousy time. We have some good people, but never enough. I don't mean that we don't have a lot of bodies floating around. If you can cut through the morass of horseshit, Marcus is right. Our problem is quality trained black personnel. If you don't hire black, you don't keep the faith. If you keep the faith, you don't maintain the schedule."

"That's what I heard," Paul said casually. "Things aren't quite what they're supposed to be."

"Hey, listen, Paul," Mack said with sincerity, "we have our problems. But we are going to finish that building, and we are going to survive. What we are doing matters." He pointed a long finger at Paul. "I'm not going to sit here and lie through my teeth, and tell you that everything's perfect. But, if I think that you're barking up the wrong tree, I am going to say so."

"I can't ask for more, Mack. Are you in charge of the Uhuru Project?"

"That's one part of my job. A general contractor in a job this size is like an orchestra conductor. It's our job to get the trades—steel, concrete, carpentry, and so on—together and moving in unison. All the equipment and materials have to be in the right place at the right time. Now, if everybody blows his horn on time, and in the proper sequence, sure enough, the building goes up."

"Don't you have trouble finding black subcontractors for some of the trades?"

"We have trouble finding black subcontractors for everything."

"How about the masonry trade?" Paul asked.

Mack looked up at him from under beetled brows. "Now, I thought that you and I had decided that we weren't going to pull each other's chains. That didn't just pop into your head. You don't know much about construction. And you don't know shit about masonry. So what do you mean?"

"Okay," Paul acknowledged. "I hear you have a bad masonry subcontractor. True?"

Bell's face went blank. "You'd better ask Marcus."

"Fine. I will. But what's your opinion?"

"My opinion." A tinge of hostility crept into his voice. "My opinion is that you'd better ask Marcus about Gaines. He's his buddy. Not mine."

Bell got to his feet and looked at his watch.

Paul rose to leave, then threw out a last question. "If you were going to rip this place off, how would you do it?"

"You've got some fucking nerve. You know that? That's not funny."

"I didn't mean it to be funny."

Bell put his hands on his hips in exasperation. "I can't tell whether you're a part of the problem, or a part of the solution. All projects have problems. This one's not going to be any different."

"I don't have a fix on the techniques. If I don't know how people steal, how can I tell if they're stealing?"

"Are you looking for nickels and dimes? The timekeeper is probably raking off a couple of hundred a week covering for people. Does discovering that make you a big-time reporter? There's no big money, except the payroll. The only thing that you could really steal is building material. And for that there are requisitions. Miles of paperwork. Everything else is small change."

"Who handles the paperwork?"

"The estimator, the processor, and Marcus."

"Who are the other two guys?"

"The estimator is Marcus's brother, Charlie. The guy who takes care of all the paperwork is Malcolm Woodruff. He spent forty years with the state. He's sixty-plus." Bell wiped his forehead with the back of his hand, and said, "You're barking up the wrong tree. There's a system of checks and balances. No supplier can get the money for a delivery unless he has a state-approved authorization. A requisition for cash for the bank. They're damn particular to whom they give money."

"Okay, Mack. Thanks." Paul stepped out of the door. He turned back and said, "You're sure you don't have anything to say about Gaines?"

He snapped, "I'm not only particular who I talk to, I'm particular who I talk about." His eyes locked with Paul's for a moment, then he looked away and walked to his chair.

Paul walked down the hall and knocked at Hawkes's door.

"Come on in. I'll be through in a minute." He sat at his desk writing. "Sit down. Did you have a good talk with Mack?"

"Yes and no. I didn't get the answers to all of my questions, and there were some others that I didn't get to ask."

"He's a busy man," Hawkes said, finishing his work and folding the paper. "I'm sure you wouldn't say that he was uncooperative."

"No. Not at all. But he's certainly a company man."

"I would hope so, Mr. Curtin. This isn't the Darktown Strutters Ball. We've all worked very hard for this opportunity. We're all very proud of what we've accomplished. If you expected us to make painful confessions about our ineptitude, you came to the wrong place."

"I'm doing a reporter's job, Mr. Hawkes. Like you, I have a vision of my trade, and I keep my nose to the grindstone. What I am after here is the basis for a story about urban renewal and housing under the O'Neil administration. Just the truth. No more, no less."

"We're staying out of politics here at Hawkes Building. We're pro-us. We're pro-urban renewal. Your paper carries a hatchet for Governor O'Neil. That's no secret. But Governor O'Neil is only one of our staunch supporters. Mayor Greene, his opponent, is one hundred percent committed, too."

Paul smiled. You son of a bitch, he thought. It's all worked out in your mind. You've got all the answers. "I have heard that Uhuru is quite a bit behind schedule."

"There's a little truth in that, in one trade or another, but nothing that isn't common to other projects of the same magnitude. And frankly, Mr. Curtin, I don't think our being a month behind schedule in one building is an offset for being three centuries behind in getting to build it."

"Is there something wrong with your masonry contractor?" How's that for a kick in the nuts?

"Not at all. I have worked with him for many years. He enjoys my complete confidence."

"Is it a matter of concern that one of his foremen was killed on the job? There's no question of carelessness?"

"Mr. Curtin, you were at the funeral. You met George Gaines. The death of Lloyd Gibbons was an unfortunate accident which has taken a little of the joy from our accomplishment. In economic terms, it didn't cost us an hour of lost work, and it in no way reflects on the competence of George Gaines or his organization." He had a pained expression, as a teacher might when speaking to a dreadfully slow but earnest child. "Is there something else we can show you that might interest you?"

Paul shook his head. "I'd like to digest what I've seen. Perhaps you'd favor me with more time later."

"Of course, Mr. Curtin. And if you do find something here that doesn't bear up under your scrutiny, you let me know. And you go ahead and print it. We want this program to be up front."

"Thank you, Mr. Hawkes."

"Good day, Mr. Curtin. You're very welcome."

As soon as Paul had disappeared through the door, Marcus Hawkes poured himself a glass of water from the carafe on his desk and took two Valium. He sat quietly for a moment, then took his private phone from the hook, and called George Gaines.

"George, I think I owe you an apology. I just had Paul Curtin up here. He's been nosing around everywhere, George. He's been to see Englander. He's on to something. He knows. He can't put it together, but he knows. I can smell it."

"Do we run?"

"It's much too early. I told you. He's guessing."

"Does he need to have an accident?"

"No. That's the last think we want. It will only confirm whatever suspicion he may have."

"I meant a permanent accident."

Hawkes wet his lips with the water. "No, George. He may have passed his conjecture along." Hawkes paused to think, then continued. "Let's see if we can cut off some of his avenues of approach. Call down to the Department of Housing and maybe to the comptroller's office and ask our contacts there if Curtin's been looking into our affairs. See if he's got any contacts of his own. Maybe we can discourage them. I'll try to find out how high up he's reached."

"I'll take care of it, Marcus."

"No rough stuff, George. I don't want anybody hurt."

"You leave it to me, Marcus."

Paul Curtin continued his walk through Central Park, trying to work off his frustration and annoyance. Hawkes knew that he was aware of something. And he didn't care.

He dropped onto a bench and watched a pair of sparrows collect twigs for a few minutes. He had pushed as hard as he dared short of an outright accusation. Mr. Hawkes had said, in effect, print what you like. You can't prove a thing. And I have the whole world behind me.

Paul chewed over what he heard from Mack Bell. Perhaps the answer was more attention to detail. Another visit to the Division of Housing might be in order. He took out his address book to look up the name and number of his contact.

37

Eustace McGee, the contact that Paul had made at the Division of Housing, was a man of habit. Out of the modest income provided by his job, he had constructed a comfortable family life.

He had a wife and two little girls, eight and ten. After years of careful management, he had parlayed his savings and his wife's salary as a dental technician into a substantial down payment on a house just on the wrong side of the tracks in Lawrence, Long Island.

Each morning at six-fifteen, he rose and breakfasted with his wife, then dressed. While she dealt with getting the children out of bed, he went for his morning constitutional with his energetic two-year-old golden retriever.

The girls satisfied their maternal instincts by lavishing affection on the dog and a huge tomcat named Elvis. Eustace had found him in a garbage can just before the elder girl was born.

Beyond his wife and kids, Eustace had developed friends in Lawrence and the surroundings. He had a two-year-old Chevy that he kept in immaculate condition. The house was a model of efficiency and cleanliness. As each new gadget had come on the market, the McGees had acquired it; two years late, sometimes three, but eventually, they maintained their uneasy par with the Joneses.

This particular morning, Eustace felt the call of spring. He stepped out smartly down the country lane that led away from his house, his dog dodging and circling ahead of him. He walked all the way down the road to the white colonial church at the crossroads, then across the street and around the massive modernistic synagogue that dominated the hill.

It was eight when he got back to his block. The girls would have bathed and dressed and would be descending the stairs to the kitchen for their breakfast. The dog sprinted ahead onto the lawn, kicking up his heels and wagging his tail.

Whistling, Eustace crossed the gravel path that led to the back door. A piercing shriek rent the air, making the flesh crawl up his arms and the back of his neck. He stretched his legs, taking the two short steps to the porch in a single bound. The screaming continued unabated. There were three voices, now, both his daughters and his wife.

He burst through the door into the kitchen. His wife stood in the middle of the room with her hands over her ears, screaming wordlessly over and over again. His elder daughter was on her knees gagging. His youngest child, her eyes rolled almost into her head, clutched at her mother's skirts, howling in terror. From the smell Eustace could tell that she had soiled herself.

He crossed the room and slapped his wife sharply on the cheek. She drew a sharp breath, then was quiet. The elder girl threw herself at her father's legs, making animal sounds in the back of her throat and trying to hide. He shook his youngest till she stopped screaming. Then she fainted. The room was all stench and hysterical breathing, but there was quiet enough to think.

He looked at his wife, who dabbed her hand at the stinging cheek. "What in the name of God is the matter here? Sweet Jesus, Nancy, you scared me to death. What are you all carrying on about?"

She tried to form the words, but they stuck in her throat, and all she could manage was a racking sob.

"Nancy, child, for God's sake, what's the matter?"

She raised her hand, which trembled so that it threatened her fragile equilibrium. Eustace reached out to steady her, then turned to follow the direction of her hand.

He rushed to the sink to vomit his breakfast. He stood with his head bowed between his elbows, letting the cold water wash away the mess. He splashed some onto his face, dried himself with a dish towel, and walked across the room.

The brand-new microwave oven stood like a jewel box on its shining pedestal where it had been for a week, the newest sign of the McGees' grip on the good life.

Eustace looked through the clear glass at the body of the cat. A wire had been wrapped around its jaw to shut its mouth. Then someone had added a broad red ribbon and a bow. The internal heat generated by the radiation had vaporized the liquid contents of the cat's head, and its skull had exploded.

Eustace McGee led his two girls upstairs and ran them a warm bath. He rinsed their clothes in the sink and then threw them in the hamper. When the girls were clean, he dried them and put them back in their nightgowns, and sat them down in front of the television set.

His wife was sitting on the living room couch, with tears trickling slowly down her cheeks. "Why? We ain't never had no trouble in this neighborhood. What kind of person would . . ." She began to sob softly.

Eustace took a bottle from the liquor cabinet and poured

them each a stiff drink. He downed his in a gulp. She sipped at
hers. He knelt in front of her and removed her slippers, then
swung her feet around onto the couch so that she was lying
down. She took another sip and put the glass on the floor,
closing her eyes.

He covered her with the jacket that he had been wearing and
went into the kitchen. It took him ten minutes to bury the
remains of the cat in the garden, and a half hour to scour the
oven and the kitchen with Lysol. When he was through, he
washed his hands at least a dozen times.

38

After reflecting on his meeting the previous day with Marcus
Hawkes, Paul Curtin decided to risk a call to Eustace McGee at
his office. After a confused pause that lasted several minutes,
he was told that there had been an illness in the family and that
Mr. McGee wouldn't be in. He didn't leave his name.

Paul would have preferred going to Melanie Parsons with a
better hand of cards. He had hoped that McGee would be able
to support some of the conclusions he'd come to since their
meeting. Well, he said to himself, there isn't any point in
putting this off any further. It's just a matter of selling the old
lady on the idea.

"Mrs. Parsons's office," Madeleine said.

"It's Paul Curtin. May I speak to her, please?"

She picked up the phone immediately. "Yes."

"I'd like to see you. I have some copy."

"I hope it's worthwhile."

"It might be a little daring for you," Paul said kiddingly.

"Don't smartass me, young man. If it'll sell newspapers,
we'll print it. Be here at eleven."

Paul sat down with Melanie at the appointed hour and made
his case. "You can see what I concluded from the information.

These forms are the key to milking money from a public project. The signature has to be that of the governor and/or the comptroller, or a facsimile thereof, signature guaranteed and stamped with the Great Seal of the state. The facsimile machines are in the comptroller's office. There might be others in the governor's office. If you could get these requisitions in blank—"

"If pigs had wings," she scoffed. "I don't see what you've accomplished at all. All I see is more surmises."

"Mrs. Parsons, do you think that the destruction of Al Jenks's building was an accident? You know that he worked on a crew with Lloyd Gibbons. You know that they both worked for Gaines on Uhuru Towers. You know that they are both dead."

"I know that the New York Police Department has determined to their satisfaction that both deaths were the result of accidents."

"We've been told—"

"The mystery source. Name him. Have him come forward and make an accusation. Then the police would reopen the cases—maybe. On your slim surmise I am supposed to accuse the governor and the mayor of complicity in a multimillion dollar swindle at Uhuru Towers, and by corollary, in mass murder? Impossible. You have a speculative case against O'Neil, nothing at all against Greene."

"I want to say that it is our understanding that Uhuru Towers is far behind schedule. We've spoken to Hawkes. He doesn't deny that he's behind schedule. We've talked to his partners. They're nervous about the building. Suddenly, an employee in the area where we believe they are having the most trouble has a fatal accident. Then, shortly thereafter, the building of a man that worked with him goes up in flames. I want to print that, and ask a question. What the hell is going on here?"

"Do you have a single piece of this bogus paper you're positing? You do not. Do you have anything beside your instincts to tell us that there is anything substance wrong with Uhuru Towers? You do. The invisible man. In his absence, you do not. You have been less than subtle in your search for evidence. Assuming that you're correct in your assumptions, you have probably shaken them to their roots. They have no doubt been covering their tracks as fast as they can. They might even put back the money that you think they stole. Then, all you'll produce with your story is a black eye for the *Advocate*, and the mistaken impression that we oppose the project on its merits. I think you're in a blind alley."

"But, if you're right," Paul said, "and they know that we're on to them, our silence will aid and abet them. They'll finish whatever it is they're about, sweep it under the rug, and walk away scot-free. We have to press them, upset their timetable. If we push them maybe Gaines and Hawkes will run. But Greene and O'Neil can't run. Whatever their involvement, or their aims, they're stuck. If we let it pass, we're going to have a choice of unconvicted felons for governor come November. Do you want that?"

"You won't expose your source. I don't blame you. I won't print unfounded libelous accusations. Who shall we say burned down that building? Hawkes and Gaines? Greene and O'Neil?"

Paul ran his hands through his hair and stared at his notes, seeing only a blur where he hoped to find inspiration. "Okay," he admitted. "You're right. It's too soon to shoot the whole wad. It's too risky. We could be embarrassed. We could get sued. But, for Christ's sake, Mrs. Parsons, can't we make a compromise?" He held his story up in his hand. "If you don't want this, let me at least try to put together something that will let them think we're getting close. Something to force a mistake."

"Make a suggestion."

Paul composed himself. She was giving him another try. "Let's say that we keep them in suspense. Maybe you're right." She'd like it better if she thought it was her own idea. "We'll give it to them a little at a time. Establish the fact that we're going to do a series on housing under the O'Neil administration, to run one piece a week, for four or five weeks. The first article can be 'The O'Neil Housing Policy from One Extreme to the Other.' Put two pictures on the page: one of Uhuru Towers, the other of 523 East 135th Street. For public consumption, it's just two buildings, one under construction, the other after demolition. To Hawkes, it'll mean something else. It will be more than a coincidence. Let their imaginations do our work for us, Mrs. Parsons. Let them chew on what we're going to come out with next week."

"I understand the juxtaposition of the pictures, and the motivation, but what do you intend for the body of the text?"

"Here we are, the people of the state of New York, seven years into the O'Neil administration, and this is what we have for housing." Now's the time to wing it, Paul, he thought. "In the private sector, we're stuck with co-ops from a hundred grand and up for three rooms and a thousand-a-month rentals. Who the hell can afford that? At the other end of the spectrum, instead of making inexpensive housing projects the first priority, we have sleight of hand like Uhuru Towers. As a result, housing reality for too many of us is the rundown stock whose end product are death traps like 523."

"Rousing," she said. "A good swipe at O'Neil."

While I'm on a roll, Paul thought, I might as well try another shot. "We could also mention that Mayor Greene has failed to take a critical look at Uhuru."

"I don't see," she said, putting her pencil on the desk carefully, "how that has to do with a story on housing in the O'Neil administration."

"Mrs. Parsons, if there is a swindle at Uhuru, don't you think that Greene has, at least, got to be looking the other way?"

"Speculation." She straightened her glasses. "All right, Paul. If you can convince the rest of the editorial board that the series has merits—without including the mayor—I'll go along."

He sat back in his chair. "You'll go along? No support?"

"This newspaper is a business. It has a *modus operandi*. Feature stories and serials are passed upon by the senior personnel. I am not solely responsible. If you want to write this piece as an anti-O'Neil exposé, then I'll lean with you. Even to the degree that I'll go with this five-piece concept, to let you try to flush out your boogeyman. If you are going to insist on making a whipping boy of Uhuru by questioning its intrinsic values, I maintain my neutrality."

"That's as good as a veto. And that's not the story. What can I say about Uhuru?"

"That O'Neil has backed it because it's his only accomplishment in the housing area. You can say that it's the only thing he's done for Harlem in seven years. You can say that that burnt-out shell is the result."

"Do you think the senior personnel that you mentioned before will buy that?"

"You can't do more than try, can you? If you want to sell them more than that, you can always try to impress them with your surmises. If you really want to print your original story, you can always reveal the name of your confidential source, or say that you are ready to make a statement to the police."

Paul started to protest, then shut his mouth. She'd let him talk. Maybe she listened, maybe not. When he was through, she told him what she wanted. If it was about housing, that suited her fine. She didn't want Hawkes or Gaines, and for sure she didn't want Greene. She wanted O'Neil. If somewhere along the line he'd forgotten that he was a pawn, she was reminding him.

"Whatever you say, Mrs. Parsons. I'll make my case. You do what you want. But, if they agree that my story makes sense, we print."

"Fine. I'm sure they'll like our idea. You have my word," she said with a little smile, reaching for the intercom.

"Madeleine, ask Mr. Bornstein and Mr. Fabrikant to come up here, please." She looked down at Paul. "Keeping the meeting small will forestall any leaks."

He was tempted to get up and go home. He didn't like being sandbagged. Max and Oscar wouldn't throw their lot in with him without her agreement. On the other hand, Paul thought to himself, if I don't try, I'll never know.

When the door opened, Melanie said, "Come in, Max. Sit down, Oscar. Paul wants approval for a series of articles. I've heard him out. I want you to decide whether or not the *Advocate* should go along with him."

My God, Paul thought, if she got any more distance between herself and the idea, you'd think it had leprosy. The patient is going to die of nonsupport. He looked down the table. Bornstein wore his look of chronic circumspection. Fabrikant looked like he was about to get even for all past slights, real and imagined.

"What have you come up with, after all this time, Paul?" Max asked.

"I want to do a series on building under the O'Neil administration."

"And what will it say?"

"I envision it as a five-part series. I want to start with the state of housing in the urban center. I'd like to use New York as an example, though it's as valid in Buffalo, or any other urban area."

"Where's the zest? What's new?" Fabrikant persisted.

Bornstein shook his head and interjected. "Oh, Max, you're making it sound like a seder. The next think you'll ask him is why he's eating bitter herbs. Paul, get on with it. Where are you going? I'm sure that Mrs. Parsons didn't invite us up here to hear a recital. I assume you've already come to some agreement."

Paul looked at Melanie. Oh, Oscar. If looks could kill, you'd be in your urn already. "Oh, yes. We want to open with a comparison study between Uhuru Towers and the Willis Avenue fire. There's a sociological connection that's easy for the reader to see." There's a hell of a lot easier one, Paul thought—Gibbons and Jenks—but that's off limits. "Here's our governor," he continued, "gassing about his shiny bauble that's representative of his commitment to the inner city. From evidence I've uncovered, it's behind schedule and over budget. It remains a hazy dream. On the other hand, we have the reality of the Willis Avenue fire. Twenty-two corpses. When is the governor going to deal with the horror of the reality by making the fantasy come true?"

"Wouldn't you say that Uhuru at least represents progress in the thinking of the administration? I hate to knock a good idea. Isn't there something else to pick on?"

Melanie folded her hands decorously and looked at her father's portrait.

Paul said casually, "I'd think you'd have more confidence in Mrs. Parsons's judgment than that, Max. Why would she have let me go this far if she weren't satisfied that I had something to go on? That would beg the question about her confidence in you. If she's going to pull someone who reports to you off of his regular beat, she must think there's a damn good reason. If I'm not sharp enough to sell you her idea, that doesn't mean it should be shot down." He added piously, "The fault lies with my sales pitch." Go ahead, Melanie. Tell him I'm full of shit.

Melanie ground her teeth.

"I was just worried about the possible repercussions. But if you can show that there is a problem at Uhuru, then I suppose we ought to go ahead," Fabrikant said.

"Certainly," Oscar said.

Paul looked up at Melanie Parsons. She started to say something, then changed her mind. She'd made the rules. Now she was stuck with them.

"Thank you, Max," Paul said. "Mr. Bornstein. I'll have the copy in a couple of hours."

"All right," Max said, thinking aloud. "We ought to run it either on page two or opposite the columns on twelve. Let's make it two, with the photos. We'll run it that way from the first Wall Street Edition. Listen, when should we expect the rest of the pieces?"

"Let's make it weekly."

"That's a long spread. I'd think we run it five days in a row." Fabrikant turned to Mrs. Parsons.

Paul jumped in, "We want to give people a chance to think about the piece. To wonder what's coming next."

"Compromise," she said. "Run today, Thursday. Then run Tuesday, and so on. That way, you maintain continuity and still have some sense of suspense. That's what you want, isn't it?" The question was directed at Paul.

"Yes, it is." *Now she's pinned me. If I don't get some reaction which leads to hard evidence by the next deadline, I'm not going to have anything to say.*

Melanie's face flickered in a smile. "Good day, gentleman."

39

There was a trailer on the front page. "New Real Estate Scam—Paul Curtin Speaks. Page 2."

The story's subhead, printed in red, was "The Decline and Fall." The first sentence, in boldface, read, "Are the citizens of New York being treated to a fiddle concert while the city burns?"

> For seven years the O'Neil administration has sat with
> a smug look on its face as the Big Apple has gone the way

of the Roman Empire. The housing stock has either declined or deteriorated in all of the city's major residential areas except for those which can take care of themselves—the luxury quarters of the well-to-do. Instead of coming to grips with the needs of the city—a completely new urban housing approach—the present administration has leaned on inequitable tax practices and the placebo of rent control, which cheats both landlord and tenant, to put off the day of reckoning while the housing conditions of the large majority of the city's citizens worsens.

When pressed into action by an upcoming election, where does the administration turn? Not steak, but sizzle. A bauble for Harlem—Uhuru Towers.

The story continued for five hundred words, with a picture, almost half the page.

When the paper came out in midafternoon, George Gaines had just settled into his chair at Marcus Hawkes's office.

"You've dealt with the leak at the Division of Housing?"

"I think so. How did you find out about this fellow McGee, anyway?"

"There's a man down at the division who's an ear for the governor. He must have seen McGee with Curtin. Do you really think McGee will keep his nose clean from now on?"

"Oh, I think he got the idea," Gaines said.

"What did you say to him?"

"Nothing. I killed his cat."

Hawkes shuddered and turned away.

The door burst open and Mack Bell entered, in a rage. "Have you seen this shit?" He dropped a fresh copy of the *Advocate* on Hawkes's desk.

Hawkes picked up the paper, opened to its second page, and quickly scanned Curtin's story. "Questionable advisability of the project . . . questionable capability of the builders. . . ." He read it through a second time with care.

Bell leaned forward on the desk, his voice full of anger. "How about that shit? I mean, how about it?"

Hawkes looked up at him. "If you can't stand the heat, then the kitchen's no place for you, Mack. We're just a tool to get at O'Neil."

Gaines picked up the paper and read it, his face darkened in a scowl.

Bell threw his hands in the air in frustration. "It's like inviting somebody for dinner, and finding the silverware missing when they go home. He didn't just come here for information. He violated our hospitality. He used us." Bell stalked around the office with his hands jammed into his pockets, fuming. "Of all the people in the world, Marcus, I'd think you'd be bellyaching the loudest."

Hawkes sat quietly behind the desk. "You ought to get ahold of yourself, Mack. There's nothing to be done."

"We ought to make the bastard put in a retraction. Who is he calling incompetent? I'm the first to say we got problems, but where the fuck does he get off ridiculing us? He all but calls us crooks."

"Retract what? His opinion? This doesn't call itself a news story. See, it says right up top—Political Analysis. It's his opinion. He's entitled. And if they printed a retraction? It would be two lines on page sixty-six. The damage has been done. We're just going to ignore it."

"I'd like to break his neck," Bell said.

Hawkes frowned. "That's a stupid thing to say, Mack. It makes you sound like a fool or gangster. Have you done anything you're ashamed of? Do you think that this building is a rip-off? If the answers to those questions are no, then you'd better go back to your office and do your job, and let Mr. Curtin do his, whether you like it or not. That's the best way to prove that he's full of shit."

Bell slammed the door in frustration behind him.

Gaines gnawed thoughtfully at a knuckle. "He's right. We should kill him."

"Don't be a fool. You'll slip the noose around our necks. There's nothing conclusive here. It's only the beginning of a series on urban housing. It's possible that we may never be mentioned again."

"What if we are? What if he keeps pushing? We're going to have all kinds of press people around here now asking questions."

"Possibly," Marcus said. "But we're not going to be in this alone. We have friends. Lots of them."

"Marcus," Gaines said grimly, "once a newspaper gets on your back, they don't let go."

"We're just poor black folks trying to make a living. I wouldn't be surprised if the publisher didn't start getting a lot of negative letters about the treatment of Hawkes Building Company. We're going to see a ground swell of support . . ."

Gaines shook his head in disgust. "Sometimes I'm afraid you believe what you say."

Hawkes gave him a hard look. "Don't you worry, George. I know just what I'm doing. You can't solve all of your problems with brass knuckles. I'm going to get on the phone and call in a few markers. There are people who owe us."

Gaines studied his nails, then said, "There's a lot of money in the bank, Marcus. Three million dollars. We can just get on a plane and disappear. Today."

Hawkes rounded on him angrily, his voice low but shaking with emotion. "I have waited all of my life to make me a score, George Gaines. And I'm not going to run off without the money because of some damn honky reporter who's guessing at things." He grabbed the paper from the desk brusquely and pushed it across at Gaines.

"There's another four or five million dollars to take out of Uhuru Towers, George, and I want every damn dime. Now, if you want something to worry about, I'll give it to you. Why do you suppose, of all of the fires that take place in the city of New York a year—it says right here that there are eight thousand—he picked the fire in Al Jenks's building? Did you want me to tell Mack Bell that there was a coincidence? Do you suppose that it's by accident that the story mentions that there are slowdowns in plumbing and particularly in masonry?"

He shook the paper under Gaines's nose. "You want to know what this story really says, George? It says, I know you're running a scam. I know you got rid of Gibbons and burned down that building. I know it. But I can't prove it. So blink, nigger. Goddamn you, blink." Marcus put the paper on the desk and sat back in the chair. "Well, we aren't going to blink. We are going to sit tight and pull strings until we're ready. Because if there were any proof at all, we could have all of the political connections on this earth, and we'd still be in front of a grand jury. Now, I'll tell you what I want you to do, instead of sitting there and making threatening noises. First, you're going to get our money out by the end of next month."

"Jesus, Marcus, that would mean ordering all of the bricks at once."

"You only have to worry about that if you want to survive the next monthly audit of materials. Order this month's supply and next, today. Double up as usual. Cash in the requisition forms. On the first of April, you order all of the rest of the bricks."

"All the way through September?"

"All of them. Then double the dollar amounts on the blank requisitions. Cash them in a few at a time each day. Use different banks. By the end of the month, we have all of the money, and we'll be on our way."

Gaines thought about it for a while, then nodded in agreement. "If we've got to run anyway, getting found out after the fact doesn't make any difference."

Hawkes said, "There's something else. I've been thinking. There's no way in the world that Curtin could have made these connections without a tip-off. It wasn't intuition that brought him to our doorstep. I want you to get our personnel records from Eleanor. You go through them and try to figure out who might have tipped off Curtin."

"It couldn't have been Gibbons," Gaines said. "I saw him looking over that damn manifest. He was comparing it to the materials on the skid. He was still at the guessing stage. That's why I dropped those damn bricks on him. And it couldn't have been Jenks. You heard him, Marcus. He was too busy trying to figure out how to rip me off to think about anything else."

"You're right," Hawkes said. "This has to be someone who's just passing along his suspicions. As I said, if there was any proof, we'd be having this little talk in a jail cell." Hawkes picked up his copy of the *Advocate* and stuffed it into the wastebasket. "You do what I said. While you're looking, I'll get on the phone and see if I can buy us the time to cash in our chips."

40

After spending most of his adult life developing a high profile, it wasn't easy for Christopher Greene to move about the city unnoticed. He would have liked to think that his private driver would ferry him where he wanted to go in the ordinary sedan that he affected instead of a limousine for the sake of his image and to keep it to himself. But Chris Greene had done nothing to promote his loyalty and expected none.

The night that the *Advocate* carried Paul Curtin's first article on housing, Greene had his girl friend, Jennifer Ashton, go to a West Side office of a local agency and rent a subcompact car.

When Jennifer arrived at Eighty-fourth Street and First Avenue, she double-parked and called the mayor's private number.

"Greene."

"Chris, I've got it. I'm around the corner."

"I'll go down through the service entrance and meet you on Eighty-fifth Street in five minutes."

Green took one of Jennifer's woolen caps and pulled it down over his forehead. He looked down the hall before he closed the door behind him and slipped into the service elevator. He felt foolish as he pulled up the lapels on his dark trench coat and quick marched down the linoleum alley, past the soap smell and women's small talk of the laundry room, and out into the rear court and onto the street.

Jennifer was parked between two lamps on the opposite side.

"You drive," he said, getting in. "Go down the drive to the Brooklyn Bridge."

He had been undecided about taking Jennifer at all. He'd toyed with the idea of leaving his hairpiece in his pocket until he reached his destination. In the end, the best he could come up with was a small truth. Jennifer was an adult. She had a license. She could lay claim to being the mayor's intimate friend. It was perfectly plausible, if they were spotted, that she had rented a car for personal purposes and just taken him for a little ride.

After a while, Jennifer cleared her throat. "Chris."

"Yeah?"

"Where are we going?"

"Brooklyn."

There was a pause. "Why?"

"Shut up, Jennifer, will you?" He slumped in his seat and pulled the hat down, then turned on the radio. He looked at her out of the corner of his eye.

He wondered, as he often did, how she had gotten into his life, and why he let her stay. They had met at a party in the Village a year before he had decided to run for mayor. She had been twenty-four. One of the prettiest girls in Minneapolis. That's what everybody said.

By the time she was twenty-two and had graduated from the university, a mile from her home, she was bored to extinction. With only a little coaxing, her executive father settled a thousand-dollar-a-month allowance on her, and she went to New York to be a model. Her face was pretty, but just a little wide at the jaw, and in the pressure cooker of the New York modeling industry, that meant life on small change.

By the night that she met Chris Greene, she'd been in New York a year and a half. She knew that she was a flop and was wrestling with the idea of returning to Minneapolis, full of failure and white lies. She had begun to console herself with increasing dependence on grass and coke, when she could get it.

Jennifer had been sitting on a bench in the garden of a Village brownstone when Chris Greene had arrived. His voice carried from the front door. She saw that the flow of the crowd was in his direction. People went out of their way to stand in his shadow, to talk to him, to pass an aimless word. She took a pinch of powder from an aluminum foil packet in her purse and snorted it.

After she had watched the guests swirl around him for a while, she lurched to her feet and wove toward him.

"Hello," she said. "Are you important?"

He was about to give her a smart answer when she was thrown against him by the crush. He looked down into her face. He could feel her bare breast through the silk of her blouse. He cupped his hand surreptitiously. She smiled.

"I'm very important. I'm your city councilman, Chris Greene." He shrugged himself loose from the circle of homely amateur politicians. "Excuse me, won't you?"

As the band on the balcony played ragtime, they contrived to meet in the master bedroom on the floor below.

Jennifer leaned against the door and took out her silver packet. "Want some?"

Greene suffered a moment's trepidation. Was this a setup? She snorted. He looked into her eyes. The pupils were dilated and she wasn't focusing. She leaned back against the door. Her helplessness made him angry.

He reached out a long arm and undid the sole button on the blouse, then pulled it over her head. For reasons she didn't understand, she felt afraid and tried to cover her breasts with her hands. He twisted her arms away and looked at her.

She felt as though his eyes burned her skin. He undid the waistband of her skirt and let it fall to the ground. She wore only a garter belt and stockings. She began to shake. He stood with his hands on his hips, looking down at her nakedness. She had shaved her pubic hair to model underwear, and looked frail and childlike.

She reached clumsily and undid his fly. Her breath caught in her throat. She was unable to close her hand around his swollen organ.

He picked her up by the waist and sat her on the edge of the sink.

"Please, let me blow you. It's tight. You'll tear me."

He slipped off his pants. His legs and lower body were covered by thick curls of black hair. His skin was hardly visible.

She shuddered and a tear made its lonely way down her cheek. "Please. Don't hurt me." At the same time, she opened her legs and reached out to him.

The pulse pounded in his throat, and he was barely able to contain himself, even without touching her. She whimpered as he pushed against her. The sound made his flesh crawl. He held her hips firmly between his hands and leaned his weight forward.

"It's too big," she said, gasping. "I can't. It hurts." She wrapped her arms around his neck, pressing herself toward the pain.

Stymied, he forced his body forward and crushed her to him. As he did, both of them were racked with spasms and left breathless and trembling, holding each other.

After a week, with some medical advice, they were able to come to grips with their physical imbalance with the help of Pond's hand cream. But the essence of the relationship remained the same as the moment when they had teetered inelegantly on the sink in the house on Jane Street. He was too big for her. His entry, whether into her body or her life, caused pain. He could not reshape himself to meet her narrow confines. She was unable to grow to meet his needs. But just the same, he for the sense of power that her subjugation provided, she needing to be mastered and prepared to endure pain for the privilege, hung together in a half-shadowed relationship, unable to pull free.

Chris Greene looked out of the window at the fast-approaching ramp of the Brooklyn Bridge across the roadway.

"Take the damn bridge, Jen. Can't you remember anything?"

"Okay. Okay." She swerved the car and skidded into the exit.

"Take the middle road. Go straight out into Atlantic Avenue. I'll let you know when to stop."

A couple of dozen blocks rolled by, tenements alternating with storefronts, small factories, and lofts, the drab ensemble occasionally dotted by a neon sign advertising fast food or laundries. At a point, many of the signs repeated themselves in Arabic, as they passed through the Syrian and Palestinian quarter that had developed during the exodus from the Middle East provoked by Israeli occupations since the Six-Day War.

In a single block, the complexions of the few street loungers turned from Levantine olive to Caribbean black, the signs from felafel to ackee rice.

"Slow down, Jen. We're not far." Greene looked up at the street signs. "Okay. Berriman Street. Turn left here."

The street was quiet and without traffic. A block beyond the intersection, someone had knocked the bulbs out of four overhead lights, leaving a patch of total darkness in the middle of the road. Greene strained his eyes as they entered it. A dark Lincoln was parked, pointed in the opposite direction.

"Drive up the street, Jen. Park there." They slid in to the curb near the end of the dark patch. Greene pulled his coat tight around him, buttoning the collar. He pulled on a pair of gloves and adjusted the watch cap on his head. "Turn off the motor and the lights. Don't use the radio."

"It's scary here."

"Lock the doors when I leave. Pretend you're a big girl. I won't be long."

He closed the door and strolled up the street till he reached a doorway not far from the Lincoln.

"Good evening, Mr. Mayor," Marcus Hawkes said, softly.

Despite himerf, Greene jumped. "You scared the shit out of me, Mr. Hawkes."

"I'm sorry, Your Honor."

"Forget it. What's this cloak and dagger crap all about?"

"I need some help."

"Don't we all?"

"Did you see the story in the *Advocate* today?"

"Of course."

"Then you must know why I called you and asked you to meet me."

"I'm not all that sure, Mr. Hawkes. You called and said we ought to get together sometime. Then, a half hour later, I get a handwritten note asking me to take part in this melodrama. Nonetheless, here I am."

"Let me clarify it for you, then, Mr. Mayor. It looks like we have a problem with the *New York Advocate*, and more specifically with Paul Curtin."

"What we? Mr. Hawkes. It looks to me, from reading the article, that you have a few technical problems up on 125th Street. As a result, Paul Curtin, who's paid to do this kind of character assassination is getting on your back and using you to embarrass my opponent. I'm sorry for your discomfort, but it suits me fine."

"I thought that you were committed to help me out. To help Uhuru out. We've gone out of our way to make sure that you get more credit in the community than O'Neil, even though it's his project."

Greene shook his head in disgust. "Come on, Mr. Hawkes. You and I know where we stand. We made a deal, all right. You were going to shift the credit for Uhuru from O'Neil to me, and I was going to ignore, or even condone the little peccadilloes that were sure to appear in an all-minority project. But those peccadilloes, Mr. Hawkes, have turned into a major rip-off. I have my sources of information, too. It is going to take my every effort, when I get to the Governor's Mansion, to keep both of our asses out of trouble by burying those peccadilloes."

"I want you to call off Paul Curtin."

"You must be nuts, Mr. Hawkes. In the first place, he is my opponent's biggest sore spot. His whole career is devoted to forcing O'Neil out of office. That's why he was hired. For your information, I have already called Mrs. Parsons once on the subject of Paul Curtin. I heard he was nosing around at the Urban Development League. I called her up to ask her support for Uhuru because it was important to my campaign."

Greene poked his finger at Hawkes the way he did when addressing an audience. "You're not dealing with ghetto intellects here. I could tell from Melanie Parsons's voice. What the hell is this, she wanted to know, that the mayor is busting my chops about one lousy project? I figured that sooner or later, she'd forget it. I'm not about to remind her?"

"Mr. Mayor," Hawkes said in measured tones, holding out a sheaf of papers, "you're absolutely right. Uhuru Towers is a real swindle. A few million dollars are missing. And I know you are aware. You're a very clever man. You've known from the beginning. Why, I have proof right here that you have received confidential reports showing how much I've been stealing, and you've had them for months and months." Hawkes let the sentence dangle.

Greene took a quick look at the papers, then shoved them back into Hawkes's hand. "Wonderful. You have proof of my knowledge of your crimes. Maybe someone might even call me an accessory after the fact. That won't do you much good in jail, will it? And I have a lot of options. For one, I can throw you to the wolves right now and take my lumps. I tried to help out a black businessman. He fucked me. *Mea culpa.* It might even sell in Harlem. I can claim that I was playing for time till I had all of the goods on you, before I sprung the trap."

"I agree, Mr. Mayor. No one is going to send you to jail, or even indict you. But I'm on the record as your all-out supporter. You've done the same for me. You've talked to Kurt Englander on my behalf. You've talked to Melanie Parsons. You're up to your neck with me, Mr. Mayor. If Uhuru is exposed before you get to Albany, I'll probably go to jail. But you'll have to go to work for your daddy, because for sure as God, when the papers I have in my hand become public, your political career is going to be over. So, please, Mr. Mayor, try to think of some way to turn off Paul Curtin." He passed the papers back again. "You can keep these. I have lots of others." Hawkes turned away from him, walked across the street, got into his car, and drove away.

Greene stood in the dark doorway and watched him, his eyes blazing in frustration and anger. Hawkes had only repeated what he already knew. They were on the hook together. He tore the papers into tiny bits and watched the wind scatter them in the gutter. He would have to call Parsons again, if only to satisfy Hawkes. As he watched the Lincoln's lights disappear around the corner, the mayor of New York City stamped his foot in exasperation.

Seething, he walked down the block and threw himself into the seat next to Jennifer Ashton, slamming the door after him.

"Is everything all right, Chris?" Her voice was foggy.

He reached out for her handbag and pulled it away.

"Please. Don't."

He opened the purse. The compact was there. She'd been snorting. He'd have to drive home.

"Damn you," he said, pulling at her arm.

She fell forward with a whimper. "Don't hurt me."

He felt his body stirring and twisted her wrist sharply.

"Ow, please." Her head fell into his lap.

"Do it," he said, his voice hoarse.

"Not here. I can't. Please," she begged softly.

He twisted her wrist again.

He felt much better as he steered the car along Atlantic Avenue and home, much more in charge than he had after his humiliating meeting with Hawkes.

In her corner, eyes closed in a half sleep, Jennifer Ashton rubbed her sore wrist and smiled a small satisfied smile.

41

At half past ten the following morning, Christopher Greene made another call on his private line to Melanie Parsons. Her voice was pleasant and noncommittal.

"I wanted to call you to talk about the Curtin article in the *Advocate* yesterday. In view of our last discussion of the subject, it was a surprise. Does this mean a shift in your position on minority enterprises?"

"Certainly not. I thought that the article was clear enough on that score. We are exploring the idea that the governor is using a big showy project to cover up the inadequacies of his housing policies. We are a hundred percent for minority business, but not as a cloak for ineptitude."

"Has Curtin been to see Hawkes? It seems hard for me to believe. He's pretty damn sharp, especially when you consider what a tough row he's had getting where he is."

Melanie frowned, measuring her words as she answered. "I'll ask Mr. Curtin again, Mayor Greene. But I cannot imagine he has not followed all the proper procedures. I've certainly taken note of your personal endorsement of Mr. Hawkes." She paused a moment, then asked, "That's what it was, wasn't it?"

Greene took the plunge. He had nowhere else to go. "In a manner of speaking. I think that attacking Uhuru Towers could jeopardize the whole concept of urban housing built by minorities. If you're committed to an editorial course, you have every right to pursue it. But I'm convinced that these are good people, and that the project is important. And to that degree, I'll go with what you said. This is an endorsement. I'm sure as the devil not trying to sway your policy, Mrs. Parsons. But I wanted to say a few words in Hawkes's defense."

"Would you like to go on the record, publicly?"

"Certainly."

Melanie tried to imagine how to maximize the impact of such a statement on the campaign and on her circulation. "How about an exclusive interview with Max Fabrikant, our managing editor? That would be a good forum for you. I'll have him call you to set up a convenient time."

"We don't have to go to all of that bother, Mrs. Parsons. Why don't we just do it on the phone. I'm ready to talk to him now, if you'd like.

"It's certainly all right with me. Why don't I call Fabrikant? When would you be free to take this call?"

"I'll be in the office for another hour or so. Or after three. I have a luncheon."

She changed phones and dialed Fabrikant direct. "Max, the mayor wants to make a statement about Curtin's article. He called up to ask for equal time. He thinks we were rough on Hawkes."

"What did you tell him?"

"I made a deal with him. We give him the soap box. He gives us an exclusive interview. I thought it would give it a little class if you did it yourself. We can run an exclusive flag on the front page. He'll be in for an hour. Run up some questions for him. Let me know when you've got the story knocked out. And Max, don't put it in the computer. Do it on a typewriter. I don't want anybody seeing it before we have it finalized."

"Should I call Curtin for some input?"

Melanie chewed her lip. "Not just yet. No. You do the interview and write the story. Let's see what this looks like without Paul Curtin's preconceived notions."

In less than an hour Fabrikant knocked at the door of Melanie Parsons's office. She scanned the article, then read it over carefully, her frown deepening as she progressed. It was more than a statement of support for Uhuru. It was a politely phrased rebuke to the *Advocate* for its criticism of the project. It was a statement in praise of Marcus Hawkes. She looked up at Max quizzically.

He shrugged expressively. "Maybe it's just one of those bi-partisan babies that nobody can afford to knock. Who knows what markers this guy Hawkes may have floating around the political community?"

"What did he say about the part about the fire? The building that burned down?"

"The subject never came up."

She cocked her head and frowned again. "Run it as it is."

"What about Curtin's second piece?"

"I haven't seen it, either. It isn't due till Monday."

"Do you want me to call him at home and let him know about this Greene thing?"

"Thank you, Max. I'll do it myself."

When he had left, she asked her secretary to call Curtin.

"Paul, this is Melanie Parsons."

"Yes, ma'am."

"Chris Greene called me an hour ago about your article. He asked for equal time." She read him Fabrikant's interview.

When he failed to comment, she said, "No surprise?"

"You know what I think."

"I do. This doesn't support that kind of thinking. If he's got some kind of illicit relationship with Hawkes, he might try to move and shake a little behind the scenes, but would he stick his neck out this far? I have my doubts. You aren't giving any credence to the possibility that he believes what he says."

"Mrs. Parsons, you have the same facts that I do. You know what I know. Uhuru Towers stinks to high heaven. Maybe he knows he's an accomplice after the fact to a couple of dozen homicides. That'll produce a lot of loose talk. By the way, what did he have to say about that fire? I didn't miss something, did I?"

"No. The conversation was restricted to Uhuru Towers and Hawkes. You're working on the Monday piece?"

"Yes. I am."

"If I were you, I'd leave both you and me a little trapdoor, Paul Curtin. We just might end up with a face full of egg. I'd hate like hell to come on strong against Uhuru and have it misread as a rebuke of Greene the candidate. Greene's a shrewd self-interested man. I can't believe he'd make this kind of commitment if there were a chance his whole political career could go down the drain because of it. You could be wrong, you know. I'm looking forward to seeing the story on Monday."

Paul's reaction, as he hung up, was reinforcement of his beliefs. When a solipsistic egotist like Chris Greene goes out on the limb in disregard of caution, and his own interests, it can only be from lack of choice. Hawkes must have his nuts in a vice.

He checked his watch. He didn't want to miss his plane to Albany. He pushed his papers into his bag, then grabbed the phone.

"Jeff Jackson."

"It's Paul. Do me a favor, will you? Take a look at the story Fabrikant is doing. It's an exclusive interview with the mayor about my story and Uhuru Towers. Its gist is that I'm full of shit. Will you dig around and see if there is something in the Greene file that could tie him to Hawkes beyond what we know? Anything at all. Or anything you see that's soft. Drugs. Anything."

"Gotcha. I'll have it tonight."

A long and expensive taxi ride brought Paul from Albany's airport to the gaping, impersonal mall which is the official seat of government of the Empire State. The gray-veined marble monoliths were as receptive to the public they had been constructed to serve as a fortress is to its besiegers.

The part of the governor's official family that Paul wanted was still in the old red brick and granite executive building, connected to its modern counterparts by long concrete tunnels in which wind whistles, mingling with lonely footsteps.

Paul's interview with the comptroller of the state of New York lasted less than half an hour. He was ushered in and politely seated by the tall and austere Jewish gentleman who had held the post through more than two decades, under administrations of every stripe.

He greeted Paul with a certain wariness, though he had come to know him well during the past four years, and admitted frankly that he would be more comfortable if he had known the reason for Paul's visit.

"Your article on housing was . . . vigorous, Paul. Perhaps a little severe."

Paul smiled. "Always a gentleman. I calls 'em like I sees 'em."

"You don't mind if I disagree occasionally, then do you?"

"No, sir."

"What can I do for you?"

"I'd like to know something about the signature machines. I

didn't really want to waste your time. If there's somebody on the staff you want to dump me off to, please feel free."

The comptroller permitted himself a smile. "No doubt you would like me to throw you at some poor naive and unsuspecting soul. I'll be glad to answer your questions personally."

"What is the process by which they are used? And who can use them?"

"It's a simple question. Anything under a thousand-dollar expenditure can be made on the signature of an authorized clerical supervisor. Over that, it goes to a location manager. Any funds that are legislated by the state need documents confirming that they reflect the strictures of the enabling act and must be accompanied by confirming documents. Any payment over fifty thousand dollars requires the signature of the governor or the comptroller."

"But you don't have to sign by hand?"

"That would be impractical. There's a facsimile machine in a safe in the next office. But there are safeguards against misuse. The facsimile signature is useless without the state seal, which is locked in the governor's office. And beyond that, anything over a million must be signed by the governor. And he'd have to have my countersignature. Does that answer your question?"

Paul rose and shook his hand. "Thank you, sir. That's it."

As Paul rode back to La Guardia on the plane, a chastened Harry Feldstein, district manager of the Division of Housing at the World Trade Center, ducking and scraping like a court eunuch in the Forbidden City, backed out of Frank O'Neil's New York office.

The essence of his visit to the governor's whipping post had concerned the virtues of loyalty, and a reminder about which side of his bread held the butter. How, the governor had wanted to know, could he possibly move anyone up the ladder when he wasn't able to keep his people from shooting off their mouths.

Harry was a clubhouse type. He had thirty years in state service, the best of them since O'Neil had become governor. He took the message to heart.

At the same time, Eustace McGee received a plain three-by-five card in an envelope. Its typed, unsigned message was, "Would your daughter fit in your microwave oven?"

Paul's plane arrived at 3:30. He took his car from the garage and rushed down the expressway and through the tunnel. Arriving and parking at the World Trade Center, he tapped his foot impatiently waiting for the elevator to the State Division of Housing.

He walked through the glass doors at four twenty-five. The receptionist was already gone. He spotted Eustace McGee in the office beyond and walked toward him.

"Hey, Eustace, Eustace." McGee kept on walking.

Paul chased after him. He went ahead, eyes fixed on the ground, and disappeared into his cubbyhole.

When Paul arrived, he didn't look up. "Please, leave me alone."

"Look, Eustace, I was up in Albany. I think I know how this scam works. All you need is two signatures; the governor and the comptroller. With those and the state seal, you're Midas."

Eustace McGee put his hands over his ears and said, "I don't want to hear anymore."

"Jesus, Eustace," Paul said. The man was shaking.

"Please, Mr. Curtin, you've got to help me."

"How? What can I do? Just tell me."

"Get out. Leave me alone. Now. I can't help you."

Paul got up from his chair. McGee's whole body was trembling. He turned away and headed toward Harry Feldstein's office.

Harry stood at the door, and as Paul approached he growled, "Get the fuck away from me, mister. Nobody talks to a fink." He went inside and slammed the door.

As Paul drove home, he found himself checking his rearview mirror. He thought about the look on Eustace McGee's face and shuddered, then closed the window against the cold air.

42

Marcus Hawkes sat behind his desk reading Mack Bell's memo for the second time. It indicated his total dissatisfaction with the pace and the quality of the masonry and plumbing work at Uhuru Towers, and suggested replacement of the current subcontractors.

In Mack's opinion, the building could still be finished by year's end if the two weakest links were replaced not later than May 1, to take advantage of the good weather.

Marcus's ring winked like an eye in the afternoon light as he tapped his fingers on the typescript. Would Bell go around him to Englander? In the absence of an answer, he might.

The memo also pointed out that inventory control in both the masonry and plumbing areas had gotten out of hand, laying them open to the possibility of massive materials loss.

Gaines and he had discussed who the leak at Hawkes Building might be. They had come to the conclusion, after a process of elimination that extended to all employees, including Marcus's brother Charles, that there were only two possibilities: Bell and Woodruff.

The outspoken memo had settled the matter as far as Marcus was concerned. No one who was carrying on a secret correspondence with a newspaper reporter would call attention to himself in such a way. And besides, both he and George had decided, Bell didn't have the art. Woodruff, on the other hand, had survived and risen through forty years in the convoluted world of the civil servant. He fit the part perfectly.

When he heard a knock at the door, he slipped the memorandum into his top drawer and said, "Come in."

"It's for you, Mr. Hawkes," Mrs. McGuffey said. "A messenger brought up the envelope."

He opened it and looked over the contents. "Good. Elly, be

a good girl and get your book. I'd like to give you a couple of letters."

When she came back, she found Marcus examining the two steamship tickets that he had booked by phone that morning.

"Now, Elly," he said, "I am going to have to rely on your discretion. No word of what I'm doing can get out, or you're going to spoil a nice surprise for some very lovely people."

"Of course, Mr. Hawkes. You can count on me."

"I knew I could." Thus assured, Marcus Garvey gave Eleanor McGuffey two letters. First, he dictated a memorandum to the staff of Hawkes Building Company expressing the thanks of management to Malcolm Woodruff for his contribution to the corporation through its difficult early years. He went on to describe the long cruise that Malcolm and his wife were being given as a token of that gratitude on the occasion of his retirement.

"Why, I had no idea," Elly McGuffey said.

"No one did, Elly. That's why it's so important that this be between us." He then dictated a short letter of resignation for Malcolm's signature, effective immediately.

"Malcolm's been planning this for some time. You know what a private man he is. He would be terribly embarrassed. He doesn't want a lot of painful good-byes. Let me have them as soon as you can."

"How many copies?"

"Oh, don't bother with that just yet. We can Xerox them later."

In twenty minutes the letters were prepared and on his desk. He read them over, then called Gaines.

"George, this is Marcus. I want you to meet me. No, not here, somewhere anonymous. The Three Ring Circus. Good. Half an hour."

He looked up Malcolm Woodruff's number and address in his Rolodex, jotted them in his pocket notebook, and left the office. On his way down the hall, he looked in on Malcolm, who was at his desk as usual, surrounded by a mountain of papers.

"Think you'll get through with them, Malcolm?"

Woodruff looked up crossly. "A lifetime of habit, Marcus. You know I never leave a piece of paper on my desk." He gauged the pile with his eye. "I'll be in front of my TV set by six-thirty."

The blocks between 135th Street and 138th Street around Lenox Avenue have been known as Sugar Hill by three generations of black people who have aspired to make their homes there, among the quality of Harlem, professionals and businessmen, entertainers and musicians, the backbone of St. Phillip's parish.

Sugar Hill has been encroached on to a degree by urban blight in all its rainbow colors, but maintains its dignity with swept stoops and cleaned sidewalks and freshly painted houses not common in Manhattan norh of Ninety-sixth Street. In such a house in the middle of 137th Street, Malcolm Woodruff lived with his wife.

Gaines and Hawkes exited from the brown Lincoln and climbed the steep steps to the door to ring the bell. Mrs. Woodruff, a slim white-haired woman in her early sixties, answered wearing a simple gray woolen dress. She opened the door only a crack, then seeing that it was Marcus, closed it again, removed the chain, and let him in.

"Mr. Hawkes, how nice to see you."

"Have you met Mrs. Woodruff, George? This is George Gaines."

Gaines smiled. "I don't think I've had the pleasure."

"Nice to meet you. Please, come in, take off your coats. Let me get you a nice cup of tea," Mrs. Woodruff said. "It was so sweet of you to call, Mr. Hawkes. I can barely wait to see the look on Malcolm's face. He's been talking about retiring on and off. I never thought that he'd take the step." She laughed. "You know he never talks any business to me."

"So you've said," Marcus replied, with some relief, as he ushered her into the parlor, decorated with bold flowered patterns on overstuffed sofas and chairs. One wall was filled with the large walnut cabinet of a TV console.

"Now, tell me what you want me to do? I'm so excited."

"Well, I think that the first thing that you should do is tell your daughter, so she doesn't bust in like a bull in a china shop and spoil things."

"You're so right," she said. "That child never knows when to shut her mouth." She put on a pair of reading glasses and took the receiver from the phone on a side table. "It's an hour earlier in St. Louis. I suppose she's waiting for the bus to drop off the baby. She just started nursery school, you know."

She fidgeted while the phone rang. "Dorothy? What in the world were you doing, child? It takes you forever to answer a phone. How's the baby? My, my. That's what I thought. Is she having a good time? Yes. Yes. And Bill? Good. You give them a kiss for Granny. Now you listen to me, Dorothy, I have some wonderful news, but I have to hurry.

"Daddy's decided to retire. He hasn't even told me about it. But his boss, Mr. Hawkes, he's right here with me. He's giving us a wonderful present. But it's got to be a surprise and you've got to play your part. We're going on a cruise around the world. It leaves in the morning. It's been all I could do to get to the telephone people, and the paper delivery, and have them hold our mail. Daddy doesn't know a thing." She clapped her hands in childlike pleasure. "Not a sound. We'll be sending postcards from everywhere. We're going out to dinner and spring it on him." She listened for a moment, a tear in her eye. "You're right there, honey. Goodness finally catches up with you, and the Lord do provide. Love you. Bye, now."

Marcus looked at his watch. "Is there something we can do before Malcolm gets here to help you get ready? Or to pack?"

Mrs. Woodruff looked down at the brochures in her lap. "We need all kinds of things. But you know, Mr. Hawkes, as you get older, you can go further and further on less and less. There is one thing you could do for me. I'm too short. Mr. Gaines, do you think you could pull those two big suitcases out of the closet for me?"

"I'll be glad to. And I'll take them up for you as well."

True to his prediction, Malcolm Woodruff opened the door of his house at 6:25, an hour and a half after his wife had begun to pack their luggage. By the time he came in, she was seated in the parlor, on the couch between Gaines and Hawkes, showing them her picture album.

"Hello, Malcolm," Marcus said, rising.

"What you doin' here, Marcus?" he asked shakily.

Marcus turned to Mrs. Woodruff and said, "George and I were in the neighborhood, and we thought we'd just drop by. We're inviting you out to dinner."

Mrs. Woodruff stepped over to her husband, gave him a peck on the cheek, and said, "I'm going to go on up and fix myself. I'll be right down again." She patted her hair self-consciously.

Before Malcolm could voice a protest she was gone up the steps. He turned to Hawkes and said, "Just happened to be in the neighborhood." His voice was a croak.

"That's right, Malcolm. I saw your lights and thought I'd drop in to say hello. We got to talking with the missus, and thought it would be nice to have you for dinner."

"I'll go up and change," Malcolm said, heading for the stairs.

Hawkes cut him off deftly with the bulk of his body. "That won't be necessary. You look fine."

They both turned their heads as Mrs. Woodruff clicked down the stairs. She presented herself, beaming, with fresh lipstick, and a small pin with colored stones proudly displayed on the bosom of her dress.

They dawdled for a minute at the top of the stoop, as Mrs. Woodruff dealt with the myriad locks with which they tried to insulate themselves from the changes that were taking place around them.

"I declare, Malcolm Woodruff," she said. "If it wasn't for me looking after these things, you'd leave the door wide open and let all this trash come in and steal us blind." She turned to Hawkes and said, "You can't imagine what this neighborhood is coming to."

"No question about it, ma'am," Hawkes agreed. "Terrible things are going on around us all the time. Robbery. Murder. There seems to be no end to it. Isn't that right, Malcolm?"

When they reached the sidewalk, Woodruff looked over his shoulder at his home.

"Come on, Malcolm," Hawkes said, holding the door open. "You can sit in back with George." He made a courtly gesture with his arm, "I'll just keep Mrs. Woodruff up here with me."

Marcus took his seat, and when they were all securely inside, depressed the electric switch at his side, and locked all of the doors. He started up the car, and wended his way east to the Harlem River Drive, then turned north.

Malcolm Woodruff was very frightened and could not muster the courage to ask where they were going. Then he thought to himself, I am here with my wife. She doesn't know anything about them. Why would they bother with her? Maybe

I could have an accident, just like Gibbons, but if both she and I disappear, there's going to be a lot of questions asked—and the place they'd start asking is Hawkes Building.

Hell, even if Marcus thought I might be shooting off my mouth, there was a limit to the risk he'd take in shutting me up. He didn't want to lose that golden goose on 125th Street while there were any eggs left. And for sure, he didn't want to face a murder rap.

Woodruff relaxed a little in his seat, and said, "Very thoughtful of you to ask us out, Marcus. I enjoy an evening out, from time to time."

"Glad to be of service. You deserve a night on the town."

"Where are we headed? What are we going to have for dinner?" Malcolm asked.

"We're going to a seafood place up on the river. Does a fish dinner suit you, Mrs. Woodruff?"

"I love fish. So does Malcolm. How about you, Mr. Gaines?"

"They're a specialty with me," he replied.

Near Yankee Stadium the car slowed suddenly.

"Damn it to hell," Marcus said. "Sorry, Mrs. Woodruff," he apologized. He seemed to be steering with difficulty. "I think we've blown a tire."

Hawkes drove down the next ramp and bumped across into the coalyard adjoining the Bronx Terminal Market, rolling to a halt thirty feet from the side of the road, in the shadow of the coal crusher. He opened his door clucking and shaking his head.

Gaines slipped out of the backseat, saying, "Let me help you with that, Marcus."

Woodruff had not time enough to voice his suspicions. After a brief moment, Hawkes reappeared from the rear of the car and opened the passenger side doors. He smiled and shook his head ruefully, extending his hand to Mrs. Woodruff.

"I'm afraid that you'll have to get out. It's flat, all right."

Woodruff emerged and looked critically along the side of the car to the uplifted trunk lid, where Gaines, partially obscured, was making clanking sounds. "It doesn't seem to be leaning. Which one's flat?"

"Left rear," Hawkes said.

Woodruff walked around the side of the car to look. When he

reached the rear fender, Gaines hit him in the groin with the tire iron. He pitched forward, gasping, and fell to the ground.

Seeing him fall, Mrs. Woodruff took a couple of halting steps toward him. As she looked down uncomprehending, at her husband's crumpled form, Gaines took the silencer-equipped gun from the trunk and blew off the back of her head.

Gaines replaced the revolver in the trunk. Extracting a heavy duty garbage bag from a box, hesitating only long enough to tear the jeweled pin from the dress, he stuffed the faceless corpse into the bag, tied the top, and threw it into the trunk.

He walked to where Malcolm was lying, doubled up on the ground. "I'd hate to see him make a ruckus," he said, and kicked him in the jaw. Then he threw him on the floor in the backseat.

In a few minutes, they had crossed the Bronx and arrived at the back door of the Gaines Masonry Company, a one-story building beneath the elevated West Side Highway. The sounds and smells of shifting garbage and marauding cats filled the moonless night.

Gaines opened the gate, and Hawkes drove into the loading bay. As Gaines closed the gates, Hawkes opened the door and swung himself around.

Gaines looked up and waved his arms frantically. "Get back in," he said in a hoarse whisper. When he heard the car door click, he walked forward, and clapped his hands twice.

Two large black and tan Doberman pinschers, which had been hanging back in the shadows on the platform above Marcus's head, jumped down with their teeth bared, and approached Gaines with their heads bowed, their docked tails wagging. He led them to a pen and told them to stay.

Gaines opened the trunk and heaved the garbage bag onto the ground, pulled it across the yard and lifted it over the side of a dumpster half-filled with construction waste: dirt, bent reinforcing bars, and shattered brick.

He stuck the revolver in his belt and helped Hawkes to drag the semiconscious Woodruff to the door leading to the basement. He unlocked it, and let Woodruff roll down the stairs to the floor below.

Hawkes blinked when Gaines turned on the light. The room was twenty feet square and filled with benches containing tools and electrical equipment.

Gaines turned Woodruff over with the toe of his shoe. "Wake up, or I'm going to give you another kick in the balls."

Hawkes looked down at him and said, "You are a miserable nigger. Do you know that? Unless I am mistaken, you have caused me no end of grief. Just how much, I don't know. But you certainly are going to tell me each and every word you've said."

Hawkes and Gaines grabbed Malcolm under the arms and dragged him across the floor to a table. They propped him up in a chair.

"What did you say, Malcolm? And to whom?"

"Nothin'. I said nothin' to nobody." The voice was a squeak.

"You ever hear of Paul Curtin, Malcolm?" Hawkes asked him. "You ever talk to him?"

"Never."

Gaines reached out and patted the instrument on the table before him. "You know what that is? That's a strain gauge. It'll show pressure up to 25,000 pounds per square inch. That's how we test brick and cinder block."

Hawkes asked, "Have you been talking to newspaper people?"

Gray-faced, Woodruff shook his head.

While Gaines held Woodruff's shoulders, Hawkes pulled his left wrist between the plates of the gauge and activated the hydraulic switch. Woodruff struggled feebly, his eyes bulged, he extended his tongue and screamed. The pressure gauge showed 656 pounds when the wrist bone snapped.

"What did you tell Curtin?" Hawkes asked.

"I never spoke to him," Woodruff panted.

"You have two wrists."

"No more." He shook his head. "It was Jeff Jackson. Old friend. A writer on the *Advocate*. A brother. Must have been him . . ." his voice shook, ". . . it must have been him that talked to Curtin. I never did."

"What did you tell Jackson?"

"Next to nothin'."

Gaines shook him violently. "We don't have all day, you old fool. Exactly what did you say?"

Woodruff's body swung like a rag doll. Hawkes grabbed

Gaines's arm as he flailed the old man back and forth. "Stop it, George. He's no use to us dead."

Hawkes sat Malcolm upright in the chair. "All right. What did you say?"

He had to lean forward to hear the response.

"I told him that there was something going down at Uhuru, and that it reached very high. Something illegal."

"That's it?" Gaines said, incredulous. He lifted his arm to strike Woodruff.

"Wait, George," Hawkes said, turning to Malcolm, who was cringing in the chair. "Malcolm, he isn't going to stop till you tell us everything. Please, Malcolm."

"I told the truth. That's all I said."

"Then what do you know that you didn't tell him? How do you know there's something going down?"

"You been kiting cash requisitions. You been getting blanks—signed blanks."

"How do you know that, you old bastard?" Gaines shouted into his face.

"That's what Gibbons must have seen. It must have been a requisition for bricks. He must have seen that the order called for more bricks than was on the skids. There ain't no way to do that without signed blanks."

"How do you know that, Malcolm?" Marcus asked.

"I been forty years in this job. I know."

"And where did we get the blanks?"

Woodruff groaned, moving the shattered arm. "There ain't but one place. They had to come from the governor's office. Ain't no other way to get them signed and countersigned. Had to come from O'Neil. Maybe, even, himself." He started to reel in his chair.

Gaines steadied him. "And how much does Mack Bell know?"

"He thinks you're stealing penny ante from the job. That's all. I didn't tell him nothin'."

Marcus sat down on the workbench and scratched at his chin. "Well, then, it depends on how much Curtin and Jackson have told other people at the paper, doesn't it? They could still be the only ones who know. But, little by little, they're trying to tell the whole world." He mulled the thought. "Of course, if they had proof, they'd have printed it. And now, their source of information is gone." He smiled down at Woodruff. "I'm grateful that they don't have forty years in the job, like you, Malcolm."

"I think we ought to kill Jackson and Curtin, too," Gaines said.

"Oh, George, you think we ought to kill everybody," Marcus said in exasperation. "I think just Malcolm will do, for the moment."

"Bye, Malcolm," Gaines said, shooting him in the back of the head. He dumped him into an empty sack and carried him up the stairs. When he got to the top, he turned and said, "Marcus, do me a favor and wipe up that spot with a rag."

The dogs were standing in the dumpster, licking at the hole that they had torn in the garbage bag. Gaines shied a brick at them, and they ran. He heaved Malcolm over the side, then crossed the yard to a dump truck.

Hawkes came to the top of the stairs as Gaines emptied the contents of the truck body into the dumpster on top of the Woodruffs' corpses.

They drove back to Sugar Hill, parking their car a couple of blocks from the Woodruff house. Wearing gloves, and using the late Mrs. Woodruff's keys, they let themselves in, and spent an hour making it look as though the occupants of the house had closed it down. When they were done, they finished packing the two suitcases that had been left upstairs. They turned out the lights and waited a few moments in the hall. Gaines opened the door a crack. The street was silent and empty. They locked the door as they had found it, and walked quickly around the corner. The suitcases were dumped into the Harlem River under the Willis Avenue Bridge.

The following morning, Marcus went into the office at eight, and after searching Malcolm's office thoroughly, packed his possessions into a half-dozen cardboard boxes he had brought with him for the purpose.

He returned to his office and sat nervously at his desk until nine-thirty. He felt considerably relieved when he called President Lines and found that the *S.S. Thomas Jefferson* had sailed on schedule at eight.

43

Paul and Jeff sat in a sleazy diner a block north of the Fulton Fish Market.

"I hate to ask you, Jeff. I know all about keeping trust. But you've got to help me out. That interview with Greene is enough to make me puke. They're laughing at us, Jeff. They're saying, 'You know. So fucking what?' I've got to talk to this guy. I have to. Do you want Hawkes and Gaines to get away with this? You want O'Neil and Greene to get elected again?"

"Back off, Paul," Jeff said heatedly. "I know what the stakes are. I hate this."

"Look, I'll help you. I've narrowed it down to three people. I figured that out from my interviews at Hawkes. There are only three people who know enough about the overall picture to see what's going on—Bell himself, Charlie Hawkes, Marcus's brother, or Malcolm Woodruff. And I don't think it's Bell or Hawkes. Bell is too plainspoken to do things on the quiet. If he thought there was something to report, he wouldn't fart around. Bang, straight to the D.A." He waited, watching Jeff's face. "It can't be Marcus's own brother. Can it, Jeff?"

"All right. It's Woodruff. You're right. But you play it safe, Paul. You'll get the man killed."

"I'd guessed who it was anyway. It's not on your conscience. I'll do the best I can."

Paul rifled his pocket for change and came up with a couple of dimes. After Jeff left for the office, he had sat at the counter with a second cup trying to build a strategy. His mind made up, he slipped into the wooden booth at the back of the diner and picked up the receiver, greasy with years of cooking fumes.

"Hawkes Building Corporation."

"May I speak to Malcolm Woodruff, please?"

There was a pause, then the operator said, "He is no longer with the company, sir."

"Since when?" he said, stunned. "Do you know where I can reach him?"

"We don't give out that information, sir," she replied in mechanical monotone. "If you would care to leave your name. . . ."

"Could you at least tell me when he left?" he asked, exasperated.

"Who is this, please?"

"I'm a friend of Malcolm's. I haven't seen him in quite a while. I wanted to say hello."

"I'm sorry, sir," she droned. "If you'd leave your name . . ."

Paul banged the phone against the cradle in frustration.

"Hey, take it easy," the cook said, scratching his two-day beard. "You wanna bust the fuckin' phone?"

"Okay, okay. I'm sorry." Fuming, Paul grabbed the dog-eared phone book and looked through it quickly, jotted a few numbers on his pad, and left, throwing a couple of bucks on the counter. He slammed the door of his car, and left a patch of rubber on the street behind him.

He parked on the Avenue of the Americas in front of Hawkes's building and flipped down his press card. When he arrived at the proper floor and got off, the receptionist spotted him and fixed him with an icy stare.

"I want to see Mr. Bell."

"I'll see if he's in to you," she replied pointedly. She buzzed and said, "It's Mr. Curtin to see you." Then she turned to Paul. "He said he'd be right out."

Bell appeared at the door in shirt-sleeves, with his collar open. He did not extend his hand.

"I'd like to talk to you," Paul said.

"What do you want? Demolition plans for Uhuru Towers?"

"No. I just want to ask a few questions about your purchasing policies."

A voice rang out behind Bell. "Well, you're going to have to go elsewhere to finish your hatchet job, Mr. Curtin. This is private property. Contrary to the myth put out by the press, we don't have to let you in, or to talk to you. Most people extend courtesy to the press because they feel obligated, or they're afraid not to. But there's no Constitutional requirement that says you have to be hospitable to someone who's trying to destroy you in print. It doesn't say that in the First Amendment, Mr. Curtin. Now, please leave. And don't come back."

Paul looked past Bell at Hawkes. "People who have nothing to fear from the press don't hide from them."

"There's a line between liberty and license, Mr. Curtin. You've built a one-way bridge of convenience over it. You want to lynch Frank O'Neil and you're trying to use Uhuru Towers as a gallows. If you don't find us obliging, Mr. Curtin, that's tough. You'll just have to find your hangman's noose elsewhere."

"Maybe others don't feel that way. How about Mr. Bell? How about Mr. Woodruff?" Paul's voice rose in anger. "Where is Mr. Woodruff, by the way? Just when I get interested in his end of the business, he disappears. Did you can him?"

Hawkes chuckled. "Before I call the security people and have you escorted off of our property, you should know that as a token of respect and affection, Mr. Woodruff and his wife are enjoying a fully paid ocean voyage. He retired, and he's enjoying the fruits of his work. We just helped him along."

"Where'd you send him, the Hudson River Day Line?"

"A sixty-day cruise to the Orient," he spat. "Now, are you going to leave, or do I call security?"

"That won't be necessary." He pushed the elevator button. When the door opened, Paul stepped through and said, "I hope you won't be going on any unexpected cruises soon, Mr. Bell."

"Smartass honky son-of-a-bitch," Marcus said. "Don't you let him in here again. He shows up, you call me, then call security. Understand?"

"Yes, Mr. Hawkes," the receptionist said.

"That goes for you, too, Mack." Hawkes turned on his heel and stalked down the hall to his office.

When the door closed behind him, Bell asked the receptionist, "What cruise? I saw Malcolm the day before yesterday. He didn't say anything about a cruise."

"Mr. Hawkes set it up. Elly told me. It was a surprise. The Woodruffs were really knocked out, Mr. Hawkes said." She took a memo out of her drawer. "I put one of these on your desk this morning." It was a copy of the letter that Marcus had dictated. He stared at it for a moment, then walked back to his office, deep in thought.

In his car, Paul checked the addresses he had looked up in

the diner. There were three M. Woodruffs in the Manhattan phone book. One lived downtown. The first Woodruff was a store on upper Third Avenue. Paul cruised past it and up to 137th Street, then west to the block where Malcolm's house was located. He parked the car and jogged up the steps. He rang the bell repeatedly. There was no answer. He was tempted to check with the neighbors, but decided that that wouldn't be safe for them, the Woodruffs, or even himself.

As he stood looking up at the building, Tyrone Giggis took the occasion to report his whereabouts to George Gaines. He was back on his motorcycle before Paul returned to his car.

Paul slammed the door of his apartment hard enough to dislodge a picture from the wall and send it clattering to the floor. Leaving it where it lay, he crossed into the living room, sat down at the desk without taking off his coat, and placed a call to Artie Winslow at the *Journal of Commerce*. He was their representative on the Newspaper Guild. A nice man. They'd gone to a few Knicks games and hoisted a couple.

"Arthur."

"Glamour boy. You want to go to the Garden tonight? It's Seattle. I have four. You can even bring your lady friend."

"God bless your generosity, Arthur. I can't. I'm in the middle of something. I called for a favor."

"Ask."

"Look at your list of sailings for today. I'm trying to find a ship that left for the Orient. It was a passenger cruise."

"From New York? I doubt it."

"It's supposed to be sixty days. I'll hang on."

Winslow was back in thirty seconds. "Only one possibility, old buddy. The S.S. *Thomas Jefferson*, carrying twenty-three passengers as incidental on a cargo run. The first port of call is Colon, Panama, then through the Canal and all points east."

"What line is that?"

"The President Line. They're right around the corner. Want the number?"

It took a little time, but the offices of the President Line were happy to cooperate. Yes, indeed. They could confirm that Mr. and Mrs. Malcolm Woodruff had boarded the S.S. *Thomas Jefferson*, and were on the high seas, enjoying good weather on their voyage south.

"Okay, Paul. Let's try another route," he said to himself. He took the phone again.

"Frank Bogulski, please. Yes, I'll wait." He drummed his fingers for a minute. "Hi, Frank. Can I come see you? Now? Thank you."

He drove himself to lower Madison Avenue to a small unobtrusive office building. A receptionist buzzed him through the door. After a short wait a brawny man with dark hair and a bent nose appeared at the door.

"It's been a while, Paul. Come in."

They sat down opposite each other over a desk. Bogulski's face was flat and Slavic. He folded his stubby fingers over his paunch.

"I want a make on somebody."

"I didn't think that you came to Proudfoot's for dental work. What's the big deal? You could have phoned it in. Not that I'm not glad to see you. What are you doing? Checking on your girl friend?"

"It's a little out of the ordinary."

"So who?"

"Governor O'Neil."

Bogulski patted his stomach with the tips of his fingers and looked at Paul from under his beetled brows. "Now, why would you come all the way down here to jerk my chain? Maybe we should start with a personal interview. Then we can have our man give us an evaluation of his appearance and his social graces."

"I'm not joking, Frank. I want you to do this yourself." They'd met at a trial a couple of years earlier and had become friends. For two hundred dollars and up, Proudfoot's would provide a prospective employer, or father-in-law, with all there was to know about a subject. From time to time, through Paul's access to the *Advocate*'s files, and Frank's legwork, they helped each other out.

"All right. You're serious. What do you want, Paul?"

"The man hands in a tax return that's open to public scrutiny every year. He's followed almost into the john."

"That's why I asked if you were kidding."

"I want small stuff. I want to know if he pays his tailor. How's his credit rating? How's his bank balance? How about his assets and liabilities? What's going on over at O'Neil

Maritime and Fuel, the family business? If he were an ordinary citizen, it would be a snap."

"Yeah, but he's not. That's why you're here. How fast do you need this stuff?"

"I have a deadline Monday afternoon. Is that possible?"

"I can work over the weekend. That doesn't mean anybody else will."

"You'll try?"

"I'll try."

"I'm dead. I'm going to get some TLC."

"I'll call you."

"I'll either be home or at this number." He scribbled Maryanne's on a piece of paper.

After dinner, Paul sat on the floor of Maryanne's living room. "It's got to be money. On the surface he does all right. The governor of New York gets the highest pay of all: eighty-five thousand dollars. It's not too shabby if you compare it to thirty-five thousand dollars for the poor slob from Arkansas."

"Honey, I wouldn't try to live on it with his social obligations, not in this town."

"That's what I'm saying. His perks are bullshit. Limos and helicopters don't pay for dinners at Lutèce."

"He comes of a long line. Lehman, Rockefeller, Harriman."

"Does he really? Well, that's what old Bogulski's trying to find out. How are the governor's private means holding up, as seen from backstairs."

Maryanne pushed herself to her feet and held out her hand. "I'll be glad when this is over. Come on inside with me if you want me, buster. We've got to make it an early night. We promised the angels we'd take them to that damn school fair."

Tyrone Giggis stood in front of Gaines and Hawkes at the Gaines Company offices and made his report. He twirled one of his dangling locks around his finger as he talked.

"Can't you stop that?" said Marcus Hawkes. "You're driving me nuts."

Giggis put his hands in his pockets and smiled. "I wouldn't want to make you nervous."

George Gaines frowned. "Get on with the fuckin' story, can't you, Tyrone?"

"After he left the Woodruffs' house, he went home. He was

there for a couple of hours. Then he went to Madison Avenue and Twenty-sixth Street. He stayed there until five-thirty. Then he went to see his fox."

"Who's looking after him?" Hawkes asked. "Whoever it is, I hope he's not just sitting there smoking these funny cigarettes and dreaming," Hawkes said.

"Don't you worry about Archie," Gaines answered. "He's sharper with a fat spliff in his mouth than most people straight."

Hawkes chewed nervously at his finger. "I've had phone calls and visits from the press, the sponsors of Uhuru—goddamn old fool McCaig came up here—magazines, even the people who work at Hawkes Building. That article stirred up a mess. But it'd blow over if he'd let it be."

"I told you, Marcus, we ought to kill him," Gaines said.

"Damn you, George," Marcus said shrilly. "Don't you know that if that man gets killed the whole world is going to fall on us?" He got up from the chair and walked a tight circle around the desk, brushing past Giggis, his head hunched between his shoulders. "Damn Curtin. If there was a way to slow him down, I'd like to know it." He stopped and looked up. "I've put all the pressure on him, and that damned paper that I can."

"How about we grab his fox, or them kids?" Giggis asked.

Hawkes shook his head sadly. "I'm telling you, no shooting, no beating, no kidnapping, no disappearances. You might as well give the cops your home address."

"How about an accident, Mr. Hawkes?" Giggis persisted.

"Hit and run is the same as shooting. You'd have to do something that wouldn't look rigged. He'd have to have the accident all by himself."

"His building?" Gaines asked.

"No. No. Buildings in that neighborhood don't catch fire, or blow up. Forget it. Shit," he said angrily, "all I want is to buy a few weeks, to keep him from writing."

"How about if he has a home accident, Mr. Hawkes?"

"Like what, Tyrone?" Hawkes asked wearily, flopping back into a chair.

"I don't know. I could take a look."

"How can you get in?" Hawkes asked.

Giggis laughed, "Shiiit."

44

By the time that he had received the New York papers, Kurt Englander had already changed from the tailored gray striped suit he had worn to the office to a pair of comfortable blue cavalry twill pants, and a black and red checked Pendleton shirt. His highly polished Church of England wingtips had given way to scuffed Bass loafers.

The rear porch of his modern redwood house stretched the full hundred feet of its length, and hung on cantilevered supports over the hillside on which the house was perched. Though it was as yet too cold to have the gardener take down the windows and roof which enclosed it for the winter season, Englander had lifted a couple of the panes to let in the refreshing evening air as he settled into a wide leather chair and put his feet on the matching ottoman. He sipped from a large scotch and soda, adjusted the glasses on his nose, and began to deal with his correspondence.

After a half hour of sorting and reading, making occasional notes on a yellow pad, he began to look through the various journals and magazines which he received each day. A one-day meeting of a charitable foundation had doubled his workload, and he was anxious to cut through it quickly.

He was about to cast the *New York Advocate* aside when he noted a leader at the top of the front page—"The O'Neil Administration and the Housing Dilemma by Paul Curtin."

He turned to page two as directed. The sight of Uhuru Towers juxtaposed with the burnt-out rubble struck him like a blow. Uhuru is a symbol of the bankruptcy of the O'Neil housing program. Ill-conceived, there is now question if it is being ill-constructed, and behind schedule.

When he finished reading, he put down the paper and emptied his glass. The last splinters of light were fading from the New Hampshire sky. It was possible that his brilliant career was being extinguished with them.

He paced the wooden deck for a while, then went to the bar, made another drink, and with the persistence born of self-discipline, returned to his chair to finish his work. Anxiety led him to open the current issue of the *Advocate* first. On page two, occupying the same space that had held Curtin's article about Uhuru Towers the previous day, was the exclusive interview by Max Fabrikant of Christopher Greene. It was an unadorned rebuke to Curtin and the *Advocate* for their remarks on Uhuru Towers, and a defense of the project, its motivation, and its builders.

Englander took a coupon cutter from the side table and removed the two articles, then read them again. There had been but one question about Uhuru Towers by an outside director at Burton Industries' last monthly meeting. It had been a random inquiry, and he had fobbed it off politely. He would not be able to do so again. Luck had given him a weekend to prepare. But he could expect that on Monday morning there would be a number of questions put to him. He ticked them off in his mind. Certainly, the half-dozen directors of Burton Industries who lived in New York would have seen or at least heard about the articles. They might have alerted some of the out-of-towners. The security analysts of Wall Street would fall on him like a pack of wolves. He could certainly expect a personal visit from analysts or investment managers from some of the investment funds that were major shareholders and were located in nearby Boston. And he would hear from the banks and the bonding company.

He took another sip and started to pace again. He'd stood plenty of heat in his time, bringing Burton up from a twenty-million-dollar building materials warehouser to the Fortune One Hundred. This was the first time he feared that he'd get burned.

He reached onto the lower shelf of the chairside table and extracted a book with a worn, green baize cover. It contained a list of the directors of Burton Industries and their shareholdings, and a list of the hundred largest shareholders. It was updated every Monday.

Englander sat on the arm of the chair and, balancing the book on his knee, began to read down the pages, searching for support. He thought seriously about the chairman of Citicorp, who sat on the board, or of the Chase, who was a major lender. He shifted in his seat. This time, he would need more than a vote of confidence from the company's bankers, he needed to have some board control. In the end, it might come down to how many shares would speak up for him.

The first name on the list was the Ely R. Burton Foundation, with seventeen percent of the stock. Not much problem there. He was a trustee. The Burtons owed him everything.

The next name was his own. Six and a half.

The third name was the Vance Charitable Foundation. Five and a half.

There were three mutual funds with more than three percent.

Then the holdings became more diverse and broad based, typical of a New York Stock Exchange listed company.

He read the *Advocate* articles again. Desperate times call for desperate measures. He walked the length of the porch and entered the house through the door to his bedroom. The room was twenty-five-feet square and took up a corner which permitted him both sunrises and sunsets, as well as a glimpse of the sea.

"Excuse me, Katherine," he said, as he passed his wife, who sat on a chaise longue, working on embroidery. In the drawer of the night table by his bed, he found an address book. He dialed a number and waited patiently.

"Wallace? Good evening. I don't like disturbing you at home. This is Kurt Englander."

"Not at all," the voice at the other end of the phone was clipped, the layer of Eastern prep school above the flat Midwestern base. He waited.

"I have a personal matter to discuss with you."

The "oh" was noncommittal.

"I'd like to meet with you tomorrow."

"Rather short notice. Is there something we can do over the phone? A point of reference?"

"I think we would both be more comfortable face-to-face, Wallace. It's not phone material."

"I see." The voice was deadly.

"Can you make it?"

"As you wish. Here in Cincinnati? Or Boston?"

"Whatever suits your schedule best."

"I'm to be at a trustees meeting at Yale on Monday. Reserve at my club for lunch."

"Lunch at the Sumner Club tomorrow then. Shall I get a private room?"

"I'd prefer that."

Englander hung up the phone and looked out of the window as the last light disappeared. He replaced the book and started to go back to his correspondence on the porch, then swung his feet up on the bed and lay back on the pillow. He felt very tired.

He awoke early in the morning and busied himself for two hours by collecting windblown dried branches broken from trees during a winter of heavy snows, and stacking them in orderly fashion where the gardener could pick them up in his tractor wagon.

By noon, he was handing his camel's hair car coat to the liveried attendant at the Sumner Club. He paced the marble hall for three minutes. From the corner of his eye, he saw a limousine pull to the door. As the doorman turned the gleaming brass handle, Wallace Harley Vance III swept into the lobby of Boston's most exclusive confederation. It was more than wealth and privilege that had permitted him to become a member among the Cushings and the Cabots and the Lowells. It required more.

"Good afternoon, Charles," Vance said to the aged uniformed black man who took his coat.

How many nonresident members would recall his name? Englander wondered as he walked forward, his hand extended.

"Nice to see you, Wallace." His hand was cool and dry.

"Good afternoon, Kurt. Have you made arrangements?"

They walked up the curved stairway past paintings of the club's former presidents and under the full-length portrait of John Winthrop, first governor of the Massachusetts Bay Colony, avoided the bar, and slipped into a meeting room in which a table for two had been set.

A waiter stood at attention, allowing them to peruse the menu. They ordered drinks and food and waited till he left.

Wallace Vance looked across at Englander. He adjusted his rimless spectacles on the bridge of a patrician nose. He sat very straight in his chair.

When it was clear that he did not intend to speak, Englander said, "I am sorry to bring you here like this." Vance did not stir. Englander continued. "I am afraid that we share a problem."

"You've mentioned that. In what respect?"

"For me, it's my career. For you, it's your daughter."

"What common ground could exist between you?" Vance asked.

Kurt restrained a laugh. *That question certainly establishes his perception of our relative social positions.*

"Our connections with the governor of New York," he replied.

Vance cleared his throat, then said, "I try not to involve myself in my daughter's sometimes confused social life. Unfortunately, she has often left me no choice. I was rather hoping that her relationship with O'Neil would redeem her prior—er—misfortunes."

Englander took the two clippings from the *New York Advocate* from his pocket and passed them across the table. "Please read these, Wallace."

Vance replaced his glasses, did as he was asked, then returned the clippings.

"Christopher Greene has voiced those same sentiments to me personally, privately."

"He doesn't seem your type," Vance commented.

"That's the point, Wallace. He's certainly not my type. But, he's just one part of the spectrum. Marcus Hawkes has friends everywhere. I've had a similar encounter with Frank O'Neil," Englander said casually.

Vance raised an eyebrow.

"Oh, yes. He went to considerable lengths to make my acquaintance. In fact, he had a mutual friend invite us both up for cocktails for the purpose of telling me what a sterling character I had crept into bed with."

Vance tapped his fingers, then said with some impatience, "What's on your mind, Kurt? Tie all this together for me."

"I need help. I'm trying to buy your support by giving you information which may prevent your name from being dragged through the mud."

The corners of Wallace Vance's mouth twitched in a parody of a smile. "That's direct enough. What do you know? What do you need?"

"Paul Curtin, the reporter who wrote the first article, came to visit me a few weeks ago. I was quite direct with him. I told him that I'd been approached by both Greene and O'Neil. I told him that the Uhuru Towers project had problems, both technical and financial. That I didn't know to what degree. That I was prevented by the sensitive nature of the involvement from dropping on my colleagues like an elephant's foot. And as a result, I wanted to voice my concerns to a disinterested third party on a confidential basis. It gives a lead to a possible big story. And—"

"It gave you a witness for your clean hands," Vance interjected.

"Exactly," Englander replied.

"And now that you've found a way to keep from being indicted, you'd like to find a way to keep your job."

"I need votes. More. I need weighty influence from on high. Then, after I've eaten a certain amount of humble pie and had my wings clipped a bit, perhaps I can survive."

"What's the damage going to be?" Vance asked.

"The project is behind schedule. At best, several millions in overage: additional cost of labor, additional interest costs, a little loss of reputation. At worst, we have the bond we've guaranteed—seventy-five million dollars." He was surprised at how easily the words came out.

"What have you offered me in exchange for your scalp?" The question was rhetorical. "You want to be saved from the lousy deal you made with Hawkes. I grant that everyone makes mistakes, but are you deserving? But that's not the question, is it? No, you have come to me with information that the governor of New York is involved in something illicit. Because you are aware that my daughter is carrying on a very public romance with him, you think that you can use this smut as currency with me, so that I can pull her out before the Vance family becomes involved in his chicanery." He paused and fixed Englander with a stare that chilled his heart.

Holy shit, Englander thought, he's going to pull the rug. He struggled to hold his steady eye contact.

Vance looked up at the ceiling. "A reasonable deal. I may want to be chairman. I may even want an option on some of your stock after the shakeout that will come when the Uhuru loss is made public. But, basically, it's a deal." He buzzed for the waiter.

They ate their lunch quickly, passing small talk while the waiter attended them. Each took a cigar and brandy.

When the table was cleared and they were alone again, Vance said, "I have a little checking to do. I don't like to interfere in Allison's life unless it is necessary. She has a strong will, and with all, is no fool. I need to know more about O'Neil. What I learn, good or bad, I will share with you. You'll have my backing. I'll expect one of your directors to resign gracefully at the next Burton board meeting. I also expect to be unanimously elected to take his place."

"Yes, sir. Thank you."

"Kurt, I want you to take a little advice. Are you interested?"

"Of course."

"Not many people are these days." He inhaled a draft of the rich smoke. "Keep a low profile with the boys from the Street. Give them the figures on Uhuru that you have in hand. You don't have to have a hemorrhage because a few busybodies are poking around. We need a little time to get our ducks in a row. If you're wrong about O'Neil, and the project, then there's no harm done. We'll just have had a pleasant lunch. If you're right, I will be well served by the advance notice, and you by my support. But the timing must be mine."

"I can't speak for Curtin," Englander said.

"You don't have to speak either for him or to him. Do yourself a favor. Go on a business trip tonight. About ten days. You like the Philippines. Go there."

After Englander watched Wallace Vance pull away in his limousine, he made two calls.

"Katherine. This is Kurt. Please pack me up for the Philippines. I'm going in the morning. Call Jan and have her get me tickets and reservations at the Manila. Open return."

Then he dialed John Holderness's home.

"Jack, I'm going to the Philippines tomorrow. I'll be gone ten days."

"When did you decide this? What's happening?"

"President Marcos wants to see me. Very quiet."

"Right."

"Listen. There's been some flack in a New York paper about Uhuru Towers. Paul Curtin—you remember him—started a series about the housing problems of the state under the O'Neil regime. You're bound to catch some static: shareholders, analysts, maybe even the banks. Just keep a low profile and a tight asshole. Exude confidence. We're on top of the problem. If push comes to shove, you can tell them you'll pass their comments and questions along to me. For your information only, I'll be at the Hotel Manila. I'll keep in touch by phone. Okay?"

"You're the boss," John Holderness said agreeably. When he hung up, he sat on the edge of his chair and started to quantify the extent of his personal debt to Kurt Englander and to weigh his own opportunity.

45

After a strenuous Saturday in the park with the children, Paul turned on the hot water and switched the shower head to fine spray. When it was the right temperature, he climbed into the tub and stood in front of the stream, letting it splash into his face and run down his body. Jesus Christ, he thought, I may never be able to move my legs again. He soaped vigorously with a sponge mitten, then rinsed himself.

His mind flickered to Maryanne on Seventy-ninth Street, struggling with the dirty, prostrate forms of her children. Thus motivated, he wiped the mist from his shower caddy mirror, and put a new blade in his razor. He stuck his hand through the curtain and pushed the button on the lather machine to start the heat cycle. He soaped his face again, then washed it off, listening to the buzz of the timer. When it stopped, he wiped the mirror again and pushed the lather release button.

The scream caught in Paul's throat as his muscles convulsed in a massive tetanic contraction, threatening to break his bones. He tried to pull away from the burning sensation at the tips of his fingers. His body quivered spasmodically, and his

heart began to fibrillate, as the current passed through his blood
vessels, the line of least resistance, from the lather machine to
the perfect conductivity provided by the running water and the
cast-iron bathtub.

As his involuntary responses were short-circuited, and his
coronary and pulmonary activity stuttered to a halt, a sudden
spasm through his powerful back muscles flung him through
the shower curtain. The rod snapped under his weight and
crashed against the lather machine, ripping it from the wall,
smashing it to pieces on the floor and wrenching the plug from
the socket.

With the contact broken, Paul's unconscious body sagged
forward. His chest and stomach bore the brunt of his hundred
and eighty pounds as he slammed across the toilet seat, striking
his forehead on the tiled floor.

An hour and a half later, Maryanne Middleton had began to
worry in earnest. What had been mild irritation at Paul's failure
to appear on time had become an unreasoning fear. She rang his
apartment for the tenth time. There was no answer.

She paced in front of the table with its two unused place
settings, then driven by a formless concern for Paul's safety,
broke her own rule. Leaving a note in front of Petey's door in
case he should awaken, she left the children alone, grabbed her
coat and ran out of the door.

When she got to Paul's house her shaking hands made
opening the door a struggle. It seemed hours before the
elevator came.

She rang Paul's bell once, then again. There was no answer.
She let herself in. The lights were on and the radio was playing
rock. Above the throbbing beat, she heard the sound of the
shower.

She put her coat on the couch and called out, "Paul? Honey,
are you there?"

The sound of running water and the absence of an answer
sent goose flesh creeping across her arms and back. She
shuddered and hesitantly made her way into the bedroom.

Paul's slacks and shoes were in the middle of the floor where
he had left them. Steam had fogged the bedroom mirror and the
interior of the windows, and the air was fetid with the odor of
damp draperies and upholstery. Little beads of condensation
dripped from the walls. The bathroom door was ajar.

As she edged forward, the drumming of the water on the cast iron reverberated in her ears. "Paul. Paul. Are you all right?"

When she pushed the door a cloud of vapor poured past her. Instinctively, she turned away. When she looked back into the bathroom, her grasp drew the moisture laden air into her lungs and caused a violent coughing spasm that left her weak and breathless, leaning against the jamb. Her eyes teared and her head spun with vertigo.

She dropped on her knees and reached out to touch Paul's back. He lay naked where he had fallen across the commode, his head resting awkwardly on the tile floor. He had bled profusely from his nose and from a cut above his right eye.

Maryanne fought the bile in her throat and kneeled next to him. His right hand was extended, palm up. The three middle fingertips were burned, the skin charred.

She lifted her knee in sudden pain. The floor was littered with the shattered plastic and metal parts of the lather machine. The torn plastic shower curtain hung over the sink from the bent chromed rod.

She clenched her fists and caught hold of her wavering self-control. Carefully avoiding Paul, she rose and stepped through the stream, reached into the tub and turned off the water. Brushing the debris out of her way, she knelt again and held her ear next to Paul's face. She couldn't tell whether or not he was breathing.

"Oh, dear Christ, please," she said, as the tears streamed down her face. She pushed herself upright and ran to the phone. She fumbled in her purse for her address book, then dialed the number of the Emergency Desk at Lenox Hill Hospital, always within her reach as a result of Petey's asthma.

"I have an emergency."

"You should call 911, lady."

"I am six blocks from you. Do you want someone to die?"

"Easy, easy. Give me the address."

She did, then described Paul's condition. "Is there anything I can do?"

"Leave him, lady. We'll be there in five minutes. You might do more harm than good."

Maryanne ran back into the bathroom. He had not moved. The steam had dissipated and the temperature had dropped. She touched him tentatively. His skin was cold and clammy.

She tore the blanket from the bed and covered him carefully, leaving his head exposed.

In five minutes, she heard the ululating siren of the ambulance as it tore around the corner of Madison Avenue and screeched to a halt in front of the house. She ran to the kitchen and buzzed them through from the street.

She was waiting at the door when two attendants in green pushed a stretcher cart out of the elevator, followed by a young paramedic in a white coat.

The paramedic put the stethoscope to Paul's back beneath his left shoulder blade. He closed his eyes and listened intently.

Maryanne stood beside the bed, her lips quivering, her hands clasped in front of her.

"He's alive," the medic said. "Come here, you guys."

Maryanne sat on the bed and sobbed quietly, her chest heaving.

The paramedic went over Paul's body quietly and expertly. "I don't think his legs are broken, or his spine. The arms seem all right, too. Easy does it. Turn him over. I'll hold the head."

They slipped him onto the gurney, face up. Silently, the white-coated man delved into his bag, and gave Paul a shot. "Get a sodium bicarb I.V. going, Lou."

He knelt next to Paul holding the stethoscope to his chest. Satisfied, he rocked back on his heels while the attendant placed the parenteral set in his left arm. He reached out and took Paul's right hand. His expression clouded with puzzlement. Slowly, he scanned the rest of Paul's body to his feet.

"There you go," he said. "I knew it."

Maryanne looked up. "What? What is it?"

"Electric shock. The burns on his fingers. See, typically depressed. That's where he got the shock. But look here." He pointed to the bottom of Paul's foot. A round black wound the size of a dime, looking like an exploded blister, leaked colorless plasma. "That's the exit wound. That's where he was grounded. He must have touched a switch or appliance when he was in the tub. Come on, Lou. I want to get this guy in. Are you his wife, lady?"

Maryanne shook her head. "No," she sniffed. "But I have hopes. Is he going to be all right?"

"I don't know, lady. There are a lot of tests. Look, he got a hell of a jolt. All I know for sure is that he's got a busted nose. There could be a lot of other things. But he's still with us. He must be tough as nails.''

"Some ways," she said, fighting another outburst of tears. "May I ride in the ambulance?"

"Sure."

It was almost one o'clock when the doctor finally came to the waiting room of the Emergency Clinic of Lenox Hill Hospital. Maryanne had read every magazine at least twice.

"Mrs. Middleton?"

"Yes," she stood, rigid.

"So far, so good. We have a way to go. Mr. Curtin has received a pretty massive electric shock. There are a number of things that will have to be evaluated over the next few days, but he's not in any immediate danger. In any case, with his ribs tightly bandaged, second degree burns on his right hand and foot, with a swollen nose, and eight stitches over his right eyebrow, he is resting uncomfortably and under both protest and sedation in room 764."

"Thank you."

The doctor reached out to catch her elbow. "Are you all right?"

She smiled wanly. "Now, I'm fine. Can I see him?"

"In the morning. I think you'd better go home, before you end up in here yourself."

Luck helped her to find a cab home. When Maryanne entered the apartment, she found the note that she left for Petey untouched. She checked the sleeping children, then went to her bedroom and dropped her clothes to the floor. Without even brushing her teeth, she crawled naked under the covers and fell into an exhausted sleep.

Paul did not awaken till the middle of Sunday morning. He remembered nothing of the previous night, and very little about the day. From time to time he was bothered by a ringing in his ears, and his vision was disturbed by luminous spots and flashes.

As he become more oriented to his surroundings, his discomfort increased. He wanted to get up, but was prevented by a general lethargy, and soreness in his arms and legs. He felt as though he had been beaten. He sagged back into semiconsciousness.

Maryanne arrived at eleven sharp, walking briskly down the hall with the commencement of visiting hours. Joe Liebman, Paul's doctor, was already in the room.

"Hello there, kid."

"Hi, Joe. How's my boy?" Her voice was tremulous.

Liebman, a short, energetic man in his middle fifties, smiled and patted her cheek paternally. "He's going to be fine. Aren't you, Paulie?" He turned back to the patient.

"Uh huh." Paul licked his lips. Hours of exposure to the humidity of the bathroom had made his throat and nasal passages sore. His broken nose made breathing laborious. "I'm ready for tennis. When can I get out of here, Joe?"

"See, Maryanane? I told you he was going to be fine."

"When?" Paul croaked, louder.

"When I let you. Last night they did a skull series. There seems to be no fracture. Your head is as dense as rock. Just the same, with these goddamn electric shocks there's always the chance of residual spinal damage. You aren't ready to walk yet, and until we see if you can navigate, we won't know. That'll be a day, maybe two. You don't have any scarring on your cardiogram. You're lucky. You can fibrillate. Most electrical shock cases die of heart failure or anoxia. The pictures show no lung damage, so you're lucky there." He turned to Maryanne. "I listened to his chest, no sign of pneumonitis either."

"What happened to me?"

"I can't tell you that, old scout," Joe said. "I was hoping that you could tell me something that might help us to figure that out. Maryanne found you on your face in the bathroom, according to the chart. You have the burns common to electric shock, and you're banged up."

"My arms and legs feel like I ran the marathon."

"Muscle soreness. It's from the contractions. It's similar to the pain of tetanus—lockjaw. It'll wear off in a day or so. We have been dripping relaxants into you." He looked at his watch. "I've got to go, kiddies."

"Golf, Joe?" Paul asked.

"Close. A grandchild's birthday party. But try to catch me later in the spring."

*   *   *

"Shut up and lie back, big mouth," Maryanne said.

He closed his eyes for a moment to ward off the splashes of colored light. "You found me, huh?"

"Like a wet mackerel on the toidy floor."

"I really don't know what hit me."

"I don't either. I'll see if I can find something when I go over later and clean up. There's bits and pieces all over the floor. The shower curtain and bar are shot, too."

Paul shook his head from side to side, trying to clear the cobwebs. "Listen, don't throw anything away, babe. Okay? Keep everything. Maybe I can figure it out. I mean everything."

"Okay, okay. Don' get excited." She sat on a chair next to the bed. "Do you want anything?"

"Nope. I feel like I was beat up by experts. Hey, listen, really, when are they going to let me out of here?"

"Two or three days, if you behave, and they don't find anything wrong with you. Honest. That's what I've been told."

"What's today?"

"Sunday, all day."

"I'm going to miss my fucking deadline. Can you get me a typewriter?" He tried to push himself upright, but winced and fell back against the pillows.

"You aren't going to play the violin with that hand for a while."

"I can dictate."

"How would you like me to get Joe to put up a No Visitors sign and take away your telephone? It would take just a word from me."

"Pest! Who's taking care of the kids?"

"Phyllis Webster, from across the hall. She's taking them to the movies with hers. She says that there's no difference between four and six. You just have to yell a little louder." She reached out tentatively and touched his cheek. "I thought you were dead, Paul."

He turned enough to look at her face, and held her hand. "Not yet, toots."

Paul spent most of Sunday in a cloud of sedation, being dragged to and fro for further X rays and poking for blood serum analyses and neurological tests. By Monday morning, he had escaped from his fog, but still felt rotten enough to let Maryanne call in to Max Fabrikant about his accident.

At two in the afternoon, a huge basket of flowers arrived. The card said, "Among the more imaginative excuses for ducking a deadline in my memory. We'll hold up on printing your series till you're on your feet and can defend yourself. Get well. Melanie Parsons."

He called her to object, but she was adamant. "You aren't going to lose momentum. This plays into your hands. You wanted them to have time to think. I will not run anything while you're in hospital and in questionable condition."

"Well, at least let them know I'm alive and more will be coming." He had a passing thought as he hung up the phone, but dismissed it. If Hawkes wanted to get rid of him, he'd have found a more certain way.

That afternoon, the Wall Street Edition of the *Advocate* bore a short message in a box on page two that due to personal illness, the second installment of Paul Curtin's investigation of the O'Neil administration and housing would be postponed for a week.

It was past five in the afternoon when Tyrone Giggis brought the papers to the Gaines Masonry Company, by the Hudson River.

Marcus had called the hospital as soon as he had heard the report of Curtin's destination after the accident. The first report on Sunday had been serious but stable condition. His most recent reply from the patient information operator had been resting comfortably. Yes, Mr. Curtin was well enough to have visitors.

"Thanks, Tyrone," Hawkes said, looking through the paper.

"Shall I stick around, Mr. Gaines?"

"Why don't you do that. I'll let you know if we need you."

When the door shut behind him, Marcus turned the paper so that Gaines could see it. "The party's over, George."

"I suppose there's no sense . . ."

Hawkes cut him off. "No. There isn't the slightest sense in sending Giggis back. I guess we ought to figure ourselves lucky. We bought another week. And the price was right, because there doesn't seem to be any idea that Paul Curtin suffered anything but an accident. There's no point in pushing our luck. How much cash do you have?"

"I put in some more chits to the bank today. Two million and change."

"Fine. Take it out of the safe. I'll take it home with me, now. Don't cash any more. Pack and put your house in order. I'll make reservations for us for Thursday."

46

The meeting of the Board of Trustees of Yale University had begun precisely at ten. At noon exactly, the chairman thanked President Giamatti for his comprehensive report and called for an adjournment.

Wallace Vance's limousine waited for him in front of Timothy Dwight College, where he had been a student himself, forty years earlier. He was whisked to the airport, where a company LearJet waited to take him to New York, cutting the trip from two hours to twenty minutes.

He was nonetheless anxious when he arrived at the Marine Terminal of La Guardia Airport that he would be late for his appointment. Planning and good fortune worked hand in hand for him, as often they did. A driver waited for him on the runway; there was little traffic.

He entered the gray stone building and made inquiry. He was expected, and with a flurry of activity, he was ushered into a large room paneled with oak in Gothic carvings.

The cardinal's sapphire glittered from the extended hand of Daniel Cardinal Demarest, Archbishop of New York.

"Good afternoon, Your Eminence. It is very kind of you to receive me."

"On the contrary, Mr. Vance. It is I who am grateful."

Vance sat in a chair before the desk, the cardinal beside him, shunning the barrier that the table would have formed. Wordlessly, he withdrew an envelope from his inside pocket and handed it over.

Cardinal Demarest took the offering and opened it carefully. Inside there was a check, and a small handwritten note. "For the use of the Diocese as His Eminence sees fit, on the proviso that the gift remain anonymous." The check was for five hundred thousand dollars.

Daniel Demarest was the son of a second-generation Irish family of no means at all. His mother had delivered eleven young souls to this earth, of whom seven had survived. Of those, three were priests, three nuns, and one a married woman with seven of her own. He was a man of wisdom and foresight and led his unwieldy flock through its perilous concrete pasture by guile when possible and brute force when not. He had met Wallace Vance twenty years before, when he was bishop co-adjutor of Cincinnati. They had not always seen eye to eye.

"I am stunned by your generosity, Mr. Vance."

"I am sure that Your Eminence will find a worthy investment."

Creases formed easily in the weathered red cheeks as Cardinal Demarest smiled. "I suppose you are going to tell me why a non-Catholic from Cincinnati is making a donation of this size to an old adversary a thousand miles away."

"I want something."

"I hope that I can grant it."

"It is merely the answer to a question."

Cardinal Demarest appraised him. Are you the old enemy that they talked about in my seminary, Wallace Vance? Not the enemy of adolescent masturbation, nor of Punch and Judy, the curse of liquor and women that scars the lonely lives of priests. Are you the spokesman for a power darker than those frailties? "Ask, then."

"Why will you not give dispensation to my daughter Allison to marry Frank O'Neil?"

"It is not for me to dispense with the laws of this Church. Six checks like this cannot buy that." There was thunder in his voice, and the red of his cheeks had deepened.

"I thought," Vance emphasized the second word with his crisp, dry voice, "that I had made it clear that I wished only the answer to a question."

The fingers wrapped around the base of the pectoral cross relaxed. The cardinal accepted the fact that he was afraid of Wallace Vance. He would do penance for his weakness later.

"You will excuse me, Mr. Vance. It did occur to me that you might have thought you were rich enough to buy the Church, too."

"Well spoken. Please, the answer."

"I am as aware of the American norms as anyone in the Church, Mr. Vance. I have tried to advise the Holy Fathers over a generation that the Church should look with a kinder eye over those suffering in the bonds of unhappy marriages."

"Doesn't my daughter deserve that same kindly eye? Is it her choice of parents?"

"Hardly. The facts surrounding her marriage are certainly not in her favor: the long Church association of her husband's family—they are Black Nobility, a Pope in the family tree—married by a cardinal, two baptized children."

"And these things can not be overcome, even with the new norms?"

Cardinal Demarest looked into Wallace Vance's eyes. He would not lie to him. "If your daughter wanted dispensation to marry a clerk in a department store in Cincinnati, three priests would sit and study her psychological state at the time of her marriage to Il Conde di Forrestiere and probably conclude that the marriage was not valid." He looked at Vance again. "The Church will not advertise through two people who have by circumstance and personal choice elevated themselves to media events that the bonds of marriage and the sacraments can be flaunted."

Vance sat motionless, absorbing his words. "I thank you, Your Eminence. You have done me a great personal service. Tell me, does the governor know your views?"

"He has been told."

Vance stood. "I hope to see you again, Cardinal Demarest."

The cardinal stood and shook Vance's hand, then buzzed. The young priest who served as his secretary led Vance through the warren of the chancellery and back to his car.

Daniel Cardinal Demarest stood next to the window, pulling aside the intricately crocheted lace curtain, watching the chauffeur close the door of the black Rolls-Royce behind Wallace Vance. When he pulled away, the cardinal returned to his living quarters and changed into his simplest priestly uniform, and eschewing his resplendant private oratory, slipped down into the cavernous body of the church to a small side chapel and prayed to God on his knees.

The press of business required that Wallace Vance postpone his meeting with his daughter until the following morning at half past nine.

It was not Allison's habit to rise early. Her children were dealt with by the staff. She preferred to sleep till eleven, read the papers until almost noon, then dress for her luncheon date.

When her father's secretary informed her late Tuesday evening that she would be expected the next day, she accepted it for what it was—a summons to the bench. She'd had them before.

Wallace Vance kept an apartment on the top floor of the Regency Hotel. The double-paned windows had been specially installed to eliminate the noise which rose from Park Avenue below.

The butler took Allison's coat and ushered her to the study. She wore basic black without jewelry and only a light coat of lipstick. Her flowing hair was pulled into a pony tail, and she wore flat shoes.

"Hello, Daddy."

"Good morning, Allison," he said. "Sit down."

She always imagined, during these sessions, that she could hear the screams from the basement, as the recalcitrant and disobedient were tortured, very expertly and slowly by men in immaculate white smocks from her father's laboratory.

He restrained a smile. One day she will show up wearing a crinoline dress, patent leather Mary Janes, and a pink bow in her hair, sucking a lollipop.

"I'm afraid that you have dug yourself another hole, my dear."

"What have I done this time?" she asked.

"This time, it's just bad luck. Do you expect to marry Frank O'Neil?"

She considered her answer. She did not trifle with her father. "I would say yes. He pays me court in grand style. The only block to our marriage is a dispensation from the Church. I need to be granted an annulment. For political reasons, Frank can't marry outside of the Church. And between you and me, he has too strong an allegiance in any case. Whatever it was Loyola said about getting them early applies to Frank twice."

"Is it that important to you?"

She nodded. "We have a good relationship. There are a lot of common interests. He's the governor of New York, Daddy. He's a very handsome, well-spoken man. With a little luck, and a lot of money, there could be a Vance in the White House."

Wallace Vance closed his eyes briefly and touched his fingertips together. "I am afraid that the probabilities of that are *de minimus*."

Allison felt the familiar sinking feeling in the pit of her stomach. "Daddy, don't toy with me. What is it?"

"You'll have to break off your relationship, Allison. You'll have to find a way to do it which will be quite public. The degree of dignity I leave to you. But it is to be done, forthwith."

"But Daddy . . ."

"I have been to visit with high Church personages. There is never going to be an annulment for you. Not for the purposes of marrying Frank O'Neil. Further, he is aware of that." He held up his hand to forestall an interruption. "It is in your best interests not to discuss anything I am telling you. If it were the matter of marriage, while I would not be indifferent, I would not be disturbed. I don't like to see you make a fool of yourself, but you're a grown woman. Marrying in or out of the Church is a matter of total disinterest to me, as is your annulment, since I consider it all to be low comedy in any case. However, you stand the risk of becoming involved—and thereby involving me—in a criminal matter. It would appear that your friend Frank O'Neil is on the take from a group of builders here in New York. I am neither shocked, nor appalled. It happens in the best of families for the best of reasons. What does not sit well is that he is about to be exposed. I cannot tell you whether or not he will end in jail, but I can tell you that his political career is at a dead end. All of the ink he gets in the paper from here on is going to be mixed with poison. Sit still and let me finish!" He lowered his voice rather than raising it for emphasis. "Therefore, you will disengage yourself. You will do it in such a way as it to make it universally known and crystal clear. You will break your connections with Governor O'Neil as of this minute."

She never cried in front of her father. She sucked her tongue between her teeth and bit down on it until she could taste the saltiness of her own blood.

"You will not contact him directly," he continued, adjusting his glasses. "I am sorry to be so abrupt, but there is no choice and very little time."

She swallowed. "And if I don't agree?"

"Good for you, Allison. A show of spunk." He did not smile. "This is not a prank, Allison. Frank O'Neil has committed a number of criminal acts. They are about to catch up with him. I want as much distance between the name Vance and the name of O'Neil as can be arranged on short notice. There is no question of your agreement. When does spring vacation start for the boys?"

She fumbled numbly in her purse for her date book. "The last week in March. Next week."

"What had you planned?"

"I was going to send them down to the Dorado Beach with Nanny for a week, and then join them with Frank for four or five days."

"You will ask the school if you can take them out a few days early. I will put a plane at your disposal. Let's see." He thought for a moment. "You'll take the house in Acapulco. Make a splash. I'll call and see that everything is arranged. Agreed?"

She looked across the Chinese lacquer table, the reflection of her father sharp on its polished black top. "Yes, Daddy."

"Good." He rose and came around the table. "I'm afraid I have a meeting at ten. Do you have a car? If not, take mine. It's downstairs."

"Thank you, Daddy."

"I appreciate your being sensible, Allison. There is no other possible solution." He leaned forward and brushed her hair with dry lips. "I'll be seeing you soon. Give the boys my regards."

Allison went home by cab. She closed herself in her room and cried until there were no more tears. Then she washed, and dressed, and decided how she would carry out her father's instructions.

47

"Ouch. Maybe you'd better give me that stick, after all."

Maryanne took the cane from the corner and handed it to Paul.

He sat at the edge of his bed in Lenox Hill Hospital, fully clothed, and ready to go home. He lifted his arm. "The ribs feel better."

"The color is frightening. I never saw a man with an orange and blue chest before. Not to mention the two black eyes."

"What hurts is the burn on the heel." He let his weight down gingerly onto his right foot, cushioned in an extra large loafer, bandaged and padded with foam rubber. He stood, partially supporting himself on the cane.

"How's the hand?"

He wiggled his fingers. "That's better, too. Joe says I'll be able to bang on a typewriter in a couple of weeks. All in all, I was lucky."

"I'll say. I'll get the nurse."

Over Paul's loud protests, he was taken from the room and down to the lobby in a wheelchair, in accord with hospital regulations. He waited, fuming, till the doorman got a cab, and they let him get up at the door. He hobbled across the sidewalk and seated himself awkwardly.

By the time they reached his apartment, Paul Curtin was glad to sit down in his big armchair. "I guess I had a little more taken out of me than I thought."

"Just stay put."

"Don't you have to work?"

"I do. But I get a lunch hour just like everybody else. I scheduled my next call at three o'clock so I could tuck you in. Do you want something?"

"My mail. A hug. Food not from the hospital."

"One at a time." She brought him a handful of letters.

He ran through them quickly, groaned, and said, "Take them back. All bills. Hey, did you do what I asked?"

"What?"

"This place looks spotless."

"I'm a good maid."

"Where's the stuff from the bathroom?"

"In a bag, in the closet."

"May I have it?"

"Sure. It'll give you something to do, like a jigsaw puzzle." As she handed him a plastic bag, she asked, "Say, who's Bogulski?"

"Frank Bogulski. He's a friend of mine. He works for Proudfoot's. Why?"

"I almost forgot. He called my house on Sunday night. He asked for you. I told him you'd had an accident and that you were out of commission for a few days. He asked that you call him when you can. Something about having your answer."

"Will the phone reach here? I don't feel like getting up."

"Just about."

It was two o'clock. Bogulski was probably out to lunch, Paul thought. He tried him anyway.

"Frank? I thought you'd be out stuffing your face. No, I'm fine. I gave myself a little electrical shock. You can bet your ass that's the last time I'll use an electric lather machine in a shower. That's right. Smart, huh? No, just a couple of burns, and some bruises. I did bust my nose, but when the swelling goes down, I'm sure it will give me character. What have you got for me?"

"A hell of a lot more than I expected. We should see each other."

"Can you come up here for a drink?"

"Six."

"Fine." Paul gave him the address.

Maryanne appeared from the kitchen with a tray which she placed on the card next to him. "That ought to shut you up for a while. I've got to push off, or I'll be late. I'll come back after I feed the kids. They want to come over and say hello."

"I'd love it."

When he'd finished his lunch, Paul pushed the plate aside, and poured out the bits and pieces that remained from the lather machine from the plastic bag. He occupied himself for an hour, trying to reassemble the apparatus from his memory of how it had looked and the logic of the assortment on the tray. All he could tell was that the part where the buttons had been had melted in the heat, and that all of the wiring was blackened and charred. The small heating element was scorched and partly deformed. He shook his head in confusion, and still affected by the residue of medication, fell asleep in the chair.

He was awakened at six by the buzzer of the front door. He winced as by habit he placed all of his weight on his right foot and used his right hand to pull himself upright. He hobbled to the button in the kitchen and asked "Who is it?"

"It's me, Frank."

Paul left the door open and hopped back to his chair. When Bogulski knocked he said, "Don't be bashful. Come on in. Put your coat in the closet. I don't mean to be less than the perfect host, but my foot hurts."

"You look like shit."

"Thanks, Frank. There's ice in the icebox. There's booze on the bar. While you're at it, you can make me a scotch on the rocks. I haven't had a drink since I tried to electrocute myself."

Bogulski fixed them drinks and pulled up a chair next to Paul. "Here's to you."

"Cheers."

"You aren't going to believe this. I didn't." He took an envelope out of his breast pocket. "I went to a lot of different places. I won't bore you with details, except one. You know about the State Bureau of Special Audits, down at 270 Broadway. I made a special stop there. I collected all of the financial information the governor makes public, either by choice, or by law. He seems to be doing pretty good."

"I'm glad to hear it."

"Except I don't know how. Because it looks to me, Paulie, like he ain't got a pot to piss in."

"How's that?"

"He nets about five grand a month from his salary. His maintenance on Fifth Avenue is three. He's got that couple that work for him. That's minimum fifteen hundred more."

"So what? He has money. And there are allowances."

"Sure another two or three grand a month in perks and paybacks. The gulf is wider than that."

"Maybe his brother is paying some of his expenses."

"Ah. Here's the crusher. Old Dennis, he's so broke he's got holes in his shoes."

"You're shittin' me."

"He sold his boat. He quit two clubs. He's slow pay to the merchants." Bogulski dropped a sheet of paper on Paul's lap. "And there's a list of contributors to O'Neil's campaign. The top hundred for this year, last time around, and the time before that. Don't strain yourself. Old Denny went from $50,000 to $25,000 to $100."

"It's early yet."

"He was always the big number up front, the keystone. I'm telling you, he's tapped."

"So where is Frank getting his money if it isn't from his brother?"

"I don't have an answer for that. But it's damn likely to be in cash, Paulie. The only securities he has are a few hundred shares of this and that—the whole mess isn't twenty thousand—and his piece of O'Neil Maritime."

"Are you sure about this business?"

"It's a private company. The bank gives out generalizations. Dun & Bradstreet don't mean shit. If you can get off your ass for a drink at lunchtime tomorrow, I've got somebody for you to talk to who owes me a favor."

"I'll manage one way or another. Where?"

"The Whitehall Club. Downtown. That's where the shipping people hang out."

Maryanne brought Paul a Chinese dinner and shared it with him and the children around the card table. She was worried. He was cheerful enough, but seemed vague and preoccupied. She was glad that tomorrow was a school day, and she had an excuse to clean up, tuck him in, and go home early. He looked like he needed the rest.

Paul couldn't sleep for an hour after they left him. There was tomorrow's meeting to consider, but it appeared that he had O'Neil with his pants around his ankles and his hand in the cookie jar.

48

It had not really been difficult for Allison Vance Forrestiere to arrange. She'd called a few old friends to ask if there was anything going on that night. Mimi Durand was having a cocktail party for the Prince de Chambord and his lovely Charlotte, who were just in from the Antilles. Allison called Mimi and asked if she might come along.

"Bringing the governor, Sweetie?" Mimi asked.

"I'm changing horses, darling."

"In midstream?"

"In midpasture. Who all's coming?"

"Just about everyone. I can't stand it. Who are you bringing?"

"You'll see in due time, my dear. I want it to be a surprise. Oh, will Aileen and Pierre be in?"

"What would life be without Suzy Knickerbocker and Pierre Du Fresne? How would the poor folks know what we're doing?"

"Bye, love," Allison smiled grimly. Between her and the rest of the blabbermouths she'd talked to, it would be all over New York, Palm Beach, and Newport before lunch.

Her next call was to the designer, Aldo Carpozzi. He understood perfectly well. Price was no object. He'd be up within an hour.

When the door rang, the butler opened it and led Carpozzi and his two assistants into Allison's bedroom. It was a large room, all pastel blues and grays on pile fabrics.

In an hour, Allison had been fitted for shoes, stockings, and underwear, and draped in a dress made from two bolts of fabric Aldo had brought with him. He cut and marked while his assistants basted.

"I hope you know I'm going to stick you for this, angel.

323

And if you ever tell anybody that I'm still doing needlework with these gorgeous hands, I'll tell them you're really George Hamilton's twin brother in drag. There we go. This is going to fit like skin."

Allison Vance Forrestiere descended from her father's black Rolls limousine in front of Mimi Durand's Seventy-first Street townhouse on the arm of Folger Butterworth. Folger was a handsome blond three years her junior. His good lucks and his excellent breeding stood him in good stead, because Allison found him as dull as dishwater and as dumb as a hitching post.

He smiled a toothy smile as they walked into the salon. She clutched at his arm possessively and batted her eyes. There was a brief lull in the hum of conversation. There had been recognition.

By nine o'clock, she had made sure that Folger had had two too many glasses of champagne. She walked clumsily with him down the corridor to the library, and looking behind her, slipped inside. By the time Mimi Durand had followed her and opened the door to say, "Oh, dear, excuse me," Folger was kneeling beside her on the couch, and her dress was around her waist.

She pushed poor, confused Folger away and straightened her skirt, making sure to leave her blue lace panties stuffed obviously in a crack in the cushions. She stepped into the bathroom and fixed her face, then dragged him back into the crowd, beaming.

"Lovely dress, Allison."

"Pierre du Fresne! How nice of you to notice."

"New, like all of the accoutrements?"

"Fresh as today, Pierre. That new. Tell me, are you going anywhere for Easter?"

"I was hoping to be invited by some kind soul."

"How about Acapulco? I'm going to be doing a real old-fashioned spring bash. You could be the centerpiece. Or, if you like, just sit by the pool and spin your nasty webs about my guests. I'll be going down in the middle of next week. You're welcome, darling."

"Thank you, Allison. I'd be enchanted. May I let you know on Friday?"

"I have all the time in the world, and thirty rooms."

"Is Folger coming?"

"That depends on his performance, Pierre. If he's a good boy—why not?"

Pierre frowned for a moment. "This is the new you?"

She looked up into his pale blue eyes. She'd known him since she had made her debut. "That's right. This is the new me—for this season. As of today."

He bent and took her hand, brushing it with his lips. "Countess, it's been a pleasure. I'll be talking to you Friday."

The next morning Paul Curtin made his way from the garage at the foot of Manhattan Island to 17 Battery Place, where the Whitehall Lunch Club was located.

Frank Bogulski was waiting for him in a chair near a Dow Jones ticker. He sat next to a tall, slender man with dark hair. They rose and came toward him.

"Paul, this is Jimmy Sullivan. He's the executive director of the New York Shipping Conference."

"Nice to meet you, Mr. Sullivan."

"Jimmy, please." There was a latticework of ruptured veins below the surface of his flaccid cheeks. He smelled of strong drink. He had the special too-even, white smile and slurred diction of people with false teeth. "Let's go in to the bar."

"What'll you have?" Jimmy asked.

"Scotch," Paul said.

"Make mine Jack Daniel's," Frank replied.

"Jimmy and I trade secrets sometimes, Paul," Frank said.

"That's right. You never know who you're going to end up doing business with. We like to check carefully," Sullivan added.

Frank failed to suppress a smile. "They want to make sure that the quality of the mafioso in the shipping business doesn't slip. It's okay to be a crook as long as you've got a pedigree."

"Frank told me you could answer a few questions," Paul said.

"Sure. I owe him a couple."

"Tell me a little bit about the tug and fuel delivery business in the metropolitan area."

Jimmy Sullivan shrugged. "There isn't a hell of a lot to say. The harbor's been going downhill for years. It's a very expensive place to do business. Taxes. Union work rules. Pilferage. Special costs." He winked. "Anyway, as the dockage drops and the movement of cargo goes to other ports, the tug work dries up. It gets very competitive, and you have to keep buying bigger, better, and more expensive, even if you have good old boats. It's coming down to where a lot of guys have dropped out. Fuel delivery's even worse."

"How's O'Neil doing?" Paul asked.

Jimmy Sullivan looked around him before he answered. "Honest? They're doin' terrible." He cocked his thumb. "That's poor Denny over there talking to the tall guy, there, near the Jap. They're on the fuckin' ropes, I'll tell you. He's here every day trying to hustle some business. He's not like his old man, I can tell you. Nobody ever fucked him over." He lowered his voice even more. "You'd think that with his brother the governor, somebody'd do him some good. But Frank O'Neil don't want to be owned by anybody on the waterfront. He knows they'd come quick to collect their markers."

"So they're not making money?"

"I don't see how they can. They lost Scandinavian Lines last year. That was their biggest customer. They just gave up their New York pier and decided to work out of Baltimore and Norfolk. It's a bitch. I tell you, if they don't work it out with their refinery, I think they could be up shit's creek."

49

Pierre Du Fresne sat in his silk pajamas overlooking Long Island from his apartment high in River House. He picked up his pen and made some adjustments to his daily column. He paid particular attention to the way in which he framed Allison Vance Forrestiere's dash for freedom from the governor. It was meant to be public, but one mustn't overdo. When he was satisfied, he made two phone calls; one to Paul Curtin, and one to George Allen Mason.

"I appreciated your card and the chocolate truffles, Pierre. Damn nice to think of an invalided colleague," Paul said.

"I have something even juicier for you."

"Aha, gossip," Paul surmised.

"What else? Allison Vance has flown the coop on Governor O'Neil."

"Really. How do you know that?"

"She was at a party last night with a vapid, good-looking schnook whose reputation begins with his father's bankbook and ends with his open fly. The hostess, who is an insufferable snoop, let it be known that she had caught them in flagrante delicto on the library couch. She even had a pair of lace panties to show. The story will be told for years."

"Have you known about this long?"

"Only since last night. That's when she let it out. But all the tongues of society are wagging."

"Do you know what brought this on?"

"I can only tell you it was sudden. Last week, Allison and the governor were like peas in a pod. A circumspect relationship, but very close. In one night, all that's past history."

"People have fights and make up."

"Paul take it from an old lounge lizard, in our tight little world, this was a stand from which there is no retreat. There is no way to kiss and make up. It was done very much on purpose. I feel the deft hand of Wallace Harley Vance behind the arras."

"What can he know that I don't?" Paul mused.

"Beware of false pride, my friend. The answer is—everything."

"Thanks, Pierre. It's another nail in the coffin."

"A professional courtesy. Get well, Paul."

Pierre dialed George Mason's office and waited while his secretary chased him down. "Hello, George. I see she found you."

"Samuel Johnson said that man is never so pensive as when he is at stool."

"Are you free for a drink?"

"In the middle of the afternoon?"

"I fear we must. I'm racing a deadline."

"I can be there in twenty minutes." Not at all like him, Mason thought. What's on his mind?

For Pierre Du Fresne the walk was a matter of yards. The River Club, a bastion of New York Society, lay one door from the front of his building. He was seated in the bar that overlooks the terrace on the East River and waited patiently, watching the sparse water traffic till George Mason arrived.

"Greetings, Pierre. Tell me what the rush is all about. Are you all right?"

"Sorry to roust you, George, but I wanted you to have this before it went on the street, for whatever it might be worth to you." He passed him the handwritten copy of his column. "Politics aren't my affair. But for an old friend. . . ."

Mason scanned the piece, surprise showing on his face. "Were you there?"

"I was. It wasn't terribly pretty. I've known Allison since she was sixteen. She's done more than her share of the things that foolish girls with too much money do. What with the tension between her convent-raised mother, and that megalomaniacal iceberg of a father, it's a wonder she hasn't done worse. But since she was married to Forrestiere, she's been very much a lady. And since her liaison with the governor, she's been straight out of Jane Austen—positively circumspect. Last night, in two words, she was preposterous and slutty. She arrived with a pretty-faced boob—you know Folger Butterworth—and proceeded to leave her underwear in the library. It was a set piece of vulgarity."

Mason shook his head and looked down at the table. "A sad way to say good-bye."

Du Fresne looked across at his friend. "That was my appreciation." He looked at his watch. "I thought you'd like a little head start."

"Thanks, I think I'll go for a walk. Don't miss your deadline."

George Mason closed his coat and stuck his hands in his pocket, looking at the sidewalk, as he meandered up First Avenue. When he came to Fifty-seventh Street, he decided what he wanted to do, turned toward York Avenue, and picked up his pace. In ten minutes, he was standing in the lobby of the Sloan-Kettering Institute on Sixty-second Street, waiting for his wife to be paged.

He took the house phone when the receptionist pointed to him. "Hi."

"Hello, George. What are you doing here?"

"Are you busy, Elly?"

She didn't answer for a moment, taken aback. She couldn't remember the last time he had come to the hospital during working hours. "I'm just dictating a letter. It'll be a minute. Shall I come down?"

"No, I'd like to come up."

He waited for the elevator, leaning against the wall, ordering his thoughts. When he emerged, Elly was waiting for him. He bent down and kissed her softly on the lips. They walked down the corridor to her office holding hands.

"What is it, George?" she asked.

"Pierre Du Fresne has come to me with an interesting story. I'd like to know what you make of it. It seems that Allison Vance made a public ass of herself at a party last night at the Durand's. Quite irrevocably. She got caught in the act by the hostess."

"My heavens, with the governor?" her eyes twinkled and her wide mouth formed into a bright smile. "I would have given anything to see that."

"Therein lies the rub. It was with a vapid twerp I know. A kid."

"Ah."

"A short syllable, long on meaning. Ah, what?"

"She's dumping the governor, for all the world to see."

"Elly, you know what I've been coming up with on this Uhuru matter. I've been stonewalled at every turn. Polite inquiries have netted me nothing. From what I've been able to gather, though, even before I saw Paul Curtin's article, things are not going well on 125th Street. I've been reticent to speak out."

"You've been right. You have enough to overcome as the Conservative candidate without making accusations in the black community with nothing more than guesswork."

"Elly, this girl is dumping the governor in public for something more than reasons of the heart. I think that O'Neil is in big trouble in the Uhuru matter. How big, I am not prepared to say. But I see the signs and sensations of bribery, and an iron hand shutting off the usual easy sources of information in the state bureaucracy. Someone has passed the word. This subject is taboo." Mason pulled his pipe out of his pocket and packed it methodically from a pouch as he talked. "I wanted your advice, Elly. I've never thought that my race for governor was a fool's errand. But we both know that minority party candidates stand slim chance of election. We'd decided, you and I, that making the race accomplished something in and of itself."

He pulled a box of wooden kitchen matches from a bulging pocket and lit the pipe, sending a cloud of smoke across the room. "I see a chance, Elly. I see a chance to win. I think that Frank O'Neil is going to come to grief over Uhuru. I don't think that Greene has a large enough constituency statewide to win. I don't know how clean his hands are either. I want to go up to Albany, Elly. I want to tell Lou Rosensweig what I know. The lieutenant governor is O'Neil's lackey. I want to offer myself for the Republican nomination if O'Neil's forced to withdraw."

"Won't they be more likely to look into their own ranks?"

"They need someone with a statewide profile, but who won't have any connection with the O'Neil machine. I think I fit the bill. I think I can make a good case, and get some support." He drew a long puff and let it out. "I have the feeling that it's a little unclean. I thought I'd discuss it with you first."

"When did you plan on going?"

"This afternoon."

"Do you think that Lou might already know that O'Neil's involved in Uhuru?"

"The Comptroller-for-Life? I doubt it. He has stayed in his job for twenty-three years, through administrations of all kinds by the cleanliness of his skirts. I cannot believe that he would sit idle in the face of malfeasance, whether O'Neil's a Republican, or not."

"Then you have to look at it as a politician yourself. You're in the right place at the right time. O'Neil cupidity is your good luck, and the state's as well. The Republicans and the state would do damn well to end up with you in Albany."

George Mason crossed the room and kissed his wife. "Thank you, Eleanor."

"Shall I wait up?"

"I'll call you."

"George, you give Lou hell. He ought to recognize salvation when he sees it."

50

"Sit down, Paul," Melanie said. "I hope you feel better than you look."

"Not a lot," he said. "Here, let me give each of you a copy of this. Read it and tell me what you think." He passed several sheets to Melanie, Max Fabrikant, and Oscar Bornstein, where they sat around the table in Melanie's office.

Paul looked up from his pages at the faces of his three companions. Each of them was intent, frowning. Melanie made notes on her yellow pad. Oscar read and reread the same paragraphs. Max drew lines and made remarks in the margin of his copy. The longer the silence lasted, the more uncomfortable Paul became. He lowered his eyes and reread the story again.

Melanie cleared her throat. "Interesting," she said. She turned to look at Max.

He nodded in agreement. "But——"

"Yes," Oscar agreed. "But . . ."

"But what?" Paul asked, his tongue dry.

"What have we here?" Melanie asked. "You have pegged your story on Uhuru Towers. You have chosen it as a unifying element. In so doing, I think that you've made the story unusable. Let's go to your main points. If I make a mistake, correct me.

"First, we have Uhuru Towers. You describe it as a mistake in public planning, a project which is ego-fulfilling for the community, but fails to meet its needs. You blame that on the governor, who sponsored it, and the mayor, who has made every effort to support it. Whether I agree or not, or am interested in printing it, is not important. You have a right to your opinion. Second, based on your interviews with the management of Burton Industries and Hawkes Building, you have concluded that the project is over budget and behind schedule. We've printed that already as a part of your projected series on O'Neil and housing. So far, so good.

"Third, you have uncovered the fact that Frank O'Neil is broke. His family business is on the rocks and isn't paying any dividends. We know what his income from the public purse is. In the absence of income which has not been declared on his publicly available tax returns, we want to know where the difference between his income and expenditures is coming. Laudable. You've discovered what I've always wanted, the location of Frank O'Neil's Achilles' heel. I am thrilled."

She frowned and put the pad on the table. "And that's where you leave reality. Fourth, you want us to accept that Governor O'Neil is making up the deficit in his income by taking graft from Marcus Hawkes. Ergo, his continued support in the face of the building's alleged problems. Ergo, the absence of available information from the state Housing Authority, and the possible—underlined—possible lack of supervisory care."

She tapped her fingers on the table and looked across at him. "And to this you add the thesis that Hawkes is not only incompetent, but that he is stealing funds and materials from the project in job lots. And, in a final stroke of imagination, you imply that lack of investigation and monitoring by the City Housing Agency is an indication that the mayor is not only going out on a limb for Hawkes in public, but is involved in a cover-up as well."

"On the basis of the evidence, what else can I think?" Paul asked. "I haven't even included the parts that deal with murders and disappearances."

"Are you ready to come out into the open with that?" Melanie asked. "You want to go still further, and suggest that the governor and the mayor are accessories to murder?"

"Would you mind letting me in on what you're talking about?" Max said. "I don't understand a thing."

Paul looked around him. There are no easy answers. Where is Malcolm Woodruff? How much can I say? I think he's dead. Can I play God? If I open my mouth, I may fulfill the prophecy myself.

"Well, Paul?" Melanie said.

"I have to ask for your discretion, Max, Mr. Bornstein. I'll tell you as much as I can. I've already told most of it to Mrs. Parsons. I got a tip that the death of a foreman at Uhuru Towers was no accident. I started to look for confirmation. Then another man who worked on the project, in the same area, died in the Willis Avenue fire I reported on. Now, the man who was the source of the tip that Uhuru Towers is being embezzled has suddenly retired and gone on a round-the-world cruise. The tip was that the embezzlement and the cover-up reached to the highest levels. With that information, what the hell am I supposed to think when the governor and the mayor make spectacles of themselves in support of the project and the builder? Add it together for yourselves. It's what you see in the story in front of you. The governor is broke. He's made a deal with Hawkes. Hawkes steals, O'Neil gets a rake-off. Gibbons finds out and gets killed. Jenks, who worked with him, goes up in flames with the rest of the tenants of his building. My source, who may or may not be alive, leaves town. And while all of this is going on, the mayor pulls down his pants publicly in support of Hawkes. Never mind the total absence of regulatory authority from the state or the city. Never mind that Hawkes's partners at Burton Industries are steering clear of the project to avoid offending the black community, and thereby losing their chance to make a buck. That's the story."

Oscar Bornstein's calm, low voice sounded to Paul like the crack of doom. "But you have no proof."

"No proof? What do you want, for Christ's sake? Signed confessions?" Paul's voice cracked with emotion.

Oscar shook his head. "I sympathize with you. I know you've been under a hell of a strain. I know that you care—a lot. You've been badly shaken by your accident. I'm sure it scared you to death. It certainly would have done that to me." Oscar arranged the papers neatly in front of him with slim graceful fingers. "I'm stunned by your allegations. You have the threads of an incredible story. I'm not denying the possibility. But, let me ask you a few questions. Is either the Gibbons case or the fire still under investigation by the police?"

"No. But that's because they don't know the background."

Oscar shook his head. "There's more to a murder investigation than motive analysis. Granted, you've given me reasons, but there was no physical evidence to make the police think that Gibbons was murdered. This—what's his name . . ."

"Jenks?"

"Yes, Jenks. The fire in that building was investigated by the fire marshals, wasn't it?"

"Yes. It was, but . . ."

"But, you suspect that both were overlooked as crimes because of the absence of background. That's good enough to foster your suspicion. It's good enough to prompt a trip to the police. But, it certainly isn't good enough to start the *Advocate* on a course of criminal accusations of the chief executives of the city and the state of New York."

Paul's head started to throb again, and the flashing lights to which shock victims are prone began to distort his vision.

"I'm not at all discouraged, Paul," Melanie said. "I think that we have a marvelous story here. You've done a very good job. We're simply going to have to reserve some of it until you come up with concrete facts, not suppositions."

"What do you suggest, Mrs. Parsons?" Max asked.

Melanie's eyes lit with enthusiasm. "We may not be in a position to make accusations, but we're certainly ready to raise some questions. What we have here is the answer to yesterday's big mystery. When I read Pierre Du Fresne's column, I couldn't imagine what had prompted Allison Vance to leave O'Neil flat." She smiled. "Now I know. He's broke. We are going to ask about his finances. We'll run the part about O'Neil Maritime and its troubles. We'll print what we know about his personal expenditures. Then, we'll ask the hard question. Where does he get the money to live that high society life-style? If he doesn't have an answer, it'll put Greene in the Governor's Mansion."

"I don't get it," Paul said. "How can you be pleased by the idea of Greene's election with what you know?"

"What do we know?" she said sharply. "You have suspicions. With respect to Greene, they are almost guesses."

"What will you say if it turns out that Hawkes is a thief? Remember your interview, Max? What did he say?"

"He said that he felt that you and the *Advocate* were unreasonable in your expectations. He said that Hawkes needed to be given a chance to prove his worth. Based on what we published, what else would you have him say, Paul? He doesn't know about any stealing or murder. All he knows is that a black contractor is finally getting a chance to build something worthwhile, and he wants us to give him a little extra operating room.''

Paul closed his eyes. God. I guess you could read it that way. But, I know. I know that Greene knows. He has to know. He lifted his head and looked at the three people across the table. But, my knowing just isn't enough.

"I'm afraid that all you have against Mayor Greene is a little extra compassion for black people," Bornstein said. "You don't want us to assume that's a sign of dishonesty.''

Max looked at Paul, then at Melanie. "I'm afraid we'll have to cut this down to nothing. Oscar, do you think we ought to seek the advice of counsel before we print any of it?''

"Not if we stick to the O'Neil finances. We have interviews and hard evidence—tax returns, and so forth.''

"How about Hawkes?" Paul asked. "You can't drop Uhuru altogether. Let me rewrite it. Break it into two stories. That way, you get the beat on O'Neil's empty purse, and I prompt a legislative investigation of Uhuru.''

"No," Melanie said with finality. "There's just as much chance that Greene is right about Hawkes and Uhuru at this juncture as you are.''

"And the murders?''

"Deaths. For the moment, they are deaths.''

"Greene is clean, and murders are deaths," Paul said with wonder in his voice.

In two hours, Melanie was triumphant, and Paul was out on his feet. They had come together again with Max and Oscar to review the story that was to be printed. The front page was spectacular. The headline read "O'Neil Finances in Question." There were two subheads: "Family Company on the Rocks" and "Who's Paying for the Good Times?''

The lead paragraph under Paul Curtin's byline was, "Industry and financial sources indicate that the family businesses of Governor Frank O'Neil are in serious trouble. No dividends have been paid in two years. Scrutiny of the governor's public financial records reveals no other source of income. Nonetheless, his high life-style continues at a pace far beyond his official salary and allowances. Where is the money coming from?"

Paul rubbed his eyes. "I've got to go home."

Max said, "You don't look great. It's a shame. This is your hour of triumph. There isn't a soul in the building who wouldn't buy you a drink today."

"I have waited some time for this," Melanie said. "I wish I could see O'Neil's face when he reads it."

"Where do you think the money is coming from, Mrs. Parsons?" Paul asked.

"Probably, it was coming from his girl friend, or her father. In any case, it isn't on his income tax, and it doesn't show on his balance sheet. Let the chips fall where they may. It's either unreported income, or undisclosed debts or assets. Whatever it is," she rubbed her hands, "we'll take full advantage. I have him, and I have you to thank."

Paul stopped for a moment at Jeff's desk on his way out. "Have you seen what they're printing?"

Jeff nodded disconsolately. "That's all?"

"They say the rest is conjecture. Maybe I should go to the cops."

"You'll get the same answer. They're all going to get off," Jeff said. "That's the Big City for you."

"It isn't done yet, Jeff."

Maryanne came to make Paul's dinner, and to keep him company for an hour.

"You did the best you know how. You can't ask more of yourself. The people at the *Advocate* seem to be more than satisfied."

"All Melanie ever wanted was Frank O'Neil's head. From her point it's a perfect story. Sure she's happy. I'm not. She went for the cheap shot and not the substance."

"Would you have stuck your neck out on your suppositions if it was your newspaper?"

"You're darn tootin' I would." He threw his hands up in frustration. "Jeff's probably right. They're all going to get off: Hawkes, Greene, and probably O'Neil in the bargain. Well, at least it won't be on my conscience."

51

Mack Bell sat in his office with his feet in his lower desk drawer. His hands were clasped behind his head, and he stared vacantly at the ceiling. He'd spent most of the day examining the material-on-hand inventories of Uhuru Towers. There had been a sudden acceleration in orders for goods, and yet he was unable to locate them physically. Just the same, he had signed notices signifying their delivery to the job. How could someone have stolen large sums of money or materials on the job without being picked up? How the hell, he wondered, had it gotten past him?

It occurred to him that Malcolm Woodruff would know the answer. Either he, or the person who was doing the stealing. Malcolm would understand the intricate web of paperwork required both to accomplish and to camouflage the act.

But he couldn't get ahold of Malcolm, because Hawkes had sent him on a sixty-day all-expenses-paid cruise. Bell closed his eyes and licked his dry lips.

Down the hall, Marcus Garvey Hawkes was arranging papers that he had withdrawn from the small safe concealed behind his framed award from the League of Harlem Mothers.

George Gaines sat silently at the side of the desk rereading the Paul Curtin article in the *New York Advocate*.

"Did you do what I said, George?"

"I went myself and stood there till the tickets were changed. I took everything out of the safe at my shop."

"Good. By tomorrow, we'll be gone out of here."

"You think that they've really got O'Neil?"

"George," Marcus said, "that man has more lives than a cat. With us gone, all they can do is count his expenditures and try to pin down where the cash came from. If we don't testify, then who will? Don't worry about the governor. When the world finds out we've skipped, he'll be the most indignant."

337

"The last of those orders for materials came through today, Marcus. They're going to pile up, without me to sell them off. In a week at the most, it'll all blow."

"By then," Marcus smiled, "it won't matter to us at all." He tidied up his desk and left a note for his secretary that he would be out looking at a site and wouldn't be in till the day after tomorrow. He took a last look at his office, then said, "You ready, George? Let's go."

In his office, Bell stretched, kicked his drawer shut and stood up. For all the good he was doing, he might as well go home. It was long past quitting time anyway. He started to take his briefcase, then decided the hell with it for once, flicked off the light, and walked toward the elevator.

As he was about to open the door to the reception area, he heard muffled voices. He couldn't make out what they were saying, but he could tell that it was Hawkes and Gaines. Not certain of why, he drew back against the wall and stood silently till they left. A bead of perspiration ran down his forehead.

He pushed the button and waited for another car. When it came, he changed his mind and turned back. He walked down the corridor to Malcolm's old office and tried the door. It was locked. He took out his pass key and opened it.

The room had been thoroughly cleaned. The blinds and drapes were drawn. Malcolm's mementoes—wall plaques, scrolls, and testimonials—lay in cardboard boxes on the windowsill, not yet sealed, but addressed. Bell supposed that they were holding everything till the Woodruffs returned from their trip.

At first idly, then with real curiosity, Bell began to go through the desk. Not a paperclip or pencil remained.

He got to his feet and walked to the closet and found it as sterile as the desk. The office had been more than cleaned, it had been sifted and dusted, and fine-tooth combed.

He turned to pull his coat from the desk chair where he had left it. His car keys slipped from the pocket, and as he bent to pick them up, he kicked them into the kneehole of the desk.

Cursing, he bent over to reach for them, but they were beyond his grasp. Finally, he pushed the chair out of the way and stretched full-length under the desk to grab the keys. To avoid banging his head backing out, he turned over.

At first, he thought that the white line was an imperfection on the gray plastic finish of the desk. He had already thought to remove and turn over all of the drawers to see if papers had been concealed there. So had those who had gone before him, he supposed.

He reached out and picked at the paper with his fingernail. He could see that it protruded from the hollow square tubing of the frame which supported the desk. Bell wriggled from under the kneehole and stood, pushing the chair out of his way. After removing the drawers, he turned the desk upside down. The screwdriver blade of his pocket knife loosened the three screws that held the tube fast. When he tapped it against the palm of his hand, two pieces of paper, rolled tightly and fastened with Scotch tape, slid to the floor.

Bell knelt and slit the tape carefully, then unrolled the papers. One was a cash requisition form for one hundred thousand dollars to be drawn on the account of the state of New York. Though the payee was not specified, it bore the approving signature of Governor O'Neil, handwritten in ink. The second was a similar form, also in blank, signed by the governor, countersigned in facsimile by the comptroller, and impressed with the Great Seal.

Bell folded the papers carefully and slipped them into his inside pocket. He fixed the desk, and took great care to efface any hint of his presence, dusting everything he had touched with his handkerchief. Only when he was satisfied that it was exactly as he had found it, did he turn off the light, and leave the office for his home.

52

Because Frank O'Neil had spent the day in his New York office, he was able to react quickly when the *Advocate* story broke on the street. Dennis O'Neil and his wife and eldest son were packed off on the first available flight to the Caribbean.

Strict orders were given at O'Neil Maritime and Fuel: no questions, no interviews, no comment.

The governor's offices in Albany and New York pled ignorance. The matter would be examined when time permitted. The governor was otherwise occupied with state business and had nothing to say at this time.

To avoid the press, O'Neil took a freight elevator to the basement and walked through the labyrinthine corridors to a connecting building, out of the service entrance, and into an unmarked sedan. He brushed past the two reporters outside his apartment house with a smile and a no-comment-for-the-moment and retreated to the privacy of his home.

A few reporters were still hanging around at nine o'clock when a dark man with Mediterranean features pulled up in a cab. They watched with curiosity as he was stopped by the doorman, then quickly lost interest when they heard him ask for the Wassermans, who lived a floor below the governor.

He went up in the elevator and was admitted by Mr. Wasserman, who ushered him to the back entrance and up the service stairs, where Frank O'Neil awaited him.

The governor showed his guest to the den and took his coat. Luigi Andretti peeled the gloves from his hands, the right one still gnarled by the scar from his old bayonet wound, and lay them on the desk.

"Have you seen the *Advocate*?" O'Neil asked.

"I have." His voice was flat and noncommittal.

O'Neil took a deep breath, then said, "It's all quite true. My brother has been a lousy manager. We've been squeezed by prices, taxes, and inflation. O'Neil Maritime is in the shit house. I haven't really seen any money out of it for three years."

Andretti frowned. "I don't get it, Frank. So you've got the shorts. So what? You could have come to me at any time."

O'Neil started to pace again. "You think it's that easy? Sure, I could have gone to you. For what? An allowance. Lou, is it all right if I help out my son Jack? He needs a grand a month to get over the hump. Lou, is it all right if I buy two tickets to the April in Paris Ball? Is it all right if I buy Allison a present?" He was red in the face. "Here I am, twice governor of the Empire State, and I'm down at the heels, with no prospects."

"You have to make up your mind what you want to be in this

world," Andretti said. "Sometimes you can't be rich and famous, just one or the other." He paused for a minute, not sure whether he wanted to go on, then said, "But isn't that what Allison was all about, Frank? I have it on the grapevine that it's dead with her."

O'Neil poured himself another drink. "I haven't talked to her in a few days." He turned back to Andretti. "I didn't even know what hit me. One minute she was there, the next she was gone."

"You were trading your public position and your good seats at the ballpark and the theater for a shot at her dough. That's a *quid pro quo*, not a basis for a marriage."

"A lot of marriages survive on less. It made good sense. We got along fine. You're right. She was the answer to my long-term financial problems. She thought I might even have a shot at the White House."

"And?"

"You know. I couldn't get the cardinal to go along with her annulment."

"And you can't give up the Church for political or personal reasons. So she got tired of being your bimbo, right, Frank? And she took a hike. Okay. I understand that, Frank. What's the real story?"

"I tried to patch over the hole in my wallet. I run five, maybe ten grand in the hole every month. I had to hold out till I married Allison. You've got to understand, Lou. I couldn't go to you, or anybody else I know, and ask him to put me on the dole. There's a lot of money involved, and I have my position to think of."

"So what did you do?" Andretti said, leaning forward on the couch, frowning.

"I was on the pad with a builder in Harlem."

"You what?"

"I made a deal with this guy. He's a black builder. His name is Hawkes. He's got a partnership with Burton Industries. I've been influential in helping him with his partners. He's served two purposes for me. He pushes hard for me in the black community, and that offsets Greene, even if it's only a little bit." He paused again, then said, "And he's given me money; close to two hundred thousand dollars."

"You're on the take? You? You're taking money from some builder?"

"He's stealing the project blind. I was supposed to blink, keep the housing people off of his back. It only amounts to a three or four percent cost overrun. No one was ever supposed to find out. He was going to end up rich. The building was going to get finished. Harlem was going to be happy. And I wasn't going to go broke. Even now, with Curtin on my back, there's no connection. I can still stay in the state house if Hawkes gets indicted. He's better off plea bargaining on an embezzlement charge than owning up to bribing a public official. He might even get off with a fine. I haven't committed murder, Lou. What he stole comes out to maybe a quarter for each of my eighteen million constituents. Is that so bad?"

Andretti shook his head numbly, trying to find the words. "So you look at this as a kind of extra tax on the electorate for the privilege of keeping Frank O'Neil in the governorship?"

"I'm not saying I was right. I'm asking you to understand. What could I do? I was broke. I couldn't even pay my household bills and my son's tuition, much less keep up the front the office requires. I didn't suborn the constitution. All I did was to take a few bucks. It happens a thousand times a year in a fifteen-billion-dollar budget."

"From laziness, and incompetence, and featherbedding, Frank." The words escaped before he could stop them. "But, you're none of those things. You're just another grafter."

O'Neil stood transfixed. "Is that what I am, Lou? Is that what my record amounts to? I've done a lot for this state. Doesn't it owe me something?"

"You contracted to take the pay. If you couldn't hack it anymore, all you had to do was to borrow enough to bow out gracefully, and then go into private practice. You could make a half million a year. You're right, Frank. On paper you've been a good governor. But that doesn't make you less a thief." Andretti drained his glass. "I'm not enjoying this conversation very much. What do you need?"

"I need a cover. I need you to say you've lent me two hundred thousand in cash over the last year." He reached into his desk and pulled out an envelope. "I've made out these notes. They're backdated. I need for you to sign them. If anybody asks you, you lent me the money. And I have a note in here for another hundred thousand, dated three days ago. I need the dough. I can't expect anything from Hawkes anymore. I've put up the apartment as collateral to you in this letter."

"For God's sake, why didn't you do this in the first place? Shit. You could have hocked this apartment to any bank in town. Even doing it with me maintains your independence. It's a collateralized loan."

"And what should I use to make the payments? This apartment is all I have left. That's what it comes down to. I have to take the place I live to the pawnbroker to buy bread. The governor of New York ought to be able to do better than that."

"You shouldn't say that, Frank," Andretti said. He leaned over the desk and countersigned all of the notes under O'Neil's signature, then wrote him a check for one hundred thousand dollars. Then he picked up his coat and his gloves. "But it's much more important that you shouldn't believe it. You've confused the dignity of your office with your personal comfort and pleasure. I still think a governor looks better on the news page than in the gossip column. You should have thought less about how you look to your constituents, Frank, and more about the kind of example you set for them." He turned on his heel and headed toward the door. "I'm truly sorry for you, Governor."

O'Neil started toward him, but he held up his hand in protest. "Don't bother. I'll find my way out."

53

Frank O'Neil lay low until the City Edition of the *New York Advocate* appeared at 10:00 A.M. As always, the first edition was a rehash of the previous evening's paper, with a new headline and a smattering of news picked up on the night wires. The front page and the lead story confined themselves to a repetition of the Curtin article. The morning editorial was a scathing condemnation of Frank O'Neil, written and signed by Melanie Parsons herself.

Once sure of his ground, O'Neil saw to it that a telephone call was made, and slipped surreptitiously out of the back door of the building to meet an old friend who was a reporter for the *News*.

An hour later, chortling with glee, the reporter ran through the doors of his building, and down the corridor to the office of Mike O'Neill, his editor. An hour later the *New York Daily News* laid on their extra issue with flair.

As the *Advocate* circulated in the streets, repeating last night's news and detailing with vengeance the unanswered questions regarding O'Neil Maritime and the governor's mysterious sources of income, the *News* appeared on every stand with a new front page. It bore two pictures: the official portrait of Francis Xavier McCarthy O'Neil and a picture taken at a War Bond rally in 1945, showing Frank O'Neil and Luigi Andretti arm-in-arm, waving to the crowd. The headline read "Governor O'Neil Answers Back," the subhead, "War Hero Buddy Came to O'Neil's Aid."

The page three story recounted the governor's heroics in the South Pacific, and the special relationship with the man whose life he had saved. Indeed, the story said, the fortunes of O'Neil Maritime and Fuel were at a low ebb and had severely reduced the governor's independent income. In order to save his friend personal embarrassment and to preserve the dignity of his office, Andretti, a wealthy importer and real estate owner, had advanced him funds to meet his needs.

At noon, the governor called a press conference in his office. He was the picture of benign forgiveness. "I don't want anyone to feel that I take this personally. I don't. I am embarrassed. Perhaps I should have handled the matter another way. I'm not mad at anyone." He looked directly at Joe Notrica of the *Advocate*, who was taking notes as rapidly as he could. "It's part of the political game. Newspapers, like individuals, have a constitutional perogative to take sides. Sometimes," he continued with a wise smile, "things get a little out of hand. I have a very busy schedule today. But I wanted to take time out to clarify these questions. I just hope that the matter is closed. Thank you."

By one in the afternoon, both the *Advocate*'s charges and O'Neil's refutation, confirmed by Andretti, had been broadcast by every radio and television station in the state of New York.

The scene in Melanie Parson's office reminded Max Fabrikant of sitting shiva for his father. Unlike most wakes, there had been little conversation. Everyone had sat staring into his own vision of the past, with an occasional moan of regret.

Melanie looked very small and old. The *News* and the *Advocate* were spread out on her desk and were marked with red pencil. "I feel as though I am reading my own obituary," she said. "Mike O'Neill had the gall to call me on the phone." Her voice started to rise. "Tough luck, Mel, he said. It looks like Big Frank has outmaneuvered you again. He said he was sorry we looked so silly." She closed her eyes.

When she opened them, she reached for her private line and dialed the mayor's number.

"Greene."

"Mr. Mayor," she said, her voice brightening. "This is Melanie Parsons. I assume you've seen the papers. I can't imagine you wanting to let this opportunity go. Would you like to give us a statement?"

"I wouldn't know what to say, Mrs. Parsons. I was certainly shocked to read your issue last night. The implications were certainly considerable. But I'm afraid that—as usual—public sympathy is on the side of Frank O'Neil. America loves a man with small sins who comes clean. I'd rather talk about the failures of his programs and the misdirection of his administration than try to blacken his name. I think I'll pass on this one. Thank you for your interest."

She hung up the phone, and in a hushed voice, repeated their conversation. "We've been repudiated by our own candidate," she said grimly. After a moment, she raised an eyebrow and looked as though she had forgotten something. "Does anyone know where Paul Curtin is?" she asked evenly. "I think his time has come."

"Why, Mel?" Oscar Bornstein asked.

"Because he hasn't done his job. We're a laughingstock. He didn't do his homework. What are we going to say in the Wall Street issue tonight? That we're boobs?"

"We'll print the news as it is," Max interjected. "What else can we do?"

Melanie whirled on him, "That's a fatuous, naive answer. O'Neil mousetrapped us. He timed it to a tee. He knew when we'd publish this morning, then held the news conference." A tear blotted a crazy course through the powder on her wrinkled cheek. She took a mimeograph of the governor's statement and looked it through again. "Condescension. Jesus forgiving his enemies from the Cross." She slammed it on the desk. "I can't even get Greene to make a comment that might enable us to back out gracefully. If he won't step forward and ask any hard questions, we'll look even more foolish if we pursue the idea. God save me from my friends, Oscar. Tell me, how do we retrieve some shred of dignity? Would it do any good to repudiate the story and throw Curtin to the wolves?"

She dabbed at her cheek with a handkerchief that Oscar had gallantly extended.

"Why are you so sure that Curtin is at fault?" Max said, almost to himself.

"What?" she asked crossly.

"So Greene is afraid to take on the issue. So what? He doesn't want to hurt his image? Who ever heard of a challenger not going for an incumbent's jugular? It doesn't ring right. Why do we have to believe Andretti? Because he's a war hero? So was Benedict Arnold."

"Anything is possible. If you had told me that this was going to happen to me yesterday, I wouldn't have thought that it was possible. As much as I want O'Neil's scalp, I'm not willing to end up with another eye full of mud. I hate to lose. But I know when to quit. I shouldn't have let Curtin wrap me around his finger in the first place. Maybe you were right about that at least, Max. O'Neil has done what Nixon failed to do. He's come clean. America loves it. If you proclaim your own faults loudly enough, you are beatified. That's what Chris Greene just told me." She slammed her hand on the desk for emphasis. "If Curtin is right, it will come out eventually. Then we will be in a position to reap the benefits by looking smart. Let the others be in a corner with egg on their faces. Let them retract. In the meantime, we don't press it, or take any more risks."

"But what about the unanswered questions?" Max persisted.

"Never mind," she blazed. "So he borrowed money. Maybe there's something, maybe not. Right now, we have a black eye. I just want to let it subside. We'll do it my way."

"Ask Curtin up here, Melanie. You'll be sorry if you don't," Oscar said. "Get his views. The milk is spilt. You're throwing away your chance to recoup if you don't hear him out. You have nothing to lose."

She picked up the intercom and said, "Madeleine, find Curtin. Here or at home. Tell him I want him in immediately."

Five minutes later Melanie fumed when her secretary reported that she was unable to locate Paul Curtin. Her angry discourse was interrupted when he knocked at the door.

"May I come in?" He was carrying his briefcase and a copy of the *Daily News* under his arm.

"Sit down," Melanie snapped. "Madeleine, get out. No calls." When he was seated, she continued. "You've set a record for the farthest an employee has ever stuck out the paper's neck. And it seems that you didn't do your homework."

"That's incorrect, Mrs. Parsons," Paul said. "It is possible that he was getting money from Andretti. I still think it was coming from Marcus Hawkes. And I think that if we'd stuck our necks out the rest of the way, O'Neil wouldn't have needed just a convenient lender. He'd have had to disprove the Hawkes accusation. I don't think he's in a position to do that. At worst, there'd have been a major investigation."

"And maybe a libel suit big enough to kill the *Advocate*. You just can't deal with the possibility that you might be wrong—even when you have no proof that will stand up in court. You're a fool," she said, half rising from the chair. "And a proud fool at that, the worst kind. You've let Frank O'Neil make a horse's ass out of you, this paper, and me. You just go right on, barging ahead, with your eyes closed and your notions preconceived. Don't be confused by the facts!"

"The Andretti story is fact? You'll accept O'Neil's hearsay but not mine. That's a hell of a note. Why don't you at least get Greene to call for an investigation? Then you won't feel so alone."

"I've already asked him," she said, her mouth in a pout.

"He doesn't want to have anything to do with your accusations. He doesn't think that mudslinging is the way to win this election."

Paul shook his head in wonder. "And that doesn't say anything to you? Does that sound like a politician? Especially a barbarian like Chris Greene? Doesn't it smell of collusion or cover-up? He should be slavering for O'Neil's blood even if the story is a complete hoax." He turned to look at the others. "Max, for Christ's sake, please say something. Mr. Bornstein? You've got to smell a rat."

"You're paranoid," Melanie said coldly. "I should have seen it before. You just aren't big enough to handle a news beat the size of New York—it's too sophisticated, too high pressured. You've gotten trapped in the story you've woven, and you can't let go. I'm sorry, Paul. I'm buying the rest of your contract. That's through the end of the year. Fair enough, I think, nine months severance. Your services are no longer required."

Paul rose, ashen-faced, and started for the door.

"Wait a minute," Oscar said. "Why? What do we have to lose?"

"Forget it, Mr. Bornstein. Why should I stick around and take this shit?"

"What shit?" Melanie shouted. "You've screwed up your story."

Paul spun and walked back to the desk. "I'll tell you something, Mrs. Parsons. You're so wound up with your emotional problems with Frank O'Neil that you can't even see the truth."

"Are you telling me that my emotions cloud my judgment?" she said, her chin protruding pugnaciously.

"You're damn right, I am!" he shouted back. "You've got him on the run. But you're so afraid that you'll look stupid, that you're letting him bluff you right out of the spot. Punch Sulzburger and Mike O'Neill wouldn't back off this story."

She leaned forward to try to slap his face and almost fell across the desk. Alarmed, Oscar pushed Paul away. "Max, Paul, would you mind going outside for a moment?"

Fabrikant pulled Paul out of the room by the arm and closed the door behind them.

"Melanie," he said calmly, "are you all right?"

She was seated slumped in her chair with her teeth and fists clenched. "What do you want to do?"

"I want to keep Curtin on. Let's see if the story unfolds a bit more. I'm not ready to accept O'Neil's story at face value. Perhaps Andretti is telling the truth, but that doesn't exclude Paul's conclusion. Let's take our lumps, make no comment, and let him keep at it. A couple of weeks or a month, at least. We can still come out a winner."

"On one condition."

"What's that, Mel?"

"I don't want to see Paul Curtin again. If he's wrong, I want him out on his ear. I want his desk packed and sent to his house. He is never to set foot in this building again. Understood?"

"And if he proves to be right?"

She sat up and looked at him. "Then give him the rest of his contract, and a one-year bonus, then throw the little bastard out of here anyway. Nobody talks to me like that."

54

"Okay, Mr. Bornstein," Paul had said. "Just how would you describe my relationship with the *Advocate*?"

Bornstein studied his polished nails. "We could call it a reprieve. You've had the rug pulled out from under you. You look like a schmuck. If you want another swing at the ball, you need the *Advocate* for a forum." Bornstein smiled. "I can read your mind from here. There are no empty slots at the *Times* or the *News*. You can thank the Newspaper Guild for that. It's tough shit, Paul. You and Melanie are stuck with each other. Who knows, maybe some day you'll kiss and make up."

"You're a lousy liar, Mr. Bornstein," Paul said, rising to leave. "She doesn't take prisoners or forgive transgressors."

"You can always run and hide."

"Fuck you both, Mr. Bornstein," Paul said. He sat in a bar on Seventy-ninth Street for an hour and had five scotches, then he went up to Maryanne's feeling sorry for himself.

"Where the hell have you been?" Maryanne asked.

"In a bar. Melanie shit on me. The *Daily News* shit on me. Everybody shits on me."

"I think I'm going to be sick," she said. "While you've been out drowning your sorrows, Jeff Jackson has been calling every ten minutes."

Feeling hurt at the cold reception, Paul stumbled to the couch and dialed Jeff's number. "What's up?" he asked indistinctly.

"Bell. Bell wants you bad," Jeff said.

"What does he want?" Paul asked.

"I don't have any idea. He won't tell me squat."

"Did he leave a number?" Jeff gave it to him. "Thanks. I'll call you at home if anything turns up"

Paul hung up, puzzled. He shrugged his shoulders. Who could guess at what Bell wanted? He sat down, stretching out the sore foot, and called Bell.

"Mr. Bell?" Paul asked.

"Who's this?" Bell replied.

"Curtin. Paul Curtin. You called me?"

"Yeah. I did." The voice was throaty and hoarse. "I've got to see you."

"When?"

"Right away. I found something. It's important." Bell was whispering.

"Are you where somebody can hear you?" Paul asked.

"No," he raised his voice a little. "Just my wife. She's in the next room."

"Shall I come to you?"

"Christ, no. I don't want to take any chances with my family." Bell's voice trembled.

"What's going on here?" Paul demanded, the last trace of whisky fog gone.

"I'll tell you when I see you."

Paul thought for a moment, then gave Bell the address of his apartment. "I'll be there in twenty minutes. Is that soon enough?"

"I'm on my way," Bell said.

Paul shook his head in disbelief. "What now? That guy was ready to kill me a few days ago."

"You can't eat dinner in twenty minutes," Maryanne said. "Have him come here."

Paul pushed himself to his feet. "Forget it. toots. This is strictly stag."

"Spare me the macho nonsense. You still need to take it easy."

"After the fight I had with La Parsons today, babe, I may be able to take the rest of my life off."

"What happened?"

He looked at his watch. "I don't have time, now. Just a little altercation. I stood up for my rights."

Paul went to his apartment and waited on the couch. It was pitch dark when the buzzer sounded, urgently and insistently. Paul rose and pushed the intercom button. In a minute, Bell emerged from the elevator, looking about nervously.

"Over here, Mr. Bell."

He stepped inside quickly and slammed the door behind him, then hooked the chain and turned to face Paul.

"I thought I'd better come over here before someone invites me on an all-expense-paid cruise. I think I owe you an apology. Can I have a drink?"

"I'll join you. Sit down."

With the candor of an honest man, Bell said, "I am six feet four inches tall. I can tell you that every fuckin' inch is scared to death."

Paul poured a couple of hefty drinks, sat next to Bell, and said, "Tell me."

"I read your story in the paper. I didn't think a hell of a lot about it. When I saw the paper this morning and saw how the governor just sidestepped you, I was pretty amused. Well, I'm not amused anymore. Yesterday afternoon and this morning, I started to get reports of materials purchases that don't jibe with deliveries or payments. I'm not talking about minor disparities. I'm talking job lots. I admit to being a little slow, Mr. Curtin. I should have picked up on it before. It's Marcus and Gaines, isn't it, Mr. Curtin? It's Marcus and Gaines and the fuckin' governor. All of them." He finished his drink.

"Yes, it is. But go prove it. I wrote the whole damn story. My paper wouldn't print it. No proof. Suppositions. Nothing concrete. Mad as I am, I can't blame them too much. As one guy said this afternoon, if I had 'em, I'd go to the cops."

"I might be able to help you."

Paul leaned forward anxiously in his seat. "You've got something?"

"It started off with little things. Irregularities. Then you came along, making a pain in the ass of yourself. I thought you were full of shit. But, you started me thinking. I almost went to Englander over Marcus's head about the shitty job that Gaines has been doing. Marcus conned me out of it. This week, it's started to occur to me that maybe we just can't finish the building alone, that maybe we just don't have the skills to hack it."

"But what does that have to do with my story?"

"If we're really pushing a rock uphill, if we're really so far behind in our completion schedule, then why this sudden upsurge in materials ordering when we can't use what we've got on hand? I gave Marcus until the end of the month to get some improvement out of the subcontractors, or I'd yell to Burton Industries for help."

"Why were you going to wait? If it's hopeless."

"You've never been black, Mr. Curtin. I'm a good engineer. I'm tired of waiting in longer lines for a job to prove the point. I'm a builder. This project was my dream. I admired Marcus for what he proposed, and I was proud to be a part of it. Now, I'm scared. The dream is going to die, and I don't want it to take me with it."

"I can't picture you scared."

"Why not? Because I'm big? I can be just as dead as Lloyd Gibbons. And you know what, Mr. Curtin? I don't believe that Woodruff went on any trip. I think that Gaines sent him someplace permanent, maybe like he did with Lloyd Gibbons."

"I'm scared, too," Paul said. "I stuck my neck out a mile on this story, and without proof, nobody's going to back me up. I just look like a dunce. We're in the same boat. Without something concrete to tie it all together, the whole thing will fade into oblivion. The project will fall on its ass. And by the time the evidence gets sifted, sorted, and obliterated by time or deft hands, the guilty will either go free or get a slap on the wrist.

"This is no two-bit scam," Paul continued. "Somehow Hawkes and Gaines got blank requisitions signed by the governor. That overordering you spotted is how they generated the invoices. They're probably selling the extra materials on the side. I think the governor's been getting some of that dough to fill the hole in his pocket. I don't give a shit what Luigi Andretti says. And you're right about Gibbons, too. But it doesn't stop there. You probably didn't know about Al Jenks. He was just a little jerk that worked with Gaines and Gibbons. Well, he must have gotten in the way, because he and his whole family, and his neighbors, twenty-two people in all, went up in smoke when their tenement exploded mysteriously. And Woodruff? Your guess is as good as mine. But there's no proof of anything. Even if Gaines and Hawkes got tagged with fraud, they'd be out in three years with good behavior, free to spend the millions they've got stashed someplace. That doesn't pay for murder or settle accounts with a greedy governor or a blind mayor." Paul wiped his eyes, filled with tears of frustration. "It makes me puke."

Bell held out a plain white envelope. "Would these help?"

Paul opened the envelope carefully and looked at the two sheets, silent and stunned. After a moment, he managed to croak, "Holy Mother of God. The goods. The real goods. Fucking Christ Almighty."

"They were rolled into a tube in Malcolm's desk. I was nosing around after everybody left. I've been trying to decide what to do with them ever since."

Paul looked up and said, "That's all, folks. They're dead and buried, hung from their own rope."

"I wonder what else Malcolm knows? Or maybe knew," Bell said.

"We could ask him. If he's still alive." Paul's mind spun like a top from one idea to the next.

"How?"

"Maybe we could arrange a ship-to-shore telephone hook-up. I don't know whether a boat like that has the facilities. We can certainly get a message to him, but that isn't the point. Would you recognize his voice?"

"In the bottom of a well. I've been listening to it for years," Bell said positively.

"If the connection were lousy, do you know enough about him to be sure it's him?"

"For sure," Bell replied.

"Let's give it a try." Paul called the marine operator and explained his needs.

"I'll have to check their location, sir, and their equipment. Then I'll be back to you. About a half hour."

Less than fifteen minutes later, the phone rang. Paul grabbed it nervously from the cradle, motioning Bell to move closer.

"Yes, Operator. I'm trying to make a ship-to-shore telephone call to Mr. Malcolm Woodruff aboard the S.S. *Thomas Jefferson.*"

"I'm sorry, sir. There is no one by that name aboard," she replied.

"Are you in contact with the ship, operator?" Paul asked.

"Yes, sir."

"I'd like to talk to the ship's captain."

"I'll ask them, sir."

Paul covered the mouthpiece with his hand and whispered to Bell, "They're not there."

There was a crackle of static, and then a voice in Paul's ear. "This is the master's mate of the *Jefferson.* I'm the senior officer on duty."

"My name is Curtin. I'm a reporter for the *New York Advocate.* I'm trying to locate a couple named Woodruff. They're black. In their early sixties. Your New York office says that they boarded your ship when you sailed from here."

There was another clicking, then the hollow voice, "There was a Mr. and Mrs. Woodruff aboard. They were black. But they were in their thirties, I would say. We've just cleared Balboa on the Pacific side of the Canal bound for Honolulu. They had some kind of personal crisis—family or something. They got a cable. They left the ship when we made port in Colon."

"May I have your name, please?"

"Sure. It's Neilsen, Gerhard Neilsen."

"Thank you very much." Paul hung the phone up slowly. "They're gone. They got off. The Woodruffs on that boat were in their thirties."

Bell shook his head uncomprehendingly.

"Plants. They were plants. It was just two people. Any two people. The Woodruffs are dead, or stashed someplace."

"Now what do we do?"

Paul tapped the papers that Bell had given him against the palm of his hand. "What we have here is all of the proof that was missing before you walked in the door. The governor steals. Gaines and Hawkes, at the very least, have lied about the whereabouts of the Woodruffs. The papers are enough to get a special investigation started, and the absence of the Woodruffs ought to be enough to put Gaines and Hawkes in jail on suspicion of murder." Paul put his glass on the table and stood up.

He walked to the window and looked out at the street for a while, not saying anything. "I think that we should go visit the governor."

"What's to keep him from just tearing up these papers?"

Paul smiled sardonically. "Too late. He's fucked. We've seen them already. The cat's out of the bag. There's no stuffing it back in."

"Wouldn't you rather go to the D.A.? Maybe to the attorney general?"

"O'Neil can't run. Hawkes and Gaines can. I've been following Frank O'Neil around like a shadow for four years. I'll tell you, it was hard enough for me to picture him on the take. I don't think that he was an accessory to multiple murder. Once he knows that we probably have Gaines and Hawkes for murder one on the Woodruffs, if nothing else, he'll bend over backwards to beg off on the lesser charge. He'll admit he took graft and try to put as much distance between himself and the other two as he can."

Bell looked up at him from under furrowed brows. "You're sure of that?"

"I suppose. What else could he do?"

"He could kill us, burn these shitty little pieces of paper, and dump us into the river."

Paul shook his head. "I can't believe it."

"It's a long fall, friend. He's the governor of New York. Things being what they are in this country, he might get off with a suspended sentence. But even so, he could go to jail. Marvin Mandel, he went to jail, and he was the governor of Maryland. O'Neil might not want to do that. And maybe he knows all about these murders. What's two more?"

"That's what I heard from Woodruff when I first got involved in this damn business. He said if he went to the cops, he'd be snuffed. The word would get out that he ratted, and he'd be killed."

"Maybe now your paper would print the whole story. Then somebody'd have to do something."

"No," Paul disagreed. "Put it on the street like that and everybody will go underground. Hawkes and Gaines will melt into the sidewalk and never be seen again."

Bell leaned back on the couch and rubbed his eyes, then said casually, "I'm too tired to argue. You pick a way we can tell the story and not get blown to hell."

55

After Mack Bell appeared, nervously looking over his shoulder, a hat pulled down over his face at the door of Paul's building, Tyrone Giggis waited until he had been rung through before he went to the corner telephone booth.

Gaines and Hawkes were sitting in the offices of Gaines Masonry tearing up and burning the last of the signed requisitions for materials when the phone rang.

Gaines took the reciever and listened for a moment, then said, "Wait." He turned to Marcus and said, "It's Tyrone. He says Bell's gone up to Curtin's apartment. He says he's shaking like a leaf."

Hawkes drummed his fingers on the desk, then looked at his watch. "It wouldn't be fair, George. Not now. It wouldn't be fair if he found something to stop us." He clenched his teeth. "Shit!" he hissed. "We need a few more hours. We'll be gone out of here, and across the ocean, and free."

"What do I tell him, Marcus?"

His face twisted into a grimace. "Tell him to kill them. When they leave the building, tell him to kill them. Kill them."

Tyrone Giggis walked back to the old gray Pontiac and

plugged in a Bob Marley tape. He pulled a thick spliff of marijuana from his jacket pocket and ducked below the level of the window to light it. He sucked in the smoke and let it sharpen his senses. Then he sat back and swayed gently to the thrumming of the reggae, his dreadlocks bobbing to the rhythm.

The ganja had altered Tyrone's view of time, but he guessed that it was a couple of hours between his phone call to his boss and the reappearance of Mack Bell, accompanied by Paul Curtin. They had a brief discussion on the sidewalk, then crossed the street and got into a Volkswagen Rabbit that Giggis supposed correctly to belong to Bell.

Giggis started his engine as they closed the doors and waited with his lights off to see what they would do. When they pulled up to the light, then turned, he flicked on his low beams, then just in time to make the signal, went down Fifth Avenue after them.

Traffic was light, enabling Giggis to keep within reach of Bell's car and still stay out of sight by hanging back a half block in the right lane. As they proceeded down the avenue, Giggis opened his window and casully swung his sawed-off twelve-gauge shotgun from the floor of the car across the crook of his left arm. He depressed the accelerator gently to pull even with the Volks, then lowered the muzzle. At Sixty-eighth Street, he looked ahead to make sure that his path was clear.

Though there was only a second between Paul's recognition of Giggis's presence and the first explosion, it seemed to him that an eternity passed. When he saw the glint of the streetlight on the metal barrel, he thrust himself across the front seat of the small car and wrenched the wheel from Bell's grasp, twisting it violently to the left.

At the flicker of movement, Giggis pulled the selective trigger twice, firing both barrels of double-O buckshot. There are fifteen pellets the size of BBs in a three-inch magnum shell. The windshield, side curtains, and roof of the Volkswagen disintegrated in a hail of lead and splintered glass and shredded metal.

Exactly as he had planned, Giggis dropping the smoking gun to the floor, and without increasing speed, drove two blocks to the Sixty-fifth Street transverse and crossed Central Park to the West Side. He continued on across town until he reached the

Hudson River. He parked the car under the crumbling West Side Highway overpass. Stuffing his tapes in his pockets, he carried the gun across the road under his jacket and dropped it off the pier into the water. He walked back to West End, took a cab to Times Square, and went to a dirty movie.

As Giggis escaped across the park, Bell's car slewed across Fifth Avenue, struck a fireplug, then spun across the sidewalk through the steel supports of an apartment building canopy, bouncing off the wall and finally coming to a halt tilted crazily against a No Parking sign, draped with the shredded green awning.

Either instinct or the smell of leaking gasoline prompted Paul to reach out to turn off the ignition.

Police guarding the Yugoslav Embassy on the next block arrived on the run, guns drawn, looking for mad Croatians. In a half minute four squad cars drawn from the 19th Precinct on Lexington and Sixty-seventh pulled into a circle, effectively barricading Bell's car from the street.

In the distance, an emergency ambulance could be heard wailing its way east from Roosevelt Hospital across the park.

A policeman from the embassy pushed the tattered awning away from the window cautiously with the barrel of his drawn gun. "Holy shit," he said. He stepped back and holstered his revolver. "Did somebody call for an ambulance?"

"Yeah," his partner answered. "From the call box. Listen, you can hear it."

"Help me get this shit off the car," the first officer said.

With the help of two more men from the radio cars, they were able to pull the twisted metal strut loose from the remains of the Volkswagen's roof, dragging the awning with it.

Dazed and bleeding, Paul Curtin was making feeble efforts to get out of the car.

"Sit still, mack," a cop said. "Wait for the ambulance."

"I've got to see the governor."

"Huh? Talk up, mack. I can't hear you."

Paul shook his head to clear the cobwebs. The words had sounded clearly in his mind, but had come out of his mouth nearly unintelligible. He twisted a little in the seat and pulled out his wallet, exposing the press card to the officer.

"Yeah, okay, mister. What do you want to say?"

"Get me out of here. I've got to see Governor O'Neil." His words were still slurred, and his voice shaky, but he'd made himself understood.

"If I were you, I'd sit still. There's an ambulance coming right up the block. You might be hurt worse than you think."

Paul looked through the deformed web of steel, little bits of glass still clinging to it. The cop was six feet tall and heavy, with a round Italian face, curiously set with blue eyes. He looked down at the name tag above the badge and said, "Listen, Officer Bonser, I've got to see the governor. That's where I was heading. I've got to get out of here. Can you get me out?"

Bonser shrugged his broad shoulders and said, "It's your ass, pally." He reached out an enormous gloved hand and slowly, straining with his two hundred odd pounds, pulled the twisted door frame far enough ajar to let Paul out.

"What about your buddy?" the cop asked.

Paul leaned unsteadily against the side of the car, trying to straighten. "Christ," he said. He hadn't even remembered that Mack Bell was there. He looked across the front seat, then turned away and vomited weakly onto the sidewalk.

The ambulance crew jumped out of the van and began to pry the driver side door away from the crumpled body of the car.

"It's a good thing they make these things out of a hundred percent pure shit, or we'd never be able to get anyone out of them. Freddie, gimme a hand," the driver said.

The driver and one of the attendants leaned their weight against the flimsy metal, and it sheared off at the hinges.

Bell lay slumped over the whell. Part of his right ear was missing and there was a bloody wound at the top of his right shoulder. He bled profusely from a cut where his forehead had met the dash.

"Leave him sit a minute," the paramedic said. "We could have a chest compression here. He's wrapped around that wheel." He listened as best he could to Bell's breathing. "No rasping or gurgling. Let's try to get him out. Get the gurney."

Paul leaned against the lamppost and watched for the five minutes that it took to extract Bell's limp, massive form and transfer it to the stretcher. The paramedic hovered over him for a moment, and said, "Get him in. He needs help. Let me look at the other one. Send somebody back for me. Come on. Move it.''

The ambulance van screeched away down the street and turned into the park. When it had disappeared, the paramedic turned to Paul. "You all right?"

"I'm a little woozy."

"Here, sit in the squad car." He walked paul to the nearest vehicle and eased him into the passenger seat. "Take a whiff of this." He broke an ampule under Paul's nose.

A few whiffs made him cough, but cleared his head. He looked down to find that the left sleeve of his coat and shirt were wet with blood. He started to reel again, then realized that it was not his own. He pulled the paramedic's hand toward him and took another sniff.

"I don't think there's anything wrong with me," Paul said.

The medic checked him over with a little light, examining his pupils, then palpating his neck.

"You're a lucky boy. I think you're right. You probably should be checked over completely anyway. Does anything hurt?"

Paul shook his head negatively.

"Not even that nose? It looks busted to me."

"That was last week's accident." Suddenly, Paul smiled. Unable to understand why the lather machine had shorted out, he'd given it to the forensic cops. When they'd drawn a blank, he'd sent it off with a nasty letter to General Electric. Maybe it hadn't been an accident after all.

A trim, older police sergeant with white hair peeking out from under his uniform cap walked forward and said, "Doc, can I talk to this man?"

"You want to talk, mister? You don't have to. You can go to the hospital."

"No, no that's fine. Make it quick. I've got to get to the governor."

"With your clothes all bloody," the sergeant objected mildly. "I think maybe you'd want to get fixed up and clean before you go to your audience."

Paul sighed, and pulled out his wallet again. "Look, sergeant, I'm Paul Curtin. I'm a reporter with the *Advocate*. I was on my way to visit the governor when this happened. It's urgent that I get to him as soon as possible." In a moment of sudden panic, Paul reached inside his jacket and felt for the envelope. It was still there.

"You got a pain, Mr. Curtin?" the sergeant asked solicitously.

"No. I thought I'd lost something."

"If you're serious about the governor, I'll run you down. It's only the few blocks. But can you tell me what happened here?"

"I'm not really sure. I was on my way from my apartment on Eighty-third Street. Mack Bell was driving. I just happened to look to my right and I saw a gun sticking out of a car window. I dove for the steering wheel, and that's the last thing I really remember."

"Did you see anything else? Had the car been following you? Could you see the driver?"

"Nothing. All I saw, or thought I saw, was a gun. I don't even know what color the car was. I don't remember even hearing a shot."

The sergeant closed his pad and stuffed it into his hip pocket. "I'm sorry you don't know more, Mr. Curtin. I can tell you that even if you didn't hear it, there was a shot. Somebody fired enough buckshot at you to tear half the roof off of the krautmobile. If you hadn't dove for the wheel, it would have taken your head with it."

Paul had a series of fleeting thoughts about his poor dumb son, Maryanne, and bits and pieces from his past, some good, some bad. He clenched his jaw. "Can you take me down to the governor's apartment?"

The sergeant closed the door of the car and beeped the siren a couple of times. Other uniformed cops had roped off the area, but a crowd of curiosity seekers were strung out along the barriers. Others hung from windows in the stately building above.

When Paul got out of the patrol car the two plainclothesmen who were the governor's bodyguard emerged immediately from their car and stepped toward him. He had pulled his coat closed in an effort to hide the worst of his dishevelment.

Paul was relieved. They were two of the regulars.

"Hello, O'Hara."

"Jesus, Mary, and Joseph! Paul Curtin. What the hell happened?"

"I came to see your boss. Somebody tried to put me away."

"Is that what all that bullshit is up the avenue?"

"That's it."

"I've got to see him, O'Hara."

"You got an appointment? You aren't exactly a favorite dinner guest."

"Let me talk to him on the intercom."

Tommy O'Hara took a step backwards. "You wouldn't fuck me, would you, Paul? I don't like long walks in Staten Island."

"It's legit. Just get him on the intercom. Please."

O'Neil was watching the ten o'clock news on Channel 5. He was emotionally drained, but with the Andretti story under him, and the hundred grand where he could get at it, he felt a lot better than he had anytime since the day that Allison had checked him out for all the world to see. He missed her. And felt bad about Lou. It would never be the same again between them. But, he was out from under the cloud with Hawkes. He thought to himself grimly, he'd have to figure out a way to disentangle himself from that mess. He'd show Hawkes that there was no percentage in both of them going to the can. Maybe he could get him off. Hell, maybe they'd be able to finish the damn building and sweep the whole mess under the rug. He leaned forward, interested by the sports news. Anyway, the *Times* poll showed that his gap over Greene had widened. He'd find himself another meal ticket.

The cop at the front door of the apartment heard the buzzer on the intercom and came back to get him.

Governor, it's the guys downstairs. They want to talk to you."

"Thanks, Kratzke," he said, climbing to his feet. "I wonder what they want. Christ, it's ten-thirty already."

He picked up the phone and said, "Yes."

"Governor, this is Paul Curtin. I must talk to you."

"Are you nuts? You can damn well call me at my office in the morning. You know better than this."

"Somebody just tried to kill me. The more I think about it, the more it seems likely that that's the second time in ten days. I thought you might be interested."

"I'm sorry, of course. Are you all right?"

"Yes, thank you."

"What does that have to do with a midnight interview in my home?"

"Hawkes and Gaines might know, Governor. If that doesn't help, maybe you'd like to see my signed blank requisitions." There was a dead silence. "Shall I come up?"

"Come ahead."

O'Neil waited for Paul at the door opposite the elevator. Paul could see the shock on his face when he emerged.

"I wasn't kidding. Somebody tried to put me away."

"Christ. Come in. Do you need anything?"

"I'd like a drink and a phone."

"Come into the den. There's both. How about a john? You could use a wash."

"I must look pretty lousy." He followed the Governor into the book-lined room. "Phone first," he said.

"Help yourself."

Paul dialed the city desk at the *Advocate*. "Listen, Sharkey, this is Paul Curtin. Send somebody to Fifth Avenue and Sixty-eighth Street. There's a 1980 Volkswagen wrapped around a light pole. It'll probably be out on the police radios as an accident. It wasn't. It was an attempted double murder. One of the victims was Mack Bell—yeah—like truck and ding-dong. He is a vice-president of Hawkes Building Company. He is seriously injured—gunshot wounds and the result of the car crash. He's at Roosevelt Hospital. The other passenger in the car was Curtin, C-u-r-t-i-n, first name Paul. No, I'm not kidding. Assorted cuts and bruises. That's all. Send somebody. There might be a follow-up. No, you can't reach me. I'll call you." He hung up the phone and took the large whisky that the governor was offering him.

"Quite a story," O'Neil said, turning away to the bar to refill his own glass.

Paul took the envelope out of his pocket and laid it on the coffee table in front of the couch. "You might want to take a look at that, Governor. The guy I started out with tonight—I don't suppose you've ever met Mack Bell—he was afraid that if we came up here, you'd take the papers in there, burn them, then have us killed and stuffed into the incinerator."

"What did you tell him?"

"I told him I didn't think it was likely, but that even if you were so inclined, you'd still have to explain how we got in and out. You want to pass some more small talk or shall we get down to the issues? I'm a little sore, in both mind and body. I'd like to get this over with and get some rest."

O'Neil picked up the envelope and read through the papers. He handed them back without a trace of emotion. "Why don't you wash up?" He pointed at a door. "You're a mess. I'll lend you a shirt."

Paul got up and stepped toward the door, then hesitated.

"It's all right," O'Neil said sardonically. "You can trust me."

Paul shuddered, looking at the governor, then nodded and went into the bathroom. His image in the mirror was no more or less than he had expected. He'd seen and felt worse in combat. He stripped to the waist, throwing the stained shirt into a wastebasket. He touched his cheek. He would have a bruise to go with the swelling. He patted his face dry gently, then combed his hair. The sergeant had been right. He'd been lucky as hell.

When he walked out of the john, the governor was seated on the couch. A dark blue, long-sleeved pullover lay on the table.

He pulled on the shirt and sat down.

"Well what are we going to do about all of this, Paul?" O'Neil asked calmly.

"What do you suppose?"

O'Neil savored his drink. "A public lynching, I expect."

"That's what I had in mind."

"Perhaps you don't have what you think you have."

Paul relaxed in the chair. "You never change. I didn't know what to expect when I came here. Maybe Bell was right. Maybe you sicced that killer on us."

"Now you're fantasizing."

"Governor O'Neil," Paul said leaning forward again, "I think we ought to change the tenor of the conversation. If you don't believe me, all you have to do is to call the Nineteenth Precinct. Somebody just tried to blow my fucking head off. And the more I think about it, the more I think that somebody arranged for me to be damn near electrocuted in my apartment. I am certain that two people have been either killed or kidnapped by your partners Hawkes and Gaines. I can prove that. And I have every reason to believe that they're respon-

sible for over twenty other deaths. Is it my fantasy that you are
an accessory, before and after the fact?''

"What are you talking about? Partners? Just a couple of
black businessmen I tried to give a hand.''

"Listen, Frank,'' Paul growled, "I came up here because I
don't believe that you are an accomplice to murder—not
willingly or consciously, at least. Don't bullshit me. You
sought out Kurt Englander at Burton Industries to make sure
he'd give Hawkes the maximum leeway. You put out the word
to the Division of Housing to keep their noses out of Uhuru,
and to play deaf and dumb to questions. Don't tell me that it
was your philanthropic instincts and love of your black
neighbors or I'll throw up. If those bastards are far enough out
in the open to try to shoot me down in the street, it's because
they're on their way to wherever they're going. I couldn't think
of anyone who could stop them faster than you.''

He picked up the papers and waved them at the governor.
"Talk your way out of the blank requisition forms, Frank.
Andretti can lie for you till hell freezes over, but I know you've
been on the take from Hawkes. You want to hear the rest?''

"Twenty murders?'' O'Neil looked at Paul, numb and
disbelieving.

"You want the details? I'll tell you.'' It took Paul ten
minutes, starting with Gibbons's death on the reinforcing bars
and ending with the attempt on his own life on Fifth Avenue.
"And that's only what I know. Christ knows what else has been
done that I don't. Now, what are you going to do about it,
Governor?''

"What do you want?''

"I want Hawkes and Gaines arrested on suspicion of murder
before they leave town.''

O'Neil reached for the telephone. His hand rested on the
receiver for a moment, then he made up his mind and dialed.

A voice replied curtly. "Greene.''

"Mr. Mayor, this is Frank O'Neil. I'm afraid we have a
problem with Uhuru Towers. I have Paul Curtin here with me.
He's just survived an attempt on his life. He has reason to
believe that Hawkes and Gaines are responsible. He has
convincing proof that they are guilty of at least one, and
perhaps a couple of dozen homicides. I believe an APB is in
order. I'm going to call the State Police, and the chairman of

the Port Authority to make sure that there's a lookout at Newark as well as Kennedy and La Guardia. You'll deal with NYPD? Good. I'll see that the Jersey and Connecticut cops are alerted, too." He paused for a moment, listening, then said, "I have no idea what I'm going to tell the public, Mr. Mayor. I assume I have until morning to make up my mind."

O'Neil made the rest of the calls, then turned back to Curtin, crossing his legs and sitting back in the chair. "Now, what kind of deal can we make?"

56

Hawkes watched Gaines rush out of his office with the remains of the tangible evidence of their crimes and saw him kneel and with shaking hands set the papers afire in a wastebasket.

As Gaines kneeled fanning the flames with his hands, Hawkes sneaked over to their identical suitcases, and looking over his shoulder, changed the identification tags.

Perspiration coursed down Gaines's face, part the glow of the fire, part anxiety. "Let's go, Marcus."

"Dump the damn Lincoln, George," Marcus hissed. "Get yourself together."

"The bags," Gaines said.

"I'll take the damn bags. Do what I said!" Hawkes took the suitcases and stood in the yard watching Gaines.

He drove a massive dumpster truck beneath the ramp. Hawkes felt a twinge of regret when he saw Gaines release the brake of the sleek brown car and push it forward. It teetered for a moment, rolled forward, and slid through the air as though in slow motion, then crash with a shriek of tearing metal into the bottom of the empty refuse van. Giggis would see to its disposal later.

Hawkes hurried to pack their bags into the unobtrusive car that had been stolen to their order earlier in the day.

He drove south on Twelfth Avenue, under the rattling overpass, and past the row of derelict autos that lined the piers and the banks of the Hudson. At 125th Street, he turned east, toward the Triboro Bridge. On his way through the evanescent corridor, smothered by greed and poverty and lassitude, he passed the looming, unfinished bulk of Uhuru Towers. Neither he nor Gaines turned to look.

Traffic was light. In a few minutes they were past the bridge on their way to Kennedy, and freedom.

They parked the car in a lot and took the airport shuttle to the TWA terminal. A porter eyed them speculatively as they stepped down from the bus.

Marcus smiled and said, "No thanks, brother. We're just going through that door."

Once inside, Marcus extended his hand. "You'd better get going. You have about half an hour to flight time."

"You're going to meet me in Grand Cayman the day after tomorrow?" Gaines asked in confirmation.

"Right. I'll meet you at the bank at noon."

"Are you sure it's all right?" Gaines said in a half whisper, looking down at the gray bags. "You've always wanted to get it under lock and key."

Hawkes looked nervously around him. "It's going to be fine. We've got to go separate ways. Just in case they start looking for us. Let's go. Just keep your hand on the damn bag."

Gaines nodded and walked to the check-in counter. When he looked back, Hawkes had slipped off and melted into the crowd.

"Yes, Mr. Jennings," the ticket agent said. "We have you booked into Trinidad for this evening. First class. Don't you want to check the gray bag?"

"No, I'll carry that on board. You just take the brown one." He waited patiently while she wrote the tags and processed the ticket.

"You can go right on board, Mr. Jennings."

"Thank you. By the way, when does the plane for St. Martin leave?"

"In an hour. You'd better hurry, Mr. Jennings," the agent said. "Your plane is boarding."

Satisfied that Marcus would have no trouble in getting out, George Gaines walked through the arched corridor and through the security gate without incident. When he was seated on the plane with a drink in his hand, he stopped to look out of the window at the glow of New York's lights in the night sky, remarking to himself that it was not likely that he should ever see them again.

He stretched his long legs and leaned back. Overnight at the Holiday Inn at the airport, then on to Grand Cayman. Marcus would make an intermediate stop in Jamaica, and be there the next day. He closed his eyes and thought about the chambermaid he'd laid at the hotel.

Marcus Hawkes tore up the ticket Gaines had purchased to St. Martin in the name of Combs and threw it in the trash barrel. He hailed a taxi. It would be very close.

At his destination, he gave the driver a ten-dollar bill, and said, "Keep the change." He hurried to the desk, but the agent held up his hand smiling.

"No need to hurry. We're just beginning to board, now. May I see your ticket?"

Marcus gave him the ticket, and the bag he wished to check.

"Smoking or nonsmoking?"

"Nonsmoking will be fine."

"Here's your passport and your boarding pass. Varig Flight 62 to Rio and São Paulo is boarding upstairs at Gate Twenty-Nine. Have a nice flight, Mr. Willis."

57

By three in the morning, there was a dwindling, annoyed group of newspeople in front of the governor's apartment house on Fifth Avenue. There had been no general release made to the press. Some had been there since before midnight. What they knew, they had pieced together from the police radio and interviews at the 19th Precinct. Paul Curtin, a reporter on the *Advocate*, had been driving down Fifth Avenue with another man. Several blocks north of the governor's house, they had been shot by an assailant in a second car. There had been a crash. Curtin's companion was in critical condition at Roosevelt Hospital. Curtin had been whisked down the avenue, apparently unhurt, and upstairs to the O'Neil apartment.

In the interim, an all-points bulletin had been issued in New York and its neighboring states for the apprehension of Marcus Garvey Hawkes and George Gaines on suspicion of murder and attempted murder. It was not understood whether the incidents were connected, but the order for the arrests had come from the mayor and the governor shortly after the accident and Curtin's arrival at the governor's home.

The air had been alive with speculation. But as time had passed, the crowd thinned. Network camera and sound crews were moved to other locations or knocked off for the night.

Shortly after three, the comptroller of the state of New York arrived in his limousine at the side entrance to the building. He looked old and drawn. White stubble marked his hollow cheeks. His mouth was compressed into a thin line, and his gold-rimmed spectacles had slid to the end of his long, curved nose.

He sneaked up in the service elevator. O'Neil himself met him at the kitchen door. The bodyguard took his coat, and the governor guided him down the hall to the library.

Paul Curtin had a splitting headache, and the bruise on his cheek had blossomed into a throbbing mass that interfered with his speech. His eyes were sunken, their whites traced with crimson.

When the comptroller walked into the room, Paul strained with his hands, pulling himself erect.

"My God."

"I'm a little worse for wear, Mr. Rosensweig, but all systems are functioning."

"Sit down, before you fall."

"Would you like a drink, Lou?" the governor asked solicitously.

"A light scotch." Rosensweig took a chair next to Paul.

"I have a problem, Lou," the governor said, bringing the drink back from the bar and holding it out. "Paul and I decided that you might be able to help us."

The older man took a sip and straightened his glasses. "I

assumed there must be some reason to pull me out of bed at two in the morning," he said acerbically.

"It seems that I have been indiscreet."

"Jesus," Paul said, rubbing his eyes. "I've been sitting here for three hours listening to you say that. You have been dishonest. I know. You know I know. I can prove it. You have been indiscreet inasmuch as you have been caught." He looked up at O'Neil exhausted. "I don't even know why I'm sitting here. I ought to be in the D.A.'s office convincing him to swear out a warrant for your arrest as an accomplice in my attempted murder."

The comptroller finished his drink in a gulp.

O'Neil turned on Paul and said, "I thought we were going to handle this equitably. How the hell can we expect to get a rational idea from Lou if he has the wrong impression from the start?"

"Goddamn it, Governor," Paul swore softly. "We're not having a debate about a sewer maintenance bill."

"If you have him over a barrel," the comptroller asked pointedly, "then why are you sitting here listening to him temporize?"

Paul shook his head. "I'm not sure."

O'Neil looked at Paul with a half smile. "He's found out that power, even derived from pure truth, is not easy to deal with. He thinks he has me dead to rights. He has his scoop-of-the-century. He came in with the wounds of just battle to claim the head of his vanquished foe. And behold! Just as he lifted the axe, he saw that there was responsibility attached to the act. What about the good things my administration has done? Should he build a pathway to the Governor's Mansion for that fraud Greene? Am I really the worse alternative?"

Paul shrugged. "Masterful overstatement with a grain of truth. You want to tell him the details? Or shall I?"

O'Neil sat in a chair opposite and began to speak in the manner of a teacher. "It has to do with Uhuru Towers."

The comptroller pushed his glasses against the bridge of his nose. "Oh yes, the building on 125th Street, Governor."

O'Neil flinched. Rosensweig never called him governor in private.

"There have been irregularities . . ." he went on.

Rosensweig interrupted. "It would appear that the builder

has stolen several million dollars' worth of materials. It is also clear that the word had been passed from a high state official that the subject is taboo. There's to be no nosing around. The people at the Division of Housing have been subject to very heavy pressure. Somene up the ladder is on the take." He stopped long enough to adjust his glasses again, then went on, his voice rising. "I haven't had long to look into it. I just heard about it after this high personnage suffered an embarrassment about his personal finances."

Rosensweig got to his feet and began to pace the floor. He stopped and looked at O'Neil's face. "Of course, I know. Paul came to see me. He asked a number of questions about the techniques of fraud. He didn't mention Uhuru, but he set me to wondering what he meant. Then, I got his article on the project from the *Advocate*. Shortly thereafter, there was the question of your finances, and the miraculous appearance of your old army buddy, Luigi. Then, your girl friend took leave in public. And finally, someone came to me and gave me the outline of Uhuru Towers."

Paul raised his head. "Who was that?"

Rosensweig looked at him, hesitating. "Before I answer your question, you tell me what you know."

It took Paul five minutes to make his statement.

Rosensweig's face was gray when he finished. He sat heavily in his chair.

The room was silent for a minute.

"Why didn't you go directly to the police?" Rosensweig asked.

"I didn't think he was involved in the murders. I don't want Gaines and Hawkes to get away. He was the fastest way to get the cops on those two."

"You took a chance."

"I don't think so. I didn't think so then."

"Have you heard anything back, yet?"

O'Neil shook his head.

Rosensweig got slowly to his feet again, his age showing. "For your information," he said to Paul, "my visitor—the one who knew about a scandal at Uhuru—was George Mason. Governor, I would like a moment with you. Paul, I would appreciate it if you would allow us some time alone. Not long, I promise."

"Maybe I'd better go to the cops, now," Paul said, his eyes narrowing in distrust.

"If you wish," Rosensweig said. "But I think you'll be better served if you wait here for those few minutes. I can assure you that neither the governor nor I will go anyplace."

Paul nodded agreement and watched them go through the door. When it closed behind them, he shut his eyes against the light.

O'Neil walked down the hall half a pace behind the stiff-necked old man. He turned in at the living room.

"Could we have some light, Governor?"

"Of course," he said, pulling a lamp cord.

They sat opposite each other in front of the fireplace.

"What do you think, Lou?"

"You're dead, Frank. Those papers are a death warrant."

"I'm not so sure." He took the phone from the table beside him and called the senior duty officer at state police headquarters. He spoke for a couple of minutes, then hung up.

O'Neil shook his head. "They're gone. Not a trace. Maybe they were tipped."

"By you, Frank?"

"Certainly not," O'Neil replied indignantly.

"That's why you're dead, Frank. No matter how you obfuscate the circumstances, even if you are never indicted or convicted, people will always ask those questions."

"Do you believe I tipped them off?"

"No. But there was a flicker of doubt. How long have we known each other? Thirty years? More? Maybe you have an explanation for those blank requisitions, Frank. Maybe you don't. I'm sure you'll make one up in any case. And I'm sure you'll never do anything like it—whatever it was—again. But them, out there," he pointed through the window, "they will not be so sanguine or charitable. I don't believe that anyone gets a second chance to violate a public trust—not if he gets caught."

"The cops say that Gaines and Hawkes left home without warning or possessions. The media are crawling all over their houses in New Jersey. The families seem completely stunned and confused. They must have just taken off." O'Neil brightened a bit. "This could be the break I need. In their absence, the investigation of the murders is going to be low-key. If there are no personalities to follow, these things are always kind of administrative. It'll drop off the front pages fast enough. Even the investigation of Uhuru might be handled in a diplomatic way. As for the papers, who knows where they really came from? Maybe we ought to think about a special investigation of office procedures in the capital. Who knows who might be fooling around in our offices.''

"Forget it, Governor O'Neil," Rosensweig said bluntly. "Even if no one else has doubts about where those papers came from, and how they got into that desk, I will. And I won't live with it. Even if you could stall an investigation, or legal proceedings, even if you were somehow reelected, inside a year, you would be facing impeachment. There isn't much bacon left to save, Frank. I've spent my whole life building the Republican party in this state. More times than not, we've held the state house and the senate, and even the assembly. I'm not prepared to sacrifice my work, and that of a lot of others to buy you the time to get kicked out of office on your ass. You're a liability, Frank. Go like a gent. Resign. The right speech will buy public sympathy. Tom Rainey becomes governor until the election. He won't be pressing too hard on you."

"You're not giving me much room to maneuver, Lou."

"You have two choices: jump or be pushed. The longer you stay in office, the worse the problem will become." Rosensweig leaned back in the chair, very worn. "For God's sake, Frank, you've gotten yourself involved in petty graft. Money. That's bad enough. They've killed two dozen human beings. Separate yourself from that, Frank. Please."

"You're going to offer the people of this state Tom Rainey as their next governor?"

Rosensweig took a deep breath and exhaled. "No. We've already talked about the top of the ticket to George Mason."

"We. Who's we? You've been busy. You think you can win with a Conservative?"

"We is me, and Senator Carney, and the attorney general, and of course, Tom. Sure, we've been busy, Frank. You'll have to forgive us. We haven't been as busy as you and Gaines and Hawkes. And as for Mason, we're a little uncomfortable with his place in the spectrum, but we'll live with it. His reputation is sparkling clean. Right now, we need that more than good positioning on the issues. That's what the electorate is going to be talking about during this election."

"I'm out, then?"

"All you'll accomplish is to take us with you."

O'Neil sat for a minute or two, staring across the room at ghostly lights that traced the paths of Central Park, and to the dark spires of the West Side beyond. In the end, he squared his shoulders, flattened his hair back with the palm of his hand, and stood up.

"Shall we go and write my resignation address, Mr. Comptroller? I'll ask Ken Miller up."

He took the phone again and dialed his executive assistant's home number. It rang twice. "Ken. It's very late, I know, but can you get your head together?"

"Yes, sir."

"Ken, I want you to come on over. Now. I need you."

"Yes, sir. But what . . ."

"Just blue jeans and a shirt. Come up the back entrance." O'Neil put the phone down gently. "That's going to be one of the hard ones. I raised him."

The comptroller stood up and straightened his tie. "They're all going to be tough. You have commanded a great deal of love and respect. The disappointment will be proportionate." He shuffled as he walked in front of the governor, bent and old.

They found Paul Curtin fast asleep in the den, lying back in the chair, his head lolling. He woke slowly when O'Neil touched his shoulder.

He rubbed the sand from his eyes. At least his headache seemed to have gone. His face hurt. "Jesus, what time is it? I thought you were going to be gone a couple of minutes."

"It's four o'clock. I have a commission for you," O'Neil said.

"Like what?"

"Ken Miller will be here in a few moments. I want you to help us to frame my resignation."

"You serious?" Paul rubbed his eyes again, then turned to Rosensweig. "Another sandbag for me? Like Andretti?"

"No," Rosensweig said somberly. "Don't expect any great admissions of guilt, though. Just a resignation for the good of the people of this state."

"I can't let it go at that. My story is going to tell what I believe."

"We know."

Miller arrived in ten minutes. He and Paul worked on the sketchy framework provided by O'Neil. When they were done, Miller cried.

"Thank you, gentlemen," Governor O'Neil said. "I'll deliver this at a press conference in my New York office at ten o'clock. If you'd like to stay here, gentlemen, you're welcome." He stood and stretched. "I am going to try to get what's left of the night's sleep." He looked over at Paul who had gotten to his feet and was pulling on his coat. "You'll try not to steal the march on me?"

"I'll think about it."

Paul slipped out of the service entrance and past the cop standing guard at the iron gate at the back of the building. He had to walk five painful blocks before a cab rumbled up empty Madison Avenue in the direction of his apartment.

It wasn't until he stood inside of the door that he began to shake, realizing that whoever had tried twice to murder him might have tried again. He dropped his blood-stained coat on the couch and walked into the bedroom. The shadow in the chair moved. Paul gasped and stepped back awkwardly, tripping over the doorsill and falling against the frame and to his knees.

When the lights came up and he saw Maryanne in front of him, wearing his old robe, he shuddered and began to sob. It was ten minutes before he could stop.

58

George Mason was taking his morning shower when the phone rang.

"George, this is Lou Rosensweig. In an hour, Frank O'Neil is going to resign as governor. We want to offer the top of the ticket to you formally. We may be forced into a primary, but I want you to know that you're going to have the support of the party leadership. I have to know now. Is this what you want?"

Mason put his hand over the mouthpiece. Eleanor looked at him curiously. "They want a commitment now, Elly. O'Neil's going to resign."

Elly Mason suffered a sudden prescience of loneliness and pulled her robe close around her. She looked across the room at him. She had no choice. "I'm behind you, all the way, George."

"It's our moment, Elly." He took his hand off the mouthpiece, and said, "I'd be pleased, Lou."

The second time the phone rang, he was half dressed.

"Congressman, this is Paul Curtin."

"You're being very formal this morning."

"Have they offered you the nomination, yet?"

"For what?"

"For governor, George. Don't play games with me. I spent all night with O'Neil and Rosensweig. I helped to write the resignation speech."

"This is not for print until after the resignation becomes official," Mason replied.

"Trust me. Congratulations, and thanks."

"I am trusting you. Don't let me down. As for the congratulations, thanks but I'm not sure that they're in order."

Paul turned back to his typewriter and added the new element to his story. He finished as his phone buzzed. It was Fabrikant. He was expected upstairs.

Paul had not seen Melanie since their argument. She did not greet him. She sat back in her chair, noncommittal and waiting.

"Will it save time if I read the story aloud?" Paul asked.

Fabrikant looked at Melanie. She nodded approval.

Paul began with the text of O'Neil's resignation.

Fellow New Yorkers:

In the past several weeks, questions have arisen about my personal financial condition. Like others in these difficult times, I have suffered reverses. As a result, to meet my obligations, I have been forced to seek funds to supplement my income as Governor of the State of New York.

Persons in public office have far less latitude in these matters than do private citizens. The power to govern is derived from public trust. When probity is questioned, and that trust is shaken, the ability to wield that power is impaired to the detriment of the state and those who believe in it.

In the past twenty-four hours, my integrity has been further put to the question as a result of my close association with the Uhuru Towers building project in New York City.

Marcus Hawkes, President of Hawkes Building Company, the general contractors, and George Gaines, one of the subcontractors, are being sought by the police in connection with serious crimes, including murder, and are assumed to be in flight to avoid prosecution.

It is clear to me that in the months which lie before us issues will arise from these matters which will occupy much of my time and which threaten to involve legislators and administrators to the exclusion of other matters, interfering with the effective government of the state. Further, it is evident in an election year that public debate centering on the honesty of an incumbent candidate can serve only to cloud the political issues from which the decisions of the electorate should be derived.

I am unwilling to risk either immobilization of the state government or distortion of the electoral process by clinging to office when questions of my fitness for office have not been fully resolved. While I am certain that time will maintain my unblemished reputation and illuminate the accomplishments of my seven years in the state house, I believe it is in your best interests that I step down at this time.

Accordingly, with deepest regret and sorrow, I herewith tender my resignation as Governor of New York State, effective immediately.

Melanie frowned. "There's no admission of wrongdoing there. What kind of resignation is that?"

"What other kind could we expect, Mrs. Parsons?" Paul asked. "He's not going to convict himself out of his own mouth and apply for a jail sentence. The resignation and the circumstances guarantee an investigation by the district attorney of Manhattan and the attorney general of the state at the very least. More likely, they'll appoint a special committee. But we have the whole story."

"Let's hear it," she said.

"I've dealt with the story in separate parts. I begin with the lynchpin—Uhuru Towers itself. I touch on the history, the motivation of the sponsors and O'Neil, particularly his desire to create some goodwill in poor urban areas. The next piece deals with Burton Industries's involvement, both their political and public relations aims, and the profit motive, and the creation of the Hawkes Building Company as their partners. From there I go into the problems that grew out of the construction of Uhuru: the delays, the lack of controls. I draw the conclusion that when Hawkes and Gaines saw that they couldn't make a go of the project, they began to steal. To do that they needed political cover. They bought it from O'Neil. He gave them cover and blank requisitions. They gave him goodwill in the ghetto and cash under the table. The next step is easy. Gibbons found out. He was killed. Jenks died the same way, and incidentally, so did his twenty-one neighbors. Malcolm Woodruff was the one who knew the most. He blew the whistle. His low profile kept him alive for a while. Then Gaines and Hawkes found him out and killed him and his wife and dreamed up the trip around the world. They must have been tailing either me or Bell, because, when he found those papers, and brought them to me, they attempted to kill us, then took off. That brings me to the governor's door."

"How is the other fellow in the car, Paul?" Oscar asked.

"Mack Bell? He must be made of iron and very lucky. I called the hospital an hour ago. He had a partially collapsed lung. They dug three pellets out of his shoulder and chest cavity. He lost a piece of his right ear. He's pretty sick. But they said he'd probably be back on his feet in a couple of weeks. He's out of danger."

"Anymore?" Melanie asked.

"Just a quick recap of the story on his income," Paul said, "to tie everything together, and of course, the resignation."

"He'll never spend a night in jail," she scowled. "Wait and see."

"Could be," Paul said. "But he's finished. His career is over. I think the best stuff I have is at the end of the last piece. How the hell does something like this happen? The project sprang from goodwill and noble motives, a sense of community pride, and an attempt at cooperation across class lines, economic barriers, and racial and social differences. And what do we end up with? A dream turned into a nightmare, all of the good intentions perverted into unspeakable acts: murder, theft, embezzlement, a cover-up in the state government, and at least a blind eye turned in tacit approval by a do-nothing city government."

Melanie looked at him coldly. "I don't see that."

"You can't still believe Greene didn't know what was going on. How about that impassioned interview with Max Fabrikant defending Uhuru and Hawkes? Where the hell have the inspectors from the municipal Department of Housing been hiding? I don't think he was on the take, like O'Neil, but I'm damn sure he knew what was going on."

"That's Pulitzer Prize material, Mel," Oscar said.

"I think parts of it are commendable," she said stiffly. "I have what I've wanted. O'Neil has fallen from his pedestal. I've always known he didn't belong there. But the story as a whole, this long, intricate jeremiad on the sins of the city—no, I think not. You can use the background on Uhuru, if you like. I'd be careful, though, about making assumptions as to what has been stolen. You don't know that, do you? Certainly, the resignation of the governor is the big news. I think it's proper to talk about those blank papers. I think it's proper to connect the papers and the governor's resignation, though I'd be damn careful how I did it? The speed at which the law travels in these matters is quite deliberate. I don't want to be out in front of it. By the way, what did happen to those papers?" she asked casually.

Paul had trouble finding his tongue. "I Xeroxed them. A half-dozen copies. I have one here. The rest I sent around; the comptroller, the D.A., the attorney general."

"You should have sent one to the mayor," she admonished.

"He probably has some of his own," Paul said. "Don't you want to put a little heat on Greene?"

"I can't see why. You are working on nothing but supposition and thin circumstance. He is our candidate. We owe him the benefit of the doubt.''

"I started out with nothing but supposition on O'Neil. You don't even want to ask him a polite question? Ask him to explain his lack of action?''

"In print? Surely not. When you have something on Greene that's as concrete as your story on O'Neil, then I'll discuss it. In the meantime, no soap.''

"Mrs. Parsons, he had to know what was happening at Uhuru. If he did, he's an accessory.''

"He was duped,'' she said. "He came out for them publicly because he was duped.''

"Greene?'' Paul said. "He was duped by a pair of con men? They just took him in? If you believe that, you'll believe anything.''

"I had a long conversation with Mayor Greene last night. He called me after he alerted the police about Hawkes and Gaines's getaway. We had a nice chat. If anything, he was victimized by O'Neil and Hawkes. He was sucked into making his public stand for Uhuru. I'm half-convinced that it was done specifically to blacken his name.''

Paul sat silent, dumbstruck.

"In fact,'' she went on, "I may even consider an editorial reaffirming our support. If you're right about the Republicans offering the nomination to that anachronism, George Mason.'' She waved her hand dismissively. "No, I don't want all of this extraneous business clouding the main story.'' She turned to Max. "You print the story about O'Neil resigning. Base it on his questionable finances and his embarrassment at being so closely identified with the two men on the run. Of course, bring up the finding of the papers, but be careful with your insinuations. You may conclude that they may have been used to bilk Uhuru Towers. You may pose the question as to why they were signed in blank.'' She turned back to Paul. "You can clean up the loose ends of the Uhuru story. You'll find, I think, that it will be slower in unraveling than you think. As to your suspicions in the Jenks and Gibbons cases, you may pose the question in this piece, but then I want you to turn over the criminal aspects of this story to someone better qualified, a police reporter. Perhaps your friend Seelig would like to do it. And you might as well let Joe Notrica pick up the Albany beat.

He's been following Greene. Since he's likely to be our next governor, it'll be all to the good."

"What do you want me to cover, then?" Paul asked, his mouth dry, his head spinning in confusion.

"Well," she said, sitting back in her chair, puffed up like a toad, "we'll have to see about that, won't we?"

Paul stood unsteadily and gathered his notes together. "Will you excuse me, gentlemen? Mrs. Parsons? I am very tired and sore. I'd like to go home."

"By all means," Melanie said. "You do that. You can trust Max to cut up your copy to fit our requirements. Under your byline, of course."

"Of course," Paul said. There didn't seem to be much point in arguing.

Oscar waited until Paul had gone and Max had departed after hashing out in detail what would appear and what would not. There was no mention of Greene. The philosophical piece on Uhuru had been severely cut. When Melanie was through, Paul's byline covered his story on the resignation, including the discovery of the papers in Woodruff's desk, drawing the conclusion that there was an implicit connection between the discovery and the resignation. The story continued to point out the obvious possibility of fraud in connection with the papers and asked why they had been signed in blank. It stopped short of connecting O'Neil directly with fraud or embezzlement. The story on Uhuru and the violence which surrounded it listed the occurrences, starting with Gibbons's death and ending with the assault on Curtin and Bell, reporting without inflection that Gaines and Hawkes were being sought in connection with the disappearance of the Woodruffs. The police had no clues or witnesses which might lead to the perpetrators of the attempted murders.

Having excised the bulk of the subjective commentary from Paul's story, Melanie approached the O'Neil matter in an editorial.

"While Governor O'Neil's resignation from office spares the state the awkwardness of investigating a reigning chief executive, the mysterious circumstances must not remain unexamined. Departure from public office is not a guarantee of absolution. We call upon newly sworn Rainey to require investigations of any improprieties which may have occurred in his predecessor's administration.

"Despite Uhuru's involvement, through the O'Neil resignation and the disappearance of its principal builders, in a skein of possible fraud and murder, the management of the *Advocate* joins with Mayor Greene in urging the speedy completion of the project. While an investigation of the rumors of incompetence and corruption surrounding Uhuru Towers is a requirement, the high hopes and high ideals which it represents should not be forgotten, nor its progress mired indefinitely as a result."

"Melanie—" Oscar began.

"You have something on your mind?" she replied silkily.

"I can't believe you're doing this. You may not only rob that young man of a chance—a very real chance—of a Pulitzer Prize, but your own paper as well. We're talking about journalistic respectability, stealing the march on the *Times*, maybe even a start on getting those ads from Saks Fifth Avenue you're always dreaming about. This is the best opportunity we've had since you bought the paper. We have a real jump on the competition. Even the *Times*, with five or six hundred reporters, can't outmuscle us on this one. Paul wasn't an onlooker. He created the story. He helped to make it happen. It should be used to its fullest advantage. He should be able to follow it to its logical conclusion. If Chris Greene is involved in this thing, our editorial commitment to him shouldn't stand in the way of our reporting the news. Let the chips fall where they may—on his head if necessary."

Melanie looked at him coldly across the desk. "I have no particular love for Christopher Greene. His political positions suit me. He's going where I want him to go, so I'm willing to help him get there. Paul's Curtin's career is something I see in function of its utility to me.

"A man I slept with a thousand years ago told me that if I wanted to express my will, I needed a medium that would command respect and attention. I have poured a number of millions of dollars into this paper for that purpose. The *New York Advocate* is my voice. I wanted to get Frank O'Neil. It suited me. I got him. I told you that Paul Curtin was through around here. Good academic marks aren't enough to get by." She smiled. "Teacher has to like you. He stepped—no, trod heavily—on my sensibilities. I intend for him to follow up on the investigation that will surely be instituted on Frank O'Neil.

I'm not prepared to give away the jump in circulation that that might mean. But that's going to be the limit of his field of focus. This paper isn't a stepping-stone to the stars for Paul Curtin. He's hired help. Let him follow O'Neil to the gallows. But that's the end of it. That's my epitaph for both of them. They deserve each other."

"Melanie, this newspaper is an instrument of public trust."

"My God, Oscar," she laughed. "Now it's my turn to be incredulous. This newspaper is exactly what I say it is. It is a forum for my thoughts and my political ideas. It hasn't always been as effective as I've wanted, but I've outlived and outlasted a lot of people who thought they were better equipped for the newspaper game than I. I've spent a lot of money, but I've had a run for it. That's what this newspaper is. That's what it means to me. I'm amazed that you've suddenly developed a journalistic conscience. I'm afraid you're getting old."

Oscar looked at her across the gulf of the years and wondered when they had set sail in opposite directions. "I feel old. If you'll excuse me, I've got a lot to do."

"I do, too," she said cheerfully. "I think I'll have dinner at the club tonight. Would you like to come? There should be much basking in the limelight of triumph."

Oscar hesitated at the door. "If you don't mind, I think I'll skip it."

"Suit yourself," she said, "but you're missing all the fun."

59

At two o'clock on the afternoon of Frank O'Neil's resignation as governor, Christopher Greene's secretary knocked diffidently at his door.

"Yes."

"Mr. Mayor, Mr. Albert and Mr. McClanahan are here."

"Send them in," he said. "I'm looking forward to seeing them."

He stood behind his desk. He decided that he would be magnanimous, then, upon reflection, came to the conclusion that magnanimity in politics is bullshit.

He had removed his suit jacket and pulled his tie down a bit from his unbuttoned collar. He tousled his hairpiece slightly and grinned his boyish grin.

Willy Albert, the black union leader of Erie County, was coming to Canossa, as King Henry had come to do homage and admit subservience to the Pope.

Larry McClanahan, the Irish ward heeler who served as Greene's campaign manager and advisor on grass roots organization, shepherded Albert through the door. A cigar stuck out of the corner of his mouth, stretched into a wide smile from the moment that O'Neil's resignation had turned his candidate from an outsider on a sloppy track into a front-running favorite in one stride.

"Hello, Willy," Greene said, smiling wolfishly and extending his hand. "I see that you finally found a little time off to come down and see me."

"It was nice of you to give me an appointment so fast," Albert said awkwardly. Three months ago, the shoe had been on the other foot. He'd stalled and backed and filled with Greene about delivering the black vote in Erie County. He'd had a pretty good feel of the electoral pulse. Willy Albert may be a Democrat in name, but no way was he going to mess around with Big Frank O'Neil while he was in the state house. A lot of state jobs and public works patronage hung in the balance. The odds were strong against Greene even if every black voter voted twice. So Willy had hung back and made excuses. He'd guessed wrong, and now, he stood shuffling, with his hat in his hand, waiting to do penance.

Greene sat behind the desk and spread his hands in a gesture of generosity. "Sit down, boys. Let me get some coffee."

Albert sat in the straightbacked chair facing the desk. McClanahan sat relaxed in an armchair next to the mayor.

"No, thank you, Mr. Mayor," Albert said. Want a shoe-shine, Mr. Mayor? he thought.

Greene smiled at him reassuringly. That's right, Sambo, eat a little shit.

"What can I do for you, Willy?"

Willy had been wrestling with his approach since he got on the plane. No Uncle Tomming, but plenty of diffidence. Greene was in the driver's seat, but he still needed the black vote.

"Since the governor resigned, I thought I'd better get down here and find out how you wanted to have the Buffalo campaign run. Before, it was easy. Just get out the brothers and have them vote Row B. I think it's going to be easier. A lot of those uncommitted folk are going to be leaning away from Mason, if they really put him up."

Greene's smile disappeared. "So you're finally enlisting, Willy. It's about time. No more trying to run down the white stripe in the middle of the road. Think you can still carry the county for me?"

"I can talk for my people." *I guess you're not into forgive and forget, honky.*

"That's what I've been told. I'd like to see a little action, Willy."

"I can speak for my organization. If I tell them to come out, they come." *What's he doing,* Albert wondered. *Challenging me?*

"It's just that you were so tight with O'Neil that I wondered."

"O'Neil delivered certain things. You could take his word."

"Everything has a price, Willy: power, patronage, even security for the guy at the top of an organization like yours. I want to carry Erie County, Willy. I need to carry Erie County big, just like I need the five boroughs. The Republicans aren't going to drop dead. I'm going to win in November, Willy, and I want to pull in a Democratic legislature with me—both houses, Willy. Then, there will be some pie to cut up."

Willy played a card. "Somebody's going to have to ring a lot of doorbells."

Greene trumped. "There are a lot of people out of work in Erie County. If they want to get back on the payroll, they would be smart to elect a governor and a legislature that will deliver some work to the big cities. If that's where the votes come from, that's where the dough is going. So I'm going to want a lot of busy hands. Lots of volunteers out on the street. Lots of folks manning the phones. Healthy contributions from union funds."

Willy Albert shifted uncomfortably in his chair. Motherfucker don't fool around, do he? "We got plenty of hands. But,
we're kind of short of cash."

"Find it," Greene said smiling again. "Find it, cause
otherwise you'll be looking at George Mason, and he might
just stall every piece of social legislation that comes before him
for four years. And what's more, he might redesign the
patronage system. He doesn't have Frank O'Neil's sense of
balance."

"Do you?"

"That's a good question. I want your people phoning and
stuffing boxes. I want to know that my campaign is going to get
matching funds for TV up there from your union. I'd like to
think we could even have an informal check off."

"Jesus. I don't know." Willy had started to sweat. The son-
of-a-bitch has me by the balls. If I don't break my ass for him
and fill his purse, he'll cut me off when he wins, and in sixty
days, there'll be somebody else behind my desk. If he loses, I
get Mason: antiunion, antispending. Four long cold years. "I'll
do the best I can."

"I hope so, Willy." Greene decided he'd better give him
some room. "You think about out little talk, Willy. Thanks for
coming all the way down here. Next time, don't be such a
stranger." The tone was friendly, the implication chilling.
"You try to figure out how you can help me, and I'll think
about how I can get some jobs going up there in Erie County."
Greene figured it was time to throw a coin into the crowd. "I'll
even try to give a little thought to an affirmative action
program, assuming things really go my way. Why don't you
have some of your people draw up a draft. That way you can
have some direct input." And that way, he thought, they'll all
think you came down here with empty pockets and came back
with a full bag. And you won't tell them that it's bullshit, will
you, Willy?

Willy stood up and shook the mayor's hand. At least the son-
of-a-bitch isn't making me go back on my hands and knees.
"Thank you, Mr. Mayor. I guess pretty soon I'll be calling you
governor."

"If I get enough help, you will. That'll be good for both of
us."

After McClanahan had put Albert into a city car to take him

the airport, he came back to Greene's office. The mayor
waved him in and offered him a chair.

"I want to tell you something."

"What's that, Larry?"

"That was one of the most professional jobs of leg breaking
I've ever seen. If you stay clean, Mr. Mayor, you're going to go
all the way."

Greene leaned forward on the desk and grinned at McClanahan. "There's nothing more exhilarating than kicking ass when
your opponent has both hands tied behind his back. I don't
want him to love me. I want him to work his balls off for me.
And when he's through, I'll give him the programs I want him
to have, and he'll owe me. Besides, it won't do any harm to
remind him that he's been keeping me on his back burner. If he
wants to fuck with me, then he pays. From now on, I'm going
to be the boss."

Greene smiled in self-satisfaction. He'd talked to the police
commissioner late in the morning. There was no question in his
mind. You could put up posters of Gaines and Hawkes in every
post office in America. They still wouldn't show up. The cops
were checking airport personnel at Kennedy, but there was no
doubt. They had left everything behind, and written off their
families, and flown the coop—probably overseas—and disappeared. And they would stay that way. Without their testimony,
there was no way to connect him to Uhuru Towers except for
supposition. He had burned the few remaining papers that
showed he was aware of the embezzlement from the beginning. His phone call to Melanie Parsons the previous night had
gone a long way toward convincing her and him that he would
walk away from Uhuru unscathed. O'Neil would take the fall
for both of them. And he'd walk into the Governor's Mansion
without a mark on him.

"Larry, what's our statement on the resignation going to look
like?"

"The boys are putting the finishing touches on it now, Your
Honor. It's one of those more-in-sorrow-than-in-anger things.
Sadness at the loss of opportunity for the community in
Harlem. Embarrassment as a citizen of the great state of New
York. Relief that the governor has taken the right step and
saved the people the pain of an impeachment proceeding.
Quiet confidence that when you are elected, you will be able to

lead the state out of the wilderness in which the Republicans
have left it."

Greene smiled with satisfaction. "Sounds good. Let me see
it when it's in final form. I want to make sure we get a good
spot in the *Advocate*'s Wall Street Edition. Phone it in directly
to Fabrikant."

Greene watched Larry walk out of the door. He spun in his
chair and looked across the river. He thought he saw the
beginnings of spring in the trees on Randall's Island. He was
going to be the governor of the state of New York, and the
problems that he would leave behind him to his successor as
mayor would be that much easier to bury with a Democratic
legislature. He turned slightly so that he could see his reflection
in the windowpane, then lifted the toupee off his head and
stuck out his tongue.

That evening, Paul Curtin lay stretched out on the couch in
Maryanne Middleton's apartment on Seventy-ninth Street. His
head was bolstered against a pillow she'd brought in from the
bedroom.

Scattered on the table next to him was the Wall Street
Edition of the *Advocate,* a letter from the General Electric
Corporation, and a glass containing the remains of his fifth
scotch on the rocks.

Paul had not showed up till well after dinner. "I just couldn't
handle the kids tonight. It's not for my sake. It's for theirs,"
he'd said.

After he'd finally gotten home from the paper he'd fallen
into bed fully clothed and slept until six. He'd changed and
showered then gone to a newsstand to buy a copy of the
Advocate to see what had finally become of his story. He'd
spent an hour on the phone with Max Fabrikant and Oscar
Bornstein at their homes. When he was convinced that there
was no more use in talking, he gave up and called Maryanne.
She had fed him chicken soup and booze.

"Both Max and Oscar said the same thing in the end. It's not
their newspaper. It's not my newspaper. There are laws about
printing the truth. There are laws about libel. There is no law
that says a publisher has to print material just because an
employee has uncovered it."

Maryanne was mad as hell. "Why don't you go to another
paper? Why don't you go to the union?"

Paul smiled a lopsided, and slightly tipsy grin. "First, what shall I go to another publisher with? My publisher is an old bitch. She only printed seventy-five percent of my story. She left out all of my brilliant guesswork. You're going to see. It'll all come out my way in the end. Uh-uh, my dear. She's not even distorting the truth, though God knows she's doing violence to my perception. The facts are there. O'Neil was broke. He failed to disclose his financial problems, or if you want to believe him, that he took large sums of money from a friend. He has been the moving force behind a program whose principals have fled from charges of fraud and murder. Papers of questionable provenance and purpose have been found with his signature on them. He has resigned under fire to avoid embroiling the whole state in investigations during his term of office. It says all those things. All that's missing are the connective fibers that transform the cold facts into the reality. She doesn't want to bring the mayor into it. She doesn't want to stretch for the truth." He frowned. "It's her paper. She told her version of the facts."

"But she's just plain screwed you. What about the union?"

"Ah, yes, she has indeed. The union? To begin with, I'm not under the guild contract. I can be fired anytime she likes, within the provisions of my contract. I haven't talked to a lawyer, but I suppose she can just pay me off and not print anything I write. While I'm under contract, what I write belongs to her. And besides, toots, all the guild can do is make loud noises about work rules issues. They're damn glad there's still a paper left in this town to work for."

Maryanne took a long swig of her drink. "I think you're a hero. She's a bitch. Why don't you tell her to take a flying jump?" There comes a time, she thought, when a woman needs to hoist a few with her man.

Paul's smile turned into a laugh. "You're going to get cockeyed. I wouldn't give her the satisfaction, now. I'm just going to follow along after O'Neil's tumbrel till he gets to the guillotine. If he ever gets there. I'm not going out on a downer, with my tail between my legs. I only regret that I have not accomplished more. If O'Neil gets off, and Greene gets off, and Gaines and Hawkes get away clean, what the hell will the point of Malcolm Woodruff's death have been? He might as well have kept his mouth shut."

"You brought O'Neil down off his high horse, Paul."

His laughter was without mirth. "I'm sick over it. I caugh him with his hand in the till. It lacks dignity. And besides, he' going to be replaced by someone worse."

"Are you counting Mason out?" Maryanne asked.

"Who knows?" he shrugged. "I think he's an honest man and the future of an honest man in this town has sever limitations. Either you get your ass kicked by the youn, hoodlums or your pockets picked by the old hoodlums." Pau snatched the letter from the table. "And when you appeal t authority for help, this is what you get. And I quote,

Dear Sir,

We have received the package containing the remains of your General Electric Lather machine, and your letter of the sixth of April. Our technicians have examined the enclosed pieces and have concluded that your warranty has been voided. In an apparent effort to repair the machine, someone cracked the plastic watertight case and the foam ejector button. In so doing, the wiring which connects the heating element to the wall current was exposed. When touched by a wet object, or a wet hand, the wire short-circuited, causing the unit to pass the current along into the grounded object. As a result, though the plastic case is highly heat resistant and safe for normal use, it was subjected to abuse and stress beyond the specifications clearly stated in the owner's manual and on the packaging. We are therefore unable to comply with your request for payment under the limited warranty, and are absolved of all responsibility in the matter as a result of the tampering.

Very truly yours,
Ena T. Louis
Legal Department
General Electric Corporation

"How do you like them apples?" Paul asked. "They aren' interested that I almost got fried like an egg. They ar interested in avoiding responsibility, up to and includin, sending me another twelve ninety-nine lather machine. And on top of it, they have referred to me as a grounded object. Pelion upon Ossa! It's not their fault of course that somebody tried to kill me." He looked up at her. "It's getting so that it's not enough to just stay out of the subways. You can't even go to the bathroom, anymore."

"Are you going to take it to the police?"

"Sure," he said, smiling. "And it'll end up in the same file with the copy for my story. But, for good order's sake, it goes anyway."

Maryanne got up from her chair and plopped down on the couch next to Paul. "Are we ever going to win one?"

"We're going to keep on giving the fuckers our best shots, toots."

She rested her face against his arm and said, "You know what day it is, the day after tomorrow? I marked it on the calendar."

"Yup. It's That Thursday, again."

She hugged him, burying her face in his chest. "You're all beaten up. Do you want to skip it? If you go, I'll go with you."

He heaved a sigh. "I'd like to go. I'm actually looking forward to it. Maybe Jerry can give me some answers to all of this. God knows, he can't be any farther from reality than we are."

60

On the third day of his Caribbean trip, as scheduled, George Gaines walked back and forth on the sun-drenched sidewalk in front of the Bank of Cayman. He walked for two hours. Slowly, damps rings of perspiration expanded concentrically until his white shirt was transparent with moisture and sticking to his skin.

Finally, resigned to the fact that Marcus was not going to

show up and exasperated by the heat, he took his car and a beat a retreat to the West Indies Club. Once inside his apartment, he pulled off the sticky shirt and stood in front of the air conditioner till the sweat had evaporated. He made himself a white rum and tonic at the bar and sat down disconsolately in a cane chair overlooking the sparkling Caribbean.

Suddenly, a thought crept into his mind. Gaines made a conscious effort to suppress it, but it would not be still. He looked at his watch again. After all, Marcus was only a couple of hours late. Things happen. Planes don't come in on time.

He put the glass down with a bang on the table and grabbed the phone. He called Air Cayman and asked if the plane from St. Martin had come in, and whether there had been a Mr. Fred Combs on board.

"Yes, sir. The plane landed on schedule at eleven-fifteen this morning. I'm sorry, there were eight passengers. None of them was a Mr. Combs."

Gaines hung up the phone and stalked across the room to the closet. He pulled the gray Samsonite suitcase out and threw it on the bed. He had attached the key to the gold chain around his neck.

He pulled the chain loose and put the key in the lock. He turned this way and that, then realized that the key did not fit. He looked about for a heavy object. Unable to find one he took a shoe. He struck once, then twice. The lock didn't budge. With an animal growl Gaines took the leg from the night table and pounded on the lock, grunting and sweating, till the wood splintered and the lock sheared off.

His breath rattled in his throat as he threw up the lid of the suitcase and stared down into the neatly cut and rubber-banded packages of newspaper which lay there instead of the million and a half dollars he had believed that he was carrying. He pawed the packets wildly, throwing them this way and that around the room.

When he had done, his heavy breathing subsided. He straightened the mess methodically and went to the bathroom to shower. In a fresh change of clothing, he took the car and returned to the bank.

"I'd like to speak to Mr. Alfred Watley, please."

"May I ask your name, Sir?" the receptionist said.

Gaines looked across at her, sitting behind the desk. She

wore a piqué blouse and matching skirt. Her skin was a subtle reddish brown, a felicitous combination of Caucasian and African blood and Caribbean sun. Her eyes were hazel, flecked with gold.

"I am George Gaines."

"Mr. Gaines, I'm afraid that Mr. Watley has taken a leave of absence. His last day at the bank was yesterday."

"Indeed?" Gaines said pleasantly, looking frankly at the girl's bare arms, and the sinuous curve where her throat sloped into a firm bosom. "Who is taking his place?"

"Mr. Alfred Jocelyn."

"I know Mr. Jocelyn. Would you ask him if he has a moment?" Gaines smiled brightly and stepped back a bit, so that the receptionist could appreciate his stature. As he had expected, she looked him over. He caught her eye and smiled almost imperceptibly. The invitation was clear without being vulgar.

"I'll call him for you."

In a moment, Jocelyn appeared at the door, wiping his forehead with a large red bandana.

"Hello, Mr. Gaines. God! It's hot even in the air conditioning today. We've had this for the better part of a week. Please, come in. My office is cooler than the reception hall. Thank you, Janine," he said to the girl at the desk.

He asked Gaines to be seated and closed the door. "Oh, dear. This is better. Now, sir, what can I do for you?"

"I wanted to check the balance of the account. I might be moving into some investments."

"Of course. I'll have it for you in a moment. Do you have the number? As you know, we don't cross-key. It's a safety measure."

Gaines took a slip of paper from his wallet and read it off. "By the way, what has happened to Watley? I asked for him."

"Alfred? I think a touch of island fever. A few days ago, he said he'd like to take a little time off. It happens to all of us, now and then." He laughed. "I suppose you Americans would call it stir crazy. The beach and water are lovely, but there are moments when one needs a little more in the way of civilization."

He riffled through the IBM cards in the metal container on his desk, jotted another number, and cross-referenced with a large ledger. "Here we are. You are just above the minimum deposit for this kind of account, $309,000."

Gaines swallowed. Smiling, he said, "Three hundred thousand, you say?"

"Yes. Let's see. The last large transfer was made last week. Half a million."

"To where?"

Jocelyn looked up curiously. "I would assume you'd know, Mr. Gaines. It's not permitted to keep that information. It is against our operating instructions to record either destinations or sources of funds of our clients after there has been a confirmation of receipt. To be blunt, it makes it impossible to trace the funds in or out of our bank. It's for your own protection."

"Yes. I'm sure. I take it that you didn't arrange for this particular transfer yourself."

"No. It must have been Alfred. He'd remember, of course, But he's not here. I only handle this account in his absence." He put the ledger away in his desk drawer. "Is there anything else that I can do for you?"

"Yes. I'd like to close the account for the time being. Could you arrange for me to have the cash in American dollars tomorrow?"

"Of course, Mr. Gaines. I'd be glad to. Any particular denominations?"

"Fifties and hundreds, please."

Gaines hesitated long enough to pick up the slip of white paper that was pushed across the desk by the receptionist. He stuffed it into his pocket and did not look again until he was back in his apartment. Janine Waterford, 58 South Sound Road. Home after seven.

He mixed a drink and sat in front of the window and watched as the sun went down. He was not surprised at his calm. After that first terrible moment when he had seen the packets of newspaper, the situation had been clear. Marcus had switched bags on him and run off with three million dollars. Not satisfied with that, he had used his power of attorney over the account to transfer the bulk of the funds at the Bank of Cayman elsewhere. In an act of Christian charity, he had left his dear and trusted friend George Gaines about five percent of their net take from Uhuru Towers. Gaines sipped slowly from the glass. There was no point in losing his head.

It was a large world. But sooner, rather than later, he would find Marcus and discuss the matter with him at painstaking length. In the meantime, there was sufficient money to maintain him in comfort.

As a first step in his effort to find Marcus, Gaines paid a call on Janine Waterford. Her house was a quaint wooden Cayman cottage on a pine-lined street. She sat rocking on the porch. She had exchanged her work clothes for a turquoise tank top and a flowing, flowered skirt.

Gaines stepped out of the car and leaned on the hood, looking at her across the redolent frangipane. "I thought I might take you to dinner."

"Very thoughtful, Mr. Gaines." She walked toward him, turning slowly from side to side. When she was within arm's reach, she caught a faint feral smell about him that sent a shiver up her spine.

"You choose," he said, his voice deep and resonant. He could see that her nipples had hardened and protruded through the fragile cotton.

She looked at his eyes. They were like jewels in a stone idol. "Welly's."

"Hmm?"

The words caught in her throat. "We'll go to Welly's. Fresh fish. Locals only. It's up the other side of the sound."

Later, just before she fell into a dreamless and exhausted sleep, she thought to herself that she had expected him to hurt her. But he hadn't. He had that rubber tube. He had wrapped it around himself.

"I'll make you three times, before you make me once," he said. Then he picked her up like a rubber doll and impaled her. And while he hugged her to his chest, thrusting at her rhythmically with his hips, he held some vibrating device against her in the back, and she came three times like he'd said, all jelly and panting and crying out.

In the morning, she went to the bank a little later than usual. At coffee break, she asked her friend Alice where old Watley had gone, and when he'd be back. Off to England, she said. A couple of months. Maybe three.

That night, she made dinner at home for George Gaines, so they wouldn't waste any time at a restaurant.

The next day, George Gaines left Grand Cayman on an Air

Jamaica plane, and entered his ancestral land as Wynford Jennings. He took with him three hundred thousand dollars, and Janine's promise that when Watley returned, she'd drop the postcard he'd given her into the mail. It was addressed to Tyrone Giggis in New York.

61

At the end of April, the Manhattan district attorney went before a grand jury and secured an indictment of George Gaines and Marcus Garvey Hawkes for murder in the first degree of Mr. and Mrs. Malcolm Woodruff.

The case rested on the testimony of four sets of witnesses: members of the crew of the *S.S. Thomas Jefferson;* ticket agents of the President Line; the agents of the Federal Bureau of Investigation who had conducted a search, which included the continental United States and the Panama Canal Zone; and Jeff Jackson, who had told all of the confidences that a newspaperman is sworn not to reveal, because their source was beyond further harm. Hawkes's secretary testified tearfully about the dictation of the letters.

In addition, Dorothy Crewes, the Woodruffs' only child, had flown in from St. Louis with her husband to bear witness.

On the day before they were to return, the vestrymen of St. Phillip's Episcopal Church sponsored a memorial service for their reverent brother and his wife.

Jefferson Jackson couldn't remember the last time that he'd been on the inside of a church. Nonetheless, the words of response came back to him, and he spoke them fervently, because he felt the heavy weight of guilt on his soul. And though he tried, he was unable to shut out the vision of that frightened, pinched face staring at him fixedly in the back room at Martell's, nor the sound of the croaking voice, begging help and protection. Increasingly since the hearing, he'd taken to blotting them out with whisky. He'd hoped that coming to the service would help, but he was too far from the habit. He felt the need to make his confession where it would count.

At the end of the service, he made his way across the back of the church and waited for an eternity while mourning parishioners flowed by, paying their condolences to the bereaved.

When only the family and the priest were left, Jeff stepped out of the shadows and said, "Dorothy, may I speak to you?"

She turned, squinting, the last tears still wet on her cheeks.

"It's Jeff Jackson. I was a friend of your father's." He walked toward her. "I want to tell you how sorry I am."

"You're the reporter he spoke to, aren't you?"

"Yes. Yes, I am. I'm so sorry."

"Thank you." She wiped her eyes with a handkerchief and tugged at the sleeve of the young man next to her. "This is Bill Crewes, my husband."

Jeff shook his hand. "Hello. I'm sorry, Mr. Crewes."

The couple stood and waited, wondering what he wanted. Jeff shifted from foot to foot uncomfortably.

"I'd like to talk to you. I need to tell you what happened between your father and me. You'd have been proud," he rushed on. "You can keep it as a memory."

Dorothy Crewes looked at Jeff and saw pain in his eyes. "I'd like that, Mr. Jackson. Would you come up to the house with us? I guess you know it was broken into. I'm afraid it's still quite a mess."

Jeff rode in the back of the Creweses' car, then followed them up the steep brownstone steps to the door. For the first time since the Woodruffs had owned the house, the brass cover of the mail slot and the door knob were dulled with a film of oxidation. Inside, too, the first inroads of dust and tarnish had begun to appear.

Jeff looked about him in the hall, aghast. Gaines and Hawkes had been satisfied to leave the Woodruff home in perfect order on the night they had murdered its occupants. When they had felt threatened by Paul Curtin's increasing proximity to the truth, they had sent Giggis to find and destroy any papers which might even tangentially refer to Uhuru Towers or their dealings with suppliers or the government. He had approached his task with thoroughness and enthusiasm. Though the cruder evidence of the ransacking had been swept away, all of the cushions and backs of the overstuffed furniture bore marks of hasty repair where tape and patches covered ragged slashes. A long cabinet against the wall was gouged where the locks had been wrenched free.

Dorothy Crewes shook her head and said, "When I think of how Momma used to keep this house, I could cry. Come on in back with us, Mr. Jackson. We've tried to fix us the little room next to the kitchen. I guess it must have been a maid's room, once. Momma used it to do the ironing or to sew, sometimes. There's a Castro convertible in there. Whoever made this mess slashed the back and the cushions, but left the mattress alone. Vandals!" she said in disgust.

Jeff followed after her somberly. More likely it was Gaines and Hawkes, he thought, trying to make sure that there wasn't a shred of evidence. Who knows what they might have found? If it hadn't been for Bell finding the papers in Malcolm's office, the whole mess—O'Neil and Uhuru—might have been covered up.

"The police went over everything with a fine-tooth comb," Dorothy said, opening the door to the sewing room. "They even sifted the stuffing and tufting that had been thrown all over the place. I would have stayed upstairs in my room, but they broke the beds."

The room was small, but unlike the rest of the house, retained the aura of human habitation. The Crewes had put the curtains and the shades back up, and there was no trace of dust. An ancient television set, whose cabinet seemed outlandish for its small screen, stood opposite the couch on a rolling cart. There were three framed pictures grouped on its polished top.

"Coffee's on the stove. It'll be along in just a minute." She offered some cookies. "I made them myself. Momma taught me to always have baked goods in the house for guests."

"I didn't really know her."

"She was a nice lady, my momma." There was a quiver in her voice, and she disappeared again into the kitchen.

"Dorothy's taken this pretty well," Bill Crewes said. "But, I'd appreciate it if you'd make it kind of short, Mr. Jackson. On the inside, she's not so . . . well . . . together."

Embarrassed, Jeff moved to get up. "I don't want to upset her."

Dorothy walked in with a tray and cups and a china pot. "Please, Mr. Jackson. Sit down. I've gotten everything ready."

"I don't want to trouble you. I just wanted to pay my respects."

"You told me you wanted to talk about my daddy. I want to hear what you have to say. It'll be little enough comfort." She wiped at her cheek and poured the coffee.

Jeff looked at Bill Crewes for guidance. He nodded, and Jeff went on. "I'm not sure what I want to say. I want to tell you that your father was a brave man. He was afraid, but he spoke out." Jeff looked down at the floor. "I wanted to share my guilt. I can't help thinking that if he'd never come to me, he'd still be alive."

"It was him that came to you, Mr. Jackson," she said. "It was him that decided, wasn't it?"

"Yes."

"Then you'd have to say he knew what he was getting into, and he did it because he was a brave man, wouldn't you? I mean, he understood the danger, but he thought that this man Hawkes had to be stopped." Dorothy's eyes were wet, but there was a proud set to her jaw.

Jeff's vision of the terrified man softened. A small white lie. Perhaps we are all as brave as we can manage. A lot of people wouldn't have come at all. Jeff blurted, "I just feel sometimes like I killed him myself."

Dorothy Crewes turned to Jeff, "You didn't do no such thing. He was killed by those no-good bastards. You did what he asked you to do. You sell my father cheap if you don't think he believed in what he was doing." She crossed the room and patted Jeff's hand. "I'm grateful that you came up here to tell me what you did. He came to you on his own. He stuck out his neck for a principle. I'd rather have my father, but if I can't I'd like to remember him that way."

Jeff was grateful that the coffee burned his tongue. His sputtering gave him a chance to mask his emotions. "Thank you, Dorothy. I'd better get along, now. I'm sure you have things to do."

He got up from the chair to leave, then looked at the

television set. He stepped over to the stiff formal portraits. "This is your mother?"

"That's her. She was the real power around here. She made every slipcover and every drape. My father said she was the busiest person in the world."

Jeff started to turn away, then looked back, puzzled. "Aren't these pictures identical?"

"It's a good thing we have them. There isn't a whole picture or frame left in this house," Dorothy said with indignation. "Those creeps broke every one, ripped out the backs, smashed the glass." She threw her hands up in disgust.

"How'd they miss these?" Jeff asked.

"They weren't here," she replied. "These two, together in the leather frame, I've had for years. They were taken on their thirtieth anniversary. They always go on my dresser. Then Dad sent me the other one, frame and all. It arrived just about a week before . . ." the words caught in her throat. She took a breath and went on ". . . before they were supposed to leave. He must have forgotten about the other one."

"Did they visit you often?" Jeff asked, trying to control his voice.

"All the time. Christmas. Easter. We even spent our summer vacations together last year."

Jeff looked past her at the picture of her mother in its obviously costly silver frame.

"May I hold it?"

"Sure."

Jeff turned it around in his hands. Surreptitiously he began to knead the back of the frame with his fingertips. The stiff cardboard backing beneath the velour cover had no give at all.

"Dorothy, do you mind if I take out the picture?"

She looked at Bill, then back to Jeff. "But why?"

"Just curious," he said. "Why would your father send you an elaborately framed photograph of your mother that he'd seen on your dresser a dozen times?"

Uncomprehending, in a shaky voice Dorothy said, "Please don't tear it." She leaned against her husband's arm.

Jeff turned the frame over and tried to slip the back out. It was stuck fast. Gingerly, he worked it back and forth, trying to get a grip. He had to restrain himself from smashing the picture on the table.

Slowly, the backing slipped away from the top of the frame, until there was sufficient room to insert his fingertips. After two or three minutes of jockeying, the contents of the frame popped out and fell.

Jeff and the Crewes remained motionless, staring at the floor. The photograph had fluttered to the ground face up, amidst the shards of the shattered pane of glass. Next to the photo, the easel had landed upside down, two white envelopes taped to its face.

Jeff looked up at Dorothy. "May I?"

"Bill?" she asked her husband.

"Okay, Mr. Jackson."

Jeff peeled the envelopes away from the backing carefully, then opened them one at a time. The first contained a memorandum addressed "Eyes Only—Mayor Green." It was a recapitulation of materials and labor costs at Uhuru Towers. At the bottom there was a footnote; difference between actual and stated deliveries $1.76 million. It was dated the third week in January, ten days before the death of Lloyd Gibbons.

The second envelope contained a similar sheet dated one week before the disappearance of Malcolm Woodruff. The stated difference was $5.44 million.

"I'd like to use the phone," Jeff said, his mouth parched, his voice uncertain.

"What is it, Mr. Jackson?" Bill Crewes asked.

"Your father-in-law was a crafty man, Mr. Crewes. This was a kind of insurance policy. We're about to collect."

"I don't understand."

Jeff had already taken the wall phone in the kitchen from its hook. He tried Paul's apartment. The phone rang ten times before he gave up. "Damn," he said, slamming the receiver. He held his hand against his forehead, trying to remember Maryanne's number, or at least her last name. The number came to him first.

"Hello."

"Maryanne, this is Jeff Jackson. Is Paul there?"

"No, Jeff. I'm sorry. He took the kids to the park."

"Do you know where?"

"The zoo, I think."

"When will he be back?"

"Not until five or five-thirty."

"Damn it. I've got to talk to him."

"I wish I could help you."

"Listen, I'm going to look for him at the zoo. You tell him if he comes back before I get to him that I think that we have Chris Greene. Tell him that Malcolm left some papers that show he knew about Uhuru for months. Will you remember?"

"Count on it."

"I am. I'm going to look for him. If I can't find him, I'll come to you. Can I wait?"

"Of course."

"Thank you." He hung up the phone and turned back to the Crewes. "Look, I can see that you're confused. This is a last will and testament. We pushed the governor out of Albany. I think this is enough to unseat the mayor."

"I don't know," Bill Crewes said warily, looking at the papers that Jeff was waving. "What if somebody finds out we've got them?"

"By then, it'll be a matter of public record. You'll see this in a special edition of the *Advocate* tonight." He could sense the hesitation. "Listen, we can't waste time. Come with me. I'll tell you what we'll do." He motioned to them as he hurried down the corridor toward the front of the house. He took his coat from the bannister rail where he had left it. "Come on. We'll get it Xeroxed. You keep a copy."

Hesitatingly, they followed after him. They had three sets made at the drugstore around the corner on Lenox Avenue. Jeff kept the original and a copy, gave one to Bill Crewes, and stuck one into an envelope. He bought a stamp, addressed it to the Manhattan district attorney, and dumped it in the mailbox on the sidewalk.

As Jeff stood on the corner, impatiently trying to wave down a cab, Dorothy said, "I'm still not sure I understand."

"You just remember that your daddy was one smart old bird. Buy a copy of the *Advocate*. You'll read all about it."

The Creweses watched as he sprinted across the street, dodging cars, and hopped into a Checker.

62

The cab dropped Jeff off at Sixty-fourth and Fifth. He trotted down the steps past the old Arsenal Building trying to remember what he liked the best when he was a kid. Jeremy the clown was doing his al fresco show under the clock at the zoo entrance. Jeff scanned the crowd of awestruck faces, warmed by the spring sun. He unbuttoned his coat and threw it over his arm.

Casting a quick glance over the sea lion pool without luck, he made his way along the lion den and up the steps to the bears' den. A giant white polar bear lay half-submerged in her pool, her head and forepaws resting on the rocks.

Half an hour later, legs aching, Jeff finally caught up with Paul and his charges leaning on the stout steel railing that separates the public from the hippopotami and their offspring.

Jeff tapped Paul on the shoulder.

"Hey, what're you doing here? Petey, Alex, say hello to Mr. Jackson."

The children said hello.

"Hi, kids. I've been tracking you down. Maryanne told me you'd be here."

"We like the zoo. What's up?"

Wordlessly, Jeff handed Paul the envelopes.

He read them two or three times, leaning against the railing, ignoring the children as they squabbled around his legs.

When he finished, he said, "Hey, hold up, you guys. Let me have a litle quiet." He handed back the envelopes. "From where?"

Jeff told him.

Paul looked at his watch. "Three-thirty. We can make the final easy. I've got the car." He knelt. "Hey, can I buy a rain check?"

"You mean we can't stay?" Alexandra asked in a tremolo.

"Not today, honey. Can I be forgiven? It's very important. Pete?"

"Newspaper business?"

"Yes, sir."

"We can always watch cartoons," Petey consoled his sister.

Paul and Jeff dropped the kids off and watched them through the front door and onto the elevator.

Fifteen minutes later, they were headed to the editorial floor of the *Advocate*.

When he saw them moving purposefully across the floor in his direction, Max Fabrikant closed his eyes and shivered. He had been having premonitions of disaster all day.

"We've got to talk to you, Max," Paul said.

"Close the door."

Paul dropped the envelopes on his desk and explained their provenance.

Max whistled as he read. "Who supplants the mayor?" he asked idly in a low voice.

"City Council president," Jeff answered.

"Hmmm." Max handed the papers back. "Write it the way you see it, then bring it in. How long?"

"Ten, fifteen minutes," Paul replied.

"That'll give me enough time to set up Mrs. Parsons and Oscar. This ought to make quite an impression on her. She doesn't much like the taste of crow. You're a winner, m'boy. She can't talk her way around this one." Max allowed himself a smile. "This ought to go well with her personally signed endorsement of Chris Greene. I'm sure you'll get the Iron Cross. Get out of here and write."

He called Bornstein first. To his relief, he was both in and available. Max didn't want to walk this plank alone.

In exactly ten minutes Paul walked back into Max's office and dropped his copy on the desk.

Max raised his eyebrow over the byline; Paul Curtin and Jefferson Jackson.

"That's the way it ought to be, Max," Paul said, "and there's no doubt about it."

"If it gets run."

"What do you mean, if?"

Max spread his fingers on the desk and studied his nails. "Mrs. Parsons isn't sure she wants to go with the story."

"It must be my hearing aid," Paul said.

"Something about mysterious documents showing up from terested parties," Max said disjointedly. "A fine public rvant. Bright future." He slammed his palm on the desk and oked up, his face suffused with blood. "Fuck it. I don't know hat she means, Curtin. There's to be nothing on the computer ll she okays the copy personally."

"Okay, okay," Paul said, as Max pushed back from the desk nd kicked his chair away from him. "Let's not get all ustered. She's a newspaper person, just as thee and me."

"Right," Max said, shrugging on his jacket. "I am very lad that Oscar's going to be there. I might just say something at I shouldn't have."

"Why, Max, I didn't know you cared."

"Fuck you, too."

The ride up in the private elevator seemed to take forever. hey cooled their heels in the outer office under Madeleine's isapproving gaze for ten minutes before they were admitted. ornstein was already in the room, sitting at the round table nder the portrait of Samuel Parsons.

Melanie, her mouth pulled down in anger, reached out npatiently. "Let me have it, this big news break."

Paul handed her both the typescript and the envelopes ontaining the papers on Uhuru. She read them slowly and arefully.

"What do you take these to mean?" she asked.

"What they do mean," Paul replied. "It's obvious."

"Not to me." Her expression as flat, her eyes cold.

"I'll explain," Paul said patiently. This is not the time for a antrum. Maybe she doesn't see it as clearly as I do. Maybe I'm o close. "The mayor had someone on the inside of the roject who was feeding him information. It could have been art of his arrangement with Hawkes. In any case, the sword ut both ways. If the mayor had not been behind Hawkes and rotecting him from the routine checks that would be made on project like Uhuru, it was likely that some city employee ould have found out that something was going wrong. ranted, it might not have been everything. But surely, there ust have been little bits of paper among the billions that asked mbarrassing questions. Greene sanded over the little bumps. 'll bet Hawkes has trunks full of evidence stashed somewhere to prove that Greene knew all along what was going on. That what Hawkes had on Greene. Greene, of course, was in position to put Hawkes in the can. A marriage of unpleasar convenience."

"Why would the mayor involve himself in a mess lik that?" she asked.

"I had some trouble with that at first," Paul answered "Then, I thought it through. What were the likely chances c Greene's beating O'Neil? Slim and none. His only possibilit lay in taking up all of the ground on the left. He needed t present himself as a man of the people, with the smalles possible p. He needed the urban poor to come out and vote and to vote for him. I figured he needed a million plus comin out of New York to take the state. No one has ever said O'Ne was a bad politician. He knew where his weakness was an tried to shore it up. Uhuru Towers was a symbol of hi intentions in his third term. It was supposed to be a terr devoted to urban rehabilitation. He was saying that it was th ghetto's turn to catch a break. Greene needed a piece of tha action. He had no legitimate claim. After all, Uhuru wa planned by the O'Neil administration before Greene even too office. He simply cut a deal with Hawkes. If you look at wha Hawkes said in the papers, you'd think Uhuru was Greene idea. The other side of the deal is easy. If I shill for you, Ma Mayor, you look the other way for me."

"You can weave that wild story from these pieces c paper?" she asked, her voice heavy with sarcasm. "It sound like Doonesbury. How do we know where these papers com from? How do we know that they aren't just plants?"

"Are you suggesting that I might have dreamed this up? Paul asked, his hands clenched on the table.

She shrugged. "If the shoe fits. . . . It could have bee anyone trying to discredit Greene."

"Including the late Mr. and Mrs. Woodruff and thei children?" Paul asked. "It says right there in the story wher these papers were found."

"I can read well enough," she snapped. "I think that yo are so anxious to prove that you've been right on Mayo Greene, and I've been wrong, that anything is possible."

"What does that mean, Mrs. Parsons?" Max Fabrikant wa surprised at the tone of his own voice.

"It means that I don't like the story. There are too many unanswered questions."

"Print it. Add a few caveats, if you like," Max went on. "Let's say 'purported' more, or 'we suppose.'"

She turned an angry scowl at him. "Are you being flip with me, Max?"

"I am not. We have written evidence that the mayor of the city of New York was cognizant of one of the biggest swindles in history. Not only is the swindle a story, having forced the resignation of the governor of the state, but the fact is, that by knowing, the mayor, like O'Neil, may also be an accessory to multiple murders. Print it any way you like, but print it. We have the jump on everyone."

"These pieces of paper could have been pulled out of thin air by anyone who wanted to put the skids to Mayor Greene."

Paul started to speak, but it was Fabrikant who cut him off. "Mrs. Parsons, I interviewed Chris Greene after the first Uhuru story. He's shilled for Hawkes shamelessly in every way."

"I told you," she said, in a rising voice, "that he was duped."

"Then let's say he shouldn't be governor because he's stupid, instead of dishonest!" Paul interjected.

"That's not what I want." Her face had begun to color with anger. "How do we know those papers aren't fakes? How do we know that they weren't planted?"

"Look, Mrs. Parsons, you write the story your way," Paul said, reasonably. "Make all of the caveats that you want. But, print that we found documents—what'd you say, Max? purported?—purported to show that the mayor knew. Let him deny. Let him explain. Let there be an independent investigation."

"It still casts an aspersion."

"For God's sake," Paul shouted, losing his temper, "what we have here is a classic collusion between a public official and a crook. It was fine enough to hang Frank O'Neil's hide to the barn door."

"There's a big difference. O'Neil stole money. What's so unusual about political logrolling?" she replied.

"If you're rolling logs with murderers? Those two bastards

have been indicted for murder!'' The cords stood out on Paul's neck.

Fabrikant said, "I don't even know what this discussion is about. It's news. It'll be in every newspaper in New York. The D.A. will have to do something with the copies that Jeff sent to him. This is a goddamn newspaper. It's our job to print the news, whatever it is, like it or not.''

"This is my newspaper,'' Melanie said. "That's why we're discussing it. And we will print what I bloody well want to print. Do I have to remind you that we endorsed Greene again two days ago?''

"Things change. I voted for Nixon twice.''

"In character, Max,'' she sneered. "We'll print the story when the district attorney makes some comment.''

"You'll let the scoop go down the drain? You'll give him a chance to wriggle off the hook?'' Paul asked. "I'll bet you're going to tip him off yourself, instead of flaying the little bastard alive.''

"There has to be an answer,'' she said stubbornly.

"I have the answer,'' Paul said, rising from his chair. "It's your ball, your bat, your glove, and your fucking newspaper, and you can do whatever you want. I quit. You're worse than O'Neil and Greene. At least they expected something in return for their moral turpitude besides a sense of self-satisfaction. You're just a spoiled old lady, and you've gone round the bloody bend.'' He rose and stalked out of the office before she could reply.

She recovered quickly and turned her venom on Fabrikant. "Well, Max, I suppose you have someplace to go, too,'' she said spitefully.

"No, Mrs. Parsons,'' he said cheerfully, getting to his feet. "But if you don't print that story and the text of those two memoranda, you can stick your paper up your ass. See you around, Oscar.'' He picked up the papers that he was certain were the shards of his forty-year career and walked out of Melanie Parsons's office a free man.

Tears of rage brimmed at her eyes, and her face glowed under the pall of chalky powder. "Well,'' she screamed at Oscar, "what are you going to do, you lousy faggot?''

Oscar rose calmly from the chair that he had occupied beside her and slapped her across the cheek with his open hand. "That,'' he said. "And it's long overdue.''

He straightened his tie, and at his usual unhurried pace, walked out of her office and returned to his own.

As he knelt by the side of his desk, packing his personal effects into a cardboard box he had found in a closet, the phone rang.

He straightened and took the receiver from the cradle. "Bornstein."

It was Melanie. "Print the story any way you like. Have the car pulled around to the front door. I'm going home. I won't be taking calls from anyone. You do with the paper as you see fit until I tell you otherwise." He had no opportunity to argue. Before he could reply, she had hung up.

Max was packing his belongings to the curious stares of his colleagues when Bornstein sprinted uncharacteristically across the floor of the newsroom. Paul had already left for home, and it was an hour before they were able to get together again.

"She's left the paper in my hands," Bornstein said. "I'm going to have to lean on you almost entirely, Max. Outside of a little commonsense input, all I've done here is pay the bills."

"First things first," Max said. "We print the Greene story, don't we?"

"Of course," Bornstein replied.

"All of it?" Paul asked.

Bornstein smiled sardonically. "I think you'll find both Max and me more unbiased on the subject, Paul. Nonetheless, if you think I'm going to let you lose the paper to a libel suit, you're mistaken. You write the story. We'll submit it to counsel, then run it."

Paul covered his eyes with his hands and said, "Oh, God, here I go again."

In the end they printed the unvarnished truth. Papers had been discovered in the frame of Rose Woodruff's picture. They indicated that Christopher Greene had known that there were sizable discrepancies in Uhuru Towers' budget even before the death of Lloyd Gibbons. Additional documents suggested that the mayor had been kept abreast of the increase in the defalcation at least once, several months thereafter. No implications were made. Only two questions were asked. Why, if he was aware that there were funds being drained from the project, did Mayor Greene not call for an investigation? Why, in view of his knowledge did he give the interview to Max Fabrikant in which he publicly praised Marcus Hawkes?

There was a painful pause and the sound of scurrying both at City Hall and in the offices of various members of the Democratic heirarchy of New York State, as an attempt was made to present a unified front and to provide a sober reply.

Ducking the media for the remainder of the day, Greene held a press conference the following morning. He had not seen the Uhuru papers, of course, though he understood copies were in the hands of the district attorney. He could not recall seeing papers like those which were described.

Paul sat back and listened with amazement. Was he going to stonewall altogether? Paul smiled. He didn't think he could be surprised anymore.

Evidently, Greene had been otherwise advised. "While the exact details cited in these papers are not in my recollection, I am not surprised by them." He stood boldly against the lectern and pointed at the reporter who had posed the question to him. "Of course, I had some idea that things were not all roses at Uhuru Towers. Why didn't I call for an immediate investigation? Why didn't someone call for an immediate investigation of the Scottsboro Boys trial? Why didn't someone call for an immediate and ongoing investigation of three hundred years of slavery, oppression, and discrimination?"

As Greene's voice rose, Paul found himself rolling his eyes.

"If my failure to come down hard on the biggest opportunity blacks have ever had to rebuild their cities is construed as an act against the public interest, so be it. I stand ready to be punished. My view is that all good ideas don't pan out. Because a rotten apple shows up, that's not an indication for a wholesale attack on affirmative action!"

The district attorney's office was noncommittal about seeking an indictment. Democrats blustered about the rights of the little man. Republicans and Conservatives screamed for blood, or at least impeachment. Investigations of the housing departments of both the city and the state were proposed from both sides of the aisle in both houses of the state legislature.

Paul found that his reservoir of absolute moral conviction was depleting in the face of reality. Nothing was actually going to happen. Nothing was going to be done.

He paid a visit to Mack Bell, who had recovered admirably

from his brush with eternity. He had still a few pounds left to gain back, but seemed his vigorous self.

"I understand congratulations are in order, Mack."

"Is that the way you'd put it? Did the Romans congratulate the Christians on their way into the arena?"

"You're the new president of Hawkes Building."

"They made somebody the captain of the *Titanic*."

"Can you finish it?"

"I'm going to finish it. Don't ask me when. Don't ask me how much. I've stopped the hemorrhage. I'm getting some real help from the people at Burton. The community and the sponsors are being very understanding. Not that any of them have any fucking choice." He smiled broadly.

"And the investigators?"

"I told them. I told them all. Republicans, Democrats, white, black, yellow, and assorted. If you ever want this building to be finished, if you ever want any salvage value, you'll leave me be. So they're leaving me be."

"And if you start to steal?" Paul asked.

Bell smiled again. "There was a time when that would have offended me. No more. If I started to steal, no one would know until I was long gone."

Paul opened his palms in supplication. "So nothing changes."

"Only the name on the door. But you can always hope you're going to run into an honest sucker once in a while."

Paul had a cup of coffee with Don McCaig up at Urban Development. "Do you think Greene's going to get elected? Do you think that black people believe what he said?"

McCaig smiled. "Do you believe in the Easter Bunny? It's the Big City, my boy. Believe in Saint Augustine. Faith and good works. The Lord will provide. Just as long as you keep trying to do it yourself and keep your eyes on the thieves, the whores, and the politicians."

A month after the revelation of the Greene papers, Paul went to the modest midtown offices of George Allen Mason. He looked tired. The good-natured smile which Paul had come to expect had been distorted by the appearance of unfamiliar lines of worry that seemed to have implanted themselves permanently in his brow.

"I'm sorry, Paul. I'm going to have to rush you through, my calendar is a nightmare."

"Bad day today?"

"Every day. Shoot. What's on your mind?"

"The polls seem to have you even with Greene, now. They've done quite a seesaw. First, you seemed to have no chance when you got the Republican nomination after O'Neil quit. Then, you skyrocketed when those papers about Uhuru were found in Woodruff's picture frame. Now it looks like a standoff. You've been pretty reticent in using the Hawkes-Gaines connection and Uhuru on Greene. I don't understand why. It seems like your strongest card."

Mason sighed and leaned back in the chair. "I can't claim the virtues of a novice at this, Paul. I ran for Congress and served a term. Somehow, I don't think that even with that training I was quite prepared for what my candidacy would impose on me. Let's say—off the record, of course—that I am imbued with a new sense of reality. In New York, politics is more the art of the impossible. I think you found out that there is an enormous gulf between what you know—as an absolute fact—and what you can prove, and therefore state as a fact in public. Let's say that I am finding out the difference between what I believe ought to be done, what I hope can be done, and finally the bottom line. In New York there is a ratio in inverse proportion: the farther dreams are from reality, the closer good comes to evil. In the end it's hard to tell the difference. If I go after Greene because he wants good housing for the urban poor— even at any price—what am I standing up for?" He frowned and shook his head. "I don't know either."

"Are you going to beat him, George?"

"I am certainly going to give it my best shot. Now get out of here. I have two Very Important People coming to see me."

"Dare I ask?"

"Sure. Wallace Harley Vance wants to talk to me about Uhuru Towers. I'm not sure I know exactly why, but I can't imagine telling him I'm too busy. And, this is another fellow I've never met. He's a labor leader from upstate. His name is Willy Albert. He wants to talk about jobs in Erie County."

Paul walked out of his office finally convinced that there are no answers to the big questions.

63

Alfred Watley put his feet up on the cool white stucco of his porch balustrade and sipped at his gin and tonic. He had been back from England for a week, and the strengthening sun of mid-June had quickly replenished the island tan which had faded during his months in Europe.

He wiggled his toes in his sandals. Quite a contrast from the spring skiing he had enjoyed at St. Moritz. He thought fondly of fat little Mr. Hawkes. After selling the diamonds he had received from him in a private transaction in Zurich, Watley had been able to deposit more than $300,000 in his numbered account at the Kreditanstalt.

He would have preferred one of the big private banks, Vontobel or Sarasin, for their better investment services, but he believed himself even more anonymous at Swiss Crédit. He had even toyed with the idea of opening an account for himself at the Cayman branch of the Royal Bank of Canada. But after considering the level of his own discretion, he had decided to avoid his confreres.

He was pleased to be at home. When Mr. Hawkes had made his last payment, and the last of the money had been transferred according to his instructions, first to another Cayman bank, and finally to South America, he had recommended that Watley take a long vacation at his expense and leave his colleagues to deal with Mr. Gaines. Never one to look a gift horse in the mouth, Watley had gratefully accepted both the diamonds and the tickets.

He rested against the wide, rattan chair back and opened the day-old *New York Times* that was delivered to his house every morning. He had begun to follow the gubernatorial race in New York with some amusement. It seemed that the incumbent had been ridden out of office because of his connection with

crooked builders. The lieutenant governor, who held the office
pro-tem, was not running again. The *Times* was torn between
the new, Republican standard-bearer, whose politics they did
not like, and the mayor of the city, whose morality they seemed
to question as a result of his ties to the same builders who had
done in the governor. Only in New York, Watley thought
cheerfully.

The editorial page dwelt on the constant backing and filling
of Mayor Greene's campaign and the seeming lethargy of the
investigations into the connections of O'Neil and Greene with
Uhuru. Farther down the page, the editors took violent
exception with the commitment of Mr. Mason to restore the
death penalty for murder. A pox on both your houses, they
seemed to say.

He put the paper down and drained his glass. As he looked
up at the rising moon, an arm reached over the balcony,
encircled his neck, and pulled him silently into the bushes.

He wanted to yell, but it was all he could do to keep from
gagging on the cold metal of the revolver barrel which had
been forced into his mouth.

Responding to grunted commands and rough pushing at the
hands of his assailant, Alfred Watley turned onto his stomach
and submitted to a gag and blindfold. His hands were tied
securely behind him. There was a moment's wait after he was
trussed, then his captor pulled him to his feet and frog marched
him rapidly forward.

After a moment, Watley almost stumbled as his feet changed
without warning from the firm earth of the roadside to the sand
of the beach. He could hear the surf getting nearer. When the
spray was in his face, his captor grabbed him by the collar,
forcing him to his knees in the water. Suddenly, he felt himself
lifted by the armpits, and thrown unceremoniously and
painfully into the bottom of a boat.

A motor roared, and he was pushed against the side of the
boat as the propeller bit. Ten minutes later, the noise subsided.

Watley was pulled to his feet, and the blindfold, bonds, and
gag were removed. Strong fingers locked into his hair and
turned his eyes toward the beach. They were a mile or so
offshore.

A lilting Jamaican voice asked, "Where did you send Mr.
Gaines's money, Mr. Watley?"

The voice was so reasonable in its tone that Watley was heartened and spoke sharply. "What the hell is this? Gaines? Money? Do you realize that you're kidnapping a vice-president of the Bank of Cayman? I insist that you release me immediately."

"Oh, dear, Mr. Watley," the voice said. "I fear that we misunderstand each other."

Watley felt his captor turn away from him briefly, then he heard a grunt as the man expelled air from his lungs while simultaneously driving his knuckles into Watley's back an inch above his belt, in the line of his hip pocket.

Watley vomited and wet his pants at the same time.

"A kidney bruise like that might not even show on the surface. But, too many shocks like that, and you have kidney failure. Where did you send the money that was in the joint account for Gaines and Hawkes?" The Jamaican voice read him the number. "Do you remember the cipher? What bank did you send it to? In what name?"

Watley's back hurt a great deal, but he reasoned that if he endured and said nothing, or told him he knew nothing, at least he would stay alive. If he could hold out till the fishing boats came out at four in the morning, he'd be able to call for help. If he told all, he'd be dead. When the fist hit him in the back a second time, he was expecting it. All the same, his breath was taken away. He couldn't even scream.

"I don't think that you understand. Fast or slow, you will tell me."

Watley lay on his side, breathing shallowly to avoid disturbing the ragged nerve endings that radiated from his bruises.

"Oh, Mr. Watley," the voice behind him said, sadly, "I do fear that you don't appreciate my sincerity." It was almost singsong.

A hand hoisted Watley by the scruff of his neck till he was upright. He felt himself pushed against the coaming. His left arm was pulled out straight from his body. Then the hand deftly cut off his thumb.

Watley's scream was drowned in the water that rushed into his mouth as he was thrown overboard. He was held by the collar of his shirt. When the bubbles thinned sufficiently to cast doubt on his respiration, he was hauled to the surface.

Watley sobbed and panted and choked all at once.

"Oh, Mr. Watley. Please tell me which bank you sent the money to. You're bleeding into the water. I can already see a fin or two."

Watley panicked and tried to grab the gunwale, banging the stump of his thumb. He cried out weakly, then sobbed again. He could feel the swishing as the powerful tail fins of the sharks roiled the water two dozen feet away.

"Banco Auxiliar, in São Paulo, Brazil. The Avenida Paulista branch."

"What name?"

The name escaped him. He shrieked as he felt the sandpaper skin brush against his own. A small gray shark, not more than three feet long, had taken a pass at his right leg, just breaking the skin.

"Willis. Frederic Willis." His head was pulled under as the aggressive little shark took better hold and shook loose a three-inch chunk of calf muscle.

"Out," Watley gargled. "Out."

Giggis let him go as he saw a dorsal fin a foot higher than the others surface and streak across the water. There was a thudding sound as the blue shark, which weighed five hundred pounds, slammed his open mouth into Watley's torso at fifteen knots.

When the boiling water had calmed, Giggis rode the boat into the dock, and tied up where it had been before he came. As an afterthought, Giggis picked the thumb up off the deck and threw it to the small fish that hung around the pilings. He watched them for a moment, then walked off to his hotel.

He had already landed at Sir Donald Sangster Airport near Montego Bay and drifted off into Jamaica's Blue Mountains when it was discovered that Alfred Watley was missing.

64

Paul sat and waited for Oscar Bornstein in the anteroom of Melanie Parsons's old office. He shuffled the copy back and forth in his hands.

Bornstein stuck his head out of the office door and said, "Come on in, Paul. I'm sorry I kept you cooling your heels."

Paul shrugged. "I'm sure it wasn't planned, Oscar." The first-name basis had been Bornstein's idea. As Paul slumped in the chair opposite him, he remarked to himself that Oscar had lost fifteen or twenty pounds since he'd taken over the paper. Those suntanned and smooth cheeks were gaunt, the eyes were hollow. Some of the graying hair was out of place. You're aging, Oscar old buddy, Paul thought.

"What have you got?"

"I had a talk with Max. We wanted to know if you want to say anything in an editorial. First, Arthur Harris and Co., the accountants for Burton Industries, say that it will take at least a year to straighten out the books of Hawkes Building. As a result, Burton is going to have to establish a reserve for the entire seventy-five million dollars of their loan and bonding guarantees. The comptroller has stated that the state of New York is willing to wait for the results to be produced by Arthur Harris to avoid duplication and further public expense, not to mention the strain on his manpower."

"What does that mean?"

"That the denouement of the Uhuru swindle is two or three years away." Paul wiped his forehead with the back of his hand. "A little birdie told me that Judge Tolbert had a meeting in chambers today. He met with the attorney general and Robert E. Lee Wampler, Governor O'Neil's counsel."

"Plea bargaining?"

"Optimist," Paul said sardonically. "Charge dropping. I

don't think that they're going to go for an indictment of O'Neil on conspiracy charges."

Bornstein looked at the ceiling and held his nose.

"It is my understanding that all parties concerned—the D.A., the attorney general, the opposition candidate, and the lieutenant governor—are agreed that a trial of Frank O'Neil will serve no purpose at all, except to create an atmosphere of public mistrust."

"And George Mason?"

"He was very frank. He said, off the record, of course, 'What do you want me to do? I'm not elected, yet. I can scream that it stinks to high heaven. That will result in the loss of my grass roots support in the Republican party. Then, you can call Greene governor. What can I do?' That's what he said." Paul smiled. "What can he do? He can just go along."

"So Greene gets off because they can't check the books. O'Neil gets off for the same reason. The only two people who can testify to their crimes are well and truly gone—Gaines and Hawkes."

"That's it in a nutshell, Oscar." Paul threw another piece of typescript under his nose. "I thought you might want to see this. Maybe Melanie would like to send flowers."

Bornstein read aloud.

Former Governor Francis X. M. O'Neil announced today that he would become president of Dal Porto Electric Corporation, effective September 1. Dal Porto, a privately held company, is one of the largest manufacturers of water purification equipment in the United States, with major undertakings in projects in Africa, Asia, and the Middle East. It has been rumored that Governor O'Neil would also soon announce his engagement to Adrienne Dal Porto, who is vice-chairman of the concern, and coowner, together with her brother Victor. The board of directors of Dal Porto Electric has released a statement which says in part that, "Governor O'Neil's long record of public service and negotiations at the highest levels in multibillion-dollar projects will add a dimension to our company in dealing with government-sponsored projects throughout the world." Governor O'Neil and Mrs. Dal Porto, whose previous husband, Alfredo Cirillio, died several years ago, have been constant companions since the governor resigned his post as a result of the investigation of the Uhuru Towers housing project.

"You want to say something, Oscar?"

"What's to say, Paul? The man's entitled to get work. He's entitled to get married."

"I hear she's worth two hundred mil."

"God bless him."

Paul dropped the rest of his papers on the desk and said, "No, Oscar. Goddamn him to hell. I quit, Oscar." Paul held up his hand to forestall the protest. "I mean it. I've had it. I quit. Frank O'Neil ran out of money. It happens to the best of us. He refilled his treasury by taking from a pair of murderers and cheats. But his buddies are covering up for him. He's been forced out of office into a half-a-million-dollar-a-year job and a two-hundred-million-dollar, silk-sheet marriage."

"He can't abuse a public trust he no longer has. You shouldn't quit. You've accomplished a lot."

Paul got to his feet, smiling. "Bullshit, Oscar. I've made a couple of waves. Nobody's going to jail. Nobody's going to get his nose out of joint. It's all going to end up under the rug, because nobody wants to get anybody mad. Next time, it could be me. And besides, what's twenty dead niggers? Oscar, I quit. You want to do me a favor?"

"Sure."

"Fire me, and let me collect unemployment. I ought to be at least as well off as O'Neil."

"I'm going to give you the one-year bonus that Melanie authorized. That much I can do. You are serious, aren't you? What are you going to do? Leave town?"

"I thought about that. I am not. Fuck 'em. Fuck 'em all. I'll be a son of a bitch if I'm going to get ridden out on a rail. I'm going to marry my lady, move into her rent-controlled apartment, write a book about all this shit, and see if I can find an agent smart enough to sell it."

Paul was amazed at how long it took to clean out the two drawers he occupied in his desk. He didn't bother to say goodbye. He'd be speaking to the people he cared about later anyway. He waited for a while, whistling, for the elevator to come up. He looked at the forlorn Linotype machine, tilted crazily in the corner against the wall. He felt a certain kinship. Still in working order, but no longer practical for the trade.

He threw the box in the back of the car, then made two stops on his way home. He parked in front of Maryanne's apartment and dropped the press card on the visor. He'd have to ask Oscar if he'd let him keep that little privilege.

He rang the bell. After a moment, she appeared at the door. "Yes," she said.

"It's me."

"Why didn't you use your key, dodo?" She licked her fingers. "I'm full of cake." She stepped back and looked him over. "Okay, what is it?"

"You remember you said that you'd follow me to Wyoming?"

"Yes."

"Would you do that?"

"Of course."

"I'll make you a deal." He whipped a bunch of roses and a bottle of Dom Perignon from behind his back. "If you marry me within the next two weeks, I can get rid of my apartment before the end of the month, move in here, and live off your earnings. I just quit my job."

"What are we going to do?"

"I have a year's severance and a book in my head. If Frank O'Neil can rise from his own ashes, so can I." He held out the flowers and the wine. "Well?"

"I thought you'd never ask."

65

As George Gaines rode the plane from Caracas, whence he had arrived as Wynford Jennings, he read in the *New York Times* that Kurt Englander had resigned as president and chief executive officer of Burton Industries for personal reasons. He was to be replaced as president by John Holderness, executive vice-president for building products. The function of chief executive officer had been delegated to Wallace Harley Vance III, who had also been elected chairman of the board. Gaines ordered another martini.

He had taken the Varig flight direct to São Paulo, landing at Congonhas airport, built on a cut-down hill in the middle of São Paulo's twelve million inhabitants.

Gaines was surprised to find a sharp cold wind funneling through the corridors of the terminal in the midst of a topsy-turvy July winter season.

A lanky mulatto in a gray chauffeur's uniform, holding a small sign bearing the name Jennings, waited at curbside next to a black Ford. The driver spoke no English, but had been well instructed. He drove Gaines up the expressway past the Bandereinte Monument and into the old part of Brazil's largest city, delivering him to the Hilton Hotel.

Gaines's trained eye spotted groups of flashily dressed prostitutes and transvestites patrolling the curb. He registered, went to his room, ordered a sandwich and a beer, watched the incomprehensible Portuguese television, and went to sleep.

At eight in the morning, his phone rang.

"Mr. Jennings, I am Alberto Fonseca. I have been asked to meet you here. Your friend is outside in the car."

"I'll be down in half an hour."

Gaines slipped on a sweater over his shirt to compensate for the temperature.

The car was the same as the night before, the driver stolid and wordless in the front seat. Fonseca was a fragile, light-skinned Portuguese in his early fifties. Tyrone Giggis sat next to the driver in the front seat.

Fonseca shook hands with Gaines. He had not known what to expect. The arrangements had been impeccable. He had been paid in dollars in advance. It was only by considerable effort that he had trained himself to stop looking at Tyrone Giggis's long sausage curls and wild eyes.

"You understand what we want?"

"Yes, señor, perfectly. This man in the pictures you have given me is a black American. He goes under the name of Frederic Willis. He has an account at the Banco Auxiliar."

Fonseca said a few words to the driver in Portuguese, then went on in English. "You will be surprised I think, to see it."

The car wound through the business section of São Paulo, past the Rua Major Sertorio, full of commercial life in the day and whores after dark, then under the elevated highway on Amiral Gurgel, past the district of Brigaderio, and onto the ten-lane expanse of the Avenida Paulista, São Paulo's financial hub. Giant modern buildings soared on every block, interspersed from time to time by some relic of Brazil's colonial era or of its imperial past.

With a grinding of gears, and a lurch, the driver made a sweeping illegal turn which left them at the curb of a side street next to a superb example of the colonial style. The walls of the colonnaded three-story mansion were ocher and white, and inlaid with painted azulejos, distinctive tiles which taken together created a landscape.

"This is the old Bonfiglioli palace. As they started to modernize here, instead of tearing it down and replacing it with another skyscraper, the family decided to make it a branch of their bank. It was once the headquarters, but now, they have outgrown it."

"Have you made any inquiries?" Gaines asked Fonseca.

"I could have shown the manager the picture. He is a friend of mine. But he was on vacation for the past three weeks. I don't know anyone else in there. It is illegal for a private investigator to pry at a bank, Mr. Gaines. I couldn't take the chance. I can tell you that the man in the picture hasn't been near this bank between eight-thirty in the morning and six o'clock in the evening over the past two weeks." He pulled the handle on the door to get out. "That's why I suggested you come down now. Luiz Freddy is back. I can ask him now."

Fonseca was back in twenty minutes. "I hope you will not be displeased. I had to make a small gift—two hundred dollars."

"Never mind about that," Gaines said impatiently. "What does he say about Willis?"

"He opened the account over a year ago. There have been some substantial transfers. About four months ago, he showed up in person again and deposited a large sum of American dollars. Luiz Freddy was able to get him a good rate in the parallel market. Luiz Freddy says he has more than five million dollars."

"I know that," Gaines said. "But does he have an address?"

"No, only a box number."

"Shit," Gaines said, between his teeth.

"But," Fonseca said brightly, "he always comes in on the third Friday of the month."

"The day after tomorrow," Gaines said.

"Exactly."

Giggis and Gaines sat in the back of the Ford across the street from the Banco Auxiliar from eight o'clock on Friday morning, scrutinizing each passerby with lightweight binoculars.

At half past eleven, an unobtrusive Volkswagen pulled up to the Avenida Paulista side of the bank. A bulky black man in livery got out from the driver's side and held open the rear door.

Gaines adjusted his binoculars carefully. He had lost thirty, perhaps forty pounds. And to go with the new, smaller waistline, there was a moustache and a goatee. But it was Marcus Garvey Hawkes.

Gaines put his hand into his pocket and withdrew an envelope. He handed it to Fonseca. "Thank you, Mr. Fonseca. You can go now."

Fonseca looked briefly at the bills in the envelope. "Thank you. You are very generous. You are sure you don't need us?"

"If we do, we know where to find you. If you don't hear from us further, you'll find the car parked on the side street next to the Hilton. I'll leave the key with the porter."

Fonseca said a few words to the driver, who slipped out of his seat, and followed him down the avenue. Giggis slid over behind the wheel.

"Now, you understand that we can't afford to lose him, don't you, Tyrone?"

"I got it."

It seemed to Gaines that when Hawkes reappeared ten minutes later, he looked around warily before he got into the car. Gaines wondered if Luiz Freddy, the bank manager, might have tipped him off. Hawkes climbed into his car and pulled away.

The Volkswagen made a wide turn at the light and headed west across the city through the burgeoning noontime traffic. Giggis was hard pressed to keep it within sight. At the end of the broad avenue, Hawkes's car began to weave back and forth through a maze of residential streets with walled gardens and impressive stucco houses.

In another moment, they burst free into a wide plaza which fronted the São Paulo River, a concrete canal with a low ebb of filthy water into which open sewers drained untreated.

Across the river, the Jockey Club stood in its park, flags fluttering. Once it was behind them, the cover of the city's bustle was gone, and the two cars moved alone, half a dozen lengths apart through the contradictions and anachronisms of São Paulo's suburbs.

As the cars rolled through the quiet streets of Santa Amaro, where high walls excluded the public from great wealth, Hawkes looked up into the rearview mirror. His eyes bulged in his head. Giggis's dreadlocks flew like banners in the breeze.

"Mais rapido. Precize perder o carro atras de nos," Hawkes said, in halting Portuguese.

The driver checked the mirror and stepped on the gas. At the next corner, he feinted a right turn, then spun the car to the left down a hill.

Giggis, in the heavier Ford, rolled beyond the intersection and was forced to back up to continue his pursuit. The substantial difference in power put the Volks back in view in a minute.

With no idea of where he was, or where he was going, Giggis stayed glued to the tail of Hawkes's car as it wound through streets of magnificent homes on the crest of Morumbi, and then slipped over the side into São Paulo's most disgraceful slum at its feet.

In desperation, at Hawkes's prodding, the driver swung up the hill into the forested park that surrounds the Butantan Institute of Herpetology.

"Jesus Christ," Hawkes yelled, wide-eyed. The road came to a dead end at the fence a hundred yards in front of them. *"No fim!"* he told the driver. "Go to the end."

The Volkswagen skidded on the gravel when the driver hit the brakes in front of the gate. Hawkes jumped out of the car and sprinted toward the fence. A wooden sign hung from a chain. The Institute would be closed from twelve until two. The next snake milking show would be at three o'clock.

Hawkes lifted his short legs over the chain and began to run across the broad lawn toward the gray, stone administration building.

Tyrone Giggis and Gaines slid to a halt next to the Volks. Hawkes's driver stared at them for a moment, undecided, until he saw Giggis draw the 9 mm Browning automatic from his waistband. The driver stepped on the gas, and the little car spun crazily across the gravel until the rear wheels hit the turf border, giving the car some traction. Then he sped away without a backward glance.

Hawkes dashed to the front door of the building, grabbed the handle, and pulled. Then he pulled again. He put a foot against the doorsill and pulled with all his weight, but still the lock wouldn't budge. He could hear Gaines behind him.

"Don't kill the motherfucker, Tyrone. We need him alive. Shoot his fucking kneecaps."

With a little cry of desperation, Hawkes scurried down the walk and around the side of the building. Open lawns spread to the top of the hills on either side. Directly behind the building, to Hawkes's front, a park a couple of hundred yards in depth, dotted with concrete walls that enclosed pens, stretched to a thick tangle of woods. He ran as fast as he could. There, he might lose them.

His heart pounded in his chest. He could hear the footsteps behind him. Gaines stretched his long legs, sweat streaming down his face despite the cold.

"I'll catch you, nigger. Then, you'll fry."

Hawkes looked over his shoulder. He could see Gaines's face, distorted by hate and physical effort, twenty yards behind him. In panic, he pulled the .25 caliber pistol from his jacket pocket. Unseeing, he slammed into the hip-high wrought iron fence in front of him and pitched headlong onto the grassy ground of the pit four feet below. The enclosure was a hundred feet long and forty feet wide, with no distinguishing features on its overgrown lawn except for two cairns of rock ten square feet at its center. Hawkes had been fortunate, in falling forward he had just cleared a three-foot-wide moat filled with water that circled the glass-smooth interior wall of the pit.

Stunned and out of breath he pushed himself to his hands and knees and began to move toward the far side of the enclosure. He heard the scraping of Gaines's shoes on the concrete as he climbed over the wall after him. Hawkes had the

presence of mind to turn on his back and raise his gun, just as
Gaines jumped the moat and hit the turf to come for him.

The little gun jumped in Hawkes's hand as he emptied it.

Half of the load, four bullets, caught Gaines in the chest,
shoulder, and neck. He dropped heavily to the damp ground.
Gaines pushed himself to his knees. He touched his sweater
above his breast pocket. His hand was sticky. He sat for a
moment, gathering his wits. He realized that he had been
wounded, but the pain was not so awful as others he had felt.
No bone, nor organ, nor major blood vessel had been hit. The
.25 caliber bullets were tiny, and he was strong.

He looked across the twenty-five feet separating him from
Marcus, who lay propped up on one elbow, pointing at him
with the empty little gun, and clicking futilely over and over
against the empty chamber. George Gaines smiled.

Hawkes let the gun fall from his hand and turned to flee.
Gaines began to rise to follow. Hawkes stopped dead still in his
tracks.

Marcus Hawkes had completely forgotten Gaines. He knelt
balanced, transfixed, looking into the obsidian eyes of the
largest poisonous snake in South America. He willed himself
to be still, but his courage and strength failed him. His hand
buckled. His eyes were not quick enough to see the bushmaster
coil its twelve-foot black body, the thickness of his forearm,
and strike angrily into his thigh. He screamed in mortal agony,
lurched a foot or two, then toppled, and lay still.

Gaines, who had been hidden from the snake by Hawkes's
body, got to his feet and walked to him. "Ain't no use playing
dead now, nigger. Ain't nobody going to help you." He looked
down into Hawkes's face and realized that, though his eyes
were open, he could not see.

A frog hopped across the grass at Gaines's feet. In
annoyance, he kicked out at the little amphibian with the tip of
his shoe.

The ten-foot-long mate of the snake that had killed Hawkes
saw the flash of the shining shoe. She coiled a third of her
length and struck, mouth agape. Her fangs sank a half inch
through the cloth of George Gaines's slacks and into his calf.
Reflexively, her poison sacks compressed and unloaded the
alkaline liquid that her glands produced.

Gaines kicked out again. The snake slithered away through

the grass, chasing her dinner. The poison began to spread immediately, attacking the neural pathways. Gaines staggered to the fence, and with his last ounce of strength, dragged himself to the top of the concrete wall. Then he fell against the iron fence, stumbled forward onto the walk, and rolled over on his back. In thirty seconds, the poison had paralyzed his autonomic nervous system, his breathing stopped, and he was dead.

Giggis saw the snake slither away from Hawkes's corpse, and in a twinkling, trap and devour the frog. After a moment of indecision, he bent over and stripped his erstwhile employer of all of his valuables and identification, and the keys to his hotel room. It would be a couple of hours before someone returned to the empty Institute grounds. Without papers, it might take hours, or even days, to identify him.

Giggis stopped at the Hilton and went through Gaines's possessions with practiced skill. He pocketed fifty thousand in cash and a small bag of trifles. He took the laundry bag from the bathroom and stuffed it with a few shirts and a sweater he had always admired. He tried on a pair of alligator shoes, but they didn't fit.

He went downstairs and dropped the key into the mail slot at the concierge's desk and returned to his car. He went over it carefully to make sure that there was no trace of identification which could connect it to him or Gaines. He left the keys for Fonseca as promised, then walked the four blocks up the avenue to the small hotel where he had stayed. On his way, he casually threw his gun and Gaines's down a storm sewer drain.

Once inside of the room, he packed his few possessions. To hide the cash, he carefully removed the plastic liner from the bottom of his toilet kit and slid the envelope in the space. He replaced his shaving equipment, cologne, and toothbrush and put it in the suitcase.

He sat at his desk for a moment and removed the chamois pouch he had found in Gaines's room. It was an odd grab bag of things. There were a couple of old gold coins, two men's rings with large stones in them, two loose diamonds in tissue paper, and a small, round gold pin with a few colored stones on it. Giggis shrugged, and put the bag in his pocket. Nothing anybody could say about that. Just personal jewelry. There wouldn't be any body search anyway.

He paid the bill and took a taxi to Congonhas. Trying to remain unobtrusive, Giggis sat down on the bench in front of the board that listed the day's departures. He had not yet had a chance to collect his thoughts and decide what his next step would be. He had twenty thousand bucks stashed away under a floorboard in his mountain shack in Jamaica. He'd earned them the hard way with Gaines. He even had eight grand legit in the Dime Savings Bank in Brooklyn. With the fifty thousand in his pocket, he was in a position to make a substantial score in ganja. He knew where Gaines's whores were. Now, instead of running them for a small commission for Gaines, he'd be running them for his own account. He thought wistfully about the big dough that would sit and rot in the Banco Auxiliar. Tough titty. Life is like that.

He looked up at the board. His best bet was to get to Rio. He could probably go on to Kingston from there.

The information booth directed him to the Ponte Aerea which serves the two-hundred-fifty mile corridor with flights every half hour from dawn till dusk. He checked his bag, bought a ticket, and waited for ten minutes until the aged Electra was loaded. It was five o'clock when he arrived at Santos Dumont, hanging like a pendant into the jewel-blue water of Guanabana Bay.

Because of rush hour, it was seven o'clock before he was able to get to Rio International. Giggis's heart had begun to beat a little faster. So far, so good. There should be no problem in getting out this evening. Another twenty-four hours. . . . Even with his care in effacing evidence of his presence, one never knew.

There were a half-dozen flights still scheduled out. One went to Japan, two to Paris and London. There were two flights to New York, Varig and Pan Am, and Varig to Miami.

He walked to the Varig counter and asked for a ticket to Miami.

"You have a reservation to Miami?"

"No."

"Sorry, fully booked."

"Even first class?"

"Especially first class," the agent replied.

"I gotta get home, man."

"I'm sorry. There is nothing."

New York was the last place Giggis wanted to go. He looked up at the clock. Other people were making impatient noises behind him.

"How about I go by way of New York?"

"I'm sorry, sir. That's booked, too." Looking at Giggis's crestfallen face, the agent said, "You might try Pan Am."

Giggis dog-trotted the length of the terminal to the Pan Am desk and waited, tapping his foot, for the line to pass. Suddenly, he had begun to take note of the numerous policemen in the airport lobby.

Finally, Giggis got to the agent. "You got room for one more to New York?"

"Tonight?" She poked at the buttons on her computer. "Yes. But, I don't think that you're going to be on time."

"Hey man," Giggis whined, looking at Gaines's Rolex watch, "we got another twenty minutes."

"There is the customs, the luggage . . ."

"Please. I gotta make that plane."

Exasperated, the girl took his small suitcase, threw it on a conveyor and quickly wrote out a ticket. "How will you pay?"

"Dollars."

"Five hundred ninety-six." She gave him the ticket and the boarding pass. "Now, run. Gate Seven."

Giggis's next impediment was at passport control. The agent, an officious-looking middle-aged man with a trimmed moustache, seemed intent on plumbing the very structure of the paper. A bead of perspiration ran down Giggis's spine and into the crack of his buttocks as the immigration officers typed his name and passport number into a computer and watched the screen. He breathed a silent sigh of relief when, after a moment of staring, the man handed back the passport and the boarding card.

Giggis was the last passenger to board the plane.

He settled into his seat and slept for an hour before the stewardess awakened him for dinner. He bought himself a couple of drinks and slept soundly through the remainder of the flight.

When he rose to go to the lavatory after breakfast, he made up his mind to get rid of the diamonds in the tissue. He laughed to himself as he threw the two packets into the plastic toilet, and pissed on them till they disappeared down the hole.

The rest was easy to explain, just in case he got frisked. Hell, he thought cheerfully, with them whores of Gaines's, he'd be on easy street. No sense risking that for a couple of shiny stones.

The plane pulled to the ramp of the Pan Am building at New York's John F. Kennedy Airport at 8:30 in the morning. Giggis stuffed his dreadlocks under his cap, thanked the stewardesses, and walked down the ramp into the customs area. He waited patiently, turned in his passport and his declaration to the agent in the booth, then followed the lines to the baggage claim area.

Though Pan Am has its own building at Kennedy, and its own customs agents, there are times when as many as a half dozen planes can come in at once. If they are full, as many as two thousand people can come pouring into the facility at once.

It was Giggis's misfortune that this was such a morning.

It was Irving Schlissel's misfortune. Schlissel was a customs agent with thirty-five years experience in baggage handling. He'd gone from the army into the service after the war. He was five times a grandfather, and normally a friendly and outgoing soul.

This morning, his hemorrhoids hurt. And between six, when he had gone on duty, and nine-thirty, in the midst of the summer holiday season, between charters and scheduled planes, he and his crew had serviced twenty-three fully loaded 747s. His feet were sore, he couldn't sit down, and he felt old and tired.

He stood with one foot up on a conveyor, looking down the line at the dozen agents who struggled manfully between the two imperatives of their duty: to keep things moving and to provide some barrier first and foremost to drugs, and secondly to the more outrageous forms of smuggling.

An Air Jamaica plane at eight had brought him to a peak of frustration. An immigrant family with a half dozen children had rolled up to the conveyor with dozens of packages, large and small, of every shape and description, including what appeared to be a large bedsheet wrapped around rumpled clothing. The kids ran in every direction. The agent at his desk was beyond his wits, as the parents and older children babbled at him in their unintelligible patois. Suddenly, Irving, picking at his pencil moustache, had smelled a set piece. He gave a signal, and amidst the howling, screaming, and crying by the family and other passengers who were held up behind them, Schlissel stopped two lines and had every parcel opened. All of the children's toys were stuffed to bursting with hashish.

Both the Immigration cops and NYPD had become involved. There had been noise and confusion. His foot had been stepped on. He had the beginnings of a headache.

All that was an hour behind him when Tyrone Giggis took his bag from the carousel and got on line. He shuffled along, humming to himself, kicking the small suitcase on the cold, polished stone floor.

He walked past Irving Schlissel and heaved the bag up onto the conveyor and handed his declaration to the customs agent.

"Wait a minute," the agent said snappishly. "Can't you see I'm doing something?" He scribbled on a form in front of him.

"Don't get excited, man," Giggis said in his Jamaican twang. "I ain't in no hurry."

"It's a good thing." The agent was a black man in his mid-twenties, trim and neatly uniformed, who, like Schlissel, was having a very hard day.

"This is all of your baggage?"

"Mmm-hmmm."

"How long you been away."

"A couple of weeks, man."

"Where?"

"Brazil."

"Business or pleasure?"

Tyrone hesitated, then said, "Pleasure, man."

Schlissel turned his head at the hesitation. One of Tyrone's dreadlocks had slipped from under his cap and was hanging over his ear. Schlissel winced at a rectal twinge.

"Let me see the bag," the agent said.

"Sure, brother," Giggis replied. He turned the key on his chain in the lock and popped the case open.

The customs agent did not take kindly to being called brother with all that that implied while his honky boss stood there watching. As a result, he carefully turned the suitcase, feeling every item. As a matter of habit, he pushed the toilet kit aside, then out of sheer spite, squeezed it, hoping he'd bust the toothpaste tube. He did it again.

His forehead wrinkled.

"Oh, shit," Giggis thought.

The agent shook his head and slammed the suitcase shut. "Next," he said.

Irving Schlissel cleared his throat. "Excuse me."

"Me?" Giggis asked.

"Would you mind showing me what you have in your pockets?"

"Hey, what is this, man? I thought I passed."

"This is a secondary level customs inspection," Schlissel said, annoyed. "And take off your watch, too." Smartass punk.

Grumbling under his breath, Giggis complied, laying out his passport and tickets, his address book, sixty cents in change, some keys, and the little chamois pouch.

Schlissel poked at them contemptuously, scowling more at his own spite than at Giggis. I'm an old fart, he thought. Oy, would I like a hot sitz bath. The pouch caught his eye, and he emptied it into the palm of his hand.

Giggis restrained a smile. That was the best piss I ever took. If he'd seen them stones . . . shit.

Schlissel felt even sillier than he had before. A couple of junky pimp rings worth a grand apiece, a few coins. He stopped, fingering the pin. He turned it over and over. He was a man whose life had been preoccupied for a third of a century with other people's possessions. Why did this little piece of nonsense speak out to him? He weighed it in his hand. Little bits of old mine diamonds, a few amethyst chips, a sliver of cabochon sapphire. What could it be worth in a store? Two hundred? Three?

"Would you excuse me for a moment?" he said to Giggis. "Please wait for me here. I'll be right back. Tony," he alerted the agent to watch him, then walked off to the office at the rear of the customs hall.

Schlissel sat gingerly on the rubber cushion on the duty desk. He felt like a prick. He was ragging the guy just because he was a Jamaican. The pin though, that stuck in his mind.

He pulled out his batch of wanted posters and started to thumb through them. Maybe it was the guy's face. Schlissel didn't think so. That wasn't it. With him, it was not often people. It was things.

Every month he went through the pile, checking to see what was current and what was not. It was the same way his brother told him they did it at the post office. They crossed out the ones who were apprehended. When he was almost to the end, he came to a missing persons bulletin. It was a Mr. and Mrs. Malcolm Woodruff. Two stiff formal portraits, the kind that you get from anxious relatives. It was four months old. Mrs. Woodruff stared up at him, her dark dress clasped closed around a white collar by the pin in his hand.

He picked up the phone and called NYPD headquarters at the airport. Tommie Vigiano, a friend of twenty years, was the senior officer on duty.

"Lieutenant Vigiano," he growled.

"Tommie, it's Irving over by Pan Am."

"You got a problem?"

"I don't know. I got a pin off a *schwartze*—a Jamaican. I remembered it from a poster. It was on a missing persons flyer for a lady named Woodruff."

"That one that had to do with the bullshit with that building in Harlem and O'Neil?"

"Yeah. What should I do?"

"Hold the son of a bitch. I'm on my way."

Schlissel stood at the door and looked through the peephole as Giggis began to jaw at the customs agent in irritation at being kept cooling his heels for no apparent reason. Three minutes later, Tommie Vigiano and three other uniformed officers stepped smartly through the Do Not Enter door with their hands on their guns.

Schlissel walked out into the hall and up to the conveyor, where he had left Giggis. He picked up the passport and the declaration and said, "Mr. uh, Giggis, would you please come over to my office. Tony, close this line and bring Mr. Giggis's bag with you."

Giggis stalled for a moment, then spotted the four cops closing on him. He'd seen that look before, with the hand down around the waist. His eyes shifted back and forth. Fuck. He didn't have anyplace to run. He shrugged and followed Schlissel while the other agent and the cops brought up the rear.

"What is this shit, man?" he asked as soon as the door closed behind him. "What you hasslin' me for?"

Vigiano said, "Would you please hold out your hands?"

"Shit," Giggis drew out the word as he offered his wrists together for the cuffs.

"Mr. Giggis, I am placing you under arrest. You have the right to remain silent. You have the right to be represented by counsel. But, I must inform you that anything you say can and will be used as evidence against you in a court of law."

"Shit. What is it I'm supposed to have done?"

"I don't suppose you've ever heard of Mr. or Mrs. Malcolm Woodruff?" Vigiano asked.

Giggis stared at him blankly.

"They've been missing. They're presumed dead. A man named Gaines and another one named Hawkes have been indicted for their murders."

Giggis remained motionless and silent.

"Let's go," Vigiano said.

"Where?" Giggis asked.

"The station."

Giggis froze at the desk.

"I said, let's go," Vigiano insisted.

Giggis thought about what he knew, in particular what he knew about Mayor Greene and all of those meetings he'd had in dark streets with Hawkes. He thought about dropping the shoe boxes off to that punchy old shoeblack in the forties and watching the governor come pick them up.

"I got a right to a phone call. I ain't going nowhere till I make my phone call." Giggis's mind raced as he had himself in dirty sneakers down so many dark alleys with a stolen purse in his hand. Maybe he'd get time off, or a plea bargain, or even a new identity. Everybody else was dead. No one could stick him with anything. But he'd have to live to make the deal.

"Okay, bud. One call. Call your lawyer," Vigiano said.

Giggis took the address book from the desk where Schlissel had left it. He flipped through the pages and dialed. There was a ringing sound, then a recording. The number had been changed. He listened, then hung up, and started to dial again.

Vigiano smiled, reached out and pushed the hook down, disconnecting him. "One call."

"Hey, I didn't make no call. They gave me another number."

"One call."

Giggis turned to Schlissel. "I didn't get to make my call."

Vigiano looked at Schlissel. "All right. Make the call."

The phone rang a half a dozen times before it answered. "Yeah?"

Giggis bit his lip. Anything you say may be used against you in a court of law. It beats the shit out of being dead. "Mr. Curtin. My name is Tyrone Giggis. You don't know me, but I know you. I used to work for Gaines Masonry Company. I'm under arrest at the Pan Am terminal at Kennedy Airport."

"So?" Paul said, his heart pounding in his chest like a trip-hammer.

"I get one call. You're it. You can call my lawyer for me later. If you want to hear what really happened to your shaving cream, you come out to the police station at the airport right quick. If not, I might not be able to answer any questions for anybody, if you get what I mean."

Vigiano grabbed the phone out of his hand and said, "This is Lieutenant Thomas Vigiano, New York Police Department. Who is this?"

"Lieutenant, this is Paul Curtin. I'm a journalist."

"Oh, yeah. The guy with the *Advocate*."

"Used to be. Where are you taking Giggis?"

"To the station. I've got to book him."

"I'll be there in twenty minutes. You make sure that you take good care of him, Lieutenant. He may have the answers to lots of questions. I mean, he shouldn't have any accidents."

"Right," Vigiano said. The message was clear.

By the time that he had arrived at the station and had been placed in the detention cell, Tyrone Giggis had developed a strategy. He'd spent enough hours close to George Gaines to learn more than the skills of violence. There were only two witnesses to his crimes. They were both dead and five thousand miles away. The Fifth Amendment protected him from self-incrimination.

His spirits were further buoyed when he was pushed before the precinct desk sergeant by Lieutenant Vigiano. They debated for ten minutes on how to book him. They finally settled on possession of stolen property—Rose Woodruff's pin. He suppressed a smile. With a charge like that, a lawyer from the Public Defender's office could have him out on five-hundred-dollar bail in an hour. But that didn't fit into his plans.

Vigiano let Paul into the cell and said, "You can have him till they come to take him downtown."

"They're not holding you on much, Mr. Giggis," Paul said. "You could be sprung by lunchtime."

"I don't want to be sprung, man. I'm better off in jail. I think I'm going to ask them to put me in solitary."

"Not a bad idea," Paul said. Jesus, he must be scared shitless. I'll bet if O'Neil and Greene knew he was here, they would be scared, too. I wonder what he knows.

He talked to Paul for about ten minutes. He had worked for Hawkes and Gaines. He'd done lots of errands for them, no details. Dropped off lots of packages, again, no details. He had heard that they were paying off. He thought maybe he could remember some conversations about who knew. He knew nothing about anybody named Woodruff. The stolen pin had been given to him by Gaines. No, he didn't know where Gaines or Hawkes were. Paul's apartment? An accident? He shrugged. Millions in stolen money? He smiled a toothy grin. "I wish I knew, man." It was like drawing teeth.

Paul closed his notebook as a couple of officers came to take him away. Foxy fellow, Paul thought. He knows a lot. He's telling a little. If they work on it, he'll be the witness that hangs everyone.

"Hey man, am I going to live to take the stand?" Giggis asked.

"If you do," Paul said, standing and walking out of the cell, "it'll be more than Malcolm Woodruff got to do. But then," he waved his pad, "you've got a better insurance policy."

Paul watched them put Giggis into a police transportation van with grill-covered windows. When they were gone, he whistled on his way down the sidewalk to a phone booth.

First, he called Maryanne at home. "You aren't going to believe this, but the cops just stopped a man at the airport who probably knows all of the connections between Green and O'Neil and Uhuru. No, I don't understand. I'll be late for dinner."

His next call was to Oscar Bornstein. It was his last dime.

When Bornstein called back, the first word he said was, "Incredible."

"I guess the only way I can really participate in this is for you to hire me back."

"I'd like to do just that. But it isn't in my power anymore."

"My God, don't tell me that Melanie has crawled back out of retirement and given you the sack?"

"No. Not quite. You're among the first to know. As of noon today, we will have sold the *New York Advocate*, lock, stock, barrel and premises to an Australian publishing syndicate. There are going to be wholesale changes in management. I'm going to retire. They're moving in this afternoon. It'll be announced in the Wall Street Edition."

66

The months between the arrest of Tyrone Giggis at Kennedy Airport and the impending election in November were occupied by a legal ballet choreographed by numerous opposing interests. While Frank O'Neil spent the bulk of his time in his job at Dal Porto Electric and continued his social life with Mrs. Dal Porto, an army of lawyers entered reams of papers on his behalf, effectively blunting the thrusts of the Manhattan district attorney. The legislature had decided to wait until the January session to form a committee for the investigation of the Uhuru matter and to consider the possibility of wrongdoing by the former governor.

The intervention of the summer slowed the impanelment of a special grand jury to hear the testimony of Tyrone Giggis, who was now being held in protective custody at his own request as a material witness. The stolen property charge had been shelved. It was decided that he should testify on what he might know of the Woodruff murders and the whereabouts of Gaines and Hawkes and their spoils.

Tyrone stalled, and gained time. As for his former employers, his concern about their discovery proved ill-founded. Neither Marcus Hawkes nor George Gaines had had so much as a slip of paper on him when found, Giggis having stripped

Gaines clean and the keeper of bushmasters at Butantan having done the same for Hawkes. After forty-eight hours in the morgue, unclaimed, they went to Potter's Field.

The mayor of New York nervously regarded both the "Prisoner of the Tombs," as the papers had come to call Giggis, and the district attorney, whose political aspirations were no less powerful than his own.

For his part, Giggis was content to wait in his cell, a private room with a television set. When the jury was finally impaneled, he shared innocuous bits of information through a tortuously slow testimony. Just enough to keep everyone interested.

As the hearings proceeded in the possible direction of indictments, and the leaves turned brown and fell from the trees, Tyrone Giggis decided to make his move. Having blackened everyone's name by inference without giving sufficient evidence to convict anyone but the deceased Gaines and Hawkes, Tyrone slipped half the cash out of the bottom of his toilet kit and purchased an exit visa from his cell in the Tombs. He had a three-hour head start.

Despite the earnest efforts of the police department, by the time they had been notified, Giggis was sitting in the crew's quarters of a Liberian flag vessel bound for Jamaica.

Several weeks later, on a steamy antipodal summer day in São Paulo, Tyrone Giggis, his pate shorn of dreadlocks gleaming in the sun, dressed in a tan three-button suit and striped tie, accompanied Albert Fonseca though the doors of the Banco Auxiliar on the Avenida Paulista. Luiz Freddy de Castro Andrade, the bank manager, greeted them both with open arms.

"Needless to say," Luiz Freddy assured Tyrone, "it will be a pleasure to continue to handle your account, Mr. Willis."

"Just for identification purposes," Tyrone said, smiling. He passed Luiz Freddy Marcus's forged passport. His own likeness and description had been expertly inserted, complete with a new, embossed government seal.

Tyrone magnanimously grabbed the check at lunch. They toasted each other in imported champagne. The alteration of his identity, including the creation of citizenship papers, birth and baptismal certificates, and the new passport, had required the other $25,000 from the bottom of Tyrone's toilet kit for payment to a deputy minister in the Ministry of Foreign Affairs in Brasilia.

Even after signing over one million dollars each to Fonseca and Luiz Freddy, Tyrone had three left for himself in the bank and a lovely house in Jardim America. As they enjoyed their brandy, Tyrone looked at his gold Rolex, then rose and excused himself. He didn't want to be late for his Portuguese lesson.

His driver took a short cut from the restaurant, avoiding the city center to get to the house. On his way, he passed an open field in which a bulldozer worked to bury the bodies of the homeless and unidentified which had been collected from the streets of São Paulo on recent dawns and where the remains of George Gaines and Marcus Garvey Hawkes had been thrown.

In New York, there was a thorough investigation of Giggis's escape from the Tombs. Two guards were severely reprimanded and suspended for thirty days without pay, a cost to them of $1,800 after taxes. The fine reduced their net profit to $10,700 each.

67

The gubernatorial election was an anticlimax. On the first Tuesday in November, forty-one percent of the registered voters of the state of New York presented themselves at the polls. As the Reverend McCaig had pointed out to Paul, the black voters of the state didn't believe either in the Easter Bunny or the soiled promises of Christopher Greene. Street wise and world weary, they either stayed away, or cast their lot in the majority for the opposition. George Allen Mason was elected by a plurality of fifty-eight percent to forty-two percent, more than one million votes. Parenthetically, he carried Erie County, including Willy Albert's home ward.

By the time that Mason was sworn in as governor of the Empire State on January fifth, his hair had begun to turn white.

The vortex of Uhuru Towers, and the ancillary difficulties which radiated from it, threatened to draw him in. He stiffened his resolve and turned away to the business of govering the state, thus extracting himself.

In the face of apathy and the absence of further incriminating evidence from Tyrone Giggis, Governor O'Neil was allowed to plead *nolo contendere* to conspiracy charges. He was fined $20,000 and given a year's probation without restrictions. He walked out of the courtroom a free man, smiling and chatting on the arm of his bride, the former Adrienne Dal Porto. In the spring, Dal Porto Electric acquired O'Neil Maritime and Fuel in a tax-free stock transaction.

Mayor Christopher Greene continued to deny that he had any part in the swindle, which was slowly and painfully being uncovered in the books of the Uhuru Towers project. He protested that continued allegations were the result of political vengeance by his recent opponent, and the ambition of the Manhattan district attorney, who was making noises about mounting a primary campaign for the mayoralty. To add to his troubles, the state committee on oversights had begun to examine stories first revealed in the *Advocate* that the city might be in violation of its fiscal agreements with the Municipal Assistance Corporation.

Paul Curtin fared better. His near passes with death and his rite of passage with Melanie Parsons added an extra layer of fiber to an already toughened hide. When he went to the offices of the *Advocate* as Oscar Bornstein had suggested, he imparted that strength to the paper's new owner. They scrapped at first, over a period of three weeks—matters of philosophy, technique, and what the paper was to be all about under new management. He offered Paul an editorship with responsibility for story selection and special material development. Once a week he was to write a column called Empire State. Paul went home to think it over with Maryanne. He accepted the next morning.

68

The Saturday before Thanksgiving, Paul and Maryanne were married. Forrest Middleton, overwhelmed by his good luck at the elimination of alimony payments, agreed to take the children for two weeks, so that the newlyweds could honeymoon in a far-off, warm climate. At first, they were inclined toward Jamaica, but after a little thought, they decided against it. "Martinique seems safer to me," Paul said, wryly.

School was already out when Uhuru Towers was completed the following June, not quite a year behind schedule, at $100 million, about a third over budget.

"I want to go to the zoo," Alexandra complained.

"Stand still while I tie this bow," Maryanne said between clenched teeth. "You always want to go to the damn zoo. There." She finished with a flourish. "And Paul wants us all to see this ceremony."

"I'd rather see the man-eating polar bear," Petey added.

"Well, instead, young fella," Paul said, pulling his tie up to his collar, "you're going to see man-eating people."

"Real cannibals?"

"Politicians. It's almost the same."

Paul led his family through the police barricade. They were accorded good seats on the aisle a half-dozen rows from the raised platform that was to serve as a dais.

"God," Maryanne exclaimed, "you ought to just print a picture of that instead of writing a column next week."

In an uneasy armed truce, Governor Mason and Mayor Greene shared the first row of the reviewing stand. Behind them sat Wallace Harley Vance III, the chairman of Burton Industries, Mack Bell, the president of the contracting company recently renamed City Reconstruction, Inc., and the Reverend Donald McCaig, president of Urban Development

441

Corporation, the project's chief sponsor. The remainder of the seats were filled by members of the legislature and the Division of Housing.

"Who are all these people?" Petey demanded.

"Governors, mayors, things like that," Paul replied.

"Who's that?" Petey asked, pointing over his shoulder at a noisy cortege making its way down the aisle.

Paul smiled and nodded at the imposing figure of Frank O'Neil as he made his way to the front, bearing his wife and several of his children in tow. They sat in seats that had been reserved for them in the center of the first row.

"Are all these people important, Paul?" Petey asked.

"They think so, sport."

Petey and Alexandra wriggled restlessly in their chairs as one dignitary after another stood to heap his blessings and praise and hope on the towering pile of masonry hanging above their heads in the humid Harlem sky.

When Governor Mason cut a red ribbon, everyone clapped.

"Paul, did those people have something to do with building the building?" Petey asked. "They all sounded as if they had almost done it themselves."

"I guess they think they did."

"They all kept saying that God helped them. Do you think He did?"

"I think He may have had more to do with it than they did."

Petey frowned and shook his head. "I'm not sure why you made us come. I don't understand what it all means." He turned his face to Paul, earnest and trusting. "What does it mean?"

"I think I might be able to explain it to you when you get older, Pete." He chewed his lip and threw off a chill. "And then again, I may not. Come on. Let's get some ice cream."